THE DOLLS' ROOM

THE DOLLS' ROOM
LLORENÇ VILLALONGA

TRANSLATED BY DEBORAH BONNER

DALKEY ARCHIVE PRESS
CHAMPAIGN AND LONDON

Library of Congress Cataloging-in-Publication Data

Villalonga, Llorenç, 1897-1980.
   [Bearn, o, La sala de les nines. English]
   The dolls' room / Llorenç Villalonga ; translated [from the Catalan] by Deborah Bonner. -- 1st
U.S. ed.
      p. cm.
   ISBN 978-1-56478-612-8 (pbk. : alk. paper)
   1. Aristocracy (Social class)--Spain--Fiction. 2. Majorca (Spain)--Fiction. I. Bonner, Debo-
rah. II. Title.
   PC3941.V433B413 2010
   849'.9352--dc22
                              2010027871

Partially funded by the University of Illinois at Urbana-Champaign and by a grant from the
Illinois Arts Council, a state agency

The Catalan Literature Series is published in cooperation with the Institut Ramon Llull, a
public consortium responsible for the promotion of Catalan language and culture abroad

www.dalkeyarchive.com

Cover: design and composition by Danielle Dutton, illustration by Nicholas Motte
Printed on permanent/durable acid-free paper and bound in the United States of America

THE DOLLS' ROOM

Translator's Foreword

> Who could ever be sure of owning
> the definitive edition of things?
> Llorenç Villalonga, *The Dolls' Room*

Llorenç Villalonga once said that *The Dolls' Room* was "the portrait, or, if you wish, the poem of Mallorca. Of a certain Mallorca, that is: mine." What many agree to be the author's most compelling work was published in both Catalan and Spanish, but essentially belongs to the island, if to anyone, as both languages do.

Villalonga was bilingual, and there is no doubt that when the novel was in the making, the political barrier between the two languages was a bitter one indeed, with Franco imposing Spanish over the other languages spoken in Spain. Villalonga lived and wrote crossing that line. In addition, he was never a careful stylist; his focus was primarily on theme, on character, and on atmosphere, evoking a lost world. Probably most of his editors in both languages were amused by the author's self-portrait in Don Toni de Bearn when he confides in Joan Mayol, "You will naturally find some oversights in my style and perhaps a few grammatical liberties and transgressions. Be careful when you correct them, Son. [. . .] I have at times had to sacrifice grammar and morals in exchange for accuracy." Although his lack of formal education in Catalan may have shown in his writing, the dialect spoken in Mallorca was his mother tongue, and, as the language his characters would actually have spoken, enabled him to develop a broad range of subtle registers; it was also better equipped to convey the natural and cultural setting for *The Dolls' Room*. Villalonga's Spanish, on the other hand, was articulate but somewhat stiff and self-conscious, with the occasional expression borrowed from Catalan.

Villalonga, a man who moved between different worlds and languages, also chose a double title for his novel: *Bearn, or The Dolls' Room*, including both the name of the fictional estate that encapsulates the lost world of Mallorcan rural aristocracy and that of the locked room integral to the novel's plot. While English editions of the novel have used only the second half of its title, in Catalan and Spanish the novel is available as *Bearn o la sala de les nines* and *Bearn o la sala de las muñecas*, respectively, and is generally referred to simply as *Bearn*.

The question as to which version of this novel—the Catalan or the Spanish—was "the original," is, however, complicated and controversial, and Villalonga was careful to cover his tracks. The first complete manuscript was published in Spanish in 1956, although a first draft seems to have been attempted in Catalan; regardless of which the original language was, the version I chose for my translation in 1986 was the Catalan edition published by Edicions 62, conscientiously edited in conjunction with the author by Josep Antoni Grimalt.

It is likely that Villalonga himself, as mischievous as Don Toni de Bearn, created a maze in which he could watch editors, critics, and translators quarrel in search for a simple explanation. In an interview published shortly after his death, he went so far as to claim that the novel had actually been transcribed from Hebrew, then translated into English, from English to French, and finally into Spanish and Catalan. He found his own form of rebellion against the forces that threatened to pull his work to one side or the other of the politically charged line between the two languages. He wanted *The Dolls' Room* to stand alone, and I certainly believe it is more than capable of holding its ground outside of Mallorca, Catalonia, and Spain.

Els meus ulls ja nó saben
sinó contemplar dies
i sols perduts...

Salvador Espriu
Cementiri de Sinera

Introduction

Letter from Don Joan* Mayol, Chaplain of Bearn, to Don Miquel Gilabert, Secretary to His Eminence the Cardinal Primate of Spain

Bearn, 1890

Dear Miquel,

 I do not know whether by the time you receive this letter you will have heard the sad news: the Senyors died nearly two months ago, on the last night of carnival, under rather mysterious circumstances. Since then Bearn has been full of clerks, notaries and creditors drawing up documents and writing out inventories. We have not had a minute's rest. Everyone is concerned with the material possessions of the dead, which in the end will amount to virtually nothing, whereas few stop to say a Paternoster in their memory. Even I, who have been in charge of the house, have not had a single uninterrupted hour, and when night falls and I am left alone, my soul feels so ill at ease that I have no strength left to commend them to God: if it were not for the Mass I say in their memory every morning, I suspect they would have

---

*Joan is the Catalan equivalent of the Spanish Juan.

travelled very light to the world beyond. At times like these, the spectacle of human selfishness seems to rule out any possibility of redemption.

Their niece and nephews arrived thirty-eight hours after the tragedy, when the Senyors had already been buried. It had been years since they had last set foot in Bearn. I can assure you, Miquel, that no one was distraught over this double death. Dona Magdalena praised the china in the drawing room and her brothers inquired about the pine forest of Sa Cova, which they assumed had been cut down some time ago. I did not judge it necessary to tell them that although it may not have been cut down, it had been sold and paid for in advance, and I have refused to answer any questions concerning last wishes until we hear from Madrid regarding the last will and testament of the deceased (between you and me, I happen to know that they never drew up a will in their entire lives). They also asked about the Senyora's jewellery and whatever money may have been in the house, but the judge, anticipating their intentions, had locked all the drawers, sparing me from having to offer explanations. At the last minute, their niece wanted to see the dolls' room, which the Senyor never showed to anyone, and believing I was interpreting the wishes of the deceased, I pretended to have lost the key. They were rather taken aback by the time they left, and I have not seen them since.

They would have been even more so had they known that in a hide-away in my dressing-table, between two boards, there are two thousand *duros** that the Senyor gave me about six months ago, with specific instructions, as you will soon see. Now that the Senyors have died, you are the only person I truly love and in whom I can confide my trials and tribulations. I need to present you with a matter of conscience. Think about it before you read on: you must take everything I tell you as a confession. If you are not prepared to receive my confidences (which, I must warn you, will disturb and upset your peace of mind), you must certainly burn these pages without reading any further.

You, Miquel, have been and still are my best friend, in the fullest sense of the word. I shall never forget the compassion you showed me when at that moment of anguish immediately after the tragedy, I

*The unit of Spanish currency is the *peseta*. There are one hundred *céntimos* to a *peseta*, four *reales* to a *peseta*, and five *pesetas* to the *duro*. In Catalan these are *pesseta*, *cèntim*, *ral* and *duro* (Translator's note).

confided in you about that misfortune, not to say that crime, which led me to finally renounce the world forever. I met you exactly a week after the affair concerning Jaume. I, who have had neither parents nor siblings, found in you at first brotherly love, and later that miraculous communion of judgement which is the greatest gift Our Lord can grant two men. Neither you nor I (*arcades ambo*, as the old rector of the seminary used to say half seriously and half in jest) will forget those conversations under the tree in the main courtyard, discussing Saint Augustine and Descartes. Our minds were opening up simultaneously to the wonder of that spiritual world which, when one succeeds in glimpsing it, constitutes a palpable revelation of the divine presence. The Senyor sometimes used to tell me that when I grew old and looked back upon my life, I would realize that it had lacked one single ingredient, that spicy sauce called the Devil. Those were the kinds of things the Senyor used to say, not expecting them to be taken seriously.

The Senyor had a generous, trusting, and open soul. All his mistakes, which were many, deserve partial forgiveness in the light of his good intentions, his confidence in understanding and his love for nature and all living things. By now his body has turned to dust — that body which he had spared no pleasures — and only his soul remains in the presence of God, his only judge. Let us pray that his mistakes be forgiven.

I must ask your counsel regarding the question raised by this two-fold death, and the instructions left by the Senyor, along with the two thousand *duros* I have hidden away. It seems impossible that a man as reckless as he regarding financial matters could have amassed a sum large enough to support an entire family. The effort it must have represented for him (even though we all know that when one of these houses collapses, there is always something left hidden away in some dark corner) makes me understand why the Senyor felt so strongly about the instructions he left me, he who over the years had become removed from so many things. If the judges and the creditors who are studying the settlement of the estate knew that I, once a swineherd and now a poor chaplain with no income other than that earned saying Mass, have so much money hidden away, they would probably think I had stolen it, and, as you can imagine, it would not be inconceivable that they should blame me for the Senyors' unexpected deaths within an hour of each other. And yet these dangers cannot compare with the moral concerns I am now obliged to face.

Before you give me your advice, however, it is important that you have full knowledge of the problem. The love and loyalty that the Senyor inspired in me could distort my judgement. The question is not a simple one, and I feel the need to start from the very beginning. Giving you all the details of that life I loved so deeply, despite its grave errors, has provided a solace for me in my solitude. I must admit that the motive of my story, written in the course of these endless nights, may not be solely the scruples of my conscience, but rather the pleasure of reviving the familiar and venerated figure I have just lost. With him an entire world has disappeared, beginning with these lands that have seen my birth and that will have to be auctioned off because the creditors have already notified us that they do not wish to wait any longer. The Senyor's nephews and niece neither have enough money to pay off the mortgages nor feel any love for Bearn, being used to city life as they are. There might be one last source of hope: they say a relative of the Senyors has arrived from America after having become a millionaire selling cardboard boxes. It seems unbelievable that anyone should become an important personality selling little boxes, but he has introduced himself with much pomp, laden with gold and determined to dazzle all of Mallorca with an electric automobile that has already killed two sheep. On his calling card, below his name, are the words *Cardboard Containers*, which no one quite understood until they realized it referred to those famous boxes. Well, this character — that is all I can call him — could, I suppose, purchase the estate, saving it from falling into the hands of strangers. I know that the Senyors would not have been pleased with the man of the Cardboard Containers, and in addition the mother of this capitalist had apparently been separated from her husband — a Bearn who had gone astray — for quite some time when the child was born, and this was the object of many a comment. But the years teach us not to be excessively demanding. To me, halfway down the path of my life, this Cardboard Container Bearn would be nothing but an intruder. Yet there is no question but that a new generation is emerging, which is willing to associate these old lands with the personality of an outsider and will experience the same feelings towards the union of senyor and lands, which it will believe to be deeply rooted, that I felt towards Don Toni as a child. Searching through the archives of the house one would undoubtedly find other similar situations, because reality is only what we make it and derives its continuity from no more than the conventional magic of a name. God, we know, created the World with the Word.

The Senyor exerted a sort of fascination over me. Dona Maria Antònia, who was so good, never inspired as much interest in me as that soul torn between God and the Devil; not even now (the very thought of it is chilling) do we know who won the battle. Perhaps this anguish was the basis for the love I have always felt towards him, and this same anguish might also be precisely that sauce which according to the Senyor is the spice of life.

One thing I do not wish to hide from you is that, regarding this moral dilemma, I could only accept a solution that would not be contrary to the Senyor's last wish, and that if an obstacle should arise, I reserve the right to take the matter to Rome. If the Pope himself should deny his consent, I would feel compelled to abide by his decision, yet if that were to happen, I hope and beg of Divine Mercy that death reach me before then to free me of my tribulations.

For your better understanding of the problem, I have divided my exposition of that strange life into three parts, as if it were a novel. The first could be called *Under the Influence of Faust*, and corresponds to the tempestuous period. The second part takes place in the peace of these mountains and could be called (albeit rather ironically, because the peace was more apparent than real) *Peace Reigns in Bearn*. Regarding the third, it consists of an epilogue written shortly afterwards, following a strange and disconcerting visit I recently received.

One last observation is that you must not be shocked at certain frivolities and crude references in my pages. Do bear in mind that I must present the Senyor as he was during his life, and given that I am submitting his character to the judgement of the Church, I can never be faithful enough to the facts, although above all possible misunderstandings there remains God, who constitutes infinite understanding.

PART I

Under the Influence of Faust

ONE

Since you never came to Bearn, I must explain that it is a mountain estate located near a small village of about four hundred souls also called Bearn. Whether the estate took the name of the village or the village that of the estate remains unknown. Year after year, on the day of Sant Miquel, the patron saint of Bearn, the preacher mentions that these lands have belonged to the Senyors since the Conquest.* It may be true, although there are no documents to prove this fact. 'Our lineage', Don Toni said, 'is so old that it can't be dated. It's lost in the darkness of time.' However, the oral tradition that made them respectable and irreproachable has had no official recognition. There is a good reason: the documents are missing. All the Senyors except for Don Toni, who was a francophile, were always quite indifferent as far as erudition was concerned. Even within the past century and a half, one of his great-great-grandfathers, also called Don Toni, was such a primitive soul that he was the object of many tales of mischief, although they probably exaggerate what he actually did. The old people remember the following rhyme:

> *Our Lord Jesus is in Heaven*
> *and in Moorish lands, the heathen.*
> *The Devil lives deep down in Hell*
> *and in Bearn Don Toni dwells.*

The Senyor found it all very amusing. 'At least,' he said, 'he didn't

*The author refers to the Catalan conquest of Mallorca, led by James I in 1229 (Translator's note).

3

waste any time.' His other ancestors were more sensible. They lived in the country, and either ignored or looked down upon the refinements of city life. The City,* in turn, ignored them.

From the village to the estate is about an hour's walk, but due to the mountainous terrain one cannot see the estate until one is practically on top of it. Bearn is thus, figuratively speaking, a lost cause. The land is poor, with only pine and oak growing between jagged rocks. It will soon be thirty-eight years since I came into this world, the son of a labourer and a farm girl. I have no recollection of my parents. I have heard that my mother was very beautiful and had jet-black eyes. When I was seven, I was sent to work as a swineherd, but the Senyor decided almost immediately that I was to be sent to school in the City. I can remember it as if it were this very moment. It was a summer afternoon and I had taken the herd over to S'Ull de Sa Font when the Senyors went by. They would spend long periods in the City, and when they returned, my respect, my fear or my embarrassment made me run off and hide every time I saw them. I barely dared to look at them anywhere but in the village church, on the day of Sant Miquel, when they sat in two red velvet-covered chairs next to the altar.

Dona Maria Antònia was very beautiful, and Don Toni, thin, graceful, and rather slight, resembled her despite his ugliness. They were first cousins. Although they almost always smiled, they were imposing because they appeared to be made of a different substance from that of the peasants, something newer and more luminous; not even now could I explain it. The way they dressed undoubtedly had something to do with it, but I do believe it was a less material, almost magical quality that surrounded the feudal and pastoral name of Bearn, revered every year from the pulpit on the holiday. Usually around Sant Miquel it rains in the mountains, and the history of the old family is as closely associated with the beginning of the cool weather and the joyful green of the first pastures as it is with the deeds of the conquerors in the battlefield.

'Look at that boy, Tonet,' said Dona Maria Antònia. 'Have you noticed his eyes?'

The Senyor stared at me and did not reply. Dona Maria Antònia was lost in thought.

---

* 'The City' refers to Palma, the capital of Mallorca (Translator's note).

4

'He reminds me of someone . . . I'm not sure who,' she said.

He remained silent. The following day I was sent to the Theatine school. I returned for the Easter vacation. My benefactors were not at the estate. Madò Francina told me that 'the Senyor was off travelling' and that Dona Maria Antònia was at the townhouse of Bearn, a stone house by the church. I thought I sensed some mystery in her words. Indeed there was: everybody was talking about it, whispering to each other, and no matter how much I listened, I could not understand a thing. Besides, whatever I could have understood would only have been the outside appearance of the matter. Years later, the Senyor, who was unreserved with me and with almost everyone, unveiled the psychological mechanism behind it in a series of long conversations which truly resembled a confession. Although I do not know to what degree they could be considered as such, despite their sincerity, and I understand that you may be shocked, as I myself am, to think that to this date, after all my years as the family priest, I cannot honestly state that he ever made a single confession.

His soul was as transparent and ever-changing as glass. Precisely because he was such a sincere man, you could never know what he was really like, just as you cannot know what images will be cast by a piece of crystal. It is strange that those people who refuse to lock themselves into a system, perhaps so as not to neglect any aspect of reality, are the ones who appear to be most dishonest. If you add to that the fact that noblemen are trained from an early age in the art of kind words that are not to be taken literally, and yet always are by those less educated, we find another reason why people mistrusted Don Toni. Ordinary people believe that only the tactless are sincere, because they are incapable of interpreting the conventional values and the things that are taken for granted in good manners. For example, I believe I already told you that he used to wear a white wig and the habit of a Franciscan. Those who compared his past and his conversation, not always edifying, with those robes, saw nothing but the disparity which undoubtedly existed, but they might also have seen the similarities (his secluded life, his love for matters of the soul) that were no less real. People who only spoke one language admired this man who spoke several. The Senyor was basically well-meaning, although some of his actions may have been disastrous; he believed that disasters were caused by errors of intelligence rather than by voluntary evil, which he refused to accept.

5

'Don't you understand,' he used to tell me, 'that the cheat or the swindler probably doesn't think of himself as such? The cheat makes thousands of arrangements so as to end up on top, which clearly does not imply evil; it implies error. Believe me, Joan, the coachman doesn't drive the carriage into the ditch out of malice, but out of carelessness.'

That may have been why he read so much and made an effort to educate himself, forgetting that intelligence can sometimes also lead us astray. He had an eighteenth-century education and could not disregard *La Raison*, despite having, as you will see, a poetic, even contradictory nature.

'I will grant you,' he told me, 'that the flame of reason is a weak one, but that doesn't mean that it should be put out; on the contrary, it should be made brighter.'

He was a skilled sophist and dialectician. I have considered his teachings with caution, but have not always succeeded in resisting his charm.

How could it have been otherwise? The school I was taken to when I was seven lacked spirit. Our education was monotonous and pedantic; the students' manners were coarse. Every time I returned to Bearn I was in awe of the aura of freedom and graciousness surrounding the Senyor. Don Toni never argued nor got angry, although he had not given up the custom of inflicting physical punishment on his servants when they misbehaved. I have seen him whip the ploughman, who looked like an athlete and moaned with every blow, and then reason out the punishment to the village priest, who disapproved of such measures. It only happened every now and then, because the ploughman would let out 'goddamns' and 'bloody hells', expressions that hardly befitted an eighteenth-century vocabulary. I found the preparations for the scene both chilling and fascinating: the gracious ease with which the Senyor pointed to the belt hanging behind the door and the way the ploughman then handed it to his master in submission.

'Let's see how long you remember this,' Don Toni said. 'Take your shirt off and sit down on this stool. Lean your head down, it's in my way.' The ploughman bent his head and it was shocking to see the tall, strong young man letting himself be whipped by Don Toni, a small man well over fifty. Because the scene defied all physical and biological laws, I believe the ploughman's submissiveness (considered base by some) was due to moral forces, to an entire order of things, disciplines and traditions honoured by both master and servant.

After the ceremony, Don Toni recommended that the ploughman put some of their best oil on his back if it stung, and then returned to read the Classics. He taught me French and introduced me to Racine and Molière; thanks to him, a poor country priest who never chose to break his vows will not die without knowing the love of Phaedra or the smile of Célimène. I think God must like it better this way; he must prefer my conscious sacrifice to those of ignorant men, which can hardly be considered sacrifices at all.

He was an extraordinary man. I know that his detractors may have many arguments against him, or even mock his moth-eaten eighteenth-century culture. As science advances (and it is doing so at an alarming rate as the end of the century approaches) his erudition will naturally seem frivolous, that of an *amateur*. In fact, he never really intended to be anything more than that, but he had moments of genius that set him ahead of his time. I have no qualms about stating that this reasonable, sceptical, weak-willed and indifferent man appeared in some ways, may God forgive me, to be a sorcerer, and that is how he was perceived, albeit simplistically, by many of the peasants in Bearn.

TWO

I believe it would be appropriate to describe the scene of the tragedy. Maybe you would be surprised by the estate's combination of peasant house and palace typical of a time when the nobleman's residence and the buildings corresponding to all the different functions of the farm were clustered together. I will not describe the oil press, the sheds, the haylofts and the barns. The truth is that my benefactor neglected these matters to such a degree that he ruined his properties and in turn damaged the good people of those lands. He was aware of his poor administration. 'Noblemen are a thing of the past,' he used to tell me. In that respect he agreed with his enemy, J.-J. Rousseau, but only in that respect, given that he was fundamentally aristocratic and, like Seneca, appeared to place intellectual prestige above the brotherhood of man. I do not mean to claim that he did not love the peasants, but rather that he did not treat them as equals. He once defined himself by saying that he avoided 'unnecessary human contact.' I believe this somewhat sibylline statement referred to physical contact when it is not a source of pleasure. Love can make a young shepherdess step up to the throne, but as soon as her sensuous charm — by nature ephemeral — dissipates, she will be abandoned to her miserable fate with the coldest selfishness. The years will go by and perhaps someday the victim and her seducer will encounter one another on some secluded path. The woman, well past her prime, will greet him humbly, calling him 'Senyor', and her old lover will reply with distant joviality. His conscience will not bother him in the least. The woman may fall ill and he will send her five *duros* with the priest. He may seek

8

to help the child who was born in sin, and spare no expense on its schooling and food, but without granting it that which is more precious than all the earth's riches: a legitimate name, a proof of honour. Such is often the nature of the powerful in the world, even those who consider themselves just: they are cold and hard as stone. Miquel, please excuse this inappropriate digression. In the case of my benefactor, I must admit that he never claimed to be virtuous. He was never a hypocrite, but when we see him recognizing his mistakes and yet persisting in them, how can we judge it as anything other than the sin of obstinacy?

The setting of interest to us is the main building of the estate. You enter through a courtyard facing south called a *clasta* (from the Latin *claustrum*) in Mallorca, where the stables and the steward's and farm-hands' quarters are. At the end, an archway leads to a smaller court-yard and then to a hall with a wide staircase leading to the upper floor. In this hall there is a rustic fireplace surrounded with stone benches covered in sheepskins. Long ago it was probably used as a kitchen, but when customs became more refined and called for more luxury, the kitchen was moved to a more secluded area. This does not mean the fireplace may not still be used on occasion to roast a kid or heat a cauldron of water. In the winter it is warm there, even though the door through which one can see both courtyards is not shut until the evening. Above the fireplace there is a small window looking out of an enclosed room. I mention this because it is important to my story. On your left as you enter there is a room with a piano that leads to the dining room.

Upstairs are the drawing rooms and the bedrooms. The staircase leads to a hallway with three large doors, one at either side and a third in the centre, framed with columns supporting classical pediments. This part of the building was renovated some seventy years ago. The central door connects with a sparsely furnished oval room, decorated with Pompeian motifs and lit by a skylight. This room leads to the main drawing room with a marble fireplace set between two balconies overlooking the garden. To the left of the main drawing room is the master bedroom, and to the right another door leads to two other rooms where the Senyor had set up his bedroom and his workroom: these rooms have direct access to the garden down a spiral staircase.

The main drawing room is truly magnificent, lined with light blue silk, full of mirrors and fine china. At one time it was always kept closed, since a series of small rooms and a corridor with a small hidden staircase connected the master bedroom with the ground floor drawing room next to the dining room; however, since their return from Rome in January of 1884, this elegant drawing room was the last to be inhabited by the Senyors. There they died in my arms; with the Senyora went her serene kindness, not always expressed to me, and with the Senyor his mind and his disconcerting enigmas. Before 1884, the room had been a sanctuary, as it is again now. I would give the entire fortune of the Baron de Rothschild to rescue it from the creditors who will soon profane it, unaware of all that has come to pass here, of the meaning of these walls and this Empire-style fireplace, next to which he pretended so often to sleep while mulling over his theories. He lived in the future and in the past. 'The present,' he told me, 'doesn't exist; it's just a point between hope and nostalgia.' It would thus appear that somewhere in his exceedingly pagan soul there was a certain yearning for eternity.

The doors that open at either end of the gallery connect on the one hand with a small room that serves as an antechamber to the archives and on the other with several rooms, one of which is a small oratory so the Senyora would not have to walk down to the chapel and cross the courtyard on rainy days. From this oratory, which had previously been a hallway, another secret stairwell led to the 'dolls' room', which I will refer to later on.

This is, briefly described, the setting for the action. Now add to it the forests and mountains, the poor lands, the rocky hillsides with their meagre, aromatic shrubs; fill it with thrushes in autumn, nightingales in spring; do not forget the forces of nature, the sun, clouds and rain, nor the moonlit nights and the magnificent storms which, in the poet's words, prove the greatness of God:

'*Coelo tonante credidimus Iovem regnare.*'

THREE

It was not until after I had entered the Seminary that I learned the reasons for my benefactors' separation, which at the time appeared to be final. The Senyors had taken in a niece* who was an orphan and sent her to school in Montpellier. Her name was Xima and she must have been ten or twelve years older than I. Her beauty was flawless, and, as the Senyor said, she was quick and affectionate as a cat. She also exhibited the lack of scruples and morality that La Fontaine attributed to felines. It was the year 1859. Lesseps was planning to open the Suez canal and Gounod was preparing the première of *Faust* at the Paris Opera. Don Toni and the Senyora liked to travel; they had already been to France and Italy. Some of their friends in Paris encouraged them to attend the première. Following the politics of Louis Napoleon, Gounod wished to please the Prussian sympathizers with his new work. The Second Empire, out of hatred towards the old Hapsburgs, who were no longer a threat to France, turned to Berlin, apparently a stronghold of the liberal traditions of the House of Frederick William favoured by the Napoleonic dynasty. That dreadful error was to result in Sedan, but for the time being no one was particularly concerned. The boulevards were anti-Austrian and nationalistic. After the battle of Sadova, the people, in their ignorance, acclaimed the Prussians. Three years before Sedan, Offenbach still ridiculed the 'Grand Duchess of Gerolstein' on stage,

*The original *neboda segona* (literally, 'second niece') in fact means a first cousin once removed. Thus, unlike the true niece and nephews referred to in other instances, Donya Xima was not an heiress to the Bearn estate (Translator's note).

representing feudalism in its last agony and thus favouring the notion of a Prussian royal hegemony. Goethe's *Faust* was the symbol of an impatient, violent race that would not settle for the promise of Heaven, but wished to possess it in this world, even at the price of making a pact with the Devil. Gounod recounted the legend, and his version was well received by the Tuileries. There was ample praise in the newspapers. The Senyor commented on the event.

'I'm already forty-eight years old, Maria Antònia, and you're no child either. We should go and find out that German doctor's secret. We'd be young again.'

It was no secret: all you had to do was sell your soul to the Devil, which for Dona Maria Antònia was a matter not to be mentioned even in jest.

'Don't be outrageous, Tonet. Do you want to burn in Hell?'

'No. But to be young again . . .'

'Hush.'

'Just think . . .'

'I don't want to.'

Suddenly uncle and niece vanished; they had run off to Paris. The news spread like wildfire. Despite her tendency to avoid drama, Dona Maria Antònia could hardly ignore the facts on that occasion. However, there were no unpleasant scenes. When the Senyor returned, he simply found that she had moved to the townhouse in the village, and a few hours later the priest appeared, notifying him of their peaceful separation, and begging him to grant his conjugal authorization.

'The Senyora,' said the priest, 'would like you to sign a document her lawyer has drawn up; she's asked me to assure you that it is not out of mistrust, but for your mutual convenience.'

'Dona Maria Antònia has plenty of reasons to mistrust me,' replied the Senyor, and then signed the document without reading a word of it.

The scandal was accentuated by the fact that his niece had remained in Paris, where she had apparently become the lover of some young society lion, a Duke of the Empire. Don Toni, who had been strong enough to lead an eighteen-year-old astray, lacked the strength to make her return to the island. The Duke was rich, elegant and far younger than he. The Senyor told me the story a hundred times, as if it did not concern him at all. 'You've opened an entire new world to me, Tonet; don't expect me to leave it just now,' she had said. 'I want to enjoy myself while I can. Go back to Bearn and don't worry about me. I know you'll understand.'

The most prominent gentlemen in Paris sought her company. Rumour had it that the Emperor wished to meet her. The Senyor returned alone, hoping that Dona Maria Antònia would let bygones be bygones as she had on other occasions, and determined to love her more than ever, like those sailors who leave a woman in each port (here I quote the Senyor) and while at sea create a synthesis of them all, turning several different, changing, vague images into the sole image of their wedded wife. This time, however, he had gone too far.

'Father,' Don Toni said, 'please let her know that I can hardly blame her. Some things can't be explained in words, but it can happen that in time one understands them when one no longer even expects to. If some day my wife were able to forget this affair (which, I grant you, would not be easy) I am and always will be here, waiting for her.'

The priest lacked a sense of humour, but Don Toni thought he glimpsed a faint smile. He would indeed have to wait for the time when forgiveness arrived of its own accord, like a divine revelation.

They spent ten years apart, although not far from each other. Dona Maria Antònia lived in the village, at the old Bearn townhouse, which she had inherited from her mother's side of the family; as I have already mentioned, she and Don Toni were first cousins. He never left the estate, and was always surrounded with books. At that time I was studying at the Seminary and spent all my vacations here. Bearn seemed to me like a great, mysterious palace. I had never known anything better; I thought it was the best on earth. The archives, decorated with old swords, recorded in their parchments the family's glorious deeds. But what were those deeds? What I most longed to explore was that mysterious 'dolls' room', which was always locked and which no one even dared to mention. More than once, since I knew how to open the door to the secret staircase, I had walked upstairs to that room, only to reach another locked door. Peering through the keyhole was useless; the curtains in the room were drawn and you could not see a thing. After asking many questions and getting my fair share of slaps across the face, I managed to deduce from Madò Francina's words that one of the Senyors' ancestors had gone mad and died in that room. I was also intrigued when I heard that my benefactor paid for the schooling of certain children without my having any notion why.

In the autumn of 1866 the Senyor introduced me to Jaume, and said I was to treat him like a brother. I had just turned fifteen.

'He's always been at school,' I was told. 'He may be as educated as you, but he's never played ball; he's never handled a gun or caught thrushes in a net. Now that the season has begun, you ought to show him the woods. He needs to run around in the fresh air . . .'

Jaume was two or three years younger than I. He looked like a boy. I was already a man. Even though I always strictly followed the Senyor's advice, I took on the child with a certain hostility. He was blond; he was intelligent and sensitive. He was afraid of the mules and even of the sheep. He did not know how to swim or throw stones. In the world of Bearn, which he found terrifying, I was his only refuge, and he did not leave my side for a single moment. I could not say exactly why I disliked him. There was something prissy about him; his manners seemed at odds with his masculinity. Youth is intolerant, as the Senyor would say, and exceedingly proud. 'The years enlighten us, Joanet, but not without making us corrupt and cynical.' Aside from my manly pride, intolerant of ambiguities, I undoubtedly harboured the jealousy a person of my condition always feels towards an intruder. Jaume threatened to take my place in the Senyor's heart. My position in the house was precarious, and depended on my master's whim. There may also have been another more complicated motive, an instinct of self-defence against unknown dangers which made me react harshly to his need for tenderness. And that poor child certainly needed to be loved. Following the instructions I had been given, I attempted to strengthen his sensitive nature and teach him to be brave. He learned not to fear gunfire and to swim in the reservoir. His admiration for me grew. A few weeks later, he looked like a different person, and the Senyor congratulated me.

'I wonder, when will you be as strong as Joan?' he asked the child. 'Didn't you say you wanted to be an artilleryman?'

Those words fired the boy with excitement and all he could think of was exercising and running and climbing trees. Because he was weak, he never wanted to be left behind. The sun and the wind had brought out the colour in his cheeks, ridding him of his city pallor. However, the transformation was only skin-deep. When he climbed a mountain, he would run out of breath and have to sit down. I still thought he was faking. To this day I could not say whether I made an effort to think otherwise; I have already said the reasons for my ill will were unclear. Yet although my contempt continued, with time I could not help but admire that child who had studied abroad, spoke French better than I, wrote alexandrines and knew the history of Rome. I was taken aback by his being so fair and so bright. He tried to compete with me in our games, and I, in turn, wished I had the intellectual qualities which, thanks to him, I was beginning to appreciate for the first time. They say emulation leads to progress. In this case it led to death. Even after all these years I am unable to distinguish the conscious from the involuntary aspect of the incident. The truth is that despite the good colour he had from the sun, Jaume was becoming more frail, and I knew it. He spent his last days in an electrified state, burning up the last bit of life left in him and willing to follow me on any absurd adventure. As his strength ran out his unwillingness to surrender only increased. It was particularly painful to him when I beat him right away in our fights, so I would prolong the games like a cat with a mouse; although it flattered him, it also drew him closer to his death. Our matches usually took place on the threshing floor, a vast, poetic arena surrounded by oaks. On the day I once told you about, the game went on longer than usual. I suddenly realized that Jaume's body was yielding, and his face was sheet-white. He said he was sleepy, and dozed off on the hay. Half an hour later, when we called him to supper, we found him dead. The Senyor kept his composure despite my being distressed to a suspicious degree. That affair, which he was never to mention again, was far more obvious to him than it was to me. The doctor diagnosed a heart attack. ('What would he know...' I heard Don Toni murmur.) I was desperate. I could not turn to the comfort of confession because I did not know exactly what I had done wrong. Anyone who had listened to me would undoubtedly have absolved me: we were playing. He got tired. He had a heart attack. At fifteen, I was unable to examine my conscience the way I can now, but I was aware of my degree of responsibility. My relationship with that child was very strange indeed. There is a cruel, arrogant tendency in me which under normal circumstances is dormant. The games I used to think of as harmless have an evil side to them, and there are few who have not felt sadistic instincts awakening within them when they fight. That is why I have never since wanted to practise those essentially pagan exercises, too close to sensuality, which I believe to be at odds with the spirit of Christianity.

Jaume's pride was as strong as mine. One of the first days after we met, I had confronted him with a verb that was an offence to the dignity of a twelve-year-old: *minauder*. I always felt I had to win at our games, which was not much to my credit. He, on the other hand, taught me the moral lesson of how to die like a hero. I may not have killed him with my hands, but I did with a verb. His French was better than mine.

FOUR

The Senyor did not like the City. He had been born at Bearn and studied in Madrid shortly after the invasion of the Hundred Thousand Sons of Saint Louis.

'Those were the years of the worst absolutism, followed by tremendous liberal anarchy,' he told me. 'The French of the Restoration didn't think they could instill any order here without a dictatorship, and they weren't altogether wrong. However, they would have liked to impose a more moderate government, as is obvious when one considers that the Duke of Angoulême imprisoned the members of the Regency of Urgell, among them the Archbishop Elect of Tarragona. Even Chateaubriand, the famous author of the *Génie du christianisme*, had denied the Regency's authority. In other words, they all found our absolutists too extreme, to such an extent that before long Ferdinand VII did not seem absolute enough to many Spaniards and the Apostolic Uprising emerged after having been planned in the forests of Catalunya. I was about nineteen at the time. It was a period of utter confusion, with different anti-liberal factions killing each other instead of the enemy.'

His criteria were clear enough to keep him from excessive accusations against Ferdinand, whose memory, like that of his daughter Isabel, is now execrated by almost everyone.

'They accuse them of the most contradictory facts, you know,' he told me. 'They'll say on the one hand that he was an autocrat, on the other that he used the support of the populace; that he sought counsel among the Dukes who favoured him or from the water-seller at the

17

spring of the Berro. If that had been true, the democrats would have honoured his memory, but are there really any democrats in Spain? Ever since the War of Independence, everything has been pure anarchy here.'

It was not easy for him to accept that when you leave the path of religious unity you fall into a state of confusion worthy of the Tower of Babel. At my age, I was drawn to discussion, despite the fact that respect held me back. Were the anarchy and the confusion my benefactor bemoaned not the natural outcome of the principles of 1789, drawn directly from the Encyclopedia?

'Your Honour,' I dared to say, 'remember that the very men who fought Napoleon proclaimed the Constitution of Cadiz and allowed freedom of the press. We won the battles, but the invaders left their mark.'

'You little devil! You're too young to be jumping to conclusions with such assurance,' he exclaimed, pulling my ear.

Even though I did not know what to attribute it to, I realized that my assurance pleased him. Due to some strange vanity, he was also pleased to see that as I grew I was becoming strong and graceful. He had asked the rector of the Seminary to let me swim and play ball; he proposed that I emulate the beautiful athletes of antiquity perpetuated in Greek statues. He even set up a small gymnasium at the estate so I could exercise during my holidays. Veneration for sports has always struck me as inappropriate in a man of the cloth. You and I, Miquel, have discussed this many a time: the fate of a vigorous body is love or war, both of which are forbidden to us. I was too ashamed to confess to him that for me physical fitness was a kind of martyrdom. Besides, since he had not made a vow of chastity, he did not share my terror of lust; and as the pagan Gautier could have asked the disciplined monks of Zurbarán: '*Pour le traiter ainsi, qu'a donc fait votre corps?*'

When you do not accept the painful mystery of Original Sin there are many things you cannot understand. I do not mean to attribute to him the sacrilegious attempt to lead me down the path of sin; if anything, quite the contrary. Even though he did not really believe in certain things, he would have liked me to face the throes of passion with strength and bravery, so that through the child he had taken in out of benevolence he could live the spiritual adventures denied him by paganism and the indulgence of his century. The fact is that he did not wish to give up any aspect of Creation. If he wished to make a handsome youth out of me, it may have been because he had a somewhat frail constitution himself, and since he was insensitive neither to the fascination of women nor to sophistical arguments, he must have enjoyed the sight of a naïve athlete, both chaste and devout: a new wax figure in the Musée Grévin of his memory.

Long before the Paris scandal, the Senyor had severed relations with almost all his family. Although he was polite in his manners, his advanced ideas were publicly known. Nobody knew exactly what they were, but everyone wanted to pass judgement on them. They went so far as to claim that during Easter he had thrown the priest out when he went to bless the house; in fact, he received him graciously and gave him a gold *duro* every year. It was also rumoured that he had slapped an altar boy in the Cathedral, which was true, but they overlooked the fact that the boy had been quarrelling with another child during the Holy Mass. Those better informed claimed he was a Freemason.

'If it goes on like this, I wouldn't be surprised if they end up making rhymes about me, like they did about my ancestor,' he once told me.

He was joking, but that baseness of spirit did not please him in the least. Besides, his wife was a Bearn from head to toe: she may have believed — and she was wrong — that in the country there are fewer dangers than in the city. For one reason or another, as the years went by, they spent more and more time at the estate, until finally they never left it.

'I don't know what they see in the old quarter by the Cathedral,' my benefactor used to say. 'I can understand that foreigners find it interesting, because they have no intention of living there. I would force them to spend a whole winter in one of those dark, dank halls that are fifteen yards long, without a ray of sunlight, decorated with black paintings, where you can't even see what's in the picture.'

His criticism was sincere. Besides, Palma made him long for the other cities he had visited with his wife. He liked Genoa, with its beautiful palaces, which he preferred to the ones in Florence; but above all, he loved Paris.

'France is the country of intelligence,' he often told me. 'Campoamor wrote that it's "*El país del ingenio y de la guerra*"* be-

*The country of wit and war (Translator's note).

19

cause he undoubtedly agreed with the Bourbons and Bonaparte. But even though Napoleon has now been taken to the Invalides, he was neither French nor good at anything but wreaking havoc and disorder. Like all good dictators, he managed to rave in the name of God. His power didn't even last twenty years, and all the victories attributed to him on the sides of the Arc de Triomphe — Saragossa, Wagram, Austerlitz — are nothing but defeats.'

I asked him whether it was true that they did not know what direction his body faced in the grave.

'It's true,' he replied, 'but you can't go on like this. I'll have to show you these wonders sometime. It was all built during the time of Louis XIV, by the architects Bruant and Mansard, two men who worked for posterity. Bonaparte,' he added (he rarely called him Napoleon) 'is in five or six coffins, one of which is made of lead. The sarcophagus, made of red porphyry, sits on a green neoclassical pedestal and faces south; but since it's symmetrical and so are the coffins, there's no way of knowing in what direction the General lies (he never referred to him as the Emperor), which would appear to symbolize that the Napoleonic adventure, ultimately, has neither head nor tail.'

Night had fallen and we were in the garden. It was a splendid summer evening. He was silent and looked up at the sky. His classical wig shone silver in the moonlight.

'Years ago, on a night like this . . .' he murmured. But he stopped himself suddenly, and started talking about the palaces of the old French monarchy.

'Napoleon III lives in luxury, not because of his uncle, who never succeeded in building a thing,' he said, 'but thanks to Catherine de Medici: the Tuileries are the work of a Florentine princess and artist who chose to live away from the hustle and bustle of the Louvre. Then it seemed suitable to connect the Louvre and the Tuileries, and they built the hall called *du bord de l'eau*, famous because the kings of France used to heal the sick there.'

I was surprised.

'Heal?'

The Senyor smiled.

'They were neither doctors nor saints, but they were kings. It's something in between. Now we're living in the century of positive science and it all sounds awfully strange to us. However, in the long run, science won't be able to part with its element of witchcraft.'

'But the Kings of France, the country of Reason ... were they sorcerers?'

'I insist: they were kings. It must have been marvellous to see them walk by, dressed in purple and ermine, as in the stained glass windows of the Sainte Chapelle, among those poor souls, touching them softly and pronouncing the magic words: "*Dieu te guérisse; le roi te touche.*" '

'What kinds of illnesses did they heal?'

The Senyor smiled again.

'Endowed, as they were, with supernatural powers, they should have cured them all, but for some strange reason they specialized in scrofula and the mumps.'

He paused and added: 'Perhaps because they happen to heal on their own.'

Was it really a hoax? The Senyor spoke in a serious tone and I did not end up asking my question; as happened so many times, he saw it coming, or asked himself the same one. Speaking softly, he added: 'Truth and lies are parts of a whole. Charcot says that hysterics have fits because their nature forces them to do so, so one can't really say they're doing it for effect. Precautions seem better than lies. Wise men in the times of Alexander the Great put chicken eggs through bottlenecks. They did it using two methods: either uttering a magic word, or soaking the egg for hours in a vinegar bath that softened the shell. Good magic supposedly called upon both methods.'

I could not help but speak up.

'If they softened the shell to get the egg through, they had no need for a magic word.'

'You really think so, son?'

He changed the subject to avoid an argument.

'It's a beautiful night out. Do you like these mountains?'

'I was born here,' was my reply.

It was a beautiful night. I wished I could have suggested to the Senyor that he join me in prayer. There was a deep silence. I shut my eyes and collected my thoughts. Behind us, the jasmine gave off its perfume, mingling with the scents of the forest.

'I too was born here,' my benefactor said, 'and I hope to die here. One of these days, the Senyora will get tired of the townhouse and come back.'

It was the first time he had mentioned their separation.

'And you,' he continued, 'will be the family priest. So you will attend to our last moments.'

I was sitting at his feet, and he caressed my ear.

'But we'll live many years yet, God willing. If we could only fly all the way to Paris and back ... there'll probably come a day when balloons will be perfected so we can travel by air.'

Sometimes he liked to rave.

FIVE

We had a good music teacher at the Seminary. Father Pi was a lover of modern music and had a preference for Wagner, who was almost unknown in Spain. He claimed that Wagner composed the music of the future.

'He has revolutionized everything,' he told me, enthusiastically.

His admiration was paradoxical in such a conservative, moderate man. Even more incomprehensible was his admiration for Bismarck and the bellicose, Protestant Germany. The truth is that nowadays there are many bourgeois raving about *Tannhäuser* and *Die Walküre.*

'It's hardly surprising,' the Senyor told me. 'The Prince Bismarck is a man of humble extraction. William I is only a descendant of some poor Marquis of Brandenburg. Dreams of grandeur are typical of those who aren't much in the first place. Such a distortion of history, a Hohenzollern proclaimed Emperor at the *Galerie des Glaces* in Versailles, has to have gone to their heads. Wagner reflects a state of things that can't last very long.'

Repeating concepts I had learned from my teachers, I ventured to ask him whether he thought that Germany was the greatest cultural and military power in the world.

'I believe none of that, and such ideas surprise me coming from a future priest. Prussian culture is merely Bismarck's *Kulturkampf*, or a war to death against Catholicism.'

He was right. However, why was Germany depicted as a virtuous, healthy country? Youth expects an answer to every question, and I found one of my own: 'Because France is a corrupt nation.' Every day the paper spoke of the immorality and anarchy of France, and one must admit that if literature and theatre are reflections of their cultures, the country of Saint Louis cannot be proud of names such as Renan, Comte, Dumas, Emile Zola and so many others.

'You're forgetting,' said the Senyor, 'Bernadette Soubirous and the miracles of Lourdes; Chateaubriand, Jean Croisset, author of *The Christian Year*, Louis Veuillot...'

One can always prove what one pleases; nothing is absolute, except for God. I was lost in confusion.

'Wagner,' the Senyor continued, 'is as excessive as Bonaparte. Therefore he isn't great, because greatness implies proportion. I admit they both knew their craft and that within the limitations of their professions they did prove skilful, but neither is a man of the future, precisely because they're incapable of seeing things as a whole. That's a shortcoming we tend to call genius so as not to call it monstrosity, which is more or less the same thing. Wagner's success blew over as fast as Napoleon's.'

'We can only find a supreme vision by coming closer to God.'

The Senyor did not seem to hear me.

'They're both excessive,' he continued. 'They didn't know human nature. Who's capable of enduring the reiterations of *Siegfried*, the din of *Die Walküre*, to say nothing of the length of each scene? No stomach can take a thirty-course meal. The French got tired of their hero before long. Even Béranger, a firm supporter of Bonaparte, interpreted the feeling of his times when he wrote:

> *Terreur des nuits, trouble des jours,*
> *Tambours, tambours, tambours, tambours!*
> *M'étourdirez-vous donc toujours,*
> *Tambours, tambours, tambours, tambours?'*

I was not interested in Wagner, whose music I did not know at all, but I certainly was interested in the moral dispute over the German hegemony. The Senyor believed that the Empire of Bismarck would not last and that Prussia appeared to be stronger than it really was. He believed it was a country of specialists, incapable of looking ahead and discerning the hierarchies of the soul.

'Those kinds of people,' he said, 'are easily disoriented. They're fundamentally anarchic.'

24

Yet anarchy was a quality my professors attributed precisely to the French.

'Paris,' Father Pi would tell me, 'is an annex of Hell. A city of atheists, indulging in pleasure and vice. The war of the seventies was a warning from God, but to no avail. They've given in to suicidal demagoguery; the Republic has been infiltrated by socialism. It can only lead to chaos.'

Father Pi always dropped the names Voltaire and Renan (I do not know whether he had read Nietzsche or whether at the time the latter had already written his blasphemous *Anti-Christ*). When he spoke of socialism and the materialistic interpretation of history (this did not occur to me until many years later) he did not seem to know that Karl Marx, who inspired the revolution of 1848, was German.

I said at the start that the Senyor introduced me to literature and that his teachings were opposed to what I learned at the Seminary. Our old professors spoke in hyperboles. The words 'immortality', 'glory', 'laurels', were frequent in their vocabulary and were repeated with cold monotony. The adjectives lavished by the poets of antiquity became insignificant, as the Senyor would have said, because they were out of proportion. The Seminary was, above all, grammatical. They always spoke of declensions and objects, verbs and adverbs.

'Be careful with grammar,' he told me. 'Grammarians are honest workers who place rocks next to each other and bind them with the cement of syntax. That's as far as a mason can see. The building as a whole, conceived by the architect, doesn't concern him; he can't even grasp it.'

Among the papers he left me I find many statements defending voluntary self-control and moderation. He was an enemy of the romanticism that has to scream and shout to express feelings and passions. 'The least literature can aspire to,' he wrote, 'is to express the states of the soul in an intelligible, or, in other words, an intelligent manner. The best writers will be the ones who come closest to reaching that end, which is, incidentally, inaccessible. Those who do not even strive for that — Victor Hugo in *Hernani*, for instance — are not even copyists. Nonetheless,' he added, 'prose that can be understood ceases to be considered brilliant by the common herd that places Chateaubriand above La Fontaine.'

Apropos of La Fontaine, a few weeks before his death the Senyor told me that writers have always attributed far too much importance to themselves. As far as he was concerned, La Fontaine was one of the few exceptions to that rule. He was an *amateur*: he only sought his own pleasure. For Don Toni art was a little like children, who cannot be conceived following a method, but only in the careless joy and intimacy of the night.

I asked him whether it was true that he had been a superficial man, who did not hold the morals of his fables.

'Certainly. For La Fontaine, the moral wasn't so important. His strength lies in his wit, his *joie de vivre*, the variety in metre and rhyme. If, for example, he attributes evil qualities to cats, it's not because he's opposed to them, which would be absurd, since every species follows its own nature. On the contrary, he does so because he finds it amusing. He himself was a cat: lazy, selfish and wild. He spent his fortune, sold the position he'd inherited from his father and always lived off others. That isn't so easy to accomplish unless you're endowed, as cats are, with some redeeming qualities.'

I chose not to ask him what those might be. The Senyor continued. 'He always had a benefactor. The most loyal one was Madame de la Sablière. Incidentally, they met in a very strange way. When a rich man with whom he lived passed away, La Fontaine walked out into the street before the body had even been buried and ran into Madame de la Sablière on a street corner. "I was looking for you," the woman said. "Where will you go now?" "Wherever you go, Madame," he replied.'

That lack of dignity embarrassed me. Without my saying a word, the Senyor suspected my feelings.

'It's true, La Fontaine had no dignity,' he said, 'but he did have wit. Save your anger for a better occasion,' he added smiling, 'and remember that dignity can be a form of arrogance, or, in other words, a mortal sin . . . and utter nonsense, too.'

I could not conceive of a mortal sin being nonsense — nonetheless, before the greatness of God, arrogance must appear as the most nonsensical of all sins.

We were talking under the stars. It was late and he gave me his hand to kiss. 'You must reconcile yourself with La Fontaine,' he added as we parted. 'If I were born again, I'd devote myself entirely to literature and adopt one of his famous alexandrines as my motto: "*A beaucoup de plaisir je mêle un peu de gloire. . .*"'

I have looked for the alexandrine, and as yet have been unable to find it. Obviously, trying to find that line among all La Fontaine wrote is like looking for a needle in a haystack. I do not know whether the Senyor's prodigious memory had begun to fail him every now and then. In any case, if the alexandrine were apocryphal, it deserved to be authentic and the fact that he could have invented it only proves the man's affinity with the lighthearted spirit of the author of the *Fables*.

SIX

According to the Senyor's instructions, my gymnasium had been set up on a landing that connects with the anteroom of the archives through a narrow staircase built into the width of the wall. It was a large space with an arched ceiling, provided with bars, vaulting horses and other such devices, and a statue of a classical athlete standing in one corner.

'You must strive to look like this athlete,' Don Toni had told me. 'Your religious calling is by no means opposed to gymnastics.'

I disagreed with that outlook, even though my nature drew me to exercise and sports. You know perfectly well, Miquel, that before Jaume's death I wanted to leave the Seminary, so at odds with my senses and my temperament. If I have sought refuge in the Church it has not been out of virtue, but out of weakness, and even perhaps because my vanity rebelled against the role I was destined to perform in life. It could be that Don Toni died without truly understanding me, because we came from such different worlds. For him, existence was easy: When he was born he found everything already achieved, and he could allow himself to live off the fortune that had been amassed by his ancestors. Such circumstances made an epicurean out of him, a man destined to die in this world and perhaps also (God forbid) in the next. Physical fitness was torture for me. *Mens sana in corpore sano* is a good maxim for a free man, but not for one who has made the vow of chastity. There are numerous ascetic authors who recommend muscular exhaustion for warding off carnal thoughts. That does not apply to all characters. For years I have been an avid sportsman and

28

mountain climber, but all to no avail; if anything, quite the contrary. Exercise may, indeed, be the main enemy of chastity, given that far from wearing down the vital functions, it excites them. The current tendency, influenced by North American Protestantism, which aspires to modernize the clergy, could have dreadful consequences.

It was not yet nine o'clock and I was doing my bar exercises when I heard a knock on the door. In surprise, I asked who it was, because I was not presentable. The Senyor's voice replied.

'It's me, Joan.'

Unaware of what I was doing, covered in sweat and almost naked, I opened the door. Don Toni, smiling, put his arm around my neck and stood me next to the statue I mentioned above.

'Excellent,' he said. 'The only difference is that the Greeks — the ones made of marble, obviously — didn't sweat.'

I blushed and asked for permission to change.

'Hush. Come with me,' said the Senyor.

He draped a towel over my shoulders and led me to the window; the shutters were half closed. I ought to mention that the gymnasium faced an inner courtyard surrounded by the steward's quarters.

'From up here we'll hear the vet.'

I remembered that the vet was due from Inca that morning to castrate some of the pigs.

'Let's listen to what that Republican has to say.'

The vet was indeed an enemy of landlords and Senyors. He had deigned to come, but only in a smart little dog-cart of his own, and he spoke in an authoritative tone. He walked into the courtyard with his sleeves rolled up, sporting a very fine shirt; as he washed his hands in a basin they had placed on the ledge, he engaged in conversation with the peasants.

'This is pretty primitive,' he said. 'These Senyors really are behind the times. They don't even have a bathroom!'

My benefactor squeezed my arm.

'They do have a bathroom, with a proper zinc tub and a mirror,' said Madò Francina.

'A tub you couldn't buy for less than eight *duros* now,' the steward added.

'I'm surprised,' the vet said. 'These people tend to think of bathing as a sin.'

'Hold your horses,' Madò Francina interrupted. 'I didn't say

29

whether they did or didn't bathe. Who are you to nose about other people's business?'

'They must use it for decoration.'

'That's none of your business.'

'At Bearn,' the steward interrupted, 'we've got everything you can find in Inca, or even in the City.'

'The house looks big,' the Republican said, 'but your quarters are old and gloomy.'

The Senyor looked at me and smiled. 'There he goes, leading them on!'

'Nobility is a thing of the past,' the man from Inca continued. 'Just look at the way they work the land. I saw some vines back there; they looked pitiful.'

'The vines are dying because of a bug that's eating away at their roots.'

'The bugs are the noblemen, who only think about spending their money in the City.'

'Or in Paris,' the Senyor murmured.

The vet began a diatribe against people who do not work, and claimed, somewhat incoherently, that he was much better off than many landowners who were swamped with debts. I noticed that he tried to avoid using the word 'Senyors'. He then proceeded to announce in a haughty tone that he was charging half a *ral* more than last year for each pig. He had finished washing. He put a new velvet jacket on over his magnificent shirt and went out to his trap. I must add that he had no servant in livery to help him into it.

'People like him,' my benefactor said, smiling, 'will be the end of us. Get dressed and come down to breakfast; your hot chocolate's waiting.'

We were leaving the table when the village priest appeared, and we immediately guessed the reason for his visit. Every year, in the last days before carnival, the same scene took place.

'Tuesday is drawing near,' he said, 'and I thought it was time to call on you to discuss this problem.'

'It's very kind of you to have come, Father. If you please, we can sit by the fire. Don't leave, Joan. You'll soon be a priest yourself, and you should know about these "problems"...'

I believe Don Andreu was not the least bit pleased to have a third party present when discussing a matter to which he attributed great

30

importance and which could only be approached with insinuations and allusions. The priest could not consent to there being a carnival ball in the village; year after year, by tacit agreement, the celebration took place at the estate. It was an old dispute between the Church and the Senyors — a concealed one, needless to say — that always ended in negotiation.

Don Andreu began a brief speech listing the dangers of carnival, originally a pagan festivity; without being pedantic, he made a historical summary of the matter.

'The Church cannot approve of it,' he said. 'The very act of covering one's face to indulge in the sort of rash or even disgraceful language that no one would dare use face to face . . .'

'We shouldn't forget,' the Senyor retorted, 'that there's much jest and playful irony in such rudeness.'

'That's undoubtedly so in some cases,' the priest granted. 'Neither dancing nor merrymaking can be considered sinful in its own right, and the Bible teaches us that David danced before the Ark of the Covenant. But unfortunately, we aren't angels of purity, so it often happens that things begin in innocence and jest, as your Honour says, only to end in sin, particularly when one's hidden behind a mask, if not from the eyes of the Lord, certainly from those of man.'

As in every other year what Don Andreu disapproved of, and rightly so, was the impunity bestowed by disguise. However, the Senyor preferred not to delve into such matters, because for him the anonymity of the disguise was the whole point of the celebration.

'Father, please consider,' he said (and this truly reflects his nature) 'that if we did away with carnival, we would also be doing away with Holy Lent.'

'Lent stands for penitence, not only because of carnival, but because of any other sins as well.'

'The nature of the sin doesn't matter,' the Senyor argued subtly, 'but it's essential that there be sin for there to be Lent.'

'On the other hand,' Don Andreu continued without picking up the argument, 'feigning what one does not feel can lead to no good. People tend to lie, and if nothing else, carnival is in that respect a school of falsehood.'

The Senyor was lost in thought.

'When Thespis invented the Greek farce,' he finally said, 'Solon judged it immoral precisely, as you mentioned, because it taught falsehood: "It will get men used to breaking their agreements, lying ..." But Solon didn't understand that Thespis wasn't a sorcerer creating something new; he was only defining something that already existed. Men ceased to be naïve, the European spirit became more complex and an indication of that complexity was precisely the pleasure of considering falsehood entertaining. But falsehood itself, needless to say, was nothing new. Lies are as old as the world itself; they give us the same pleasure as seeing our reflection in a mirror.'

'The world is slowly giving in to madness,' Don Andreu said.

It was now the Senyor who chose not to pick up on those words, and continued: 'Long before Thespis, Jacob had deceived his father pretending to be Esau. Esau was hairy, so Jacob covered his hands with a sheepskin. He swindled for money, whereas when Thespis played a character he didn't expect to be seen as such; he expected to be seen as an actor. All he wanted to do was entertain, as he openly confessed. Contrary to what Solon believed, Thespis was the most sincere of men. Have you ever thought, Father,' he continued, 'that the people in this village never have a chance to enjoy themselves? Work must have its compensations. What do you think, Joan?'

I believed such statements shared some of the notions the Republican from Inca had expressed an hour earlier. Not having recovered from the effects of his spiteful arrogance, I could not ignore the dangers of socialistic arguments. The priest remained silent. Don Toni continued, as if he were talking to himself. 'I know people, particularly some ladies, who have never been to a ball, whereas they never miss a funeral. In the long run, that must have an effect on one's character. We engage in fewer and fewer activities as time goes by; we'll end up not knowing how to do anything but die.'

'May God grant us all a peaceful death, Don Toni,' said the priest.

'Amen. But only after having had our share of life. Now that I'm no longer young, I must admit that I feel sorry for some people. The other day I heard two boys whispering under the cypress trees in the garden. One of them would have given his right arm to have a watch. He said this monstrosity stupidly, like someone who has never known the value of having a healthy, normal body.' (As he uttered these words, my benefactor stared at me.) 'I may add,' he continued, turning to the priest, 'that they weren't little children; they were both old enough to ...'

'God bless them,' the priest mumbled.

Don Toni seemed impatient.

'Let us not condemn mankind to eternal limbo. These people are poor, coarse and ignorant. They lead uneventful lives. Let us not deny them a little amusement once a year.'

'Even if they indulge in objectionable behaviour?'

'Perhaps even at that price.'

I ventured to mention that the year before a silver spoon had disappeared. The Senyor gave me a sharp glance.

'Didn't I tell you that Biel would give his right arm for a watch? If they don't know the value of an arm, how can you expect them to attribute the slightest importance to pocketing a spoon?'

'Precisely because they can't judge, Don Toni, letting them wear masks can make for all sorts of mischief. Your Honour knows I dread these celebrations.'

'I realize one can't leave them on their own, and in the village you lack the power to control them when they start going too far.'

'You know how it is. One of the guards is old; the other one is bedridden...'

'I know. It would be safer here. At any rate, we have Madò Francina, who's more than able to confront the entire village if need be. Father, it isn't that I have any particular interest in bringing them here to dance knowing that you disapprove...'

'If at least they didn't hide their faces...'

'We can't do these things half-heartedly. Let them come as they please. They'll have time to pray and reflect during Lent. As I said, I have no interest in their coming to make a rumpus and steal my spoons, but if the ball can't take place in the village for the reasons you mentioned, you know I'll be pleased to oblige, and Madò Francina won't allow...'

I don't know whether Don Andreu realized how skilfully the Senyor managed to support a celebration which the priest had not authorized while making his triumph seem like an act of submission. Don Andreu was hardly stupid, even though sometimes his modesty allowed him to seem so.

'I'm most grateful,' he murmured.

Don Toni, triumphant, flaunted his concessions.

'And do bear in mind,' he said, 'that I'm not authorizing this either; it has no significance other than its being a custom. Let them do as they please. I won't invite a soul. However, if they appear on

Tuesday and take over the house, I can hardly turn them out. That was only a joke. These "takeovers" are more and more frequent these days.'

The matter ended, as it did every year, in agreement.

SEVEN

It was shortly before the September Revolution that my benefactor, who had spent a fortune on Dona Xima, thought of selling the house in the City, which had been empty for several years. We went to stay there for the sale towards the end of summer in 1868. Don Toni chose to consult the Senyora first through the village priest. Dona Maria Antònia's response was as clear and quick as her character. 'If some day we were to live together again, and that is a matter I do not wish to discuss for the time being, I would consent on the condition that we never leave these mountains. In the City people are always talking, and we're too old to be the subject of gossip. Here in the village the scandal was so great at the time that it blew over long ago. I believe it would be good for Tonet to get rid of some debts, provided he knows how to.'

We stayed in the City for about five weeks. The sale did not appeal to the nephews or niece, who already considered the house as good as theirs. It was an old building on one of the streets near the Cathedral, with a gothic courtyard and a stone staircase. It had a hall covered in paintings from floor to ceiling, and the rooms were well furnished, with damasks and gilded consoles. The result was slightly excessive for a Christian family which, albeit old and respectable, had but a meagre income.

'In any case,' my benefactor said, 'the heirs would have had to sell it the minute our eyes had been closed. My nephews don't want to study and will never amount to much. My niece is married to a captain...'

Dona Magdalena had married a captain from the mainland with

nothing to his name but his profession. All her brothers did was sit around smoking and gambling at the club. The Senyors could not stand them, and yet did not wish to disinherit them; they had no children and wished the succession to follow its natural course. They felt it was their duty. Therefore, they never thought of drawing up a will; they simply did not see much of them during the periods they spent in the City. With the sale of the house, all relations were finally severed.

In those days the City was rather rundown, with narrow streets full of convents. The revolutionary rage of '35 had destroyed some of them, among them the Convent of Santo Domingo, considered the richest and most artistic. The reign of Isabel II, whom some called the *Angèlica*, was prodigal in acts of this sort. Finally, the mobs, who did not respect the sacred laws of the Church, encouraged by the indifference if not by the help of the leaders, went even further: in the September Revolution we saw them knock down and drag along the ground the statue of the queen who was supposed to lead us to freedom and who, much to her own chagrin — she was a good soul, after all — succeeded only in opening the door to licence.

I witnessed that act of vandalism shortly after the Battle of Alcolea. We were walking in formation on our way back from the city walls overlooking the sea. It was a cool, cloudy afternoon; it reminded me of autumn in Bearn. I thought of the thrush, of the blissful fields in the rain, the green grass sprouting up in the pastures. Instead of that beloved image, a sea of lead, menacing and motionless, loomed ahead of me beyond the pier. As we walked up Marina Street, we saw a pack of wicked-looking men in the Avenue of the Born, by the statue of Queen Isabel; they had slipped a rope around her waist and were trying to pull her off the pedestal. The priests who were leading us made us turn back down by the walls and enter by the archway of the Calatrava. Some say that it was a suggestion of one of the guards passively observing the scene, but in fact they may have received orders not to intervene. When I saw the crowd, I walked closer and did not notice when the others turned back. I was left alone. At that moment, a dark, weathered stevedore walked over to me laughing and said in a fatherly tone: 'Don't be afraid, my boy. If you were the bishop you'd be in trouble, but since you aren't anything yet...'

I was not the least bit afraid at that moment and my reply came straight from my heart. 'You have it the wrong way around. Precisely

36

because I'm nobody, you can do whatever you please to me, but if I were the bishop, I'm sure you wouldn't dare touch a thread of my robes.'

'This little brute is looking for trouble,' the stevedore said.

'I'm not, but with this rosary on me I'm not afraid.'

When he saw the cross he left me alone, but only after lifting his finger to his forehead to show I was mad. I sat down on a bench and began praying under the hostile and mistrusting glances of the mob. To this day I do not know what I thought I was proving by adopting an attitude my superiors judged thoughtless. On the one hand, I felt strong enough to knock the man over with a single blow, and doing so would have given me immense physical satisfaction. However, I knew that if I hurt him I'd be tortured by my conscience. Ever since Jaume's tragedy, violence has terrified me, and given a choice between hurting or being hurt, I prefer the latter. The small, dark man who made that insolent attempt to protect me was probably married. I could picture him going home wounded to a miserable house full of dirty, sickly children ... My ability to place myself in other people's shoes is undoubtedly what destroys the aggressive urge that courses through my veins. At Bearn I calmed my restlessness swimming in the reservoir or climbing and hunting in the mountains. None of that was possible at the seminary, and my provocative act sitting down to pray (provocative is in fact what they called it) was probably due to the uneasiness produced in a youthful character by that struggle of conflicting forces. At a certain moment, while I was praying for the ill-fated queen, I looked up at the straining, sweating men, who were not strong enough to knock the statue down and did not even know how to pull properly, and a most extraordinary temptation came over me: I wanted to join them and accomplish what they were incapable of doing. Since I am rather thin, seeing me dressed no one would suspect me to be as strong as I really am. I could imagine the surprise of the growing crowd, I could feel their admiration; and the Devil whispered in my ear that the admiration of the people can, in times of Revolution, be in the interest of the Church. I closed my eyes and gathered my thoughts. A sudden crash forced me to open them. The statue had fallen, and in front of me lay the body of the Queen of Spain shattered to pieces on the muddy street. An illustrious city had just been dishonoured.

During his stay in the City, the Senyor chose to take me to the

37

Opera. *Il Barbiere di Siviglia* was playing. They all sang admirably, and the piece itself was not immoral — the dancers did not perform as they do in others —; but the soprano played Rosina with an excess of passion that was incompatible with the modesty of a good young lady from a decent family. I voiced these impressions to the Senyor, who laughed at my naïveté.

'And what in the world makes you think she's from a decent family?'

And why, in God's name, was I to assume otherwise? Had my literary studies not taught me that theatrical works must set a moral example?

He also showed me the clubroom at the *Círculo*, with its mirror-covered walls and two galleries supported by women, sparsely clad and inspired, I was told, by the Pompeian style. This is where the musicians sat on evenings when there was a ball.

It seems unbelievable to me that a reasonably decent society should have been so eager to attend a club built on the very spot where the Convent of Santo Domingo once stood.

'Life will teach you not to be shocked by anything,' the Senyor told me. 'Everything happens for a reason, and is therefore natural. When you become a priest and listen to people's confessions, you'll understand many things.'

It is not easy for youth to accept compromise. My benefactor's philosophy and my own were following different paths. Not only did forty years separate us, but also an entire cultural background. I have always said, and you and I have argued the point many times, that the morals of noblemen are more complaisant than those of the poor. It was in the heart of the people that the doctrine of Christ first took root. With a very Prussian sense of history, Nietzsche, the sadly notorious creator of superman, says that Christianity is nothing but an insurrection of slaves. He makes the statement with contempt because he does not understand the greatness of an entire people seeking to free itself from the moral slavery in which it was kept by paganism. The fact is that noblemen must be highly virtuous if they are not to sin. We must pray for them even more than for the poor, for theirs, according to the Scriptures, is the kingdom of Heaven. On the days preceding the Battle of Alcolea, there were endless political discussions, even though the local press recommended caution. The Marquis of Collera was purported to be one of the best informed people in the City. He was a young man at the time; he travelled to Madrid and was acquainted with General Serrano, Duke of La Torre. He had already been a Liberal representative (he was later to occupy the same position in the Conservative Party) although not for long. He was a fervid speaker, and his supporters believed that if people had listened to him, Queen Isabel might not have been dethroned. There were nasty rumours about an affair with Dona Obdulia Montcada, an arrogant lady married to a Bearn from the other branch of the family, a rather weak man who died young; she was therefore related to my Senyors. I must add that this side of the family, in which the eldest have the title of Baron, claim that the Bearns are related by marriage to the Princes of Nemours and the Kings of Navarre. According to the Senyor, there are no facts to support such a claim, and there is indeed no reference to that effect in the archives. However, we have no right to deny it, and Don Toni can be accused of treating the subject too lightly in his *Memoirs*. The affair with Dona Obdulia did not dishonour the Marquis; quite the contrary. We must assume nothing serious came of it ('because they were both too stupid', according to the Senyor) and that Dona Obdulia's spiritless husband never heard any of the rumours. The Marquis added to his glory as a speaker the reputation of a Don Juan he was to flaunt all his life, even though in his latter years envious tongues may have hinted at deeds as monstrous as they were inconceivable. That is high society for you: claiming to be Catholic and yet given to self-indulgence. It is not always perversion, but rather frivolity, no less pernicious, that moves the gracious and carefree people of the world.

Apart from the act of vandalism I already mentioned, the authorities tried to maintain order. There were nonetheless some surprises that prove how little is to be expected of human nature. One of the Senyor's cousins was leaving the church of Sant Gaietà, and when she reached Carasses street she had to hide in a doorway so a 'civic rally' could march by. At the head of the group, waving a flag and shouting wildly with her hair loose and tangled, was the lady's cook, a peasant from Caimari who had been a servant at her house for almost forty years. I also heard a story about a little old lady from Pina, the village with the kindest, loveliest people on the entire island. Apparently, the priest of Sant Jaume was rushing off to Mass when he heard the old lady say to him in a low voice: 'You can't run because of those robes. We'll take them off you, don't worry.' What is so strange and gives you a notion of how distorted people's minds have become, is that this woman was also on her way to Mass and listened to the priest with the same devotion as usual. I have also heard, although I could not be sure that it is true, that the coachman of the Count of Biniamar told his Senyor that from that day on he would be the Count and the Count would be the coachman. What is certainly true is that some Senyors in Lluchmayor whose daughter was ill with typhus had their house burned down. They managed to get the girl into a carriage, and on their way into the City they saw the entire estate go up in flames. The fire was so dreadful that it spread to some nearby houses and destroyed the home of the man who had planned the whole thing; he was so horrified that he died on the spot. Revolutions are blind, heedless forces, like lightning. May the Lord preserve us and keep us from them.

At Bearn there were also attempts to revolt, and two extremists started ringing the churchbells without the priest's permission. But the people here have a fair amount of common sense, and when they went down into the square the men were received with a beating they will not forget in a long time. They were embarrassed enough not to make any further attempts of the sort.

These circumstances were hardly the most propitious for the sale of an important property such as the Senyor's town house, and in that respect his relatives were right when they suggested that we should wait. Don Toni listened to no one. Apart from his needing the money, he was in a hurry to leave the City, and all he could think of was going back home to the country, as was only natural.

EIGHT

On September 28, having sold the house at a low price, because there was not much money around and also because he had refused to wait, the Senyor returned to the country. I went with him: the following day was the Patron Saint of Bearn's day.

During the time that they had been living apart, the Senyors only saw each other on that occasion. In order to avoid any unpleasant comments, they had agreed to continue to sit in two chairs placed next to the altar, side by side. After the service, Don Andreu used to go over to greet them and the three would then leave the church together and talk briefly outside the door, facing the village. After a few minutes the Senyor would look at his watch and say out loud: 'It's getting late, and it's quite a way from here to Bearn . . .'

Dona Maria Antònia would reply: 'Especially with those roads that look like riverbeds. It's a good thing the mules are used to them.'

They would say their goodbyes graciously and not see each other for another year. However, that day the conversation was drawn out on the subject of the political developments. Rumour had it that Queen Isabel had fled to France. It was not true just then, but it would be a day later. The priest was uneasy.

'How does your Honour think these people will react if we have a Republic?'

'Stupidly, I should think,' the Senyor replied. 'We'll have to put up with music and speeches, but I doubt if anything important will happen.'

For the moment the villagers were more interested in the Senyors

41

than in the fate of their Queen. When Don Toni disappeared into the coach and his wife had returned to her house, as every other year, the chatter began.

'You'd never guess they weren't getting along.'

'Who says they aren't?'

'Well, then, why aren't they living together?'

'That's another story.'

'It's like the gentlemen in the City, who can be in the midst of a lawsuit and still greet one another in the street.'

'I wonder when they'll get back together...'

'The Senyora can't forgive him. When he left with his niece...'

'And then there was Barbara Titana.'

'That's a lie.'

'A lie?'

'Lies and envy.'

'So you also think it's a lie that the Senyor keeps his light on all night long in his room?' said a voice, shrill with indignation yet held back in fear.

'All night long?' the women asked. 'What could he be doing up so late?'

'You don't know?' asked the indignant and fearful voice. 'Well, neither do I.'

'The one who knows it all is Madò Francina, but she won't open her mouth. She keeps things to herself.'

'I've always heard,' an old woman exclaimed, 'that people who keep their lights on at night are calling for the Devil.'

The priest appeared all of a sudden.

'Enough of this chit-chat. Gossip will be the end of you. Go home and cook your soup, or your supper will be late.'

Existence seemed uneventful in these mountains, and yet was pregnant with psychic life. The Senyor spent his days buried in papers. There was some entirely unjustified gossip about him and Margalideta, a fair girl who died after less than a year at the estate. By then, he already wore a sort of Franciscan habit and a Louis XV wig because he had gone bald. He was thin, with a face as wrinkled as Voltaire's. Rumour had it that he had lost his fortune, but he knew how to reason out the causes of his ruin. Since the workers' revolution of 1848, he believed the world was being re-organized and that the era of bourgeois capitalism was on the decline. He thought socialism would triumph in the end, as he sometimes explained to the priest.

'May the Lord have mercy on us, Don Toni,' he replied.

Then the Senyor uttered one of his prophetic statements: 'They may give it another name and call it something else, but the governments that are determined to fight the signs of the times will only manage to foster them.'

In that respect, he has since been proved right. In regard to nobility, I don't know whether to call his ideas modern or feudal. He was convinced that families improve on their own in the course of time, like good wines. Kings are often no more than parvenus, and, besides, what power do they have to grant certificates of nobility?

'It hasn't yet been proved,' the Senyor even ventured to say to the priest one day, 'that James I* was his father's son.'

'That sort of statement is horrifying.'

'Not really, Don Andreu. Nobody really cares.'

The priest used to come by every so often and try to convince him to destroy his Encyclopedist library. Don Toni made reference to the permission he had requested to read banned works. The reply to his request was being delayed. I cannot believe that he made use of his influence at the Palace in order to defer a response he expected to be negative. I prefer to believe that the bishopric did not want to deny the permission, but they did not wish to grant it either. I think they were more concerned about what he might write than about what he might read. He was said to be working on his *Memoirs*. The people who lived at the estate knew he stayed up all night. He was always expected to do something outlandish. The *Memoirs* he has left, in addition to a few stories and essays, are indeed disconcerting. His wish was to have it all published after his death, and to that effect he gave them to me a few weeks before he died, as if he had a premonition. He gave me the manuscripts and the money I have mentioned to you, pointing out that the *Memoirs* were still incomplete and that he would give me the rest as he wrote it. He did not add much to them. I would have liked to persuade him to hand the matter over to someone else.

'Your Honour must understand,' I said, 'that there are some points, as we have sometimes discussed, that do not seem to agree with the dogmas.'

*James I of Aragon was the Catalan King who conquered Mallorca in 1229.

'That isn't so,' he answered. 'You know a great deal about theology, more than enough to be able to find their good sides. I have always written without thinking about theology, which I don't believe concerns this life so much as the one beyond. However, your point of view is different. You have my permission to add to my work and say whatever you please about it. If it turns out to be immoral or antidogmatic, you can moralize and present it to the reader's consideration as a bad example, as an example of what should not be done. And if my death were not "proper",' he added, with a melancholy smile, as if he were foreseeing an outcome soon to come, 'you could even present it as a natural consequence of my life. Morality would win in the end. I believe that even from a literary point of view, that double aspect could add interest to my work.'

'Your Honour hardly needs me to add interest to it. Besides . . .'

'Besides, what?'

'I understand you perfectly. I could write a prologue praising your literary skill and regretting your errors and follies.'

'Such an apologia would probably get you a canonry. It would please the bishop and wouldn't bother me in the very least. Quite the contrary.'

He did not mind having his beliefs refuted and opposed, but if that was so, why was he intent on perpetuating his work? I understood the Senyor all too well, as over the years he evolved towards pernicious Socratic scepticism. Ideas had no value to him, or rather, they had equivalent values, and he felt no need to condemn some in order to accept others. That gracious attitude was built upon his fundamental immorality, an immorality which the Athenians punished with hemlock. Clearly the Senyor, being a sceptic, could not object to having his 'errors' refuted. He was not determined to defend a doctrine, but to exercise the reader's mind as in a gymnasium, and to immortalize all his recollections and loved ones through art. If I were to sum up his life, I would say: 'He lived and loved.' *'Homo sum: humani nihil a me alienum puto,'* Terence wrote. Knowing this, was I to distort the problem pretending to place importance upon those things that were if anything accidental to the Senyor, leaving without comment those he considered paramount and perhaps even justified?

'I could write the prologue you propose,' I told him. 'I don't know whether it would get me a canonry, but I have not grown up at your Honour's side for nothing. I'm too honest for that.'

44

He ran his fingers through my hair with unusual tenderness.

'Son,' he said, 'I have no one but you. All my friends are dead. Do as you see fit.'

He gave me the *Memoirs* to read and said he wished to be alone. Although I could not be certain, I thought I noticed something strange in him, but he seemed calm, and smiled. I glanced at him with curiosity. He wiped his eyes with his handkerchief, and when I reached the door, he said in a perfectly natural tone: 'I must have conjunctivitis.'

Therefore I knew he was crying.

NINE

The *Memoirs* are the Senyor's most personal work. You can imagine
how thoroughly I have read them. The alexandrine he attributed to La
Fontaine,

'A beaucoup de plaisir je mêle un peu de gloire'

seems to have presided over a creation which is more the fruit of
pleasure than of study, although one must not forget that for him
certain studies were a pleasure. The work has the spontaneity of
improvisation and the charm of sincerity. True talent is revealed under
its careless appearance, much like those thoroughbreds whose inner
strength can be perceived even when they are standing still. It
undoubtedly contains reprehensible statements, so intimate and
sometimes so puerile that only in confession would they not seem
cynical. For example, how are we to accept that a respectable
nobleman should tell us that when he was all dressed up for a meeting
with a lady, he poured a bottle of paraffin on his head, thinking it was
cologne, and had to change all his clothes? 'My skin,' he wrote, 'still
reeked of it, and I had to take a bath. When I finally arrived, my sweet
friend had left, tired of waiting. I never found her again. She had
probably gone off with some other gentleman who did not smell of
paraffin.' Right after such an improper anecdote you find valuable
thoughts that prove the greatness of his soul. All of us, including the
humble, because existence is ephemeral, aspire to immortality not
only in the other life, but also in this one. That desire is, in a sense,
fulfilled by having children. Don Toni had no succession, or at least

none that he acknowledged. His name, that old name in which he claimed not to believe, even knowing that names shape the reality and continuity of history, would die when he closed his eyes. When the name was lost, that magic word, what would be left of fatherhood and family? I believe that not recognizing his illegitimate children was an act of cruelty and arrogance that I find hard to explain in a man as benevolent as he. And yet I, Miquel, am hardly in a position to judge his conduct. Besides, men such as Don Toni are wary of seeing themselves reproduced in a living organism that could disappoint them; they prefer to survive in the immaterial world of the pages of a book. He, the sceptic, believed in *la raison*, and only in *la raison* did he feel capable of holding his ground and not being dragged along by the currents of time. The *Memoirs* thus contain his share of immortality; in them he has recorded recollections and circumstances; for them he has sacrificed, among other things, the pine forest of Sa Cova which he loved so and which by the grace of God he did not have to see cut down (they start tomorrow, I was told just a moment ago). I repeat that his setting aside these two thousand *duros* gives you an idea of how he placed the *Memoirs* above everything else. Lately our life here had been precarious. This did not bother the Senyors, who were capable of living in great austerity. I had at times the utmost trouble to get together two *reals* so they would not have to do without their hot chocolate and their *ensaïmades* in the morning. Despite her failing memory, Dona Maria Antònia still had as fine a palate as ever and laughed at the quality of her breakfast, which sometimes left much to be desired.

'Goodness, Joan,' she said, smiling, 'they call this chocolate? I doubt if it's Swiss.'

'There hasn't been any around for a while,' I replied.

Don Toni, distracted, lifted his head and exclaimed. 'There hasn't been any around? Why don't you take a trip to Barcelona and stock us up for the whole winter?'

The Senyors were rich in land, but poor in income. The rents they received were more titular than real. Part of them went to religious groups that used them for charitable causes and to collect the money would have meant they did not wish to contribute to those causes. The other rents came from small properties owned by people who could not afford to pay. The main crops on this estate, not to say the only ones, are acorns, which are virtually worthless, and olives, which

47

are profitable when the harvest is good; which unfortunately does not happen very often. The pine forest is also a good source of income, the safest in my opinion, provided that the trees are not cut too young as can happen in times of need.

These circumstances, in addition to a windstorm that did considerable damage to the olive grove years ago and to my benefactor's inordinate expenditures, had forced him into debt. Besides, there was another factor: although the income of the estate was meagre, the credit was ample and as soon as the peasants saved up some money they took it to the Senyor, who gave them a reasonable interest and made use of the capital, usually on things that were necessary for the upkeep of his estate, but sometimes, I must admit, for other superfluous things. Such an administrative system became ruinous in the long run. I realize he sometimes accepted these unsolicited loans so as not to slight the poor people who did not know what to do with their money; but even if his motives were legitimate, the consequences were dreadful, and one year when many crops froze and some creditors reclaimed their capital, the Senyor had to go to a bank and draw up the first mortage, which would soon be followed by others.

I sometimes wonder what he would have done if the situation had become desperate, and whether he would have sacrificed his wife's comfort for the publication of his *Memoirs*. The dilemma is so unsavoury that I would rather leave the question unanswered. Despite his reckless life, he always loved Dona Maria Antònia, and in his old age he felt real tenderness towards her. She deserved it, and the contempt she may have shown towards me during a certain time must not cloud my judgement. She improved with age, re-emerging in the last decade of her life as the little cousin the Senyor had played with in the forests of Bearn. 'She was a little stubborn then,' the Senyor wrote, 'and would lose her temper at the drop of a hat, but her resentment never lasted long and gave way to a marvellous gentleness. When she was angry, her features turned awkward and ugly; that only accentuated and heightened the beauty that appeared a few moments later, the charm of the best smile in Europe.'

The Senyor draws his portrait with the technique of a Dutch miniaturist. He was aware of it, and wrote the following comment: 'Just as impressionist art expresses dispersion, miniatures depict density and concentration; in other words, love. Millet does not know how to love close up, which is much like not knowing how to love at all. Women are not spots or light effects; they have come into this world to be caressed, be it by hands or paintbrushes.' Later I will explain how he rationalizes his 'accessory' marital infidelities (that is how he qualifies them) and how he sophistically proposes that infidelity can represent a homage to matrimony. For him there was only one real woman in one's life. He does not necessarily refer to a man's lawful wife, but to the woman he sees close up over a long period of time. 'How is it possible,' he asks, 'not to love what you know well?' Such an optimistic thought is a homage to the perfection and the greatness of God. It is followed by another frankly orthodox and even more beautiful notion: 'Romantic exploits are a product of that reckless curiosity for which our forefathers were banished from Paradise . . . Don Juan searches, tries, and yet never finds . . . To find you need time; you must take your time and choose. When you have spent half your life by a woman's side, then you can say she is your wife.' Here he no longer refers to those scabrous 'accessory infidelities' that I tried to make him renounce, to no avail. I am a witness that my benefactor persevered many years by his wife's side without deceiving her, but also, and this is what makes his work immoral, with no regrets about his unstable, disastrous past. That belief would give us the answer to the dilemma I preferred to leave unanswered. The *Memoirs* in which Dona Maria Antònia is depicted with the painterly detail, sweetness and harmony and the pure colours of a Vermeer of Delft are undoubtedly, as he said, a homage to his wedded wife. This being the case, we must consider the fact that Dona Maria Antònia has already turned to dust and that the irate little girl in the gardens of Bearn with the best smile in Europe only exists in the Senyor's manuscript. Can we blame him if in order to preserve her image he subjected her to a few financial hardships when she was alive?

In fact it never came to that, thank God, because they never left the house and did not spend a penny. You know that in these mountains you can live sparsely off the land without tilling it. Some time ago, a Reformist representative referred to our backward agriculture and spoke against large land holdings, defending the division of property. He was a very modern man who claimed every peasant ought to have a hectare of irrigated land and grow tobacco. 'Who are those noblemen,' he questioned in Congress, 'on the northern mountains of

Mallorca, who own thousands upon thousands of hectares and only manage to produce a bit of grass and a few harmful goats?' The Senyor laughed when he read such nonsense.

'What would you do with a hectare, Joan, with a little patch of mountain land? How many "harmful goats" could live off a pile of rocks?'

Dona Maria Antònia looked up.

'Why on earth are you insulting the poor goats, Tonet? They're such marvellous little animals; they survive on almost nothing, no one takes care of them, and then they even give us milk and meat!'

The truth is that at Bearn (poorly cultivated, as it was, I must admit) there is no need for agricultural engineers, and whatever fruit does not grow of its own accord, such as olives, acorns, and carob beans, does not grow at all. My benefactors were happy in these surroundings. They had been born to be so and tended to adapt to the circumstances. The first time they went to Paris, Dona Maria Antònia was shocked, and rightly so, when she saw the scanty costumes on the dancers at the Opera. However, she never lost her composure.

'It's true,' she said, 'that the dancers don't wear much in the way of clothing, but the way the light shines on them they look artificial; they look as though they're made of porcelain.'

In the last few years her memory failed her, even though her love for precision remained intact, and only grew as she realized it was slowly slipping through her fingers. One rainy afternoon by the fireside, she said she would not go out into the garden even for one hundred *duros*; a minute later, looking at us inquisitively, she added: 'Well, for a hundred *duros*, maybe I would.'

In fact she had no idea of how much that really was. A few weeks before she died, she asked us whether it would be best to give her maid a diamond ring or a handkerchief. We suggested the latter.

TEN

The Paris adventure had lasted almost half a year and finished the day Dona Xima realized they were running out of money. The Senyor had taken a large amount with him, but his niece was wildly extravagant. It seemed unbelievable that a young lady from a good family, raised at an excellent school, could be so depraved at the age of eighteen. The fact would have an explanation if we could attribute it to the sinful books that wreak such havoc these days, particularly those romantic, libertine French novels. However, it appears that Dona Xima did not read. And why should she, when she had an imagination capable of eclipsing Victor Hugo and Alexandre Dumas together? The spirit of evil adopted the form of the most refined innocence in her. Under those light, winged forms lurked indecency, selfishness, greed... They said she had a good character because she had none: the Senyor has described her carefreeness claiming she was 'the woman who never loses her temper'. Small wonder: she had no shame.

Forgive the harshness of my words, my friend. When you reach the end you will be able to judge whether I am being fair. In a case such as this, the sadly famous Zola, who created the Rougon-Macquarts, searches for the laws of inheritance to justify a crime, because the last novelty of this century that is dying amidst mud and tears is that criminals are praised and victims are declared guilty. That is the thesis of *Les Misérables, La Dame aux camélias,* and so many other fashionable novels. We cannot accept such doctrines, but after studying the archives of this house, I must admit that within the family one finds

51

exemplary lives such as those of the Bishop Rigobert and Venerable Maria-Francisca alongside other less fortunate cases. Some have been kept a secret. Others, such as that of Dona Anna, a great-grandmother of Dona Xima and an aunt of the Senyor, were publicly known. Around the middle of the century, one Bearn ended up in prison. Therefore the Canon of Binimelis, who was not one to mince his words, would mumble out of the side of his mouth: *Bearn, fish and fowl* implying that there was a bit of everything in the family. These blunders are rather widespread even in the most illustrious genealogies. They should be a lesson in humility.

The object or the excuse for the trip was to attend the première of *Faust*. In Paris, the Second Empire was richer and more ostentatious than the Third Republic. I have lived the rapture of those days through the pages of the *Memoirs* and long conversations with my benefactor, speaking softly by the fireside while Dona Maria Antònia crocheted or said her prayers. Those conversations could have been taken as a confession had it not been for their degree of objectivity, which prevented pain from emerging and unfolding like a flower.

'We all felt the temptation of selling our souls to the devil,' he said, 'specially those of us who were no longer young. Paris was magical. There was gold everywhere and the boulevards were bustling with luxury and elegant women. Alboni was having a brilliant success at the Théâtre des Italiens with *La Sonnambula*, and *Le Prophète*, a French work playing at the Opéra, was the subject of much discussion. Lesseps, protected by Eugenia de Montijo, strove to join two oceans. Haussmann was opening up avenues, railways were being built, the telephone and the sewing machine were invented . . . France had been very rich, but never before had it reached such a degree of comfort and luxury.'

Nor had it ever reached such a degree of dissipation, for that matter. Vice was out in the streets, on stage, in the theatre boxes and in the lavish *équipages* driving along from the Bois de Boulogne to the Porte de Saint-Martin. Offenbach had created a comic and grotesque genre that delighted an audience eager for novelties. The Empress was admired more for her dresses than for her virtues. However, the real queen of the boulevards was La Rigolboche, a miserable can-can dancer who, according to Alarcón,* was neither beautiful, virtuous

*Pedro Antonio de Alarcón (1833–1891), Spanish novelist and journalist (Translator's note).

nor much of an artist, her only attribute being her ability to lift her leg high enough to kick the hats off her admirers.

The best lodging in Paris at the time was the Grand Hotel, on the Boulevard des Capucines, and there they went, paying eighteen francs a day per person. The Grand Opera, not the one we know today, was on the rue le Pelletier, a little farther away than it is now, but too close, according to Dona Xima, because it seemed inappropriate to take a coach from the hotel. The Senyor, however, could not sleep at night on account of the noise in the neighbourhood, so they finally rented a furnished townhouse near the Etoile, with a garden, a bath and electric bells. Thirty years ago that area was not as popular as it is now; only the rich and idle lived there. But Dona Xima, who had not a penny to her name, never worried about prices.

'She wanted an ermine coat,' my benefactor told me, 'dresses, a carriage waiting outside her door . . . I didn't argue, even though it all seemed excessive to me.'

Dona Xima found the perfect setting for her fantasies. Dumas *fils* has immortalized Marguerite Gautier, Marie Duplessis in real life, in *La Dame aux camélias*, a work that extols vice and embellishes it with the best of colours. She did not suffer from tuberculosis (her body was as sound as her soul was unhealthy) but in every other respect Dona Xima was the queen of fashion just like Dumas' heroine, a dazzling star in a society as fictitious as the Empire itself. There is an anecdote about Louis Napoleon that my benefactor assures me is true. Napoleon III had been a disciple of Senator Vieillard, a renowned Freemason who had been so bold as to give him a book with the following epigraph: '*Le dieu de l'antiquité n'est plus; aujourd'hui l'Humanité est Dieu.*' The disciple read the epigraph, looked at his master, reread it, pondered for a while, and finally said: 'Disrespectful, but true.'

Man above God. The anecdote gives us a notion of the Humanism that characterized the Second Empire. In his *Viaje de Madrid a Nápoles*, Alarcón described the materialism that infiltrated the customs and reached the throne, causing so many bitter tears.

The setting could hardly have been more appropriate for the success of Dona Xima, a mortal and dangerous beauty, an incitement to rebellion and war. Her reign was short-lived and collapsed with the defeat of Sedan and the horrors of *La Commune*. The Emperor was lucky enough to die shortly afterwards, while she continued to live and spread evil, fulfilling her destiny, as you will see when this story reaches its conclusion.

Faust had its première in March '59, and despite all expectations, it was not particularly successful. The audience did not appreciate Gounod's beautiful score until ten years later, when it was staged again. However, the theatre was a sight to see. The Emperor seemed blind as a bat concerning international affairs (in that respect he was much like Napoleon I), and thus mistrusted Catholic Austria and turned to the godless kings of Prussia. Faust, as we all know, is the most authentically Prussian of all Germanic legends: that sufficed for the Emperor to support it to a certain degree. The Empress was dressed in white and covered in jewels. Dona Xima appeared in the box next to them, also dressed in white, but without a single jewel. Since they entered simultaneously a murmur of surprise ran through the crowd. Whether it was a coincidence or not, it looked like an act of rivalry and was interpreted by many as such. Dona Xima, more beautiful and graceful than Eugenia de Montijo, also surpassed her in natural distinction. 'She seemed so sure of herself,' the Senyor wrote, 'that the fact that she was wearing no jewels — because she had none — was interpreted as what they now call a handicap, an advantage granted to the Sovereign by Dona Xima in that contest. Society is frivolous and gossipy; Dona Xima was the winner. Few listened to the opera, their attention being divided between the two Spanish ladies; I have often thought they were the reason why the performance passed unnoticed. I went to congratulate Gounod during the intermission. I wanted to express my admiration, but he spoke only of Dona Xima: "*Je vous serais bien obligé, Monsieur, de vouloir me nommer Madame.*" He was a charming man. We went back to our box and there, in front of all Paris, he kissed Xima on both cheeks. Some applause started up and it seemed to me that Eugenia de Montijo was made rather uncomfortable by the scene. However, she smiled and we heard her say to the ladies in her company: "*Elle est ravissante.*" Louis Napoleon had picked up his opera glasses and stared at us insistently, which was hardly polite considering we were virtually next to him. They assumed we came from some great family. Paris is generous in that way. A few days later, Gounod appeared at the town house at the Etoile. He came with a young *beau* from the court who was friendly with Louis Napoleon, and, apparently, even more so with the

Empress. This cub had the title of Duke of Campo Formio and seemed to be in charge of some extremely important mission. His master was rather naïve to trust certain embassies to such a rich and fashionable man.'

These lines are followed by a series of rather bold considerations on preferment that I would rather leave without comment. My benefactor does not hide his contempt towards the nobility of the Empire. 'It was all a hoax,' he writes, 'imitation, *pastiche*, like the Pompeian style, the sphinxes and the bronzes of Bardienne. In Paris I heard a story about Campo Formio's father. He had been granted the title of Duke by Napoleon I, who would touch a washerwoman with his magic wand and turn her into a princess, or so he thought. Apparently one day a friend went to call on him and the servant said he had gone off to see the painter "to order a few ancestors".'

The anecdote may be false, because Don Toni liked to draw upon his imagination for the sake of amusement. The matter ended as could be expected of people with no moral sense whatsoever: Dona Xima accepted the ambassador for the time being. 'You understand, don't you, Tonet? You're so kind . . .'

Feelings can hinder understanding. To the Senyor, Campo Formio was a fake. He could not get used to the man's insolent courtesy, his monocle, his Prussian clicking of the heels. It all seemed ridiculous in the eyes of an old Mallorcan nobleman, but besides, Dona Xima's preference for a younger man would have been enough to displease the wisest philosopher.

'When I get tired of Campo Formio,' she said, 'I'll ask to be introduced to the Emperor.'

'That's some company you're keeping!' replied her uncle, who did not accept the First Empire and even less the Second. 'Do as you please. You will anyway.'

'You're so right, Uncle Tonet. But I hope you won't start lecturing me about morals. Do you know that Lesseps is also in love with me?'

They parted on friendly terms. He sought comfort in the doctrines of Zoroaster and returned to Mallorca with his curiosity equally divided between Hormuz and Ariman. For him, not only were the Bonapartes not entitled to the throne, but Louis Napoleon was not even a Bonaparte.

'It's a known fact that he isn't his father's son.'

Paternity seemed increasingly doubtful to him: in the last years of his life, he ended up questioning everyone's ancestry. However, in that specific case history seems to be on his side. Queen Hortense, who in his opinion was not a queen either, had a rather public relationship with the Admiral Verhuell, and, in fact, Louis Napoleon does not resemble the Bonapartes; he has the face of a Dutchman. It is strange that the Senyor, for whom only natural laws applied, should speak of the right to the crown and condemn a man, or, in other words, a free spirit, for his illegitimate origins. The human heart is full of contradictions.

'In fact,' he would sometimes say, 'every man is his father's son; who really cares whether his name is Peter or Paul? There's nothing more adulterated than lineages. Those who still believe in them are fools. If they had archives that date back centuries, as we have here, they'd know a lot more. Have no regrets, son,' he added, stroking my head, 'about coming from a poor family. Not even I can be sure that I'm a Bearn.'

ELEVEN

Dona Xima stayed in Paris, where it took her only a few weeks to become better known that Alboni or even La Rigolboche. She carried herself like an experienced woman. Instead of yielding to the desires of Louis Napoleon, she told the Duke that she had never entered a house through anything other than a main door, and that if the Monarch wished to see her at the Tuileries all he had to do was arrange for an official introduction and she would be glad to pay her respects to 'the Imperial family' (the Emperor alone would not suffice). Campo Formio was shocked by a response that not even he, with his title and his millions, would have dreamt of making, and he delivered it, duly modified, to his master. It appears that he also recounted it more faithfully to the Countess of Teba,* with whom he was on excellent terms. The lady, whose reactions were quick, was very pleased by her fellow citizen. '*On ne badine pas avec une femme espagnole,*' she told Campo Formio, who, being young and arrogant, was tempted to reveal to what extent the honour of a Spanish lady is incorruptible. Meanwhile, the Emperor, who could not quite make up his mind whether to allow an official introduction, felt more desire than ever after receiving such an unexpected reply. Thus, Eugenia de Montijo lost her husband and her '*chevalier servant*' all at once.

Among the adventures of Dona Xima in Paris, the Senyor used to tell the story of a fight with a local celebrity at that time: La

*Don Joan sometimes refers to Eugenia de Montijo in this manner, undoubtedly because the Senyor did so in his *Memoirs*, giving her the name of a Spanish countess instead of her title as a Napoleonic Empress (Editor's note).

Rigolboche, whom I have already mentioned. 'I do not know,' he writes, 'exactly how their rivalry began, as I was in Mallorca. Yet it is hardly surprising, considering they both aspired to the same thing. It appears that at the Jardin-Mabille the dancer had her eye on Campo Formio during her can-can solo, despite the fact that he was in the company of a lady, or perhaps for that very reason. Since her attempt was unsuccessful, she must have felt humiliated, and when that same year of 1860, she published her *Memoirs*, she included a passage that was an offence to Xima and to our entire family. Needless to say, she would have been incapable of writing them herself, so she found a journalist by the name of Ernest Blum — who was no great writer either — to write them for her. Tradition, Joan '—I find it touching that the Senyor thought of me upon writing these lines—' leads us to believe that the Bearns are honourable noblemen who have occupied a well-known position if not since the Conquest, because that is not certain, at least since the fifteenth century. We have set an example with Bishop Rigobert, Don Ramon of Bearn and *La Venerable*. But there are so many exceptions to the rule!

'You know the story of my aunt Dona Anna, Xima's grandmother. You already know the rhymes they made up about my great-grandfather Toni. If you look in the archives [he continued to address me] you will find even more things, episodes that have been voluntarily forgotten. The legend of our coat of arms reads specifically: "Better to die than to let in new blood."' The three following lines are crossed out, and I could only make out two words: 'I myself.' The account continues: 'When we were in Paris, we considered ourselves as noble as we are among these mountains. However, we were considered suspect. We spent a lot, particularly at the beginning. Xima was too beautiful; I was too tolerant. When we stopped spending, which was before long, when she became acquainted with Campo Formio and started accepting jewels, there was no question about it: we were a hoax. However that may be, it is particularly unpleasant to have it said by a can-can dancer. Xima, the woman who never loses her temper, was angry that time. Fate gave her a chance to take revenge. One of La Rigolboche's most popular 'numbers', which she performed every night at Mabille, was *La Toilette de Mam'zelle*. She stepped out of bed and chose two gentlemen at random from the audience to comb her hair. It was long, thick and splendid, and there was not a single fool or man of fashion who did not wish to claim he had touched it and knew it was not fake. Participating in the raffle cost fifty francs. The scene had appeal because of its idiocy. I mentioned that the actress rode around the park in the morning in a cabriolet: she was always changing her horses, and the older she became, the younger she liked them. That morning she was out with a magnificent Spanish three-year-old, which she treated as absurdly as she did her admirers at the Mabille, until she was finally thrown against a tree. Xima, who happened to be riding by in her carriage, took the unconscious woman to a nearby restaurant, where she asked for a pair of scissors and cut off all her hair. The waiters were so astonished that when they finally tried to stop her it was too late. Xima wrapped the woman's head up in a bandage, even though she was not hurt, and revived her with a cup of coffee. Kinder then ever, she even took her to her carriage and saw her off with a kiss of Judas. The story spread like wild fire. The dancer tried to take her to court, which only added to Xima's popularity. By the time her hair grew back, she had been forgotten: she was dead and ready to be entombed in three lines of the *Petit Larousse*.'

That sentence, more worthy of a Marchioness in the court of Louis XV than of a Mallorcan nobleman, is all that death inspired in Don Toni: a three-line entombment under the letter R in an encyclopedia, without the slightest mention of the poor woman's soul.

TWELVE

You already know that after the première of *Faust* the Senyor had to return to Mallorca and that his wife refused to live with him. They spent ten years two leagues apart, yet spiritually more united than one would have suspected. Those years were not spent in vain by Dona Maria Antònia, who devoted herself to religious practice and household virtues. After they were back together, she used to tell her husband (she was a Bearn after all, and knew how to laugh about most serious matters) that she had not missed him very much because she had kept herself busy crocheting a bedspread. It was true to a certain extent, although not entirely so. She drew the strength of her temperament from religion. She was sure that she would reach salvation, and I, who listened to her confession on the night she died, have no doubts either. Just as there is hygiene for a healthy body, so is there hygiene for a healthy soul. The materialists believe praying is a waste of time, the very time they spend mumbling in conversation at clubs, and that it makes no sense to repeat the Ave Marias of the rosary fifty times when you have said it all in one. Following this purely rational criterion, there would be no need to educate children, either: all you would have to do is give them a list of sins and virtues. However, we know that it would have no moral value and that without the example of praxis rules serve no purpose whatsoever. A philosopher such as Pascal once said that to have faith we must begin by crossing ourselves with holy water. Even my benefactor acknowledges that Dona Maria Antònia was strong because she was at peace with the angels of Heaven, while he only was with those of the earth.

60

Those angels undoubtedly inspired the Senyora, who was highly esteemed by all. They believed she was honest and sincere. In fact she had the necessary discretion to live in a tiny village for ten years without having an argument with anyone. She respected the beliefs that prevailed in her surroundings; in other words, she kept her own to herself. She was very polite and I cannot say for sure that she was altogether sincere. If she had been, she could not have appeared to be, just as the Senyor did not seem sincere because he really was, and did not hide his sins. The local peasants are used to living slightly on guard, because the village is small and everything is remembered far too long; therefore they tend to hush up their faults and, in general, anything out of the ordinary. They thought it absurd that the Senyor should stay up all night reading, because for them it would have been, and even though he was the most understanding man in the world, they did not understand him, and thus found him mysterious.

When he returned from Paris, the slander about Margalideta began. She was a blonde, blue-eyed girl, just as the real Marguerite in *Faust* must have been. In *Faust*, Marguerite is seduced, has a child and kills it. Margalida of Bearn had no need to kill a soul: she died within the first year she spent at the estate. She was buried in the garden, under a magnolia tree, and the Senyor ordered a white marble monument that was never built. However, a sculptor did come to study the site which raised even greater suspicion. Not for a moment did they think his intentions could have been innocent, nor did they consider the possibility that, not having any children with Dona Maria Antònia, he may have wanted to adopt the girl. The political climate at Bearn was already askew, and by then we had two Republicans in the village who went so far as to say at the café that Don Toni should go on trial. 'You poor devils,' replied the sacristan, who was an intelligent man, 'if you insult the Senyor, you're insulting the entire village along with him.' But they would not budge from their theories; they did not acknowledge noblemen, popes or kings, and the worst is that they did not lack people who listened to them.

Shortly after the incident, Barbara Titana, a skinny, dark and half-crazed young girl, finally went stark raving mad, and since she came by the estate fairly often, rumours began going around about the Senyor having cast a spell on her.

'What do you think of that, Joan?' he told me. 'So now I'm a sorcerer.'

'That must prove to Your Honour,' I replied disrespectfully, 'the dangers of universal suffrage.'

'Steady, son. Don't jump to conclusions. These people are uneducated, uncompromising and coarse. The ones to blame are the upper classes, who have been on the decline for some time. We'll have to go through an enlightened dictatorship before democracy wins out in the end.'

I did not express my lack of faith in historical interludes that presuppose a better world 'in the end', as if there were any definitive ends in history. The truth is that he was appalled, and rightly so, by human stupidity.

'If I were capable of casting spells,' he continued, 'I wouldn't waste my time on a woman as ugly as Titana.'

The poor soul had fallen in love with him and lived in a sort of mystical delirium in which Don Toni appeared in angelic forms; she remained in this state until her death only a few years ago. Titana's spell was all the peasants needed to redouble their fears. These good people can also be brutal, and more than once, when we went to the village through the woods of Sa Creu, they threw stones at us from the bushes. 'It appears,' the Senyor wrote, 'that man, contrary to the doctrines of Rousseau, is endowed with a natural portion of cruelty, either directed towards others in a sadistic manner or towards himself, leading to a masochistic nature. One cannot be too cautious. When La Fayette asked the Queen whether she loved her people, who had just invaded the courtyard of Versailles, she replied that she did, "*mais avec les grilles fermées.*" With those beneath them, the nobility must always take the initiative. They must love their people from a distance and not appear friendly unless they wish to do so, since love can draw them near, but intellectual communion is almost impossible. They can kiss them, but they can never shake hands with them.'

Later on, still thinking of the stones that broke two carriage windows, he wrote the following words, more reminiscent of recent German philosophy than of the doctrines of Christ and in which he seems to relive the spirit of some legendary Bearn of times past: 'If the Senyor does not use his whip, surely the farmer will rise up against him sooner or later,' only to end with a scientific and optimistic rigmarole very typical of the sources which he had been drawing upon: 'It may all be due to a nervous disorder, and over the years they may discover a drug that affects the sympathetic system and gives us back the tranquillity we seem to have lacked ever since Cain.'

The drug the Senyor referred to and which he hoped to find in the materialism of chemistry has existed for centuries: it is called Christian humility and fraternity. But so much for that.

THIRTEEN

A few weeks after the house in the City was sold, I was at the estate on a leave granted to me by my superiors when the events I will now recount took place. But first I must explain my bad habit of listening behind closed doors. It was partly a practice I had picked up from the Senyor, but there are also other causes. I was already eighteen years old, and my ignorance of certain matters had heightened my curiosity. This natural impulse went hand in hand with others which were the product of very personal circumstances. You are aware of the things that have been said about my birth. For others, love and the fruits of marriage can make up for the misfortune of having no parents, whereas for us men of the cloth, there will never be another woman to replace our mother. At eighteen, I was not unaffected by earthly temptations, and my eyes eagerly searched for anything that could satisfy my curiosity. I now understand that the punishment that was inflicted upon us at the Seminary was wise, because my quest for knowledge was entirely opposed to resignation.

That day, to be more specific, and I certainly must, it was a night (in November 1868), the Senyor was sitting by the fireplace, surrounded with books and papers. He had already begun to don the Franciscan habit he wore the day he died, as well as a Louis XV wig, which he needed to keep his head warm after losing his hair. At least that was his explanation. I think there was another one: to him that wig must have symbolized eighteenth-century culture, with its frivolous appearance masking truly exuberant latent forces, a time when the Regent of France left his ladies in order to search for the soul in

64

chemical distillations and spent endless nights on the hill of Montmartre, 'where that man who did not believe in God searched for the Devil in a paradox that can only be conceived as a punishment of Providence.' The clock had just struck eight and we had finished supper. I went outside. The night was cold. The moon shone on Margalideta's tomb and I was about to pray a part of the *Requiem* in her memory when I saw the village priest coming up the road. Don Andreu was close to seventy, and yet still as strong as a young man. I remembered that in the morning he had announced his visit, although he had not mentioned a specific time. He did it to avoid their sending him a carriage. He felt it was unnecessary to bother the farmer and the mules when there was no real need, for 'a half-hour stroll' as he called it, even though it was closer to one hour. He was praying as he walked by; he was so absorbed in his devotions that he did not see me. A visit at that hour of the evening and coinciding with the rumours about the Senyor's supposed sorcery had to be for an important reason. My curiosity overruled my sense of duty and I crept through the kitchen door and up to the dark room with the small window overlooking the fireplace where Don Toni was writing.

My heart was beating as if at that moment the fate of the Bearns was at stake — and thus my own fate as well. From the window I saw the priest enter the room. His figure stood against the background of a starlit sky. By the fireside, surrounded with books, sat the Seynor. The fire cast shades of red on his face, giving him a disquieting appearance. I have never believed the rumours one heard then, and still hears now — perhaps more than ever after this mysterious double death — concerning his sorcery, but he certainly contributed to the hearsay with his behaviour. Next to his bed he had set up a small laboratory where he performed analyses and distilled liquids. I have never known what he intended to achieve with it. The first bottle of soda water in Spain was the one that arrived at Bearn just around that time. He frightened Madò Francina by telling her about sewing machines and if he did not have a telephone installed it was because the French engineer who was to direct the operation asked for a fortune to come to Mallorca. He did not consider those extravagances inappropriate for a Senyor who had the responsibility of showing wisdom to the superstitious peasants. He even managed to build a little cart that moved on its own — an *automobile* — using steam, according to the principles of Fulton. The Church authorities kindly suggested that he refrain from such experiments, so he put the cart away, although he did not resolve to burn it. Not only did he not destroy it, but he sometimes took it out to examine it and modify some device, since he had not entirely got over the idea. That day he had been examining it near the fireplace. He was quite skilled in mechanical matters and using a simple kettle of boiling water on a kind of burner with a series of iron tubes that collected the steam and led it to the wheels, he had managed to make it run and drove it all the way round the courtyard. I am certain that it is true because I saw it with my own eyes. Unfortunately, others saw it too, and spread the word in the village. Those of us who have been to school know that steam is a force capable of moving machines, and that there are large boats, actually called steamers, that are propelled by this force. There are already railways that work with this system, too. They are natural inventions, not the least bit diabolical, that are transforming modern life. But try to explain this in a tiny village like Bearn, and, above all, to the Bearn of a quarter of a century ago. Luckily the Senyor hardly ever left the estate, because if he had gone to the village often I hate to think what it all may have come to. I do not mean to imply that he was not respected, but the villagers were afraid of him, and fear makes people unreasonable. The people who sent their daughters to work on the estate despite Don Toni's romantic adventures — and I refuse to believe that, as the Republicans claimed, they sent the girls on purpose — no longer allowed them to go; it happened more than once that the olives were not harvested for that reason. The day the *automobile* drove around the courtyard, the old steward in charge of the estate decided to leave and has never been back since.

Don Andreu stopped in the doorway for a second. He was a simple, uneducated man, but gifted with natural intelligence. With one look he took in everything: the *automobile*, the books, the Franciscan habit and the white wig, reddened by the firelight. Don Toni looked up.

'Come in, Father. Have a seat by the fire. I was expecting you. Did you come on foot?'

His words were warm and kind, as usual, but he did not rise from his chair. It appeared as if he were doing it out of humility, so as to counteract the solemnity of the conversation and create a more congenial atmosphere. Don Andreu came closer: 'It's only a half-hour walk.'

66

It was closer to an hour. The Senyor scolded him for not having announced a time for his visit so he could send the carriage. The priest smiled. He had walked over saying his rosary and gazing at the moon. He interrupted his explanations to glance at the books.

'Your Honour is always studying. When will we get around to burning a few of these?'

The Senyor eluded his question.

'You know, Don Andreu, that we requested permission from the Palace for all kinds of books. Lord knows when it'll get here; they don't seem to be in much of a hurry.'

'Such matters can't be decided in a moment,' the priest replied. 'The permission is being considered. It would appear that the Palace doesn't object, but . . .'

The Senyor waved his hand in a vague gesture he often used to imply that one had to be patient.

'Don't put the cart before the horse, Don Andreu.'

'Of course not.'

My benefactor was rubbing his hands. Nothing was more contrary to his stubborn nature than an argument. As for the priest, he had already lost his incisiveness. The Palace delays were convenient for both of them. Don Toni courteously inquired to what he owed the pleasure of his visit. There were two reasons, and the priest said he would begin with the one that was least important.

'Your relatives would like to join a religious order, and, if your Honour has no objection, they would like to consult the archives. The proof of nobility they have now doesn't appear to be sufficient.'

'Well, they'll have to settle for it anyway. The fact is that the family tree only dates back to the sixteenth century. We purchased this land in 1504. It was never granted to us by the King.'

'But your Honour's lineage,' the priest objected with a look of concern, 'dates back to the Conquest. That's what I've always preached on the Day of Sant Miquel.'

'There's no proof, Father. If the Bearns had really been "lords of lands and great estates in Navarre" as some genealogies claim, they wouldn't have stayed in Mallorca. The noblemen who came with King James returned to the mainland.'

'However, according to tradition...'

'That's true,' Don Toni said. 'You'd agree with that Italian princess whose name I can't remember ... A noble family dating back to before Christ, perhaps descendants of Romulus and Remus,' he added with a smile. 'One day a journalist asked her whether that genealogy was authentic. She replied that at least it had been considered so for over two thousand years.'

Madò Francina came in with a message from the steward. One afternoon, in a state of despair because he could not pay the labourers, the man had used bad language, uttering something almost blasphemous, as if that would make the money appear out of nowhere, and the Senyor had punished him with a whipping. After the incident he had behaved particularly well for a week or two, as if the blood in his veins were running faster and had cleared his mind. Madò Francina asked whether he could sell some wheat and whether they could begin sowing the following Monday. It was obvious that this is what he should have done in the first place instead of cursing and swearing.

'Let him come, sow and pay.'

Madò Francina retired. The priest gently admonished Don Toni. How could an enlightened nobleman who spoke French and wrote Latin hexameters ... ? Don Toni smiled, thinking, 'why should Latin hexameters or even French alexandrines be incompatible with a whip?' However, he realized it was beginning to seem like an anachronism in the nineteenth century. 'How many years do you think it'll take,' he inquired, 'for the Enlightenment to reach these lands? Besides, I've developed a rather unusual view of the world. What I mean is that over the years I've come up with a philosophy of my own that may be rather eclectic: I believe the more refined we are, the more cruel we become, because everything is always balanced. The nineteenth century is the century of great inventions, of brotherhood and also of the most dreadful wars. Everything has its counterpart. If something has a front, it must have a back, too. God, for all his mercy, condemns countless souls.'

Don Andreu looked solemn.

'The Devil is the one who condemns.'

'The Devil? I've never been quite sure of that.'

'Or, rather, we're the ones who chose the path of evil. Free will ...'

'Well,' said Don Toni, changing the subject, 'be that as it may, Creation is always harmonious. Look at this starry night...'

'On the way here I was looking at it. It's a lovely evening...'

My benefactor seemed to be lost in thought.

'The Universe,' he said, 'always turns right on time, like an enormous clock. Are you interested in machines, Father?'

I caught a glimpse of mystery, the mystery of strange coincidences. I remembered the poet's words:

> *El hombre está entregado*
> *al sueno, de su suerte no cuidando,*
> *y con paso callado*
> *el cielo vueltas dando*
> *las horas del vivir le va hurtando.* *

The priest said: 'From what we have seen of them, I think they can do a lot of harm, Don Toni.'

'They can do harm, but they can also help us. The world is a harmony of opposites. See how good we feel by the fire, you and I? Come closer and sit on this sheepskin. It's because the night's getting colder. In the morning the fields will be covered in frost. Then the sun will rise and melt the crystals, and the trees and flowers will be clean, as if they'd just been washed.'

The Senyor was drawing from old Oriental doctrines: Good and Evil, two aspects of one sole principle, of one Supreme Being. It smacked of Manicheism, a heresy in which powerful minds have gone astray — even Saint Augustine, before he became a saint. However, the Senyor knew how to express things without offending anyone, without malice or confrontations. Thus his mistakes were doubly dangerous.

'Getting back to where we left off, Father,' Don Toni continued, 'my nephews and niece would love to pass as *botifarres*† as if that were something to be proud of. As you know, *botifarres* comes from *botifleurs*, from the *fleur de lys*. They're the ones who joined the Bourbons about one hundred and fifty years ago simply because they'd won the War of Succession. And look at the Bourbons now. You see how Dona Isabel has ended up, after all that nonsense about crazy nuns and everything else we've heard. I'm not particularly fond of my relatives. They all vanished into thin air the moment they saw our

*Man yields to sleep/heedless of his fate/and with their silent steps/the heavens turn around/stealing away the hours of his life, (Translator's note).

† The *Botifarres* are the old Majorcan noblemen (Translator's note).

money was running out. Besides, I don't like to spread lies, and I wonder who gave them these strange ideas.'

'His Lordship the Marquis of Collera, who I believe is related to you ... or at least that's what Dona Magdalena implied.'

'Collera's never been related to us. Magdalena's inane enough to think that makes her more important. You mean to say now Collera's breathing down their backs?'

'Apparently he's offered to attend to the matter. He knows so many people in Madrid, you see ...'

'Castelar and he are the two biggest parrots in Spain,' the Senyor muttered in resignation. 'He'd do best to stay put in Parliament telling stories.'

'Dona Magdalena asked you to excuse them for not coming, but they haven't got a carriage...'

'Tell her not to worry; they'll come whenever they can.'

The priest was slightly exasperated, realizing he was making no headway whatsoever.

'But, you know, before they come, they'd like to know whether they'd be well received.'

'And why shouldn't they be, Don Andreu? They will always be welcome at this house. But they will not see the archives. These genealogical matters ...'

The priest decided to drop the issue: 'We are all the product of our actions,' he said.

'That's what we're taught by religion and the laws of nature,' the Senyor replied with a sigh.

They continued to talk about general subjects, as if they were trying to avoid a specific issue that was on both their minds. I sensed it, and could not imagine what would happen next. Suddenly Don Andreu said: 'Now I must come to the more difficult part of this visit. [I took my hands to my heart, trying to stop it from pounding]. I'm very sorry, Don Toni, but it's my duty ... someone has just arrived in Bearn ...'

The Senyor interrupted.

'My niece Xima.'

FOURTEEN

I had to hold on to the windowframe. Dona Xima in Bearn! The Senyor already knew! I felt as though the earth had collapsed under my feet. Dona Xima in Bearn, right when my aging benefactor had finally settled down and everyone had begun to think that Dona Maria Antònia would finally return to the estate. You must understand, my friend, the horror I felt at the wild age of eighteen. Dona Xima, at the height of her beauty and her depravity, was, in my fantasy, the Devil incarnate. A thousand times, up in these mountains, I had thought of her as Saint Anthony must have thought of the Queen of Sheba in the desert. At the time, Dona Xima was a woman of about thirty, a desirable, open rose exciting sad, mortal passions. The most dissolute city in the world, the most licentious society, had moulded in its image that poor soul, born for evil.

There was a pause. I closed my eyes and prayed. The priest lowered his voice. 'She's travelling like a queen: a carriage, pageboys, everything ... There aren't enough servants at the inn to attend her needs. In the morning she bathes in warm milk. It's the talk of the town. The worst part is that children and sick people will be left without nourishment. Not even I had an *ensaïmada* yesterday morning: the maid told me that Dona Xima's coachmen walked into the bakery and ate everything in sight. They look like princes, all covered in braid. They only speak French, and no one can understand a word they say.'

'But they do manage to find the *ensaïmades*,' murmured Don Toni. The Senyor did not happen to be very fond of sweets nor

71

particularly demanding at the table. Don Andreu continued to speak softly.

'The entire village thinks Dona Xima has come to take your Honour away. I certainly hope it isn't true.'

'So that's what they think?'

He had a tender look in his eye, as though he were daydreaming. He was no longer the devilish Faust who strives to steal land from the sea and seduce young maidens, but a poet reminiscing. Seldom did he let himself be seen with that expression. 'I understand,' he said. 'For a long time I've been meaning to make a confession, and you've come just in time, Father. Would you like anything to drink? A glass of wine, perhaps?'

Don Andreu accepted a glass of water. The Senyor now spoke frankly. It was true that Dona Xima, with whom he had not ceased to correspond, had come to the island to try to take out a new mortage on Bearn in the hopes of leaving for Paris with her uncle. The priest was speechless.

'There's no stopping that woman,' he said when he regained his speech. 'With what authority did she dare to conceive of such criminal notions?'

'With mine,' Don Toni replied.

Don Andreu was speechless and had to drink a sip of water. For a moment he must have considered that his mission had been fruitless and that Don Toni was completely determined to go back to Dona Xima. I knew him better than that, even though I did have my fears. The Senyor's reply was only a protest against Don Andreu's expressions. He disliked the word 'criminal', and applied to his own niece he found it offensive. The Bearns were used to taking responsibility for the follies of the ladies whose company they kept. Besides, in the heat of his indignation, Don Andreu had referred to her as a 'woman' as opposed to a 'lady'. However, not being the resentful sort, the Senyor smiled when the priest finished drinking his glass of water.

'You may think I'm too old for certain things,' he said, 'but everything's relative. Ten years ago I already thought I was old when in March 1859, Xima got it into her head that I had to take her to see the première of *Faust*. You remember that.'

The priest certainly did. He recalled how they prayed in church in an attempt to prevent such recklessness; how they took Sant Miquel

72

out in procession; how there were two astonishing conversions, that of the barber, who had recently declared himself a Protestant...

The Senyor interrupted. 'There were two conversions, but I never converted. I lost my head instead. You have no idea what it means to take a lady the likes of Xima' — he said 'lady' staring at Don Andreu and smiling so imperceptibly that the priest did not even notice — 'to the opening night at the Paris Opera.'

And his colourful language led the village priest through the extravagance and the splendour of the Second Empire. Years later, when I finally went to France, during the time of the Third Republic, I was still able to witness that the Senyor's words were no exaggeration. To give you a slight idea of how it was I will just tell you an anecdote that is rather inappropriate here, but that shocked me deeply. A lady of high society (even though morally it should be called the lowest) was walking through the Champs Elysées followed by a lamb on a leash. From what I could see, such extravagance was far from unusual in the cities that are thought of as civilized. A young friend walked over to her and, after kissing her hand quite lavishly, asked after her husband. 'He's right behind me,' the lady answered, pointing to the lamb. Her husband, who had in fact fallen behind, walked up and greeted the young man quite effusively, calling him *mon cher*. The passers-by smiled. The three of them stepped into a carriage and headed off to dine together at a restaurant.

Don Toni never covered up embarrassing things nor sought to extenuate his behaviour. Don Andreu listened in silence. When they reached the scene where the Emperor sent the Duke to the town house at the Etoile, the good priest was astounded.

'I hadn't heard that one before,' he mumbled.

'Campo Formio,' Don Toni said, 'was an opportunist, a rich, good-looking nobleman of the Empire. Louis Napoleon didn't accomplish his objective, but his emissary ousted me right away. He was twenty years younger than I.'

The priest tried to take the opportunity to prove a moral point and boldly adopted a rather declamatory tone.

'Ah, Don Toni, youth doesn't last ... Every day that goes by draws us closer to death, and when we're old and remember our follies, we feel sadness and regrets. Isn't that so? Ashes in our hearts and a bitter aftertaste. Then we meditate, and what does our conscience tell us?'

I feared a Voltairian reply. It seemed to me rather imprudent on the part of Don Andreu to venture into such dangerous realms, and I was right.

'Our conscience,' he answered, 'doesn't always tell us the same thing. I know people who regret not having sinned a little more when they were still in time to do so.'

The fire shone red on his face. He looked like a condemned man consciously defying the laws of God. I wished to believe that he did not mean those terrible words in earnest, but who could be sure of that? Don Andreu rose from his chair as if he had taken it personally.

'Man is not so depraved,' he exclaimed. 'I hope your Honour can't give me a single example.'

The Senyor's features softened and he waved vaguely with his hand as he often did.

'Certainly not,' he replied. 'The two of us, you and I, are alone in this house.'

With that sentence he ruled me out. How distressing, my friend. Not only did I live in the house (apart from the workers, who are also the children of God) but I had occasionally confided in the Senyor and he knew some of the complications that in times of doubt tempted me to abandon my ecclesiastical career. When I felt that moment of rejection, my pride got the best of me and I could have cried out to remind him of my presence. But if he had known that I was listening, he would not have been angry. And then, would his indifference not have wounded me even more?

Don Andreu had to accept things as they were, even though he was not really satisfied and felt ill at ease. Despite his simple appearance and his lack of education, he was no fool.

'Your Honour had mentioned a confession,' he said.

'I believe this is a confession.'

'With the pain of contrition and the intention of never repeating the offence?'

The Senyor eluded the former and only responded to the latter.

'At my age? I'm beginning to feel quite worn out.'

His health was enviable. He spoke of his physical decline as he did of his financial ruin, as a rhetorical device and probably intending to inspire sympathy, because, knowing human nature, he realized that neither health nor fortune were qualities that one easily overlooked.

Don Andreu, eager to know specific facts, was thrown off course and did not realize that the penitent had not answered the essential part of his question. As is often the case, material and contingent details draw attention away from matters of the soul.

'But Dona Xima has come to take you with her, your Honour,' he said, 'is that not so?'

'In January,' the Senyor observed, 'there will be a new production of *Faust*. I'd written her that I'd love to see that opera again. Capoul will be singing it. Last time, *Faust* rejuvenated me.'

'At what a price!' said the priest. His subject smiled imperceptibly.

'In exchange I lost something,' he said, 'as is only natural. I was disconsolate when my wife left me; I've always loved her. Ever since then I've worn the habit of Saint Francis.'

He had made a vow? I truly doubt it. He never told me so, and now he has taken his secret to the grave. But if the habit were a sacrifice to implore his wife's forgiveness, what meaning could he attribute to the eighteenth-century wig?

'Your wife,' said the priest, 'is a saint.'

'I know she is. Everything requires some sacrifice, Don Andreu. You know the legend: in exchange for youth, Faust sells his soul to the Devil. However, there are several versions of the story. According to some, Faust, redeemed by love, was saved. According to others, he was condemned.'

'Which happens to be what I believe,' the priest concluded.

Don Toni smiled.

'It may not be so, Father. You know that a moment of contrition is enough to save a soul.'

'Yes,' said Don Andreu. 'God is merciful.'

'And we must not censure that. We should pray for Him to absolve even those of us who don't deserve it . . .'

'We should never lose hope, Don Toni. But believe me, Faust . . .'

'You aren't very fond of him. Neither am I. He isn't a clear enough hero. We don't know what the Germans meant by that myth, whose origin, according to the scholars, is English, even though it seems utterly Germanic to me. Excessive, like everything those people do. You see, both versions we mentioned refer to the same trap: Faust, condemned, is a victim of Mephistopheles. . .'

'I'm pleased to hear you say that.'

'But Faust redeemed is a cheat: he cheats the Devil.'

'We can cheat the Devil: he isn't a fellow man...'

'Isn't he?' asked the Senyor. 'He's always so close at hand...'

Suddenly Don Andreu feared that the conversation had wandered too far from the purpose of his visit to the estate.

'Don Toni,' he said, 'after the scandal you made, your Honour can't go back to Paris ten years later. Think of your wife. Didn't you say you loved her? That would rule out any chance of a reconciliation. She's willing to forget, but obviously only if your Honour is willing to be reasonable.'

Without giving a specific reply, my benefactor had to admit that if he returned to Paris everyone would assume it was because of his niece, not for the opera. However, he found that the truth outweighed the lie. If he went, it would be for the opera.

He used the conditional: he had not made up his mind to return to Paris. The priest was astonished. The clock struck nine and suddenly Don Toni said: 'My niece told me she would be coming after supper. I haven't seen her yet. I'm telling you in case you'd rather not meet her.'

The priest got up to leave. What a shock! What would they say in the village? I was thunderstruck. Dona Xima was a legend to me, as Don Juan is to so many maidens who are seduced before they even meet him. Her image had troubled my soul for years and almost made me renounce my ecclesiastical career. Prudence and holy reason advised me to leave my hideaway and lock myself up in my room, but I decided against it. I would not move from the window until I had witnessed her visit. Judging by the cold night, they would probably sit by the fire. I was moved by an uncontrollable urge, and all the reflections in the world would not have succeeded in changing my behaviour.

The Senyor tried to reassure the priest and begged him not to leave. Before his niece arrived, they would hear the carriage; if Don Andreu did not wish to meet her, he could leave through the garden. That solution was safer than leaving earlier and risking the possibility of an encounter at the entrance to the estate.

'You're right,' said the priest. 'That's what I'll do.'

Lowering his voice again, he continued to describe details about Don Toni's shameless niece.

Since he was already old, his disapproval of the magnificence he described was mixed with an involuntary admiration, the product of the very magnificence he censured. Two days before Dona Xima's arrival, a foreign man had come from the City to the village inn. He spoke French and brought a big cart full of furniture and curtains; he had gone up to the living room and the bedroom on the upper floor overlooking the square, facing the Bearn town house, and with the help of two men who came with him he covered the walls with damask, hung mirrors and filled the rooms with vases of flowers and silver candelabra as in a chapel. Word spread that the Field Marshal was on his way, and a woman was sent to the priest's house to ask if they would lend her their linen sheets. Don Andreu, proceeding with caution, did not agree before he knew what it was for.

'When I found out, naturally, I said no. And I hope your Honour will forgive me if I offend you in this matter.'

'You are the one who ought to forgive me for the wrong I have done,' Don Toni replied.

'That is our mission.'

'And for what I still may do,' the Senyor murmured almost inaudibly.

'That's impossible.'

'You're right. It's impossible.'

And to please him, knowing his weakness, because the priest detested progress but enjoyed discussing it, Don Toni brought up the subject of inventions and travel.

'The first time we went to Paris, instead of travelling by carriage, we travelled by railway from Bayonne. There are many trains in France. Do you know what a railway is? It's a row of cars attached to a locomotive. The passengers share the cars. You buy a ticket and you can ride in any one of them. I remember there was a man from Bordeaux who sat down next to us; he looked like a Marquis, but he claimed he was a shop-owner.'

Don Andreu looked up.

'And your Honour didn't leave the car?'

'It was already moving, and when a railway car starts moving it doesn't stop for anyone.'

'So if you see a lovely landscape and want to go out for a stroll or have lunch by a spring...'

'You can't. You see, you'd be imposing upon the other passengers.'

'You have to suit the others' needs instead of your own, then?'

'Exactly. That's socialism for you. As you see, it isn't only a political theory, but also a technological necessity. Progress leads to socialism, whether we like it or not. Have you sent any letters by mail yet?'

'Last Sunday I sent one to the Palace. I spoke to the Post Master personally — we now have a postmaster in Bearn — and he helped me attach the stamp.'

'Some time ago,' Don Toni replied, 'you'd have sent the letter with an emissary, by hand. Now you have to send it through others whose families and opinions you don't know. Along with the letter you sent to the Palace, there may have been other very different ones, written by Protestants, for example.'

The priest pointed out that there were no Protestants in the village, but that it was a known fact that the secretary's wife was corresponding with a young man. They sent each other poems.

'It's the worst scandal in the past fifty years,' he said.

'Not counting mine,' the Senyor murmured.

The priest responded with a discreet silence. Then he said: 'By the way, Don Toni, a minute ago I noticed that little cart . . .'

He had not taken his eyes off it since he had walked in the door. As much or more than Barbara Titana's madness, the *automobile* reinforced Don Toni's reputation as a sorcerer in the village. Don Andreu stared suspiciously at the device.

'I'll burn it soon,' my benefactor said, vaguely.

'There's no rush,' the priest replied in a conciliatory tone. 'However, it would be advisable . . . and besides, Don Toni, allow me to remind you about the dolls' room.'

'It's locked up. No one can get in,' the Senyor interrupted firmly.

Don Andreu dared not harp on the subject and continued to talk about the advances of the century, which he considered somewhat diabolical.

'At any rate, they're dangerous inventions.'

'They will impose themselves sooner or later,' the other man argued. 'Have you ever heard of the telephone? They've used it in some important experiments. The same as the balloon. Ever since the Marquise du Châtelet went up in a balloon, in the company of Newton* . . .' And he showed the priest a commemorative engraving

*Who died, obviously, long before Montgolfier's invention (Editor's note).

78

with some verses written below it which had always fascinated me:

A côté de Newton, l'immortelle Emilie
s'élève dans les airs,
et parcourant des cieux la carrière infinie
mesure l'Univers.

'I don't know French,' the priest mumbled, 'but I think it says she wants to measure the Universe.'

The Senyor nodded.

'Burn this print, Don Toni.'

'As you please,' he said, and threw it in the fire.

That very moment they heard the carriage. The priest left in haste and when I expected to see Dona Xima appear through the courtyard doorway — I had unwittingly closed my eyes to open them the moment her striking figure appeared against the starlit sky — I witnessed a very different image, yet no less marvellous: a graceful, proud young man dressed in red and gold who seemed to radiate light. Angel or demon, I had never imagined anything quite like him. Years later, visiting the Musée du Louvre, I discovered in Poussin heroes and gods with that same French liveliness and that classical profile.

The young man stopped, clicked his heels and announced in an insolent tone:

'*Madame de Vidal demande si Monsieur de Bearn veut bien la recevoirrr...*'

He drew out the word '*recevoir*', already emphatic by nature, singing it in a baritone and adding a few consecutive r's. The Senyor lifted the spectacles he only wore for reading and examined the man from head to toe. The splendid valet let himself be admired without moving a muscle, as if he were a painting on a wall. A moment later, neutralizing his French insolence with some sound Mallorcan common sense, the Senyor replied softly in his own tongue: 'Tell the lady to please come in.'

Before the valet retired, the house was invaded by a waft of perfumes and colour. Dona Xima advanced, smiling with open arms.

'Uncle Tonet...'

FIFTEEN

Beauty is a tragic force. Paganism sees it as the joy of life. To me it represents sadness. The Renaissance placed the intensity of artistic pleasure above all else. What an aberration, my friend! The ancients left lovely sculptures of animals, innocent lambs, noble horses and placid cows. After visiting the fauna kept in the Vatican Museum one's soul feels light, as if it had been bathed in purity. The artists who created such beautiful sculptures did not intend to take things out of their place nor act excessively on our sensitivities. They were indeed true classicists. Unrest and sin begin with the exaltation of humanism. It has been said that art ennobles everything, but the more artistic it is, the more delicate the representation of feminine beauty, the more intensely it will address the senses of man. A kind, modest woman, appropriately dressed, even though dangerous, can also offer something pure and comforting. Venus, the deified woman, is sacrilegious. Those who insist that art is always pure are either hypocritical or rhetoricians with no sensitivity. Art is sometimes intoxicating. The temptations of Saint Anthony by Pafnuci are full of beauty; Lucifer was beautiful.

Xima looked stunning. She was wearing a deep green coat and a feather hat. Her appearance was that of a porcelain figure painted with the most delicate and artful colours. Her eyes had a mysterious depth to them; her mouth was exquisite. Despite my trepidation, I realized she resembled the Senyor, who was thought of as ugly. Years later, the Senyora, who had begun to lose her senses and decline, assured me that Dona Xima resembled me. Mysteries of the human mind.

80

SIXTEEN

'Our fireplace. . . Do you remember our fireplace, Uncle Tonet?' said
Dona Xima, sitting down beside him. 'I like to call you Uncle.'

She had taken off her travel coat revealing a light spring dress in pale
ivory. She moved with aplomb and was always smiling. I remembered
the masks of early Greek theatre, where each character was comic or
tragic from beginning to end. She had banished the word 'no' from
her vocabulary. 'Xima, the woman who never loses her temper. . .'
she was used to getting everything she wanted with her smile. Either
she had no feelings and behaved like an automaton or she was
endowed with the ability to manage them. I have sometimes thought
that people like her, provided with moral stupidity, are not
responsible for the catastrophes they unleash; instead of being
condemned like deliberate criminals and burned in Hell, after death
they will keep on smiling equally to Truth and Error from the
darkness of limbo. The Senyor compared her to a cat, and it seemed
obvious that a soul such as hers could not be entirely rational.

'Isn't it true,' she said, resting one knee on the bench, 'that you'll
come to Paris with me as you did last time? Capoul will debut in a new
production of *Faust* at the beginning of the year.'

'*Debut* is a gallicism, Xima.'

'And what am I, but a gallicism?'

'A delightful gallicism. How is Campo Formio?'

'I'd rather not talk about him. *Tout à fait snob.*'

'I warned you.'

'He still thinks he's in love with the Empress. Do you like Eugenia de Montijo? Don't you think she's a little withered? She's fiery, as a Spaniard should be, but her virtue goes to her head. She loves to let everyone know that she's righteous. Since she's no child any more...'

The Senyor closed his eyes.

'Never a kind word...'

'That's all I have to say about her. She doesn't know how to behave like a queen.'

'Do you think Louis Napoleon knows how to behave like a king?' Xima fluttered her eyelashes.

'*Il est charmant*. And awfully dignified. Imagine that I still haven't managed to get an official introduction. But I will this winter. I have his word. I refuse to enter the Tuileries through the back door.'

'His conversations with Bismarck,' said Don Toni, 'don't strike me as particularly dignified. He oughtn't to have agreed to speak to the Chancellor, but rather to the King. He has humiliated France in the eyes of the other countries. The Hohenzollern, who are not really kings, but marquises, are far more effective.'

Dona Xima remained silent because she was not interested in politics. He noticed she was getting bored and took her hand.

'Let me see this bracelet...'

She caressed his cheek.

'Oh, how did you guess? They're magnificent diamonds, aren't they?'

'They could be bigger. And what else?'

'This ring.'

'In exchange for...?'

Dona Xima feigned the sort of indignation she was incapable of feeling and replied — things must be called by their names — with a cynical sentence.

'*Mais voyons, Monsieur, je suis une honnête femme.*'

'You're worth a lot, Xima,' said the Senyor. 'You're a gift from God.'

'In Bearn they think it's from the Devil. Oh come with me, Tonet. I bought the town house at the Etoile, remember? It will all be just the same as the last time, only this time I'll be paying for you. I'm rich.'

The Senyor did not reply. She had picked up a book and began to read:

'*Un soir, t'en souvient-il...?* Are you a poet now?' she asked. 'That's why the Emperor's diamonds seemed small to you.'

The Senyor waved his hand indecisively, as he always did. She laughed.

'Poets are generous. Instead of giving diamonds they give moons and stars... The Emperor of France, poor thing, could only buy me this.'

Was it a request? Had she really come for money? Everyone knew the Senyors did not have much, that there were heavy mortgages weighing on their lands, whereas Dona Xima arrived in a carriage drawn by two English horses, with a footman and a valet in livery. But her heart was cold. I expected her to make a specific request at any moment. If she had done so, I believe the peasant in me, violent and attached to material possessions, would have overlooked all the conventions and given the intruder the answer she deserved. This is a poor land, and we have been taught that because we live in poverty any change could make things even worse. What I did not know was that women such as Dona Xima do not ask; they wait for others to offer.

He looked up: 'So you're rich now? I'd already heard through the mail that Campo Formio was ruined.'

She looked at him, flattered to see such evil powers attributed to herself.

'Don't be mean, Tonet. I'd never ruin a man. And if I did, he'd always be welcome at my table. I still haven't paid for the town house, you know; but I told the Emperor about it and he laughed. That's a good sign, isn't it?'

'So you don't need anything from me? In your letter...'

'Oh,' she quietly interrupted, 'that was before I spoke to the Emperor. Didn't I just tell you that he laughed?'

I let out a silent sigh of relief. Suddenly, the twitching silhouette of Barbara Titana appeared on the doorstep; she had already gone mad some time ago. She was tall and shabby, covered from head to toe with a dark cloak.

'Oh, Xima, my child,' she cried, 'let me kiss you. You're an angel. I can't touch you with my hands, child...' In her excitement she started speaking in the third person: 'There's a carriage with two generals waiting for her outside. The Kings of the Earth bow down when she goes by. What do you think of that, Senyor? We've never seen anything like it in Bearn.'

'Never, Titana,' said the Senyor.

Dona Xima looked at her in surprise: 'Is that Barbara Titana? I wouldn't have recognized her.'

The madwoman walked up to her.

'Xima, the priest wants to set you up on an altar.'

'That's right, Barbareta,' laughed Dona Xima.

Barbara stared at her in ecstasy.

'Senyor,' she whispered, 'touch her. Touch her face, even if it's only for a second.'

Dona Xima graciously consented: 'You touch me, Barbareta.'

She fearfully dared to touch the lady's bracelets.

'How lovely . . .'

She was kneeling down and praying. Dona Xima smiled as you would at a dog or a cat.

'Has she lost her mind?' she asked.

Don Toni explained that she had, and that the villagers therefore considered her in the odour of sanctity. The young woman seemed pleased.

'Good. Now I have a saint on my side,' she said. She took everything the same way.

'God will protect you, dear,' Titana continued in a somewhat declamatory tone. 'The good you have done will have its reward.'

'But I'm a devil, Barbara.'

'An angel, an angel from Heaven . . . we all adore you.'

The intensity of her feelings was such that it seemed theatrical. She declaimed like a bad actress. I have since realized that many of the insane are affected, contrary to what one would expect. The observation, in all fairness, was Don Toni's. 'When one lacks a critical sense,' he said, 'all that's left is to play to the gallery. Just look at all those "sincere" love letters the world round. Don't they seem ridiculous? Isn't Ophelia, poor thing, a prime example of pretentiousness?'

Suddenly Titana grabbed Dona Xima and kissed her. Then she flung herself on the floor and cried: 'Now I can die in peace! Kiss her, Senyor!'

'That's enough, Barbara.'

'Kiss her, Senyor,' the madwoman repeated, getting more and more excited.

The Senyor kissed Xima, and Titana disappeared with a howl.

84

'I didn't know she'd gone mad,' his niece said. 'Didn't you tell me she'd fallen in love with you?'

'A long time ago...' the Senyor granted.

'And what about you?'

'I was a saint.'

'You didn't like her?'

'She's always been ugly.'

'Look what your sanctity has done for her.'

'She's satisfied,' the Senyor objected. 'And now you seem to be the one she's in love with.'

Dona Xima, who knew all sorts of people in Paris and had picked up the latest scientific trends, smiled like an expert: 'No, Tonet. She was putting herself in my place.'

'Goodness!' said the Senyor. 'Since when do you know about these things?'

'We're awfully up-to-date in Paris.'

My heart was heavy after witnessing that scene. Uncle and niece were impassive, cold as the powerful often are, sometimes seeming to be utterly selfish in the eyes of the people. They were like two surgeons, two vivisectionists applying their scalpels with no regard for the pain they may cause. For a moment I loathed them. They were the 'Senyors', the enemy. My resentment did not last long. We are all what we are brought up to be. The ladies at the Court of France fainted at the sight of a spider, but watched the torture of la Brinvilliers and the quartering of Damiens.

SEVENTEEN

While I was lost in such thoughts, Dona Xima and the Senyor had vanished. I assumed they had gone into the dining room to eat something, and expecting them to return, sat down on a rocking chair and fell asleep, exhausted as I was after all the day's excitement. I do not know how long I slept. When I awoke the house was silent. I looked out the window again and saw no one. On a bench, abandoned amidst papers and books, lay Dona Xima's green coat and feather hat. Lying in the firelight, those objects were full of latent life. The owners of those belongings would be back before long to continue their tempestuous activities. Meanwhile, the coat, books and flames seemed to throb in the silence of the night.

The culprits arrived. They did not come from the dining room, but from the rooms upstairs. Dona Xima, pleased as usual, sat down by the fire and repeated as when she had arrived: 'Our fireplace...'

She shut her eyes and smiled. Suddenly she asked: 'Will you show me the dolls' room?'

The Senyor shook his head.

'Why not, Uncle Tonet? You know I've always been dying to see it. I thought you...'

There was a moment of silence and she realized it was best to drop the subject.

'Where's Margalideta?' she asked.

'She died.'

'Ah, that's right.'

'Tell me about Paris,' said the Senyor. They were talking to fill the silence, like two people who no longer have much to say to each other. She answered: 'It's better than ever. The Exhibition two years ago was magnificent. The Empire is secured for a couple of centuries.' That was not long before Sedan. 'Lesseps is about to inaugurate the canal. Offenbach is a success on the boulevards. Do you know *La Grande Duchesse de Gerolstein?*'

And she parodied, lowering her voice:

'*Voici*
le sabre, le sabre,
le sabre de mon père...'

'So Louis Napoleon is paying for your town house?'

'Didn't I tell you he laughed?'

'And that's all?'

'He said, "We'll have to pay a visit to the Minister of Finances."'

The Senyor gave his usual wave with a look of surprised approval, opening his mouth and lowering his head, as if to say 'that's much better'.

'France is so rich...' Dona Xima continued. 'What are 600,000 francs after all, divided among all the French?'

And she proceeded to expose her economic and sentimental plans.

'There's a dragoon...'

'What?'

'A lieutenant dragoon, very young, tall, poor...'

'You have such a good heart, Xima,' the Senyor interrupted.

She pretended to be offended at his mockery and pulled at his hair.

'Why do I tell you these things? You're very naughty, Uncle Tonet.'

'Don't mess up my wig. Are those earrings real?'

'Yes. Why do you ask? Oh, I'm not telling you any more. This sounds like a confession.'

He explained that when her carriage had arrived he had been in confession with the priest.

'Where is he? Where are you hiding him?' she asked. 'Well, you'll finish your confession tomorrow. You'll have more to tell. Let's see, how will you explain...'

'I'll tell him a devil came in...'

'Aren't I a gift from God, a seraph?'

'Lucifer was also beautiful.'

'But he couldn't have been a gift from God.'

'What, then?'

'I've never understood these things,' she said, fluttering her eyelashes.

Don Toni began some explanations and she interrupted.

'Now, none of your heresies, Uncle Tonet.'

The Senyor continued, ignoring her.

'I believe that between God and the Devil there must be some kind of coordination, a certain balance . . .'

Dona Xima was looking serious, searching for arguments her mind could not find.

'Stop, it isn't true,' she finally said. 'I do have principles, you know.'

The Senyor pointed out that they were rather poorly applied, and she lightened up again; no matter what was said, she was always pleased to be the centre of attention.

'But I couldn't be all that bad,' she said.

'You heard Barbara. What does the dragoon say?'

'He says I'm an angel.'

'See? We should all reach a consensus. Because the village certainly doesn't think so.'

He changed the subject with his usual skill: 'Have you ever seen a sewing machine?'

'I have one. I had it sent from London, but as you might imagine, I never sew.'

'Have you got a telephone?'

'Every morning I lie in bed and use it to give orders to my coachmen.'

Don Toni pointed out: 'Do you know that your servants left the priest without his *ensaïmada*? Where did you find that valet?'

'He's rather elegant, wouldn't you say?'

'Rather insolent, is what I'd call him.'

'Exactly. It's more imposing.'

She then proceeded to explain that she had seen Dona Maria Antònia several times, or rather, that they constantly saw each other, but pretended not to do so, as if they had never met.

'And you can imagine how difficult that is in a village the size of Bearn, Tonet.'

'I'm sure you're both marvellous at it.'

He said both out of courtesy, because Dona Maria Antònia was the only one who really deserved any credit. Dona Xima explained that she would have gladly gone up and embraced her aunt. She had no capacity for bitterness, as for so many other feelings. Her aunt was not very resentful either, but she knew how to keep up appearances. She was a master at the delicate social art of ignoring. The first time a peasant came up to tell her that Dona Xima had arrived from Paris, she talked to him about the Seine and Notre Dame. Since the Bearn town house is on the square next to the church, and the village inn, as I already mentioned, is right across the square, Dona Maria Antònia's balconies overlooked not only the entrance to the inn, but also Dona Xima's rooms, which as the priest mentioned had been covered in damask and filled with vases and silver candelabra. But Dona Maria Antònia never looked out from her balconies; they were only opened when there was a procession. The niece's carriage was always waiting at the door; her aunt always left through the garden gate that faced another street.

'She's still beautiful, you know,' said Dona Xima.

'I always thought she was,' Don Toni replied, and then added an extravagance improper for a mind as lucid as his: 'In a quarter of a century, you'll be just like her.'

Dona Xima was flattered and silent. The Senyor caressed her hair. For a moment he did indeed look like a sorcerer predicting the mysteries of time.

'You'll turn fifty,' he slowly explained, 'and your hair will be grey. You'll become a respectable lady, give to charity . . .'

Dona Xima smiled at the thought of her problematic regeneration. The idea of practising virtue at the age of fifty seemed fine because she had not yet reached thirty.

'I'll become a respectable lady,' she said, filling a pause, because she never dared to interrupt him when he spoke of her, 'and when I die . . .'

'When you die, you'll have a proper funeral, and up to Heaven you'll go.'

She embraced him.

'You're so kind, so generous. . . Come to Paris with me!'

That was her reaction to her uncle's plan for moral regeneration. He gazed at her with a look of irony and perhaps a little sadness.

'What about your dragoon? And the Emperor?'

Xima tried to scare away the two ghosts with a wave of her hand.

'Oh, don't you start making up problems, you who are so kind, you who make everything simple and sweet.'

The Senyor continued to stare at her with the smile Houdon attributes to Voltaire. She said nothing because she enjoyed being looked at up close and did not like to interrupt comments concerning herself. In a clear, low voice, Don Toni uttered eight words that filled my heart with joy.

'I will not go to Paris with you.'

I heard a loud, almost desperate bolt of laughter.

'What on earth is this? I thought... What's come over you, Tonet? When did you change your mind?'

'Perhaps just this minute. I must tell you something I've never told any other woman.'

She was exultant, because, as Don Toni observes in his *Memoirs*, she was as nosy as a stray cat.

'Oh, Tonet, you're so kind... You want to tell me a secret? Is it something intimate and naughty? Will you allow me to tell it? Psychology has become so fashionable in Paris...'

'You'll do as you please.'

'You're so good, so marvellous... Tell me. I'm all ears, Uncle Tonet.'

She had coiled up on the bench like a snake and stared straight at him, fluttering her eyelashes. The Senyor uttered another decisive eight words: 'I did not like you much this time.'

I was breathless with joy. Blessed be the Lord a thousand times! Praise His Holy Name! Dona Xima was thunderstruck. Then she let out another shrill laugh.

'You're admirable, Uncle Tonet. I've never met anyone like you. Is this the first time you've said that to a woman? How very original... It's also the first time anyone's said it to me.'

Her expression finally turned more sombre and she searched for a mirror in her purse.

'Don't bother looking at yourself, Xima. You look magnificent,' the Senyor said nostalgically.

'That's what I thought.'

'You may continue to think so. I'm the one who's changed. And yet I haven't...' he continued, closing his eyes. 'Now I see you... There. We're walking into the Opera. You're dressed in white.

90

Gounod greets us. The Emperor has noticed you, too. Of course he'll pay for your town house, if you set your mind to it. Six hundred thousand francs... it's nothing. But the diamonds on that bracelet are quite small. You're marvellous, Xima. There's no one as marvellous as you.'

He was dreaming out loud, like a sibyl. Seeing him in such an unusual state, I could not help but recall the rumours about his sorcery. Something was running through him and his words came out inspired and somewhat mad, straight from his heart. Dona Xima had risen and looked out of the courtyard doorway. She may also have felt moved at that moment.

The Senyor continued: 'Quiet, don't say a thing. I had never seen you as clearly as tonight. When I kissed you, I couldn't see you. To see each other, we need a certain distance. Give me your hand. Where are you? Xima!'

He opened his eyes and found he was alone. She walked back to him with a tender look in her eyes.

'I'm here, Tonet,' she said as she sat down beside him. 'I was looking at the stars. You could see me clearly with your eyes closed and from far away?'

The Senyor had returned from his reverie.

'Wait a moment,' he said. 'I have a surprise for you.'

He left the room. Dona Xima went over to the wooden cart and studied it closely. I thought I heard her say to herself: 'An *automobile*?'

Don Toni produced a little case with the diamond necklace that had belonged to his mother. It was the only valuable piece of jewelry left in the house. My benefactor had once shown it to me, telling me that if he had to he would sell it to pay off his debts. Dona Xima flung her arms around his neck, exaggerating her joy, which was undoubtedly genuine.

'A diamond necklace? Uncle Tonet, you're marvellous. Oh, I'm so happy! Louis Napoleon...'

He smiled modestly.

'These *are* bigger, aren't they?'

'But why are you giving me this? And you're not coming to Paris with me?'

He shook his head.

'My goodness,' Dona Xima laughed, 'never have I been so lavishly rejected. What can I do for you, Uncle Tonet?'

'Enjoy yourself with that dragoon.'

'Are you jealous?'

The Senyor looked at her sadly. He wasn't exactly jealous of the lieutenant, as he has expressed very well in his *Memoirs*: he had just understood that one does not reach Eternity by selling one's soul to the Devil, but by stopping time, freezing it. The eternity he yearned for (eternity in this life, as he was too pagan to think of any other) he had to create himself. It was too late to repent, but not to remember. He no longer needed Dona Xima. Now her image was enough: his *Memoirs*, the seclusion of Bearn, his pen, ink and paper.

'Look,' he said, 'when I was a child I loved my skipping rope; when I was older, the trapeze... Now that would all be absurd. Besides, I don't really want to give up my childhood. I'll always have fond memories of what I did on the trapeze.'

'It seems too late for the trapeze,' said Dona Xima.

'Not really. It's too late to repeat, not to remember. I won't be leaving this place any more. I know what I have to do now. I assume you don't understand.'

She moved closer to him, gentle as a cat.

'Oh, Tonet, you know I'm nothing but a stray. And you're so kind and understanding. Now I really feel ashamed. Who would think it, ashamed for the first time at the age of twenty-eight.'

She leaned her head on his shoulder and said something I could not make out.

'Yes,' said the Senyor, holding the necklace. 'Look at this one. You could make him a ring out of this stone. How old is your dragoon?'

'Twenty.'

Don Toni was already fifty-eight.

'Twenty years old...' he thought out loud, 'Lieutenant Dragoon. How did it occur to you to ask my permission?'

She kissed his hand, moved by such generosity.

'Come now, don't be silly,' he said. 'Don't you remember our motto, "always above the heart"? It's half past ten. Do me a favour and leave for the village now. Maria Antònia will still be awake. Pay her a visit on my behalf.'

'Don't frighten me.'

'You're not the least bit frightened. You'll be splendid. Tell her you've been here and found me in bed, ill and lonely...'

'At death's door?'

'Not quite. She doesn't like extremes.'

'And she should come?'

'No. That's up to her. Oh, and allow me to give you a bit of advice. Don't have that general in livery announce your arrival.'

'Well, then, what should I do?'

'Leave your carriage a little way down the street, go in alone and say, "Aunt Maria Antònia, I'm leaving tomorrow. Do you need anything from Paris?"'

'Very well.'

The Senyor helped her on with her coat and made her button it up to her neck so his wife would not see her décolleté. He was very attentive and always respected conventions, at least minor ones. Dona Xima vanished into the night leaving the sound of bells and horses in her wake. He stood still in the doorway for a moment. Then he walked over towards the entrance to the kitchen and said: 'Madò Francina, please get the Senyora's room ready. She's left a message that she'll be coming in a little while. See if anything's missing and put rose water on her dressing table.'

EIGHTEEN

Dona Maria Antònia arrived an hour and a half later. The Senyor had told everyone to go off to bed, including Madò Francina, who would have liked to welcome her. I was the only one exempt from the general order. He assumed the Senyora had come back to stay, and he was right. He was as happy as can be and rattled off plans to make her life as pleasant as possible.

'She'll find the house a little dirty, but that's her obsession, and it will give her something to do. We must tell Madò Francina to call some women in to whitewash.'

'Your Honour thinks she's coming to stay?' I dared ask him.

'Naturally,' he replied. 'That's what she said in her message. The priest has made all the arrangements. Where have you been since suppertime?' he added, looking at me with curiosity. 'My niece from Paris was here. Didn't you see her?'

'No, Senyor,' I said, trembling.

'You didn't hear the carriage? Well, it wasn't for lack of bells!'

But his attention wandered at once; the thought of his wife's arrival obsessed him.

'She'll want a priest, Joanet. It's a pity you can't say Mass yet. You should also learn to play ombre.'

We kept on looking into the courtyard every few minutes. Finally, in the silence of the night, we heard a sound. Biel, the Senyora's coachman and factotum, was talking to the mule as he drove. Unlike Dona Xima with her insolent luxury, her landau and her servants in livery, Dona Maria Antònia arrived in an old open carriage drawn by a single mule. I have since mentioned that contrast to the Senyor, who did not think it was particularly significant.

'What does luxury have to do with moral qualities, or even with social standing?'

'Your niece,' I replied, 'oughtn't to have appeared with servants in livery and English horses when the Senyora...'

'Why do you lose your temper over things that are only natural? Dona Maria Antònia doesn't need to impress anyone, whereas Xima is essentially what in France is known as a *cocotte*. Don't you realize that she needs to show off more than my wife? There's a letter from the Empress of Austria to her daughter, Marie-Antoinette, that you should know about. You know that Marie-Antoinette was very fond of luxury and fashion. Her seamstress was a German Jewess by the name of Madame Bertin; if we go to Paris someday I'll show you where she lived, on the rue de Saint Honoré. She was always firing Marie-Antoinette's vanity. In one year she made her seventy-two new silk dresses. The Empress scolded her daughter for it. She wrote to her in a letter that such ostentation was "unbecoming in a queen". The memory of Du Barry was still fresh in everyone's mind.'

The Senyor had recognised Biel's voice. Before the carriage drove into the courtyard, he had an idea: he grabbed me by the arm and led me to the dark room where I had spied on his conversation with Dona Xima.

'From up here,' he said, 'we'll see her enter, but she won't notice. We'll see how she walks in, what kind of luggage she brings — she's always had the strangest luggage — and the look on her face. And don't forget that listening behind doors,' he added, laughing, 'has always been a dreadful sin.'

As the carriage pulled up to the entrance of the estate, the clock struck twelve. Dona Maria Antònia was already about fifty years old. She was still lovely, with a captivating simple, self-assured look.

'The prie-dieu first, Biel,' she said. Her voice was calm.

'Where should I put the fly-swatter and the velvet cushion?' Biel asked.

The Senyor put his arm around my neck and smiled at me.

'Just put them all in the same place,' said Dona Maria Antònia. 'The crucifix with the bottle of holy water and the little silver bucket.'

She had sat down by the fireplace and looked at the books as she continued to give orders.

'Don't put the brooms near the prie-dieu,' — Biel had just walked in with six new ones — 'I don't like the toilet water near the holy water, either; put my toiletries on a chair.'

The Senyor was tapping me on the neck.

'Anything else?' Biel inquired.

The Senyora told him to go to Inca the following day to fetch a priest and buy some violet soap.

'If you can't find a priest, bring back a friar. A friar ought to do for saying our rosaries.'

'And what should I do if I can't find any violet soap?'

'Bring some other good soap.'

'Good night.'

'Goodbye, Biel. And be careful on the curve going down the hill; the mule can't see where she's going.'

'She can see better than you can, Madam! She's just naughty, that's all.'

When she was left alone, Dona Maria Antònia looked around at the walls.

'What is this? Nobody home?' she murmured. The Senyor finally decided it was time to leave his hideout and he walked out with theatrical ease. I can see him now, advancing down the length of the hallway in his grey Franciscan habit and his white wig.

'How are you, Maria Antònia?'

She smiled without moving from her seat.

'Hello, Tonet. I'm feeling very well, sitting here by the fire.'

'It was awfully kind of you to come so late. Were you very worried about my illness?'

'Not at all, Tonet. I know you too well.'

Their strength was matched. He tried to make a subtle reference to the past and his wife did not allow him to finish.

'Let's not talk about it. We might lose our tempers all over again.'

'You're right. You'll find rose water and violet soap on your dressing table.'

'You were listening to my conversation with Biel, weren't you?'

'You could have guessed so.'

Naturally, she had. They knew each other well; knowledge and understanding, Don Toni used to say, are the equivalent of forgiveness. When I think that such intelligence and kindess have also led him to fall into heresy, I feel as though I were living in the greatest and most tragic of situations. I will always remember one day — the day I sang Mass — when over breakfast he whispered in my ear that between God and the Devil there was only a misunderstanding. If he had punched me in the face it would not have been as great a shock. Without knowing what I was doing, I rose from the table, much to the astonishment of the guests, who had not heard the sacrilegious statement. The Senyor immediately sent me a note with a message in pencil. 'The chocolate is getting cold.' It was an order. Instead of obeying, I replied with a manifesto saying that when the impious Voltaire studied with the Jesuits, he put pieces of ice in the holy water fonts so the monks would light the fires, which remained unlit until the water froze; that I didn't care if the chocolate got cold, but that I had been horrified by those words that were colder than ice, and that I would not return to the table until he asked God's forgiveness for the nonsense he had dared to utter. Many years have gone by and I still do not know whether that reaction stemmed from my virtue or my arrogance. I had not sacrificed my youth with all its temptations for a 'misunderstanding'. The Senyor read the manifesto and returned it to me with a single word written in the margin in his own hand: 'Sorry.' My eyes swollen with tears, I returned to the table, and there, in front of everyone, he gave me two slaps that made me see stars. Then he made me drink a glass of some strange beverage.

'That's the only way to cure a case of nerves,' he said. 'I read it this morning in a German book.'

The Senyor went over to Dona Maria Antònia and kissed her forehead.

'I had to catch your first impression,' he said, 'watch you walk in, look at the fireplace, see what you'd brought with you. You've always had the funniest luggage!'

'Well,' she interrupted, 'we have a lot to talk about. Xima came to see me. By the way, her entry was particularly unnatural: from the street she started bawling, "Aunt Maria Antònia, do you need anything from Paris?" What manners! Do you think that's usual in France?'

The Senyor looked alarmed.

'How should she have done it?'

'In a more natural way. What good does it do her to always be followed by two servants in livery? I kissed her. What was I to do? I asked her how long she'd been in Bearn, even though we've been running into each other everywhere.'

'And what did she say?'

'She said she'd just heard I was in the village. You should have seen the innocent look on her face when she told me about your illness . . .'

'She's so candid . . . I know there have been rumours that she came to take out a mortgage on the land. Not only is that false, but knowing that I was penniless, she invited me to go to Paris with her.'

'Poor Tonet,' said Dona Maria Antònia. 'She's spent these last few days running all over the place trying to find out how much could be got for your property. When she discovered the land was going down in value and that nobody's willing to lend a penny, because you've already mortgaged everything, she decided to invite you. And she probably got something out of you after all.'

A diamond necklace. All she had got from him was a diamond necklace worth as much as the best house in the village, including all the furniture. And she had got it without asking for it, graciously inviting her victim. The Senyor lowered his head and replied in a slightly confused tone: 'My mother's necklace. After all, it belonged to her great-grandmother. Seeing as you wouldn't have it, because you returned it the day we separated, it seemed natural to . . . do you mind?'

'Not at all. I'd returned it, just as you said. But given the circumstances, you can be sure your mother wouldn't have found it so natural.'

He did not reply, and sat down by the fire with his head in his hands.

'Are you sure you heard that they'll give no more money against the estate?'

'The mayor and the town clerk came to tell me. It's the talk of the town. That's why she asked for the necklace instead of money.'

The Senyor felt defeated. He was trying to convince himself more than his wife.

'That's not exactly true. She didn't ask for it.'

'She preferred to have you offer it. And who's the lucky man now?'

'The Duke, as usual . . . and the Emperor too, it seems. There's a young dragoon from a poor family . . .'

'What an exciting story!' said Dona Maria Antònia. 'I wouldn't be surprised if the dragoon ended up with the necklace.'

'She's only planning to give the dragoon one diamond for a ring.'

'That's what she told you? That woman must be out of her mind!'

'She's candid, I tell you.'

'Either that or she came across someone else who was.'

He meditated, sitting by the fire.

'A few hours ago,' he said, 'by this same fire, Xima was sincere. She asked my permission to give a diamond to the dragoon. Her sincerity was real, even if she then gives him the entire necklace. Everything changes, Maria Antònia. Those moments of sincerity pass like all the rest: immortalizing them is up to each one of us.'

His wife caressed him as though he were a child.

'You're either very kind or very stupid, Tonet.'

'And you're marvellous. I have never loved anyone the way I love you.'

'How many have you said that to?'

'It's true, but not in the same way. Will you stay with me?'

'If you behave.'

'I'll have to,' he said.

'If you promise to burn these books... because I'm sure there are quite a few bad ones among them.'

'That depends on what they answer from the Palace... We'll see what they say.'

'If you confess...'

'That's all I want.'

'If you repent, if you can forget...'

The Senyor gave her a cold glance. Suddenly poor Dona Maria Antònia really did not understand him, despite her intelligence and her intuition. Please do not think I am vain, Miquel, but it is true that the Senyor, who had travelled so much and known so many different people, was never understood by anyone but me. I realized right then and there that Dona Maria Antònia had touched upon a sensitive point, the only one that should have been left unmentioned. Don Toni would agree to anything, even burning the library, but he would never forsake his memories. There was no doubt that those memories were often sinful, but they were so deeply embedded in his soul that it would have been impossible to eradicate them. He could condemn them or try to dignify them, but not suppress them. The Senyor's last and most faithful lover, the one who kept him company in his solitude, was Memory, and in his *Memoirs* he has in effect sacrificed everything: money, a good name, even Dona Xima's beauty. Therefore, when he heard his wife's words he stood up and went to sit at the other end of the room.

'Never,' he said. 'Don't ask that of me. I can't forget a thing.'

He pronounced his words with acrimony. Seeing his reaction, she had a moment of pain and wiped away a tear. Then, without saying a word, she started collecting her luggage.

'I'll leave early in the morning. I won't leave earlier because I'm afraid of the dark. You'll have my things sent.'

He embraced her tenderly. He was back to his old self.

'You silly thing, you're just like a little girl! Afraid of the dark...'

Since they were now at the opposite end of the room and spoke softly, I could not hear them, but it was obvious that they would soon be reconciled. Even if Dona Maria Antònia did not succeed in understanding certain things about her husband, she knew how to forget and leave questions unanswered if necessary, realizing that time and oblivion are the only ways to solve insoluble problems. She was endowed with the gift of diplomacy and the ability to choose what she wished to hear. Her husband's answer had been ambiguous because Dona Maria Antònia had proposed 'repenting and forgetting' and he had stated that 'he could not forget a thing', as though the important part of the question were the second instead of the first. It seemed fairly obvious that he had not repented, but to avoid admitting such a painful truth, the Senyora's practical instinct drew a veil over the ambiguity and proceeded to negotiate other aspects. It was necessary to burn a few books. Why wait for the bishopric's decision? Did they not know that Voltaire was evil, that Diderot was an atheist? She had gone over to the fire and had one hand on the Senyor's shoulder.

'Burn these things, Tonet! Look, this one at least... Voltaire, fancy that. And this one, Renan: "Life of Jesus..." Oh, this one ...'

'If it pleases you...'

Without waiting for a reply, he threw the books she had chosen into the fire. His docility comforted Dona Maria Antònia. 'I must admit,' she thought, 'Tonet is quite good after all. We oughtn't to pay attention to little things when he's so accommodating on truly fundamental matters.' Such reasoning was hardly the product of anaylsis or precision, but it calmed her and served her purposes the same way an umbrella would have, not because umbrellas reveal any truth, but because they protect us from the rain. Watching from the little window (although now legitimately, so to speak, since the Senyor himself had taken me there) I was not fooled by Don Toni's

100

docility. Years later, he himself explained to me how littled he cared about those books.

'It's only natural,' he said. 'It's fine that a man should read until the middle of his life, but past a certain point it's time for him to write. Or have children. If we enlighten ourselves, we must then enlighten others, perpetuating what we've learned.'

NINETEEN

For a moment she was moved by the Senyor's acquiescence.

'Poor Tonet,' she said, 'what will you do now without any books?'

'I'll have you. You'll stay in exchange for the books. Watch out, you're burning Thomas à Kempis!'

'Oh,' Dona Maria Antònia cried, 'Why didn't you tell me? What's this?'

'The Encyclopaedia. But these volumes are *The Christian Year*. They have the same binding.'

'They shouldn't have been bound the same. Look at those lovely flames!'

The Senyor smiled mischievously.

'What will Don Andreu say? We're doing him out of his canonry.'

She looked at him inquisitively.

'If Don Andreu,' the Senyor explained, 'had been able to present himself to the Bishop as the author of the *auto-da-fé*, Monsignor might have made him a canon.'

'Who told you that? Are you serious?'

'Just an idea I had.'

'Ah!'

And she kept on burning books, although not quite as hastily. After a while she stopped.

'And what if it were true?'

I think she felt sorry for the Senyor and wanted to change the sentence she herself had dictated. Don Toni took her hand and briefly praised her thin, delicate fingers.

102

'I don't know what you see in them . . . You've always told me you liked my hands. Poor Tonet,' she continued, 'what will you do now without any books?'

'Now I'll have to get everything from within myself. Goethe was a primitive soul. Who would ever think of Faust being redeemed because he took land from the sea? It's all fine and well that a peasant woman from Bearn should think that happiness consists of inheriting one hundred thousand *duros*, but Goethe had the obligation to delve a little deeper. Look, when I was a boy, I went up on a trapeze, remember?'

'Xima told me you'd mentioned that.'

'She did? So your conversation was actually quite friendly.'

'Quite friendly, indeed.'

'I won't give up the trapeze, Maria Antònia. In my mind, that is. Nor anything else.'

'But didn't you give me permission to burn . . .'

'Yes. Everything. These books no longer mean anything to me. Now I'll write. You'll see!'

She replied apprehensively: 'I hope you won't write anything outrageous.'

'I'll try my best. I'd like to explain the harmony of the world and work towards the concord . . .'

'See? I like that,' said Dona Maria Antònia, not really wanting to reach the heart of the matter, just in case. 'Good harmony . . .'

Suddenly she looked at him mischievously (she was a woman after all, even though she considered herself old) and asked: 'You have to answer one question, Tonet. Were you sorry that Xima had a dragoon?'

'No. It's only natural.'

'Natural for her,' the Senyora clarified. 'Is that why you wouldn't go to Paris? You would have been second on her list, poor Tonet.'

'As far as I know, I would have been fourth.'

'Oh, my God! Three before you?'

'Well, there's the Duke, the Emperor and the dragoon.'

'We certainly have a pretty wild niece. To think that I had to kiss her . . . But what else was I to do?'

'It's silly to hold a grudge.'

'I'm not at all angry with her, but I must say I am happy that she's leaving and taking her scandals elsewhere.'

'I doubt whether she'll make much of a scandal where she's going. In France everyone does as he pleases.'

'What haven't we heard about the Emperor's mother...'

'About Queen Hortense? Yes, and about her aunt, Pauline Bonaparte...'

'From what I can see, they're just right for Xima. That's quite a circle of people she's found herself...'

Like an authentic Bearn she professed, as did her husband, the belief that it takes centuries for good breeding to develop, and felt little veneration towards royalty. 'Our family,' the Senyor used to say, 'is not indebted to any king. On the contrary. When Charles V came to conquer Algiers (which he did not succeed in doing) our ancestors gave him eighty sheep and two mules. He ate the sheep and didn't even thank us.' It is true that the real Bearns were never offered a word of thanks. Don Toni claimed so in his *Memoirs* with pride and perhaps, may God forgive me, with a little resentment. The word *botifarra* irritated him and he could not stand hearing about titles such as those of Collera or Sant Mateu which date, at the very most, from the beginning of the century.

'Kings are sometimes bad people,' said the Senyora.

'Parvenus. Particularly these.'

'And others. Look at Isabel II.'

'That's why I didn't want to authorize our relatives to snoop around in the archives.'

'You did the right thing; they would have messed everything up. They're worried to death about it. The two youngest ones visited the village some time ago and came to see me. I was very nice to them because I didn't recognize them at first. I hadn't seen them in ages.'

'They oughtn't to come if they don't feel like it. Ever since they saw we were ruined...'

'Wait, Tonet. I'm not quite ruined yet, thank God. You know I really love you, but I'll never let you touch what's mine, no matter how much or how little that is.'

The Senyor laughed.

'Take care of the pennies and the pounds will take care of themselves. You're admirable.'

'No. I know you too well. But don't worry, because as long as I have something you'll always be welcome at my table.'

'You're so much like Xima!' he said, with a melancholy look in his eyes.

His wife stared at him in surprise: 'I've never heard you say that!'

'Morally speaking,' the Senyor clarified.

'Morally? Have you gone mad?'

He did not reply. What he undoubtedly thought was that all women resemble each other a little. 'Isn't it just the same, Joan?' he's asked me a thousand times. He always discovered similarities between things, and when he could not find them directly he found them by contrast. Aunt and niece, so different, had coincided in their maternal reaction.

'Well, well,' said the Senyor. 'So you're willing to stay?'

'Yes, as long as you behave.'

'I can't live in the City, and even less in the village. This is where I have to be. Don't you think you'll be bored?'

'No, I'll start to crochet a bedspread.'

My benefactor's face was transfigured.

'We'll work together, each on his own. You'll see, Maria Antònia. You'll find the courtyard with the well full of begonias, and a hydrangea such as you've never seen before; that was Madò Francina's doing. We'll raise animals. It will be wonderful, you'll see. I love you very much, Maria Antònia, but we mustn't tell each other so too often...'

He had stopped himself and I completed his thought: 'Remember our motto: always above the heart.' Things resemble each other even to that extent. He continued: 'You'll have to eat whatever there is in the house.'

'My God, who cares? What I want is a priest to say mass in the morning and help me with my accounting. Do you know how much you owe, all in all?'

'Not exactly.'

'Have you been paying the interest, at least?'

'Every year, when the oil's ready, the creditors come and take it away.'

'The priest and I will do what has to be done. I don't want you to meddle in my affairs, but I will take care of yours.'

That was in keeping with the Senyor's ideology: an enlightened dictatorship. He had no objection.

'First of all,' she continued, 'this house needs to be whitewashed.'

She suddenly caught sight of the cart and looked concerned.

'What on earth is this? Tonet, Tonet...'

But she was overcome by curiosity and wanted to know the details of its operation. Had he managed to get it moving?

'Of course!' he replied. 'It moves on its own. That's why it's called an *auto-mobile*. See? You fill this kettle with water, put this iron cover on it and light a fire underneath... Would you like to go for a little drive? It's past midnight. Everyone's asleep.'

'Even if they're sleeping, Tonet. If they found us out...'

He went to fill up the kettle and put it on the fire.

'The world's changing, Maria Antònia,' he said. 'A hundred years from now no one will have mule carts anymore. Oh, I have to show you something.'

He returned with a bottle of Seltzer water and a glass. At the time there was no such thing as carbonated water in Spain, and it was supposed to have many healing properties. It was used against fevers and pneumonia. There were even people who got drunk on it.

'Taste it. It cures every kind of illness.'

'I feel fine.'

'So what? It makes you merry.'

She drank a sip.

'It's like white champagne. It looks full of gas. Couldn't it explode?'

Don Toni shook his head, but gave her a few notes of precaution: not to shake the bottle nor let it get too cold. The Senyora was afraid.

'Take it away, Tonet. I don't really like it, to tell you the truth.'

'Everybody's drinking it in France.'

'But we're in Bearn.'

The water had started boiling and the Senyor went back to the *auto-mobile*.

'Today,' he said, 'is the happiest day of my life. What objection could you have to our going for a little drive around the room? We'd go from that corner to the fireplace and back.'

Dona Maria Antònia looked at the machine with curiosity.

'But... it isn't dangerous?'

'Not at all. I'll bring a lot of embers from the fire, and since the water's already boiling, it'll make steam in no time. The steam comes out here, see? There's a valve...'

'Don't bother explaining. I don't want to understand it. You say it's perfectly safe?'

106

'Get in.'

I listened in terror. The Senyora was about to give in. I saw her look around as if she wanted to make sure that they were alone. She would finally yield to an adventure disapproved if not condemned by those in a position to do so. But she was extremely resourceful and her sharp instinct found a formula that harmonized whim and duty, just as the poet knows how to use the limitations of rhyme to his advantage and only add beauty to his verse.

'I consent to riding around the room on the condition that tomorrow the priest comes and burns the cart in front of everyone.'

The Senyor's eyelashes fluttered in a way that reminded me of Dona Xima.

'I have no objection.'

Why was that incorruptible man being so acquiescent? Had he really forsaken the *automobile* or did he plan to rebuild it later on? I do not know whether at that time the English were already ahead of him and there were a few driving around London. If that were the case, he certainly would have known, and that would have explained his acquiescence. Whereas if he had believed his invention was the only one in the world, he surely would not have destroyed it. A few weeks later, referring to the books they had burned, he laughed as he told me:

'Even though you aren't a clergyman yet, Joan, I must confess to you that I have fooled the Senyora. She stayed here in exchange for my burning the library, and unlike the medieval caliph, I didn't need to have it copied before it was burned. With the printed letter, the great Gutenberg guaranteed free thought to such an extent that nowadays burning books is the same as propagating them. The more editions are burned in Bearn, the more will be printed in Paris.'

Primo avulso non deficit alter, writes Virgil in Book VI of the *Aeneid*. But there is a difference: the poet refers to a beautiful bouquet of flowers, whereas Don Toni was alluding to the poisonous fruits of false philosophy.

They had stepped into the *automobile* and sat next to each other, stiff and motionless.

'What are we waiting for?' she asked.

'We have to wait for pressure to build up from the steam.'

'How strange! I'll never understand how a cart can be moved by a kettle of water, no matter how big it is. Don't go too fast, Tonet.'

'Are you scared?'

'Not particularly,' Dona Maria Antònia specified, 'but a little, I suppose.'

The *automobile* let out strange rumbles and whistling noises. It appeared to be animated by some vast inner energy, as though it were possessed by spirits. It could be compared to a beast in chains: without moving an inch, it heaved and shook like the demoniacs of Jaca on the Day of Santa Orsia. I assure you that it was no sight for a lady. I looked at her and she seemed serene, perhaps slightly pale, but calm and composed. The beast kept on shaking and I expected the whole thing to burst into pieces any minute. The Senyor's expression changed: he was aware of the responsibility that he had taken upon himself. I saw him hesitate between two levers, as if he had suddenly become disoriented; he finally pulled one energetically and cried:

'Hold on tight!'

The *automobile* let out a screech and jolted forwards. The entrance hall in Bearn is a large room. The corner the Senyors were in was more than forty steps away from the fireplace. The car bolted towards it like lightning.

'Not so fast,' said Dona Maria Antònia.

'Hold on tight!' the Senyor repeated, while trying to manoeuvre one of the levers.

'Stop, Tonet, we're going to crash!'

I had shut my eyes. Suddenly, in the silence of the night, I heard Don Toni's agitated voice: 'I can't stop it!'

Almost a quarter of a century has gone by, and I can still hear it now. 'I can't stop it.' For years the Senyor had searched for Truth and Life in the theories of a science that have been declared omnipotent. 'When the forces of nature threaten mankind, Franklin comes to the rescue and stops lightning,' reads the caption of a French engraving from 1754, exactly one year before the Lisbon earthquake. Scorning the power of God, a false philosophy had created a multitude of idols and revered the atheists Diderot, Voltaire and Condorcet. And when the Lisbon earthquake proves the impotence of Man, when the railway crashes or the most dreadful Napoleonic wars begin, natural consequences of the French Revolution, then Science will fall silent and all its advocates will manage to say will be 'I can't stop it.' You cannot stop that which you yourself have unleashed. Lucifer will never return to Heaven because no one, my Lord, can undo what has been done.

108

TWENTY

I heard a loud crash and opened my eyes. The *automobile* had run into the fireplace. I saw the Senyors below me, fallen on the embers, and somehow I managed to jump out of the window and drag them out of that inferno. I first attended to Dona Maria Antònia, who was unhurt, and then lifted the Senyor's body: he was unconscious. I have always been very strong and you know that at the Seminary I was in charge of moving the piano on holy days. Unfortunately, my physical strength, which serves me no purpose whatsoever, is no reflection of my courage. The Senyor's forehead was bleeding and Dona Maria Antònia told me to carry him over to the sofa in the nearby drawing room. When I had fulfilled her request, my head started to spin and I collapsed on the floor.

In the fireplace, the *automobile* had started to burn.

PART II

Peace Reigns in Bearn

ONE

Twenty-two years have gone by, Miquel, since Dona Maria Antònia returned to the house and the *automobile* burned up in the fireplace. Twenty-two years in these peaceful mountains, with the sole interruption of a trip abroad in the company of the Senyors. I will recount it all in the course of this Second Part, which takes place for them, even if not for me, in the most perfect serenity.

Dona Maria Antònia had begun to crochet a bedspread and the Senyor was writing. We seldom saw them before lunchtime. Madò Francina, who had been the Senyor's nursemaid, brought him his breakfast until the last few years, when she was replaced by Tomeu, a young farmboy whom I will mention again further on, as in a way he contributed to the unfolding of the tragedy. As in all tragedies, we find that fate has carefully choreographed numerous different causes. Each one of them is blind to all the others, and yet they operate together with the accuracy of a precision instrument. Tomeu is now almost twenty-three, and last week he was married to Catalineta, Dona Maria Antònia's maid. He is dark and his hair is always uncombed; the Senyor used to threaten to cut it. When he was still a child, a foreign woman wanted to paint him in a mythological scene surrounded by nymphs; it was quite a scandal. Women sometimes seem mad to us, or so different that we cannot understand them. Six years later, this catastrophe has occurred. Yet I must not jump ahead of the events.

During the first period after their reconciliation, I was at the seminary and only returned every now and then during my holidays.

113

Before I turned twenty, the Senyora used her influence to make sure I would be ordained as a priest, even though I did not say mass until later on. Since then I have not left Bearn, apart from our trip to Rome, and I would have liked to spend the last days of my life here, too, had Providence not determined otherwise.

At the beginning, our life was monotonous and disciplined, although towards the end we lived in a friendly sort of anarchy. Dona Maria Antònia got up at ten and went to hear mass at the chapel. Then I would go off to the archives. The three of us met at lunchtime. The Senyor would come down from the rooms upstairs, his wig combed and his mind sharpened by the acute thoughts he had just put down on paper. He was usually in an excellent mood. At the table, he would recall his travels and tell me stories about Paris and Rome.

'Maria Antònia, we must go back before we die. Joan has to see the world.'

I was dying to visit Rome, but I realized that we could not really allow ourselves such prodigality. Together, Dona Maria Antònia and I had managed to put the administration of the estate back on its feet to some extent, but we had not succeeded in paying off the main mortgages, the interest on which took most of the profit from the harvest. Dona Maria Antònia neither approved nor disapproved of her husband's plans.

'Don't you think we're a little old for that, Tonet?'

Over the years she had become less and less concerned with monetary problems. If I explained that a trip to Rome would cost far too much, she would calmly reply: 'You may be right, but I believe that given a chance a priest has the obligation of visiting the Pope. Be quiet and stop behaving like a child.' Patting my hand, she added, 'If the Senyor wants to take us, I think we should take advantage of it. This is our chance.'

After lunch, my benefactor and I used to go walking in the woods. We usually took our guns, but we hardly ever hunted; we preferred to sit under an oak tree and discuss the ancient poets. I do not know whether it was out of perversity or refinement, but he preferred the French classics.

'They're better than the Greeks and the Latins, for one, because they're less original; having drawn from the ancients, they're capable of surpassing them. Assuming Homer really existed, he was too primitive; his works are like compilations of folk tales. Socrates is a

114

sort of *nouveau riche* of reason. Think about it; he'd just discovered it. In historical terms, he's a keystone of civilization, but how can one avoid preferring Candide to Plato's Dialogues.'

He was an optimist about Creation, and, in his own way, an admirer of the greatness of God, only his God could prove at times to be rather strange. I found it disturbing to hear him speak of Voltaire's religious sentiment.

'Voltaire was a deist, Joan. It's a known fact. "*Si Dieu n'existait pas, il faudrait l'inventer.*"'

Invent God! I cannot think of a more blatant misrepresentation of the problem.

At seven o'clock sharp we said our rosaries in the chapel. Afterwards we always sat in the courtyard, or by the fireplace in winter, until it was time for supper. Rumour had it that the Senyor never went to bed before dawn, but it was hard to know, because he always left the table as soon as he had finished eating and we would not see him until two o'clock the following day. He always reappeared looking pleased, as if the world were new to him day after day. He would ask us how we had spent the night and we would walk to the dining room rather ceremoniously, the Senyora and I ahead and the Senyor a little further back, to the left of the Senyora. That order, that precision worthy of a convent or a palace, prevailed until only a few years ago, when they started getting up late and disrupting their schedule.

Lately, when the bell rang at lunchtime, instead of coming down to the dining room, Dona Maria Antònia called Catalineta, asked her to comb her hair and disappeared off to the left. Then the Senyor, who had not yet washed, asked for hot water and disappeared to the right. If truth be told: life in Bearn was enviable. In the place where so much had happened (and happened still in the realm of the soul, as the Senyor was constantly writing) nothing seemed awkward. Dona Maria Antònia never had the slightest doubt that their tranquillity was perfectly consolidated. She carried peace within her and considered the disorder of the last few years to be some new sort of order in itself. Bearn was like an anticipation of Paradise, with forests, lambs and sunsets, the stone house and the old fireplace, spring and winter, hydrangeas and snow . . . How I will miss it all when in just a few weeks I leave this place forever! Nonetheless, Miquel, here I have suffered more than you could possibly imagine. This paradise was ephemeral for me; it was earthly, the one man is bound to lose. The tree of Good and Evil grew here, but Dona Maria Antònia grasped only one aspect of the tragic duality revealed in the Senyor's posthumous and supposedly frivolous writing. Her calm blue eyes were far removed from the beady, bright eyes of her husband, surrounded with wrinkles, and from mine, too black, having seen so little happiness. In her unsurpassed serenity, no matter where she had been, she would have succeeded in reliving the maxim written by Horace: 'Of all the corners of the earth, this one smiles at me the best.'

TWO

Bearn continued to smile at them during twenty-two years: an eternity. Now that I see it from afar, I understand that it really was paradise. In this world the only paradises we know are those we have lost. Now I can cherish the oak woods, the sunsets and the beauty of the Christmas snow on the pine grove of Sa Cova. I feel the same towards those who are no longer here: I miss them more and more each day. The name Bearn, full of old pastoral memories, is associated with the Senyor's eighteenth-century robes and the calm politeness of Dona Maria Antònia. As the years went by, she became kinder to me. Her death, as I will recount later on, was exemplary. Suspecting that it was drawing near, she did not attempt to prolong it, and preferred to spend her last breath on a good, holy confession. I have no doubt that she is in Heaven. It would be difficult to conceive of it being otherwise, as she was one of those people who know how to make something heavenly out of the elements that surround them.

I remember that on one occasion, when we were out walking, we came upon a shack built on a *rota** of our property. An old woman by the name of Madò Coloma lived there. She lived alone, with a goat and a mongrel called Trinxet. She told us that every week her nephews brought her two loaves of bread. She lived on bread and milk. She showed us an orange tree that gave her oranges for almost half the year and six pomegranate trees that bore fruit without needing to be cared for. Apart from these things, which are riches for those who know

*A *rota* is a small plot of land that the lord of an estate leases to a peasant for him to harvest, either free or in exchange for a service.

117

how to see them as such and are in the grace of God, she had a well with the best water in the region. Once two thieves appeared at her house; it was the greatest adventure in her entire life. But when they saw all she had was a goat, and not a very good one at that they decided not to steal it. ('They turned it down as if she had been trying to sell it to them,' the Senyor told me.)

Dona Maria Antònia offered to send her three hens so she could have eggs, but Madò Coloma did not accept the gift.

'I wouldn't know how to take care of them,' she said, 'and neither Trinxet nor the goat like to have other animals around. It would only make for trouble.'

'Well, then, I'll send you a sack of sugar for your milk,' Dona Maria Antònia replied.

'That would be lovely, Senyora, but don't bother sending me so much: I don't think I'll make it through to next year, and if I die, there's no need for the sugar to go to waste, prices being what they are these days.'

As we parted, she gave us a pomegranate each, like a *grande dame*. When Dona Maria Antònia was about to leave, my benefactor grabbed me by the arm and opened a small door to show me a courtyard. There, under a vine, was a magnificent hydrangea, just like the one at Bearn. I glanced at him inquisitively and he smiled, raising a finger to his lips.

'Are you coming?' asked Dona Maria Antònia, looking back.

But the Senyor had already shut the little door and we all walked out together. The sun was about to set and the air was cool.

'Oh, Tonet,' she said, 'I feel so sorry for that woman! If I were left all alone and the socialists took everything away from me, I'd live like her. What does she lack? She has no tapestries or mirrors, but she has a bed and a rocking chair, and those are the most comfortable things in the world. And did you see that hydrangea?' (The Senyor and I looked at each other, thinking it was impossible that she could have seen it.) 'I think it might even be better than ours. Oh, Tonet, spring in Paris ... do you remember the flower market on *la Cité*? Let's see,' she continued, descending a few notches in her lyrical enthusiasm, 'if these pomegranates are sweet.'

The Senyor was walking, lost in thought, and missed her last comment.

'You'll be like her,' he said.

118

'I noticed,' Dona Maria Antònia replied, 'that she was wearing a pendant with a gold chain around her neck.'

'How would you know it was gold?' the Senyor asked.

'The pendant looked like copper, but it was a very old gold chain. We have many feet of that same kind of chain; we inherited it from our great-grandparents. You've never had the faintest idea about these things, poor Tonet.'

It was dusk. We were silent. We heard the Angelus and stopped to say our Ave Maria. For a moment we could think we were eternal, at one with the olive trees that had seen twenty generations, with the fifteenth-century belfry, new and perfect as the day it was built, with the rocky cliffs. A nightingale sang, I remember. When a few months before his death the Senyor handed me his *Memoirs*, the first thing I did was look to see whether he had recorded that evening. He had indeed done so, and it is one of the best pages in the book, perhaps the only one in which nature breathes and moves like a living thing. He who so rarely described landscapes vibrates here with the spell of the Angelus, when people walk back from work, with the poetry of the huts where fire is being lit, so a quotation from Virgil's first eclogue of the passage

et iam summa procul villarum culmina fumant
maioresque cadunt altis de montibus umbrae,

loses all its rhetorical quality and seems as natural as if the Senyor himself had just improvised those famous lines. The miraculous moment was revealed to us (and has remained exquisitely consigned to a book which deserves not to be destroyed) through the sensitivity of Dona Maria Antònia, who some of us have often judged to be cold. The Senyor draws from that revelation the most transcendent part of his philosophy. 'My wife felt a spiritual identification with Madò Coloma,' he writes, 'because they truly did have something in common: the better they knew their surroundings, the more they loved them. Love, being the deepest of human feelings, is the most contradictory, and based upon it one could construe all sorts of theories. During my youth I confused love and curiosity (imitating our very first parents, who were also young). The sexual instinct is eminently investigative. Nothing is as intriguing as knowing how a person will react to a caress; it is a source of both pleasure and torture. It can turn you into a Don Juan, and can also lead to the vice of Sodom: two different paths to Hell. Don Juan is a tormented soul, what they

119

now call a *tourist*, travelling across the desert to know what is behind each dune of sand, only to find another one exactly the same as the last. The curiosity of the homosexual is also sterile, since the object of his desire will react only by yielding (and becoming, thus, the most deplorable caricature of a woman) or by virility, putting up a fight. Love as Curiosity has all the sad monotony of melodrama. One cannot deny that while the tourist travels miles in search of that which he will never find, or while the homosexual attempts to love a virile being (who, as such, cannot reciprocate his love) his fevered imagination works fast and sometimes makes for noteworthy cultural progress. In my opinion their creations will always be unwholesome. To quote the examples of animals or primitive man would be sophistic. Cave men could do without their women, who were hairy and resembled them. Now femininity is an exquisite and necessary product which has to be seen and enjoyed close up and without haste. Time demystifies Love as Curiosity, and makes us appreciate the infinite range of Love as Habit, or, if you please, Love as a Miniature. "What will you find elsewhere that you cannot find here?" Thomas à Kempis inquires. The masters of the Dutch school shared that view and applied the techniques of miniaturists, unlike the dreadful school of Barbizon that is now in vogue. They had no need to search for "interesting" subjects, as in an adventure story, because all that which is observed closely is interesting.'

As I read these pages, written one year ago, God is merciful enough to fill my heart with hope, and I believe there must be some mysterious law capable of stopping two beings who have loved each other in this world from being kept apart in the world beyond. In the Eighth Book of the *Metamorphoses*, when Jupiter wishes to reward Philemon and Baucis for rescuing him from his captor, he gives them a common fate and changes them both into trees so their roots can intertwine in the earth.

'Naturally, there must be a law like that,' my benefactor used to say. 'They can't be impolite in Heaven. If they invite a married woman, they have the obligation of inviting her husband as well.'

'Assuming he weren't unworthy of her because of his conduct,' I replied.

'If he had been that bad...'

There lay the essence of the entire problem.

I have already mentioned that he hardly ever argued, because deep

120

down he was stubborn; besides, being a sceptic, he thought it improper to reform in conversation 'all the mistakes accumulated', as he would say, 'over centuries of experience'. Besides, who has not defended unreasonable convictions which sometimes turn out to be true? About fifty years ago, George Sand judged the Mallorcans uneducated because they believed tuberculosis was contagious. Pasteur and Koch have proven those ignorant peasants to be right. My own benefactor, supposedly such a liberal, had his own taboos, certain dogmas — few, but inexorable — that could not even be mentioned. One memorable night by the fireplace, had he not refused to satisfy Dona Xima's curiosity? She wanted to see the dolls' room, clearly an unfortunate episode in the history of Bearn, yet how many other dreadful events are mentioned in the *Memoirs* he has chosen to publish!

From what I have managed to infer from sparse words and one misplaced document I found in an old accounts book, towards the end of the eighteenth century, Don Felip de Bearn, a distinguished cavalry captain from Aranjuez and one of the young 'lions' of the court, after befriending an Italian parvenu who made toys, began to dress dolls and 'exhibited more than twenty' — according to the document — 'in the flag room at the barracks.' 'He sewed all the dresses,' the document continues, 'and crocheted the lace with his own hands...'
He was expelled from the Army, despite the efforts of the Prince of Peace, who tried to dissuade him from such an odd pastime, and locked himself up in Bearn, where he spent the last years of his life in the throes of his madness. He wrote many letters, and apparently corresponded with personalities from the courts of Charles IV and Frederick of Prussia. However, the Senyor never mentions these affairs in his *Memoirs*. Only in the last few chapters are there some general considerations regarding effeminacy (which he believes to be a romantic degeneration) that can lead one to suspect that he was referring to his ancestor: 'When I was in school,' he writes, 'I was surprised to see how some of my friends who used to spend time with the girls started to be considered effeminate. When I was older, I observed that the most manly ones went to brothels to insult the vestals and throw their furniture into the street. They turned against me the night I disappeared with a blonde girl; my behaviour was attributed to fear, since in fact their debauchery was not only unpleasant, but also dangerous and lacking in camaraderie. "You must understand," they told me, "that among men, first things come

first".' Perhaps they were right, but thinking that the Universe is curved and that serpents bite their tails we would reach the conclusion that an excess of virility can lead to homosexuality. It is undoubtedly best not to pass judgement on these matters. *In the eighteenth century there were colonels who knew how to embroider and who were also perfect gentlemen.*'

I have underlined the last sentence, and this may be the only reference the Senyor makes to the dreadful event. The affair had psychological consequences: it appears that the day after an eminent gentleman had come to visit him from the City, Don Felip was found at the foot of his bed after what had apparently been a violent death.

THREE

For all her piety, Dona Maria Antònia shared a certain pagan nature with the Senyor; one could see that they were cousins. I point this out, however, admitting that she knew how to overcome her instincts. The Senyor claimed that the legend of her coat of arms, instead of alluding to blood and battles, could have been the following phrase, which he attributed to her: 'I will listen to no voice that disturbs me.'

She was endowed with what is called sound common sense and was convinced, like the ancients, that man is the measure of the Universe.

Columnes sereníssimes t'aixequen una arcada
que retalla la glòria, però enmarca el fracàs. *

'Would you like to be a queen?' the Senyor once asked her.

She needed no time to consider her reply.

'I wouldn't have minded being the Queen of Mallorca. A small country would be fine, but not a nation; I wouldn't dream of it.'

For years my benefactor had been asking people whether they would like to be kings or queens, and almost all the replies were negative.

'It's strange,' he told me, 'that so many people request positions of twenty *duros* a month and yet so few would like to be kings. Naturally, that only proves that people don't know themselves well enough. I believe the Senyora's reply may be the best. It would be

---

*'Serene columns lift an archway/that shapes your glory, yet frames your defeat.'
Jaume Vidal Alcover, *Poem for Maria-Antònia*.

amusing to see the court she would set up here at home. She'd name Madò Francina Director of National Security, because she's energetic and knows everything that happens in the village. She herself would be in charge of the relations with the Church, like Charles I. And maybe if she were religious enough she'd end up at odds with the clergy. Not too much, though. She wouldn't attack Rome nor associate with an ungrateful man like the Duke of Bourbon. She'd know how to use subtler methods.'

There was in fact something incorruptible in Dona Maria Antònia's character. When Don Andreu, the village priest, died and Don Francesc arrived, young and ready to make all sorts of innovations, I was surprised to see how little heed she paid to his advice and how she did not seem to take his words into consideration. I have already said that certain dangerous modern trends had begun to reach us from overseas, particularly from the Americas. Priests who go to cafés or participate in races are not really committing criminal acts, provided they do not attribute undue importance to such vanities. But adapting to fashion in order to draw people to religion is something I find abominable, because it could easily happen that instead of the priest leading the sheep, the sheep could mislead him. Don Francesc was perfectly willing to make concessions, and had no objections whatsoever to founding a sort of clubhouse where people could gather and read magazines and newspapers from Madrid which were hardly proper for the simple life among these mountains. He always liked to do things his way and I remember how stupefied I was when one Sunday he stood by the altar and said to his parishioners: 'Monsignor has sent a pastoral letter for me to read from the pulpit, but it's very long, so I'll explain what it says.'

And he made a brief summary — quite a good one, I must admit — instead of following orders and reading the text. Ever since he came to the village, he spoke of a 'devout family' instead of a 'noble family' at the celebration of the Patron Saint of Bearn.

'I see, Don Francesc,' said the Senyor, smiling, 'that you have done away with our nobility.'

He apologized with arguments of a democratic nature.

'These matters of ancestry,' Don Toni told him, 'are old and on their way out. In the twentieth century nobody will pay attention to them anymore. Socialism will take their place.'

Don Francesc, though wishing—up to a point—that he was right, was taken aback. Dona Maria Antònia smiled. She spoke to me softly: 'Joan, the Senyor seems quite sure about what will happen in the twentieth century.'

'Bear in mind, Don Toni,' the priest continued, backing down slightly, 'that if socialist doctrines took over, it would be utter chaos. I chose not to say "noble family" precisely in order to avoid . . .'

'You did the right thing, Father. We will be the same, whether we are called noble or merely devout.'

The priest did not notice the 'merely' that seemed to me so very embarrassing. Dona Maria Antònia looked up.

'You're absolutely right, Tonet. Either way, we'll be just the way we are.' There was a tender look in her light eyes.

'Let us pray to God that He may absolve us all,' she added a little incoherently, unwittingly quoting the last verse of the *Ballade des Pendus*.

The village priest was convinced that her words had been dictated by humility, because despite his modern ideas he had not invented gunpowder. The Senyors were not proud, but neither were they humble. They valued themselves according to what they were and represented. They must have considered it foolish to have their nobility questioned. The estate of Bearn had always set standards for the village of Bearn. There has probably never been a single fifteen-year-old girl who has not dreamed of marrying a prince — a Bearn, in other words — nor any farmboy who was not delighted to be granted a smile by the lady of the house. It was through that house that the civilized world, the world of refinement and fantasy, blinding like a hall full of mirrors, could reach these far lands, serving as an incentive for progress and yet also fostering restlessness and a yearning to break loose from that small world. Sometimes the Senyor's influence was frankly demoralizing. His somewhat whimsical teachings made people imagine all kinds of nonsense. He had made up his mind that Margalideta would learn to play the piano. He had an English teacher sent to a poor boy who was born to live and die among these mountains, merely because he was blond. All of this was absolutely unheard of, and in the end he was accused of sorcery.

We Catholics do not believe in sorcery, but the accusation could never have had the same effect without the magical prestige of the five letters in the name *Bearn*. Honest maidens who never would have given in to young men their age, gave in to him, who was neither

125

young or handsome. When I think of those poor souls (and of one in particular, whom I have never met), I can still feel my blood boil; I have often felt the impulse to avenge them, remembering Seneca's pagan statement according to which mercy is a weakness of the heart. One day when I judged it my duty to confess these thoughts to the Senyor — I was very young at the time, not even eighteen — he stared at me with a half ironic, half curious expression. His eyes were small and piercing. He took my hands in his, and as I held forth, proffering insolent remarks mixed with insults and becoming increasingly excited in the face of his silence, he squeezed them hard, as if he wished to test my physical endurance. Then he touched my arms and shoulders in admiration, seemingly proud of my constitution. When I finally stopped, terrified by what I had said, he recommended that I read a poem by Heredia, *Le serrement de mains*, which had just been published in a French magazine. He left me alone. When I reached the triplet in which the Cid challenges Don Diego (according to tradition, he even struck him) the magazine dropped out of my hands and I burst into tears.

It is however true that he was a father to many a humble family, that he knew their many needs and tried to help them. I have already mentioned that he sometimes incurred debts in order to help the people in the village who did not know where to place their savings, and how these debts damaged the soundness of his fortune. In the discussions between villagers, since the peasants mistrusted lawyers and preferred to turn to the counsel of the Senyor, he always ruled with a strict sense of justice, and more than once, if the culprit was very poor, he gave him money and made him promise to keep it a secret. However, word always got out, and although that enhanced his respectability, it also made him seem rather gullible and caused certain people lacking in scruples to conspire and fake a litigation only to get money out of him. Dona Maria Antònia was smarter in this respect and let them get only sweet words out of her. She was also a master at the art of not understanding what she did not wish to hear, and developed a most convenient deafness that allowed misinterpretations and saved her from many a conflict. I do not wish to imply that she was pretending, because at times she really was hard of hearing. Yet on other occasions, her hearing was excellent. A specialist from Barcelona had diagnosed a case of intermittent deafness.

FOUR

On August 11, 1883, after a very hot night, I awoke at dawn to read Virgil's eclogues under the oaks at the Puig de Ses Llebres. Through the mist you could just barely see the pink light of the Cathedral of Mallorca in the distance. The sun was beginning to rise and the golden moon wondered whether to set. I found that moment of indecision deeply moving. I sat down thinking of the sadness of Meliboeus banished from the land where he was born. In the poem, Meliboeus, young and unlucky like myself, appears standing as he contemplates Tityrus — Virgil, that is — who is sitting under an old oak. 'You are fortunate, Tityrus,' Meliboeus tells him, 'to be able to rest in the shade of these trees . . .' 'Shepherd,' Tityrus replies, 'this rest has been granted to me by a god.' 'Poor Joan,' the Senyor had said to me the first time I read that passage, 'poor Joan; the god Virgil speaks of is not God with a capital G, but merely a triumvir. It's unfair of the old poet to use trickery to make you or Meliboeus cry, you noble souls who know how to admire without envy. Virgil, or Tityrus, had been to Rome, where he used his cunning and his influence to convince Octavius to exempt him from the general confiscation of land.' Voltaire put ice in the basins of holy water. I was hurt by the Senyor's words.

'Does your honour mean to say that Virgil was a deceiver, an ignoble soul?'

The Senyor stared at me with curiosity.

'Don't use excessive words, Joanet; they don't mean a thing. Virgil had talent.'

I dared not reply.

As I meditated, I was distracted by a muted noise that sounded like distant gunshot. It seemed to come from the City, and since at that time there had been more talk about Carlist insurrections, I looked towards the bay, but it was covered in fog and nothing could be seen. I was about to warn the Senyor when I realized what I thought to be gunshot was coming from the opposite direction, from S'Ull de Sa Font. I climbed the hill to see the other side and found men felling pine trees. Such boldness at six in the morning was brazen, and as I was closer to the house than to the pine forest, I ran to tell the Senyor. When I entered the courtyard it occurred to me that he would be sleeping. The steward, whom I told what I had seen, suggested sending for the Civil Guard, or that we all go, he and the farmers armed with guns and myself with the double authority of priest and administrator, to speak to the delinquents. Neither one of the two solutions pleased me, least of all the first; for some reason — you will soon see that my instinct was right — I was horrified at the thought of mixing strangers into the affair. The only solution was to wake the Senyor. I knocked softly on his door and he immediately asked me in. I was astonished to find him awake and dressed. He was sitting at his desk, pen in hand, examining some papers.

'Look, Joan,' he said, handing me a drawing. 'Let's see if you can guess what this is.'

He seemed perfectly happy, not the least bit surprised at such an early visit. Without looking at the drawing, I tried to apologize.

'*Audaces fortuna iuvat*,' he replied, laughing. 'Sit down and stop that nonsense. You know that in principle I've always defended boldness.'

And he wandered off into a literary digression, witty and perhaps ever so slightly sophistic, only to end up saying that our writers had never been bold, and therefore could never be amusing.

'Bold, amusing ...' he continued. 'The secrets of charm are feminine. One can't possess anything, and least of all a woman, without being a little bold. Don't you agree?'

'Your Honour knows that I have no opinion on such matters.'

'It's true,' he said, taking it back, 'I'm pleased that you're such a good boy.'

I was intrigued. When did the Senyor sleep? For years it was rumoured that he kept his light on all night. Suddenly, hearing his

128

brilliant, fluent speech, seeing the ease with which he found timely quotations from the classics, lightly underlined with irony in order to neutralize whatever solemnity they conveyed, I understood that Don Toni was one of those people for whom the first moments of the morning are those of the greatest lucidity. That lucidity must have diminished in the course of the day, and by the evening, when he excused himself after dinner claiming that he was going off 'to write,' he must have collapsed into bed, exhausted, without even remembering to put out the candle. That was the explanation that occurred to me at first, although it has since changed somewhat: he probably left the light on purposely, so that in the morning, when he really did work, everybody would think he was asleep and allow him to rest; expecting them to allow him to work would have been asking too much.

The Senyor chattered on merrily and I could not find a way of telling him what had happened.

'What do you know!' he told me. 'Fourteen years ago we burned all those books, and now I've been left with no maps. That night, the Senyora and I went too far: we even destroyed *The Christian Year* and Thomas à Kempis. Now I need a map of Rome and I wanted to draw one up from memory. But Rome, unlike Paris, is a centipede. The heroes of Italian culture are no longer the Italians. There must be a reason why the platinum standard metre is kept in Meudon. Look, this is Michelangelo's Porta del Popolo. This is where the three main streets start from. The one in the middle is the famous Corso, which joins the Popolo with the Capitoline Hill. But it's a narrow street, and it would be hard to widen because it's bordered with old palaces, which probably aren't as artistic as they're supposed to be.'

He sat, lost in thought, and I took the occasion to tell him what was happening at S'Ull de Sa Font.

I assumed he had not heard me when he continued: 'Nevertheless, it's a unique city, if only for its fountains.' But then he added: 'The pine forest they're cutting down has been sold. As soon as the hot weather is over, we'll leave for Italy. A priest has the obligation of visiting the Pope.'

I was astounded.

'So your Honour has sold the pine forest? Hadn't we decided that whatever we got from it would be used to cancel part of the mortgages?'

129

'You'd made the decision ... but in order to travel we need a full purse. However,' he added, seeing the look on my face, 'I haven't sold the entire pine forest; only the largest trees' (which happened to be the most expensive). 'Cheer up, Joan. Fourteen or fifteen years from now it will be just the same as it is now.'

'Fifteen years from now, your Honour will be close to ninety!'

'If I'm alive,' he replied.

I did not know what had hit me. To see the Pope was what I had most desired in life, but the pine forest of Sa Font was our last resort. How had he managed to sell it without my knowing? I later discovered it had all been done by means of letters that I myself put in the mail; that is what it is for, after all, and inventions must serve some purpose. I dared to tell him that he ought to have warned us, because the steward had almost called the Civil Guard.

'You're right,' he said. 'I forgot.'

I assume that given his reluctance to discuss monetary matters he had preferred to not say a word until the buyer had begun to fell the trees and we were faced with a *fait accompli*. The pine forest of S'Ull de Sa Font can only be seen from the Puig de Ses Llebres. The Senyor must have assumed that we would not notice until a few days later. Fate would have it that I found out that very morning.

'When are we leaving?'

He smiled and put his arm around my shoulders.

'Slow down. There are a thousand arrangments to be made ... First of all, we must arrange for a private audience with our Holy Father. Leo XIII is an enlightened and liberal man, as he has proved during his five years as Pontiff.'

It was not the first time he expressed his admiration for the enlightened Pope, as he called him. I noticed that on the table lay the encyclicals *Diuturnum* and *Humanus generis*, which had just been published.

'Does the Senyora know ...'

'Of course. She knows everything.'

I remembered that Dona Maria Antònia had announced a surprise a few days earlier. But did she understand that it meant spending the money from the pine forest on travel? My mind was set on finding out. I said goodbye and turned to leave, but the Senyor stopped me.

'Listen, Joan: don't say a word to anyone ...'

'Very well.'

130

He stared at me with curiosity: 'Are you trying to outsmart me? What do you mean by "very well"?'

'That I shan't tell anyone you wake up so early in the morning.'

'Under the seal of confession,' he laughed. 'You can go now.'

I went out into the room with the fireplace. It was not yet eight and Catalineta told me the Senyora was sleeping. She was frightened and wiped her lips with her hand. She had chocolate stains around her mouth. I gave her a gentle scolding (she was not even fourteen) and sat down by a balcony. A few minutes later, the Senyora appeared. She greeted me with the following words: 'Joan, we can get the trunks ready.'

She knew that they had started cutting down the pine forest and seemed quite pleased.

'Joanet, that means we'll have money. I hardly get excited over *cèntims*' — like all country ladies, she said *cèntims* even when referring to large amounts — 'but I'm happy that we can still find some when we need them. One can make any sacrifice whatsoever in order to see the Holy Father. Aren't you pleased?'

'It's what I've dreamed of all my life, but . . .'

'Hush,' she interrupted, striking me softly with her fan, 'don't tell me we're getting old. Thank God, we're still strong and healthy.'

Her gesture with the fan proscribed any possible discussion. Until that moment I had not suspected that Dona Maria Antònia's mental faculties were beginning to decline, and it still took me quite a while to acknowledge it. The sale of the pine forest made her feel optimistic and, by the same token, child-like. In fact neither she nor the Senyor had ever been deprived of anything. Whenever money was needed, money appeared. Such experiences tend to give the powerful security and a certain hardheartedness; that is why Jesus Christ said salvation was not as easy for them as for the rest of men. It also gives them a certain kind of blindness. 'You're ruined, you're swamped with mortgages,' I could have cried, 'everything will be sold in a public auction . . .' I was reluctant to upset their happiness. It was a lost cause.

FIVE

The arrangements for the trip lasted a few months. Obtaining a private audience from Leo XIII was not easy. The Holy Father adds numerous cultural activities to his solid piety. He is both a mystic and a humanist; in his spare time he writes Latin verse. All his encyclicals, renowned for their concepts and their style, are written in his own hand. In the mundane world, where his name had been Count Pecci, he had received a thorough education. A fine diplomat, he strives to separate the spiritual interests of the Church from political struggles. His occupations leave him little time to devote to private visits. Given our moral and material difficulties — we were hardly in a position to give a large donation to the Vatican — Dona Maria Antònia would have settled for a public audience, but the Senyor did not easily forsake his plans.

'It won't hurt us; one thousand *duros* more or less don't matter. I won't settle for a blessing, Maria Antònia. All popes give blessings, when they don't . . .' He looked at Dona Maria Antònia and stopped himself, because he had been on the verge of mentioning the excommunications and anathemas of the medieval papacy. 'They all give blessings,' he continued. 'Pius IX already blessed us once, but Leo XIII is an intelligent man, in addition.'

'Don't start up with your heresies, Tonet. Benediction is above intelligence.'

'As you please. But once we're making the financial sacrifice of going to Rome' — it was quite a time to think of finances — 'we shouldn't deny ourselves an interview with Leo XIII. Joan is young

132

and will benefit from it. And you're dying to see him, too.'

'That's true enough.'

In my opinion, the Senyor knew better than to be deceived by his own words. If it is true that a blessing confers a spiritual benefit and does so all at once, by divine grace, a half-hour of conversation operating by rational means could not change a grown man like myself, already thirty-two years of age.

Dona Maria Antònia had an idea: 'Jacob will arrange it.'

'Jacob? That parrot?'

She protested at her husband's aggressive, bold reaction, worthy of some legendary ancestor.

'My God, Tonet, what a way of judging your fellow men! You've a merciless tongue. Collera, a parrot?'

Don Jacob Obrador i Santandreu, third Marquis of Collera and representative in the Spanish Parliament, was the most prestigious man on the island. All the newspapers had printed his speech in reply to a representative of the Opposition who had referred to him as a 'poet' because he wanted a better naval squadron than the English. '*Poetry, poetry, if only I could dive into the magical world of poetry and witness the Battle of Lepanto . . .*' They claimed it was an oratory piece worthy of Castelar. A Latin scholar, he had written commentaries on Seneca and Cicero. He was also an archaeologist. 'His life is charmed,' said his many female admirers (in the best sense of the word). 'Charm, grace, elegance . . .' However, the Senyor could not stand him.

'I know him all too well. He's emptier than a snailshell.'

He also mocked the ridiculous title Don Jacob had been granted by the Queen Regent.

'She's not really a queen, since she has no number in history, nor does this Collera Don Jacob business make any heraldic sense. Seventy years ago the Obradors were known as the stupidest people in Selva. Since they only opened their mouths to make asses of themselves, once, on the Senyor's saint's day, they were given a *collera*.* They didn't take it as an insult — they were too stupid to do so — and when they thought of asking Dona Cristina for a title (she would grant one for five hundred *duros*, and for even less than that) they signed Obrador de Ca'n Collera†. Dona Cristina, who was a scatterbrain,

*Collar of a harness (Translator's note).

†*Ca'n*, a widely used contraction of *casa de en*, could be translated as 'the house of Mr' (Translator's note).

133

left out the Obrador, so they've been the Colleras ever since.'

I believe the story he told was true, and even though he claimed that such matters belonged to the *ancien régime*, he was interested in the ancestry of the families on the island. He sometimes surprised us with statements that seemed whimsical and turned out to be accurate. For most people, at any rate, Don Jacob was an eminent personality. His office and his title provided him with good relations in Madrid, and in the end it was he who, through the Spanish Embassy in Rome, succeeded in getting His Holiness Leo XIII to grant us, in principle and barring unforeseen circumstances, a thirty-minute audience for the last day of the year, at eleven in the morning.

We left the island on November second, when a French steamer called in at Palma before sailing to Marseilles. It was called *Le Lion du Louvre et de Belfort*, and was, as the advertisement in the shipping office said, a veritable floating palace. The Senyors had travelled in their youth and were no longer surprised at almost anything. To me, that steamer seemed like magic.

Don Jacob Collera, not content with obtaining the audience for us, had recommended us to the captain of the ship, who came out to greet us on deck and showed us into a drawing room with a red carpet that was a feast to the eye: lights, mirrors, plush chairs, china, electric bells ... even a piano! Right then and there, he had a glass of wine and pastries served, and asked the Senyor if he would be so kind as to introduce him to Dona Maria Antònia. As we were told later, that is a French custom, and although we knew perfectly well that we were with the captain, which was obvious right away, he pretended, out of politeness, that no one knew him but that everyone knew the Senyora, and thus he had to be introduced to her, though in that fantastic world he was the maximum and sovereign authority. Two handsome young men appeared to serve the wine; their hair was slicked back with pomade. They wore black trousers and red jackets; I cannot remember whether they wore gloves. When they were not busy with something, they would stand at either end of an ebony sideboard against a wall covered in mirrors, so it seemed as though you saw four identical figures, serious and stiff as if they were walking in a procession. Unaware as I was of the world and its vanities, all I could think of was that, as we sat there talking, those young men could have reaped a quarter of an acre of wheat.

Before retiring, the captain sent for a steward to see us to our staterooms. The one they had ready for me made me blush: it too was full of mirrors, scented with violets, with a carpet and pink silk curtains. If I had dared to, I would have asked for another one. The steward showed me a button and I understood it was an electric bell; he told me that if I rang it once the valet would appear; if I rang it twice, the *femme de chambre* would come. I noticed there was no water jug by the sink and pointed it out to him. The steward smiled, walked over to the sink and opened what they now call a *robinet*: out poured the water.

We had a pleasant crossing; the sea was calm and nobody even felt sick. As we had lunch the glass doors separating the dining room from the drawing room opened up and from the table we heard the piano, played by a young lady who did so quite well and who apparently had won a prize at the Conservatory. *Le Lion du Louvre et de Belfort* had sailed from French Morocco carrying Moors, Jews and Negroes, but they were not allowed into the first-class section. I watched them from the deck, and the Senyor decided to go down to meet a Negro personally — a man-eater, according to him.

In Marseilles, where we were supposed to rest for three days, we stayed at the Grand Hotel, on the famous Cannebierre, a wide avenue full of cafés, theatres and stores selling everything you could possibly dream of. My room was covered with floral paper, more fit for a young lady than for a poor priest raised in the mountains. Once again, there were mirrors and curtains everywhere.

'What do you think of all this elegance?' asked the Senyor, peering in.

I felt stifled, as if the flowers on the wall were real. Even the bowl in the basin had a floral design. The mirrors made my head spin. The door that opened into the corridor had four square mirrors facing the inside of the room; since it was just opposite the balcony, with four panes of glass set in the same position, when I got up in the morning to let a little air into the room, I opened the wrong one and instead of ending up on the balcony I found myself half naked in the corridor, with a young English lady staring at me in astonishment.

Marseilles is a rich city, and its harbour is perhaps the largest in the Mediterranean. Unfortunately, the mixture of races and the freedom or licentiousness of their customs has slowly undermined the city's moral foundations. I do not mean to say there are not good people there, but the shamelessness is sometimes so extreme during festivities that the decent families leave for the country so as to spare themselves. However, most people are very respectful, and the waiters at the hotel bowed at me and called me *Monsieur l'abbé*, which I found embarrassing, since I have never been and probably never will be an abbot.

I will not even mention the inventions that French civilization had gathered in Marseilles and that were nothing but a preview of what we would see shortly afterwards. I will only point out the great use made of electricity, a form of energy applied to light, medicine, the telegraph and even, impossible though it may seem, to music.

On the fifteenth we took the train that would take us to Ventimiglia and to Rome, passing through Florence, where we would stop for a week.

'You'll see,' Dona Maria Antònia had told me, 'how beautiful the Côte d'Azur is. Instead of planting wheat in the fields, they plant carnations.'

Unfortunately, night was falling and we did not see a thing. When I awoke at dawn the landscape was striking: tall, tall trees, water, beautiful pastures and cows. I had always heard that the Côte d'Azur looked like Mallorca, but what I saw was very different indeed. Even the sky and the infinite softness of the light seemed strange. I pointed it out to the Senyor when he awoke.

'What I don't understand,' said Dona Maria Antònia, 'is why we can't see the sea.'

The Senyor was smiling. He looked at his watch, consulted a guide and then uttered the following words, which left us dumbfounded: 'In six and a half hours we'll be in Paris.'

'Weren't we going to see the Pope, Tonet?'

'Certainly. But we'll stop to rest in Paris.'

They say all roads lead to Rome, although that one hardly seemed to be the most appropriate.

'It isn't a shortcut,' the Senyor granted, 'but I suppose we'll all enjoy a week in Paris.'

I looked at Dona Maria Antònia. The name Paris had suggested that of Dona Xima. Luckily the Senyora did not seem to lose her composure.

'I think it's a good idea, Tonet. Once we've crossed the sea, we might as well take advantage of the trip. Don't you think so, Joan?'

136

'In a sense,' said the Senyor, addressing me, 'it's a way of saving money. In Marseilles we were already halfway there.'

'Besides,' Dona Maria Antònia corroborated, 'we're already old and this will be our last trip.'

They were both staring at me. Since I did not open my mouth, she gave me a chocolate and started talking about churches.

'You'll see Notre Dame, Joanet. And that other church that's so old and is also on the Ile de la Cité . . .'

'The Sainte Chapelle.'

'That's it. What a beauty! That's what I call stained glass. And the Madeleine . . . There's a very good restaurant right across from it, you'll see. Only the best people go there — usually men, ambassadors or politicians; not many ladies. Isn't that so, Tonet? A few old ones like me, perhaps. Where will we stay?'

'At the Louvre, like the last time.'

Since I did not know Paris, the word Louvre made me think of the palace of the Kings of France; ever since we had left Mallorca, the Senyor kept me living in a world where the absurd seemed possible; but the Louvre he was referring to was a hotel, one of the best in the city, and in fact quite near the palace after which it was named, at one end of the Avenue of the Opera. Incidentally, right next to the Opera was the Grand Hotel, where at one time Don Toni had lived with Dona Xima. What crossed the Senyor's mind every time he walked by? And how did Dona Maria Antònia, who knew everything, agree to go to the Café de la Paix one afternoon, on the ground floor of the very same building? You know how I have loved the Senyors; my pen refuses to condemn them, and yet I must admit that at times they proved surprisingly insensitive. Reading certain authors we are struck by Napoleon's kindness. Alas, did that great captain, adored by his *grognards*, about whom such moving anecdotes are told, ever hesitate to declare war, or renounce a crown so as not to send them to their death? We may feel compelled to accept the sweet Napoleonic legend, but the millions of lives sacrificed for that captain are a no less tangible reality. I would be horrified to have to agree with the Senyor when he implies that Good and Evil stem from the same source. No: that dreadful error is definitively refuted, and glorious Saint Augustine, who had fallen into heresy, has since been the most illustrious advocate of catholic orthodoxy. In any case, earthly greatness implies cruelty. How could it be otherwise? Could the surgeon

137

amputate a limb if he were moved when he heard his patient moan? The night the *automobile* burned, I fainted and Dona Maria Antònia had to help the two of us. I am ashamed to think of it; I was a strong young man, the strongest in the Seminary. I still am. And an elderly lady kept her composure and asked for a mule to be harnessed, sent for a doctor and cleaned the Senyor's wounds. That is what happened, Miquel, and my honesty forces me to acknowledge it: when they behave as such, noblemen also have their place in this world.

SIX

By 1883, Paris had completely overcome the twofold disaster of Sedan and the Commune. Some missed the splendour and riches of the Second Empire. Everything seemed magical to me. The Third Republic claimed to be austere. It was said that President Grévy was a good man. However, the ways of a country do not change that fast. An entire troop of servants was mobilized at the hotel for each meal, and at the Café de la Paix we were served by an authentic Turk who insulted us one day in his own tongue because the Senyor had asked him whether the cap he wore could be used as a jelly mould. I will not even mention the Café de Paris, on the Avenue of the Opera, where you do not pay for what you eat, but for the waiters' dashing tails. Such establishments are wildly expensive. Seeing money spent so frivolously when so many poor people suffer in utter misery is hardly very edifying. I have seen a couple of lovers sit down at a Café, order two ice-creams, eat one spoonful, hold hands under the table, get up and leave in a carriage, all in two minutes' time.

'The rich,' the Senyor assured me, 'have the obligation of making money circulate. Their luxury feeds many of the poor.'

'How can you say such things, Tonet? What does a poor man gain when you let your ice-cream go to waste? Isn't it better not to order it and give the three *rals* it costs to someone who needs to eat?'

The problem was that the Senyora, who at times was so reasonable, forgot that our purse was now emptier, and tried to relive times long gone, thus becoming too extravagant.

'I think,' she said one morning, 'we should have lunch at the Restaurant Vefour.'

It was supposedly the most expensive place in Paris. The Senyor approved. The famous restaurant, located in the north façade of the Palais Royal, was just a few steps away from our hotel. We walked up a carpeted staircase. The dining room was a regal hall lined with wallpaper that looked like red velvet and was framed in strips of gold. It occupied the entire width of the building and had balconies facing the street and others across the room facing the palace garden. The arched ceiling was decorated with mythological paintings. I need not mention that the entire room was covered in the same carpeting as the staircase. As we entered, we were approached by a steward, or *maître, d'hôtel* as they call them, and two waiters in tails who took our hats. I will refrain from describing the details of that meal, served on porcelain plates and silver soup tureens and platters. One of the main dishes was golden pheasant, the speciality of the house. I also remember some sort of flat fish that may have been fried or boiled and tasted of butter, and an ice-cold white wine that seemed inoffensive and was, may God forgive me, as treacherous as the children of the Seine.

I, Miquel, could not help thinking that it was all fake. That magnificent palace, built by Cardinal Richelieu, had belonged to Louis XIV, who then handed it over to the Duke of Orléans. The details of the Peace of Westphalia may have been discussed in that very hall; the ill-fated Philippe-Egalité may have conspired against Louis XVI in those rooms. Now all those historical events, glorious or ominous, were eclipsed by a sauce or a wine called, if I am not mistaken, Sauternes. The kindness of the steward and the waiters was so extreme that it could not be sincere. One of them, who seemed to be in charge of all the staff, offered the Senyora snails as an hors d'oeuvre with the following words: '*Madame, j'ai six escargots arrivés pour vous de Bourgogne.*'

I could give an endless description of the comings and goings, the unnecessary manoeuvres, the 'pardons' and 'messieurs' with every word, to bring a plate, to take it away, to fill a glass. The art of eating took on a ceremonial stature, and the ceremony was one of the most pagan materialism, presented among flowers and served on a silver tray. I prefer to forget such things. What I have not forgotten is the price: for three people, we spent thirty-two francs for lunch that day, not counting the tip.

140

The life we led in Paris was carefully organized. After mass at Saint Roch we took a carriage through the Bois de Boulogne, and then returned to the hotel for lunch, after which the Senyors went to sit at the Café de la Paix, located on the ground floor of the Grand Hotel. It is true that almost a quarter of a century had gone by since that scandal, but Dona Xima was still living in Paris, she had lived in that very neighbourhood and, since that was the centre of the city, they risked finding her seated at a nearby table any moment. None of that seemed to bother them. I believe they did not even think of it. I thought of it constantly. It was almost fifteen years since I had seen her arrive at Bearn, dazzling in silks and colours, preceded by a valet in red livery. In fifteen years and a city such as Paris, fashions can change twenty times. Elegant ladies now wore simpler dresses. However, there were always those who refused to forsake excess. What would Dona Xima look like now? She must have already turned forty. The last time she had been to Bearn she was at the height of her beauty. She might still be beautiful; she might be dead. If that were so, what would have become of her soul? I was overcome by a feeling of deep pity for that unlucky woman, perverted in her adolescence by the man who had the obligation of ensuring her chastity.

When I gave in to such thoughts, the Senyor appeared as a monster. Later, studying his *Memoirs*, I realized his heart was not as cold as I was willing to believe. Yet even so, I would have had serious qualms about absolving him. Besides, did Dona Xima not carry the blood of that great-grandmother about whom so much was rumoured, even in connection with the Senyor, who could have been her son? And had Don Toni not also inherited something from the other legendary Don Toni, whose name is still mentioned in rhymes by the peasants of Bearn?

> *Our Lord Jesus is in Heaven*
> *and in Moorish lands, the heathen . . .*

In those anonymous rhymes we find the same pain and anguish as a great poet of the middle ages left in the *Ballade des Pendus*:

> *Pies, corbeaulx nous ont les yeux cavez*
> *Et arraché la barbe et les sourcilz.*

Don Toni de Bearn i Torre Roja had violated the honour and peace of humble, decent families who did not deserve such treatment:

Pine and sigh, dear women,
the whirlwind is here;
cry salty tears . . .

They say that the rhymes accuse him of more calamities than he actually committed, and I am inclined to believe it is true. There have been plenty of scholars who claimed that some of them do not refer to Don Toni but to a real whirlwind that did great damage to the village at the beginning of the eighteenth century: that is the degree to which history is distorted in the course of only a few years. Responsibilities fade away and end up disappearing in a cowardly way when we attempt to find them in the actions of others (of our ancestors, that is) instead of looking deep into ourselves. Our soul is, after all, to use modern terms, 'personal and untransferable', as it said in our passports.

One night, the unlucky woman appeared in my dreams: she was older, still beautiful, with a melancholy gaze in those deep eyes Dona Maria Antònia had once compared to mine. I asked her whether she suffered very much.

'My suffering is bearable,' she said, 'but I know it will only grow until my final despair, which will be eternal.'

I gave her a cross to kiss. She refused to do so, smiling sadly.

'I owe twenty-three francs for the room,' she said.

I awoke covered in sweat.

SEVEN

After that dream, Dona Xima was my obsession. I thought I saw her everywhere, and, like Proteus, she appeared in any number of different forms. Even though I knew she was a grown woman, I found her in the Bois embodied in a fifteen-year-old girl playing diabolo. In the hotel dining room I recognized her in an Italian countess, and one evening when I was half asleep waiting for the Senyors to return from the theatre she appeared in the form of an angora cat who had her eyes and movements.

One morning, on the electric tram, I was surprised to see a graceful lady who I thought to be her on the Quai de la Mégisserie. The tram was racing along at top speed. I asked the conductor to let me off and he replied that there was not a stop there. The lady was left farther and farther behind. One more instant and I would have lost her. I was about to jump off the car when someone grabbed me by the arm.

'You're not allowed to do that, sir.'

My reaction was involuntary. It had never happened to me before: I flung my fist at the man, who turned out to be a police officer. The tram came to a halt even though it was not a stop and two other policemen asked me to come with them. I was embarrassed to death. I saw them take the wounded policeman away in a carriage. I had split his eyebrow. When I saw him covered in blood I was so distressed that I thought I might faint. Thank God I reached the police station on my own two feet, and was led up to an officer who upon seeing my habit bowed and greeted me, calling me '*Monsieur l'abbé.*' After we sat down, he kindly inquired whether I was familiar with French law.

143

Before I answered, he added with a smile: 'I assume you had not been drinking.'

When he saw my surprise he laughed cordially and offered me a glass of wine, which I did not accept. Finally, turning in his chair and half closing his eyes, he said: '*Mais racontez donc l'affaire, Monsieur l'abbé, je vous écoute.*'

I began my story, sparing no details. When he heard I had wanted to get off the tram to meet a lady, he lifted one eyebrow.

'She was my master's niece,' I added.

He opened one eye.

'*Mais je ne vous demande pas cela, Monsieur l'abbé.*'

That statement disconcerted me.

'It was of the utmost importance that I speak to her. With all this mess I've lost track of her, and now it will be impossible . . .'

'You came to Paris in the company of your master, and you don't know where to find this lady?'

'That's right. I came with my master and mistress.'

'And couldn't they give you her address?'

'They don't know it.'

'Ah!' exclaimed the Inspector, lifting the other eyebrow.

I realized he did not believe me. That was all I needed to fall into utter despair, and precisely because I never tell lies, my entire story seemed like nothing but a lie from that moment on.

'I'm awfully sorry to have to arrest you for a few hours, sir,' the inspector said, 'but until the doctors determine how serious the officer's wound is, you'd best not leave. I assume you know the penalty you would incur for assaulting a police officer.'

Instead of frightening me, his threat gave me courage.

'No, Inspector, I don't,' was my reply. 'That point is exclusively of your competence. I'm ashamed of what I've done. I find it so base to have used my strength against a man who only meant to fulfil his duty that I'll never forgive myself. I know God will punish me for it, so the sentence I receive here may help to extenuate the one that awaits me in the afterlife.'

The inspector looked at me with curiosity.

'It's strange . . .' he said, and the telephone suddenly rang. The Inspector spoke for a moment with the receiver stuck to his ear and then turned to me: 'The doctors say his nose is broken.'

'Is it bad?'

'No . . . but it is serious. *Monsieur l'abbé* . . . '

I was heartbroken. In my distress all I could think of saying was: 'Inspector, I'm not an abbot.'

'Oh,' he exclaimed. 'Well, what are you, then?'

I understood he was about to take me for an impostor.

'I'm only a chaplain from the House of Bearn.'

'*De la maison de Béarn?*' He looked at me inquisitively. I took out my wallet and gave him a hundred-franc note.

'On behalf of my master, I beg you to have this delivered to the man I wounded.'

'That's awfully kind of you. Where are you staying?'

'At the Hôtel du Louvre. And by the way, the Senyora had asked me not to be late for lunch.'

He seemed to hesitate.

'I could let you go on probation,' he said, 'as long as you're escorted by two officers. But that may shock the Princess,' he added inquisitively.

Not knowing what princess he was referring to I kept my mouth shut.

'Very well,' said the inspector, 'You may go now. I assume you'd rather their Highnesses didn't find out about this. Next time, proceed with more caution. Believe me, it's good advice.'

The inspector was convinced that the whole affair was nothing but a typical Parisian romantic adventure, and as a good Parisian, romance, even for a priest, appeared to be an extenuating circumstance. But what royalty was he referring to? He himself gave me the answer to the enigma.

'I hope you will give my thanks to *Monsieur le prince de Béarn* for his donation.'

I hadn't the courage to point out that he was not a prince. It was late and I wished to see the wounded officer who was in a nearby hospital. In fact it turned out to be farther away than I had imagined, and finally, after keeping me waiting for quite some time, they did not let me see him. I told them to give him on my behalf the pendant with the Virgin Mary which I always wore around my neck, and, alarmed to see how late it was, I asked them to let me speak with the hotel using the electric telephone. When I asked for the connection, the young ladies at the switchboard transferred me to the Museum. That confusion made me lose a few precious minutes, and when they finally put me through to the hotel and I had already recognized the concierge's voice, it let out a spark that made me fall unconscious on the floor. When I came to, they called a cab that took me to the hotel, upset and with a bruise on my forehead. A servant opened the glass door and as he bowed to me I thought I heard him say that the Prince and Princess were waiting for me in the winter garden.

I heard him as if in a dream. I did not know there was a garden in the hotel. Luckily, through the French windows of the nearby drawing room, covered in a red carpet and lined like a jewel-case, where a grand total of five palms justified its being called a garden, I saw the Senyors saying their rosaries. The first words uttered by my benefactor, who was dying of hunger, were these: 'You devil! I thought you'd been kidnapped by some beautiful lady. How on earth did you get that bruise?'

I cannot remember how I explained it all, and after the meal I locked myself up in my room. I needed to pray and collect my thoughts. I had to think of some explanation for the money I had given to the inspector. I had some savings at Bearn which may not have reached that amount but were not far from it; however, for the time being I had to say I had lost those hundred francs even if only to avoid our spending more than we could. It would have been nobler to confess the truth, yet it seemed wrong to stir up the past and raise the sensitive issue of their niece. Tired of going over it time and time again in my mind, I fell asleep, and immediately Dona Xima appeared: 'The lady you saw,' she said, 'was not me.'

She seemed sadder than in the last dream and I asked her whether she prayed.

'No, because it's too late,' she said, and disappeared.

I woke up and walked over to the balcony. In the foreground, leaning against the columns of the Théâtre Français, I noticed two gentlemen who did not take their eyes off the hotel. They could only have been policemen; it was improbable that they were robbers, at that time of the day and right in the centre of town. Suddenly, one of them signalled to the other. Don Toni had gone out, crossed the square and disappeared down the rue de Richelieu. The one who had signalled went over to his partner, who was younger than he, and said something to him. Then he went into the hotel. His partner lit a cigarette and pretended to read the theatre advertisements. When he had thus proved his indifference, as if he could guess that I was

146

watching him and had performed that pantomime exclusively for my benefit, he walked away down the rue de Richelieu very fast, because Don Toni was already far ahead of him. A minute later the one who had gone into the hotel came back out and went over to the same place, also pretending to read the cast list of that evening's performance of *Phèdre*. I found the events disturbing and decided not to move from my observation post. Less than a quarter of an hour later the Senyor returned with a package of books in his hand. At a reasonable distance, smoking and pretending to look at the ladies, the young policeman followed him.

When I went down to supper a few hours later, my benefactor was in the hall, scolding one of the bellboys in Mallorcan. The youth listened with his mouth open.

'What is this nonsense about *Monsieur le prince*, you little cockroach? Get out of my sight!'

Over supper I had to give a more elaborate explanation of how I got my bruise. I had already prepared a few lies, because one muddle always leads to another. As I piled falsity upon falsity, I remembered the verse Father Pi made us recite in school:

> *On the path of sin*
> *not taking the first step*
> *is the very best thing*

However, one thing leads to another in such a way that it was difficult to determine which was the first step. If a graceful lady (who I was now convinced was not Dona Xima) had not been on the Quai de la Mégisserie, I would not have tried to get off the tram nor attacked an officer. But why on earth did I have to speak to Dona Xima? To convert her? Would she have listened to a poor country chaplain? Could it not have happened that she would have tried to see the Senyors, again disrupting their placid existence? It is true that Don Toni was already old; he was already over seventy. But who knew . . . ? It was certainly impossible to discover the initial cause of that tragedy. Was it Don Toni's frivolity, morbid inheritances, circumstances, coincidences? All these ingredients and many others had helped unleash the events.

As we had our dessert, the boy came over and announced that Monsieur Garellano wanted to know if *Monsieur de Béarn* wished to come to the electric telephone. I had just told them my adventure with the spark that knocked me unconscious.

'And now,' said Dona Maria Antònia, 'you have to talk on the telephone? Who is this Mister Garellano? If he has something to tell you, why doesn't he just come here himself?'

At that moment I remembered that after lunch the Senyor had said to the boy, thinking I could not hear him: 'Tonight you'll come over to our table and say that this man is on the telephone,' and handed him a slip of paper. Not until now did I realize the importance of that exchange. The Senyor went out and returned almost immediately.

'That little urchin ...' he said, referring to the boy. 'He insists upon calling me Prince! What he needs is a good whipping.'

He said it to distract our attention and make the telephone call seem less important. In my case he succeeded for the moment. It was obvious that the police were watching us and that the title of Prince of Bearn, mentioned for the first time that day at the hotel, where we had already spent almost three weeks, had something to do with the officers waiting in the square of the Théâtre Français. I did not like it one bit. Our life had become complicated. I did not know whether those policemen were protecting us as people of importance or spying on us as impostors. If it were the former, the latter would prove true before long.

'What did the gentleman who sent for you want?' Dona Maria Antònia asked.

'He's a fellow Spaniard. I don't know him, but he heard we were going to Rome and wanted me to deliver something for him. I'll go see him tomorrow. He lives in Auteuil, so don't worry if I'm late for lunch.'

I was shocked by his lies. What was the Senyor up to? Dona Maria Antònia seemed vexed.

'I'm getting old,' she said, 'and the world has changed very much; but Tonet, I don't think that's right. Making you go to the electric telephone is already rather bold. How does he know whether you want to talk on the telephone? And now he asks you to go all the way to Auteuil ...'

'He didn't ask me to go; I offered to do so. A daughter of his is ill,' he improvised.

'But you aren't a doctor, Tonet. The whole thing is quite suspicious,' she added, pretending to take it in jest. 'Don't you think so, Joan? I think the Senyor is fooling us. Maybe he didn't even get a telephone call and he's made it all up so we'll let him go off on his own. Very well. You and I will also amuse ourselves: we'll go for a boat ride down the Seine.'

They went to bed before long. I stayed in the hall. I wanted to speak to the man in charge of the reception desk to see if I could stop the nonsense about the Prince and Princess. The receptionist was always madly busy: he took notes, added up bills, answered clients' questions and spoke on the telephone. The man was too quick: he understood everything at the first word, and since he could not wait for the second, he never quite grasped things, even if in turn he answered ten questions in the time anyone else would have taken to answer one. Such qualities made him unpleasant despite his artificial smile. I had not even reached the *comptoir* when he looked up and flashed his teeth at me:

'. . . *sieu désire?*'

He had used a word and a half, but I could not manage to answer with a single one, as I would have liked to. Eager to be specific, I fumbled for words, which irritated him: '*Dites, dites* . . .' and while he pronounced these syllables he wrote numbers down on a piece of paper.

'I'm sorry to bother you . . .'

He looked at me in anger and flashed his teeth at me again.

'*Dites, sieu* . . .' and he leaned over to bow to an elderly lady covered in jewels. I had to be quick.

'My master would appreciate . . .'

'*Oui,*' he whistled loudly while ringing a bell and flashing all his teeth at two Americans who walked by. At that moment five very elegant travellers walked in and the receptionist lost interest in me.

'My master,' I shouted, 'would appreciate your not addressing him by the title of Prince, because . . .'

The receptionist looked at me for a second and offered his smile to someone wearing a diamond in his tie.

'*Oui, monsieur,*' he retorted rapidly, looking at me again. '*Incognito. C'est compris.*'

I saw it would be impossible to make him listen to one more word, and due to his inordinate mental capacity he would end up not knowing that the Senyor did not want to be addressed as a prince because he had never been granted that title.

In exchange for having painted a truly malicious portrait of the concierge, I must admit that during the entire remaining week of our stay in Paris no one pronounced the word 'Prince' in our presence up to the moment we left the hotel.

EIGHT

I could not sleep thinking of all that had happened. I had to tell the Senyor that I had taken one hundred francs from the travel fund, but I did not know how to. I was not willing to mention Dona Xima under any circumstances. I had no objects of value other than a gold chain and pendant. The pendant I had already given to the wounded police officer and the chain alone would probably not be worth the amount I needed. Even if it was, sooner or later I would have to make up another lie to explain how I had lost the chain. Yet would I not have to do so anyway since I was missing the pendant? Around dawn I managed to doze off and I was sleeping soundly when the Senyor walked in and sat at the edge of the bed.

'I'm here,' he said, 'to ask you for three hundred francs.' My eyes were open and I thought I was dreaming.

'Don't open your eyes. You'd never guess whom you look like.'

I preferred not to make a guess. Even though I was the administrator and depository of the funds, two days prior to our departure he had asked me for forty *duros* in case we were separated at any point. Since until then we had always gone out together, I could not imagine how he had spent all that money. His request was highly suspicious. Who else could it be but Dona Xima? I suddenly decided to talk and told him everything that had happened to me without omitting a single detail. He listened with a look of satisfied curiosity. When I told him about my conflict with the officer, he put his arm around my neck.

'You hit a policeman, my dear boy? He dared to grab you by the arm? Very good. Who did he think he was?'

At the very thought that a foreigner (even though in that case we happened to be the foreigners) had dared to touch my clothing, all his love for the French seemed to vanish into thin air. He pondered for a moment.

'You say you thought you'd seen Dona Xima?'

'I was probably wrong. Does your Honour know where she is?'

'No,' he said. 'I don't have the faintest idea,' and he looked towards the balcony.

I thought he was lying and felt my anger rise within me.

'So your Honour needs three hundred francs? Yesterday I took a one hundred franc bill to give to the poor police officer. Until we're back in Bearn I won't be able to pay you back.'

And so as to leave nothing unaccounted for and to purify myself after telling all the lies I had told (and the ones I had been about to tell), since I had already mentioned Dona Xima, I confessed that I had also given away the gold pendant that he and the Senyora had given me. He smiled.

'You seem to be awfully concerned about this policeman,' he said, with a mischievous look on his face. 'Now you can't say you haven't had an adventure in Paris. I'm having one, too. Give me the money I asked you for and stop thinking about what you spent ... on the policeman. Poor Joan, don't you see we're older than you?'

His words expressed kindness, authorizing confidence, so I dared to ask him how he had spent the forty *duros* I had given him in Bearn. Far from being taken aback, he answered in a pleasant tone, as if he did not find my question the least bit inappropriate. 'I only have ten *duros* left.'

I understood I was not to press the issue, but he added: 'The village priest is in charge of giving one *duro* a week to Madò Coloma and we hadn't settled our accounts for weeks. Are you and the Senyora naïve enough to think that someone can really live on the milk of one goat and two loaves of bread a week?'

I gave him the three hundred francs. One hour later I was saying mass at Saint Roch, in a state of mind you can imagine and with Dona Maria Antònia as the sole member of my congregation. After the celebration of mass, God chose to favour me: 'Before lunchtime,' a voice within me said, 'you will have proof that the Senyor is not with the person you suspect.' When we returned to the hotel, the

Senyora had not given up her idea of taking a boat down the Seine. There were boats leaving the Quai du Louvre every quarter of an hour. She decided to go to Passy and land on an island.

'You'll see, Joan. They're beautiful desert islands. On Sunday they're full of people, but today there won't be a soul. We'll sit under a tree between the sun and the shade and say our rosaries.'

In addition to being a famous river, the Seine is a place of great beauty, with its placid, abundant waters and lush forests nearby. Past Saint-Germain, the banks form a majestic valley full of avenues and rich in game. We landed on an island that was indeed deserted — there was no one there but us — yet full of birds who offered us a concert worthy of being performed at the Opera. Ahead of us walked a bellboy from the hotel carrying two red velvet cushions trimmed with gold braid, which were apparently used during the visits of the Duchess of Edinburgh. The Senyora asked to use them to sit in the boat, and also asked for the boy to come and carry them, which gave us prestige in the eyes of the hotel staff. We said our rosaries. The bellboy fell asleep on the grass. After we had been listening to the birds sing for quite some time, Dona Maria Antònia said, as though she were talking to herself: 'The Senyor is so strange sometimes, Joan. I've never managed to understand him.'

There was a pause, and since I had dared not open my mouth, she continued: 'Neither you nor I believe he has gone to Auteuil. He used to be better at telling lies. Now that he's getting old . . .'

She fell silent and stared at her hands, once so beautiful and now frail and withered. Her blue eyes were full of melancholy.

'I don't know,' she added, talking to herself, 'whether he made up that silly story about Auteuil because he's become old or whether he thought it would do now that I'm so old and forgetful.'

I was moved by the subtlety of her thoughts.

'We have no right to think ill of anyone,' I said.

She dropped her pensive tone and regained her usual liveliness.

'We have no right to be stupid, if you ask me. What could he be up to at his age, my God? You who know him better than I . . .'

'Who, me?'

'Yes, Joan. I've known him longer and more intimately. But you . . .'

She stopped and looked at the sky of the same irresolute blue as her eyes, inherited, according to her husband, from a Norman ancestor.

They were bright eyes, sometimes a little hard, yet at that moment they seemed misty with sadness. They would have been even more so if she had known everything I knew and could not reveal. Only three hours earlier, the Senyor had said 'I'm having an adventure, too,' and asked me for three hundred francs. For a moment the turbulent scenes from his past ran through my head. Dona Maria Antònia tried not to find out about unpleasant things, but we will never know to what extent she was successful. That day I glimpsed an intimate, painful suffering in her: that of moral incomprehension. May God forgive me if I dare say that in the presence of the Senyor, Dona Maria Antònia gave me the impression of a savage in front of a piano. And nonetheless they were cousins, they bore the same name and shared part of the same blood. They loved one another. 'But love between man and woman has never implied intellectual understanding, but rather the fusion of two opposites, the amalgam of two metals that lose their characteristic qualities,' my benefactor proclaimed. Dona Maria Antònia's last words had struck me because I did not know exactly how to interpret them. 'Yes, Joan, I've known him longer and more intimately, but you ...' She never finished her sentence, and I never asked for an explanation. My pride did not stop my eyes from filling with tears, and I kissed her withered hand.

'In a sense,' I told her, 'I'm an offence to you, Senyora.'

And how poorly endowed, my God, was I to live with this old family of Bearn! Fourteen years ago, I had fainted in a moment of need by the fireplace, and Dona Maria Antònia, a Senyora, had given me an example of strength. Now, at the age of seventy, the same lady again defeated me on a desert island on the Seine. When she heard my words, her eyes, which before being of gauze, like the sky of the Île de France, had been of agate, became two spring flowers, two weightless marvels, two little bouquets of forget-me-nots. Her gaze seemed to smile and point with delicate mischief to the boy half asleep on the grass.

'Joan, for God's sake, that boy has already seen abbots kissing the hands of marchionesses in the museum ... My goodness,' she added, 'what if the boat didn't come by again? Wouldn't we be scared?'

She was not. We suddenly heard a low sound which seemed to come from the east. The birds cried and flew away. We saw a sort of cigar-shaped balloon coming from the direction of the Bois de Boulogne. Then I remembered that in the paper I had read that the

Tissandier brothers had announced their second scientific flight in an electrically propelled balloon of their invention.

'How can they drive a balloon in the air?'

'The same way one would drive a steamship, I've heard, with a propeller revolving and a rudder.'

She remained pensive.

'Anyone who has any sense,' she said, 'can't approve of such things, and yet who knows whether eventually we'll end up travelling by balloon. Years ago the Senyor invented the *automobile* and we all censured it. Nowadays it would seem that the *automobile* is here to stay.'

She may have felt remorse about having opposed the invention, now that the idea had triumphed. But that's how all the Dona Maria Antònias of the Universe are and always will be. The Senyora, strong and cautious like the Biblical Leah, was bound to the earth.

The balloon was drawing closer. It was the shape and colour of a cigar, thick in the centre and almost pointed at the ends. It also reminded me of a whale, and in neither case was it pleasing to the eye. As I was to learn later, it was twenty-eight metres long, or more than seventeen Mallorcan *canes*, and full of a very poisonous gas that was also explosive. We could already see a sort of large basket hanging from what one might call it's belly; it seemed to be made of woven reeds and carried a lot of machinery. Three men stood there making signals to each other, pulling levers and pushing buttons. Two of them, large and tall, with beards and moustaches, must have been the inventors, the Tissandier brothers. The other man, Heaven help me, was the Senyor. Dona Maria Antònia and I recognized him at the same moment and looked at each other without saying a word. The monstrous whale flew very low over our heads and disappeared slowly to the south, vibrating and swaying like a big bumble-bee. Despite the danger my benefactor was in, I felt deeply comforted, and I remembered the voice I had heard during mass: Don Toni was not with Dona Xima. The three hundred francs had not been spent on a romantic adventure; they had probably been given to the Tissandier brothers, since in France, as in many other places, you rarely get something for nothing.

Our boat arrived a few moments later; we embarked in silence and moored by the Louvre. The Senyora entered the hotel preceded by the bellboy with the two velvet cushions of the Duchess of Edinburgh, like a real princess. The agents who were spying on us from the Théâtre Francais did not miss a single detail of our triumphal arrival, and one of them wrote something down in his notebook. I dare mention that for renting the cushions and employing the services of the bellboy for two hours they added sixty-two francs to our bill and when I asked for an explanation, assuming they had made a mistake, they answered that it was an extraordinary luxury, not included in the usual rates. ('Oh, my Lord,' Dona Maria Antònia commented, 'a luxury? That little boy who's knee high and doesn't do a thing all day? I think a half a *pesseta* ought to be more than enough to pay him.')

The Senyor was late for lunch. He was very excited; being of a sincere nature, he did not like to lie except when it was absolutely necessary, and he was dying to tell us about his adventure. However, knowing his wife would disapprove and not wanting to start an argument ('there is not a single idea that does not contain its own possible refutation,' he wrote in his *Memoirs*,*) and given that he had a fertile imagination, he found a way to reconcile whim and convenience by inventing one last lie in order to tell the truth.

'The gentleman from Auteil,' he said, 'took me to see the departure of the dirigible balloon and introduced me to the Tissandiers, the famous engineers. Have you heard of them? The papers have spoken of nothing else for days. The Tissandier brothers are very pleasant. They showed me into the crew car. It's comfortable, with chairs to seat three people ...'

Our silence seemed to disconcert him; it is so true that sin is a weight heavier than lead. The situation was becoming tense, yet I chose not to intervene. In the end, Dona Maria Antònia intervened while devoting all her attention to peeling an apple and did so with that seemingly frivolous tone characteristic of the Bearns which has even fooled me, who was raised among them, many a time.

'Joan and I saw you fly over the Seine, Tonet. Weren't you afraid of having an accident?'

The Senyor replied in a natural tone: 'No; it's a very safe vehicle. You'll see ...'

He described how it worked. She listened benevolently. The catastrophe had been warded off.

---

*The same statement has been made more recently by a French author, Paul Valéry, at the beginning of this century. (Editor's note).

155

NINE

Those three hundred francs had not been spent on Dona Xima. During the month we had already been in Paris, nobody seemed to remember her. On one occasion I had advised Dona Maria Antònia to entrust her to God. The Senyora listened to me without opening her mouth and without revealing the slightest change of expression. We will never succeed in understanding the Senyors, Miquel. They are hardhearted and perhaps cannot be otherwise. They are not interested in people so much as in the name they bear. It thus happens that an aristocrat can be more ignorant and coarse in his ways than a simple man of the middle class, and yet he will lose none of the prestige that does not belong to him, but is the legacy of a tradition exclusively connected to his name. The name is a cover for the person, and feeling to some extent invulnerable, the powerful risk forgetting even the principles of ethics and religion. I have already said that the scandalous existence the Senyor led during the first half of his life would not have been tolerated had it not been for the spell cast by the five letters in the name *Bearn*. That is why Jesus Christ proclaimed that if we wish to follow him we must abandon earthly honour and embrace the cross. Do you remember the time when the rector at the Seminary went so far as to call us socialists? May the Lord preserve us from falling for false theories condemned by the Church such as those of Karl Marx, a German Jew who died in London. This secular apostle, who created the materialistic conception of History, does not seem to know that about nineteen centuries ago in a stable in Bethlehem a Master was born whose doctrines included all that which Socialism proclaims as

156

its own invention. In addition, like a good German, Karl Marx is incoherent and contradictory, striving for brotherhood by means of class struggles and wars. These are hardly the paths we are shown by our Holy Saviour! No, neither you nor I can be accused of Marxism. On the other hand, Miquel, the objections I have sometimes made to the Senyor's morals have not meant that I did not love him, but quite the contrary. 'If a man have an hundred sheep, and one of them be gone astray, doth he not leave the ninety and nine, and seeketh that which is gone astray?' The great love I have always felt towards my benefactor rises from such a sentiment. If I have not loved Dona Maria Antònia as much it is perhaps because she was not as needful of my solicitude. Precisely because I believed the two of them were good, I found the way they proceeded with Dona Xima inhuman. It is not fair to object by saying her behaviour was a lost cause. That would be all the more reason to help her, not to forget her. When I asked the Senyor whether he knew where she was, he said he did not, and looked off into space. I was infuriated by his answer because I thought it was false. Now that I knew it was true, I found it all the more infuriating. The Senyor knew nothing about her; in other words, he wished to know nothing about her. When he had come up with the idea of visiting Paris it was, as he was to confess later on, to meet the Tissandier brothers, who claimed to have built a dirigible balloon. Such is the spirit of Faust. When he has not been able to find redemption in the sins of the flesh, the Germanic Faust seeks them in the yearning for power, in action, taking land from the sea, becoming rich . . . in anything but observing the Law of God.

A few days before our departure, the Senyors took me to the Opera to see *Manon* from a discreetly positioned box. The Grand Opera is a modern theatre next to the Boulevard des Capucines. The old theatre on the Rue Le Pelletier burned down a long time ago, as if with the disaster of Sedan God wished to destroy not only the Empire but even the stage that symbolized the scandals of that entire society. I was familiar with the famous novel by the abbé Prévost, a romantic novel that predated Romanticism, written in the middle of the eighteenth century by a man who was not the least bit frivolous and who shared the mistakes of his protagonists. The name Manon has remained a prototype of the frivolous woman who is swept away in a hurricane of passion. That is the main source of the tragedy, and I do not understand how anyone can be amused by the thoughtless mischief of

157

an unlucky woman who would have to pay such a high price for her sins in the other life, and who even in this one was pursued by Justice and met a miserable fate in the wastelands of Louisiana.

Dona Xima was the same sort of woman as Manon, and would meet a similar fate. On one occasion I saw a funambulist who danced on a tightrope at a great height and smiled as she swayed, as if unaware of her danger, until she missed a step and broke her neck. I do not know whether the spectators who had applauded her follies realized the moral responsibility that weighed upon their shoulders. I went to see the dead girl and pray a Paternoster in her memory. She was about eighteen and seemed to be smiling under her halo of golden hair.

Returning to the Senyors' niece, I could not foresee in what manner she would be forced to atone for her conduct. In dreams she had told me that her suffering would increase until it reached the point of total despair, which would be eternal. That suffering must have referred to the gradual loss of beauty and fortune, without the counsel of religion serving as a lenitive. The mundane success for which she had lived would be increasingly denied to her as the days went by. I already found it suspicious that we had not seen her in the centre of the town in an entire month. The golden city of Paris ignored her presence. Besides this Paris of luxury and riches, which extends from the Madeleine to the Porte de Saint-Martin, there are others where silks and flowers do not smile behind the shop windows, where gaslights do not shine at night, and where there are no diamonds sparkling on lovely ladies, like morning dew. In one of those Parises unseen by visitors, near the neighbourhood of Saint Antoine, beyond the Luxembourg, in some poor room with no furniture other than a bed, a tin washbasin and a chair, Dona Xima may have possibly been hiding her defeat, her irreparable decline after having dazzled the other Paris of opera boxes, Etoile town houses and carriages waiting at the door. Her friend and benefactor, the Emperor, was dead. The newspapers no longer cared about that elegant lion by the name of the Duke of Campo Formio. Her beauty and what they would call her charm could hardly resist the double ravage of misfortune and forty years of age. When these thoughts came to my mind I looked for Dona Xima among the tattered middle-aged women from the outskirts of town. At other times I could not help but evoke her just as she had remained in my memory, and I have already mentioned that in the Champs Elysées she once appeared to me in the form of a little girl playing diabolo.

158

All these increasingly precise, illusory images culminated in a real and far more distressing apparition. The day before we left for Rome, after saying mass in Saint Roch, I saw her at a distance. She was still beautiful, but her figure and her grace were lost. She was walking fast and seemed worried. She wore an old pair of shoes with crooked heels; a piece of bread and a few vegetables were sticking out of her cloth bag. This time it really was Dona Xima just before the final stage of her decline. She had the same deep, sad gaze that she had in my dream. An omnibus drove between us. Meanwhile, she turned the corner of the Rue des Pyramides, and when I tried to follow her she had vanished. Years later, Dear Lord, I would again see her in Bearn, in the very room where I now write these words, on the last day of Carnival, like a tragic mask ... Saint Francis of Borja, facing the dead body of the Empress, made a vow never to love anything but Eternal Beauty, but the body they were burying was no longer Dona Isabel, but some inanimate remains deprived of life; whereas on that tragic day Dona Xima was a ghost of herself. Those eyes surrounded by wrinkles and that shrunken mouth were still her eyes and her mouth. I was not facing a dead body, but a horrible woman whose features overlapped and mingled with the great beauty she had lost, already impossible to recapture intact in my memory. Yet I must not jump ahead. I must continue with my story. Overcome by a dreadful anguish, I returned to the hotel. There I came across the greatest affront I have ever been faced with in my life, an affront, Miquel, that will not be found in the archives of Bearn, which already contains others: as soon as he saw me, the concierge handed me a thick envelope with a Police stamp on it, addressed to the Senyor.

'It's an important matter,' he said to me rather impolitely, 'and I can't give it to you unless you sign this receipt.'

After signing for it I ran and locked myself up in my room. I foresaw something serious, but never a disgrace of such magnitude. We were being expelled from Paris. Expelled as impostors, as was specified in a long protocol which my mind refused to understand. The Spaniard 'called' Don Toni de Bearn and the 'lady travelling with him' (as if they doubted her being his legitimate wife), along with the abbé Joan Mayol, 'who professes he is performing his duties as chaplain and secretary of the above-mentioned,' were invited to leave French soil within a period of forty-eight hours 'given the excesses stated herein.' Those excesses could have been the subject of a

159

frightful novel. According to the police report, the Senyors were posing as the Prince and Princess of the House of Bearn, demanding royal treatment at the hotel and having a bellboy precede them on their outings to carry the red cushions of the Duchess of Edinburgh. In addition: the 'so-called' Don Toni had flown in the electrically propelled balloon of the Tissandier brothers using the false name of Bernat Villar (which turned out to be true, because he did not wish to appear in the press for fear of Dona Maria Antònia finding out). As far as the *soi-disant* abbé Don Joan Mayol was concerned, he was a dangerous subject who had assaulted a police officer on the Quai du Louvre because of some affair concerning a lady.

The sad and astonishing fact was that almost all they had reported was true, but we are undoubtedly as indulgent with ourselves as we are demanding with strangers. Nothing is more surprising than the discrepancy between the notion we develop about our own selves and the notion according to which we are judged by others. In 1859, a dancer with a pitiful reputation had dared to mention the name Bearn, and I have already explained that the Senyor records this in his *Memoirs*. In the eyes of that sinner, Don Toni was something that my pen refuses to put in writing. And nonetheless my benefactor lucidly points out that such criteria are hardly surprising at all. In Paris, the Bearns of Mallorca were unknown. Yet everyone knew the other facts, such as Dona Xima's behaviour, the visits of the Duke and the compliance of Don Toni, followed by a timely disappearance at the very moment when the new lover began lavishing generous presents on his beloved. All of that, for those who did not know him, had a name, and La Rigolboche had uttered it. 'I didn't believe I deserved it,' the Senyor had told me many times, 'but when I saw it had been applied to me I had to admit that she had plenty of reasons. I don't know whether La Rigolboche, who sold her favours every night, would have accepted another clear, unforgiving appellation that also appears in the dictionary . . .'

God was kind to us. The police had asked us to leave within forty-eight hours and we were planning to leave the following morning. I resolved not to say anything to the Senyors. I was the main culprit of that ignominy: it was only fair that I alone should suffer the consequences of not having stopped that whole princedom affair from the start. Neither could I deny the fact that I had assaulted a poor police officer. I wanted to carry the weight of the affront without

160

sharing it with anyone else, and since I was leaving the City of Light with a heavy heart, I would at least allow the Senyors to leave with a smile on their lips, their heads high and honoured as Prince and Princess. The last time we crossed the hall, those were precisely the words pronounced for the last time — and with such irony! — by the monster at the reception desk: '*Bonjour, messieurs les Princes.*'

He said it flashing all his teeth, and God knows I felt the impulse to beat him to a pulp. Instead of doing so, I took the golden chain from my neck and begged him to accept it, telling him that it was made of old gold. When he realized how much it weighed he turned pale with greed and bowed all the way down to the floor.

'What kind of carriage have you ordered?' he cried out to the *garcon* who was carrying our luggage. 'Couldn't you have found an older one in all of Paris? Go get the cushions of the Duchess of Edinburgh so this lady and these gentlemen will be comfortable on their way to the station.'

The policemen who had been watching us walked over to observe the ceremony of the cushions, pushing back a few children who were in our way. One of the officers personally closed the door to the carriage and took off his hat when we departed.

'The French are so attentive and charming,' said Dona Maria Antònia.

The Senyor agreed. And thus we left Paris, with their majestic smiles and my heart heavy with gloom.

TEN

One's first impression of Rome is disappointing. All those who have studied some history and know that the city was the capital of the world are surprised by its layout, its ruins and the disorder and poverty that abounds. I was particularly distressed at the chatter and lack of devotion in the houses of worship. Most of the parishioners do not even kneel down during the Elevation.

'And you have a lot more to see,' the Senyor told me, 'that will make you doubt about the place and its history. Nonetheless, Joan, and in spite of everything, this is Rome.'

Not until a few weeks later did I understand those words.

The Senyor wished to stay at the Grand Hotel, but due to the state of our finances, quite meagre after our Paris adventures, we went to a *pensione* on the Corso. The lady of the *pensione* received us with an effusiveness that did not please Dona Maria Antònia in the least and that certainly was not appropriate. She assured us that she had the best and most pleasant rooms in the city, but what we saw bore no relation to what she said. The Corso, the main avenue, like the Ramblas in Barcelona, for instance, is really not much more than a narrow, crooked street. That was the street our rooms overlooked. The weather was humid, and grass was growing in the cracks between the pavement cobblestones.

The Senyor wanted to show me ancient Rome first of all. Dona Maria Antònia stayed in the *pensione*. It was raining and we could not find a carriage. Armed with an umbrella, we went to the Capitoline square, one of Michelangelo's more beautiful works. From there we

162

walked down to the ruins. What dereliction, what an absence of grandeur, compared to what I had expected! Even the Coliseum struck me as small.

'Rome,' the Senyor told me, 'is too ancient. It's like a wine: to be good it has to be old, it has to be a vintage wine. But it oughtn't to be too old, or it might turn sour. Rome did so quite some time ago.'

He was referring to the Rome of the Caesars. The Rome of the Popes, praise the Lord, is not dead, as we were able to witness later on.

The audience with Leo XIII was set, barring unforeseen circumstances, for the last day of the year, and we devoted the two previous weeks to visiting churches and museums. The Senyor was right: that was Rome. We were escorted by a sturdy fair-haired Franciscan from Lombardy. His expression did not seem particularly friendly (according to the Senyor, 'he had never been taught how to laugh') but he was always eager to please, one of the most kind-hearted men that I have ever known. He had been introduced to Roman high society and took us to visit some old palaces that left me in awe. I never would have thought that such a dead city, full of poverty and ugliness, still harboured such great wealth. Endless rooms covered in damask, with paintings up to the ceilings, full of engraved silver, chandeliers and swords with diamond-incrusted hilts. Neither in the house of the Counts of Montenegro nor in the Solleric Palace, veritable museums admired by the sadly famous George Sand, can such valuable objects be found. The paintings, however, are not edifying in the least. Naked bodies abound and some exceed all measure. I will not dwell upon this matter because there would be too much to say. I will only record one unbelievable instance, without mentioning the name of the person concerned. Had I not seen it with my own eyes, I never would have believed it: in a most elegant residence on the outskirts of the city (what they now call a *casino* in Italy), the property of a Prince, there is a marble by the sculptor Canova representing a naked goddess reclining on some cushions with an apple in her hand. That goddess is a portrait . . . of the lady of the house.

'In general,' Don Toni stated, 'Italian women are as virtuous as Mallorcan women, if not more. They like to talk about their honour, as do Castilian women, but sometimes their virtue and their honour collapse all at once. Then they can go to extremes.'

After lunch we usually went to the Pincio. From the Piazza del Popolo one can go up by carriage on two monumental ramps. We rode in open carriages and the Senyor amused himself by chatting with the coachmen. Sometimes they spent the entire time arguing over a *ral* and when the Senyor finally got the discount he gave the man half a *pesseta*.

'We all have our ways of losing our tempers,' he observed. 'The old ones complain and say horrible things to us, but out of respect they do so quietly. Besides, with those alcoholic voices they have, we can barely make out what they're saying. The young ones tend to be bolder, but some of them react like little girls. The other day when you didn't come along you missed one who burst into tears; he dropped the reins and almost let the carriage topple over. Only because I'd said: *L'avaro conta sempre i suoi tesori.*' Afterwards he refused to charge us.'

The fact is that either because of these scenes or because of the tip that ensued, as soon as we arrived at the Piazza the coachmen started fighting over who would take us in his carriage. The Senyor sat on a stone bench and smiled as he watched them. Dona Maria Antònia contemplated the scene from a distance, sheltered under her umbrella.

'They'll tell us when they've finished, won't they, Joan? The Senyor is turning into a little boy. Now you tell me why he has to make these men angry. Someday they'll end up calling us something we won't like to hear.'

After having argued for a while, we got into one of the carriages and rode up to the Pincio, crossing other *carrozze* full of high society ladies who went out to sun themselves. The Pincio gardens have been famous since ancient times and overlook a splendid view. Roses, cypress trees and statues compose a most beautiful image of the Renaissance. There is no path, balustrade, temple or belvedere that is not guarded by some nymph or Caesar. There is marble everywhere. The stone characters form entire legions, and as we walked down a dense avenue where the pedestals were almost touching each other, the Senyor pointed out the possible consequences.

'In Rome,' he said, 'there will end up being more statues than people, because people die, but statues live on. Each generation adds new sculptures, not even counting the ones they dig up in the excavations. What will happen the day marble rules over man, and the guides say, "Rome, with a population of one million four hundred thousand, four fifths made of stone"?'

When travelling one encounters strange characters, and the

Romans were quite unusual. Every afternoon we came across a rather beautiful elderly lady; after the second day she smiled at us as if we were acquainted. The third day, seeing we had stepped out of the carriage to contemplate the view from a belvedere, she said graciously: '*Fa molto dolce. Domani avremmo una bella giornata.*' Before leaving she handed us her card. She was a marchioness. The following afternoon we learned that she lived alone and that her distractions were art and carriage-drives on sunny days. We had started to suspect that she might be a charlatan when we received an invitation to meet her for lunch. When we arrived at her address close to the Piazza di Spagna, she introduced us to an old lady and two slightly tattered *commendatori*. In the course of the visit we discovered she was a cousin of the Barberinis, although they apparently were not on speaking terms; we therefore did not ask her to show us the *palazzo*. The residence of the *marchesa* was not exceedingly luxurious, but it had a certain charm, as did its owner. It seemed as though it had gradually been stripped of paintings and tapestries; there were still some valuable damasks and furniture. We never discovered what sort of art it was that she was interested in. She was cultured and had a melancholy, rather mysterious air about her. She claimed to know a lady who made copies of paintings for a reasonable price, but she did not press the matter nor make us feel any obligation. Suddenly we stopped seeing her. We reached the conclusion that she was indeed a lady, albeit an odd one.

One afternoon, the young coachman who had wept because the Senyor told him only misers count their riches, saw that we were taking another carriage and took out a knife; had I not stopped him, he would have thrust it into his horse's chest.

'See, Tonet?' Dona Maria Antònia said, 'That'll teach you not to fool around with these people.'

'They're a sensitive race,' the Senyor thought out loud.

'It would indeed be sensitive,' she replied, 'if we ended up in trouble. Do you really find it so amusing to listen to them?'

I think he really did. The Senyor denied the substance of Italian literature (emptier, as far as he was concerned, than a snailshell and more rhetorical than a nun's bouquet) and yet was a lover of the language for its musicality and the reactions of its people, for their primitive and histrionic nature. 'They shouldn't write,' he said. 'They'll never know how to carry out a subtle analysis. The world of

165

thought is beyond them. They shouldn't write, but they should let us write about them,' Consequently he would make them talk, and since his Italian was not very good, he would throw in any old sentence from the *Méthode de Ahn* just to test their reaction. '*Non si conosce meglio l'uomo che nell'ubriachezza,*' he would suddenly exclaim. Thinking they were being considered drunkards, they would gesticulate and spew forth all sorts of unpleasant comments, as Dona Maria Antònia had foreseen. Yet the Senyor was more interested in the euphony of the words than in their meaning.

'Have you ever heard anything more delightful than an aria from *Andrea Doria?*' he asked us.

'Who was Andrea Doria?' his wife inquired. 'Didn't Raphael paint her?'

'He was a man, not a woman,' the Senyor replied. And since Italy made him dream, he added: 'He must have been a young, energetic man; a captain. His skin was tanned from the sun; the wind tossed his hair and his forehead was always full of curls.'

Don Toni was undoubtedly caught in the same predicament as the eighteenth century: he was too lucid to seem lyrical, but lyricism was in him the way it is in the music of Rameau. What he hated was dark lyricism, shouts and exclamation marks.

'Have you ever seen the classical Latins,' he brought to my attention, 'use exclamation marks in their literature? They didn't even know what they were. It's well and good to shout at Pastora,' — a mule at Bearn — 'because otherwise she doesn't get the point. Needless to say, romantic readers are also a little deaf. Voltaire said to Rousseau: "Reading your works, one feels like walking on all fours".'

In general, he found Italy a country of outrageous gestures.

'When the gestures are the Sistine Chapel,' he said, 'we must accept and be grateful for them: genius has its privileges. But there are few artists like Michelangelo, even though he isn't always a genius. His statue of Moses, gigantic in size, is not really all that great. It's more of a caricature than anything else. In general, the Italian society of the Renaissance was histrionic. Do you know of anything in poorer taste than the banquet offered by Chigi to Giovanni di Medici? The plates were made of gold, and when they'd been used, Chigi threw them into the Tiber. But he had a net set in the river and the following day he got the entire set of gold dishes back again. How do you explain Giovanni di Medici wanting to be acquainted with a man the likes of that? Yet despite the Medicis being called princes, they were nothing but merchants. In that sense they could keep company with the Chigis. How very different, Joan, from the noblemen of Spain!'

It seemed to me that Don Toni had started slapping too many bellboys and threatening too many cheeky coachmen. In doing so he was unconsciously restating our power over a country we had dominated so many times. He was strict and made himself respected above all for his *élan*, as the French would say. I was worried that one day someone might give us an insolent reply and I would feel obliged to intervene.

'Have no fear,' he replied. 'You look so fierce that you scare them away. The other afternoon, when the waiter came in with the bill, you even showed your teeth. I wanted to say: "Don Joan will throw you off the balcony as if you were a ball," but I didn't know how to translate it.'

'Senyor, please remember that is not my duty.'

'I know,' he replied, 'and sometimes I'm sorry that you're such a good boy, because I'm sure you'd like . . .'

He stopped himself and I blushed. It was true that the Devil tempted me, awakening my thirst for combat. It had begun in Paris the day the police officer grabbed my arm; it continued at the hotel, when the man at the reception desk said goodbye with vicious irony, and now, that very morning, my blood had risen when I heard a couple of students who were staying in the room next door repeat the notes of the scale during an entire quarter of an hour, tapping on the balcony windows: '*Sono tre spagnuoli, caramaba!*' The two rooms were connected by a locked door. I could have knocked it down with one blow. God gave me the strength to say my rosary. When I finished I heard my neighbours, who according to the chambermaid were two Neapolitans, leaving their room and I ran to the door, unaware of my actions. Never in my life had I set eyes on anything more beautiful. Imagine two Greek statues, two adolescents in their prime endowed with a flexibility that made them seem to change every instant. Those expressive differences, that constant flight resulted in an appearance that I have never been able to remember as twofold, but rather as a whole. They stopped to let me by as soon as they saw me, ennobled by the serious expression that darkened their features; they suddenly looked like men. At that very moment a cat meowed and they fell on each other in an outburst of wild laughter, half-shut eyes and curls carved in stone long before the birth of Our Lord Jesus Christ. For a moment their well-proportioned, masculine bodies twisted like those of two children holding on to each other so as not to fall down and slapping each other with their hands. They immediately resumed the form of Greek statues and pressed themselves against the wall, exclaiming in a baritone: '*Prego, signore!*' I told them I was in the neighbouring room and then they smiled like proper young gentlemen. They politely put themselves at my disposal and walked off keeping their composure. However, halfway down the hall they put their arms around each other again, and as soon as they reached the staircase, their melodious voices took up the senseless song that minutes earlier had infuriated me and now filled me with tenderness: '*Sono tre spagnuoli, caramba!*'

ELEVEN

On Christmas Eve we received a note from the Spanish Embassy confirming that the Holy Father was granting us the audience we had requested. Enclosed with the note was the invitation from the Pontifical Antechamber, in the following terms.

'It is hereby announced that His Holiness Pope Leo XIII will be pleased to receive the Lord Don Antoni de Bearn and his Lady, as well as his chaplain and secretary, Don Joan Mayol, on the 31st day of this month at eleven in the morning. Formal dress. Presentation of this invitation at the entrance of the antechamber is kindly requested.'

I proposed to the Senyors that we devote that week to the deepest contemplation and begin our retreat in preparation for the grace we were about to be granted. Dona Maria Antònia was in agreement; the Senyor had some objections.

'I believe,' he said, 'that spiritual contemplation is very appropriate, but we don't all see it the same way. What the Senyora and you are most interested in is the Pope's benediction.'

'Tonet,' Dona Maria Antònia replied, 'you know that as a child I was taught that nothing can be more rude than interrupting, and I hate to do so, but I'm afraid this time I must. I wonder what can you expect from the Pope other than His benediction? Answer me, I'm interested in hearing what you have to say.'

Her eyes stared at him with intense curiosity.

The Senyor took her hand in his and caressed one of her nails with his index finger. Finally, he said: 'I believe the habit of interrupting dates back to the times of the Republic. It's a romantic vice, even anarchic if you wish, typical of undisciplined people. I must admit that people used to be more polite. Your grandfather, Maria Antònia, who was also mine, used to tell me that when they were young . . .'

'Yes, I know the story about the cane,' Dona Maria Antònia interrupted a second time.

The Senyor stared at her sternly and let go of her hand.

'Joan may not have heard it, Maria Antònia.'

And turning to me, he explained: 'There were six children in our grandfather's family. Their father, Don Ramon, made them sit in the drawing room for an hour every day with their mother, their aunts and the chaplain. The Senyora began the conversation by discussing the weather. The priest followed, drawing some sort of moral conclusion.' At that moment the Senyor looked at me. 'Their aunts participated and invited the adults to do so, too. Don Ramon presided over the act with a cane in his hand. Whenever one of the children interrupted, he hit them on the head.'

'That's right,' said Dona Maria Antònia. 'Don Ramon was a very strict man.'

'It's a pity,' her husband added, 'that in his old age he started to lose his wits like the kings of the Bible . . .'

'Goodness me, Tonet, why do you have to bring up the kings of the Bible? Leave the dead in peace. Interrupting,' she continued, 'is a nasty habit and I've just done it twice, but despite the story about the cane — which Joan already knew, by the way; you'd already told it to him more than once — and since you yourself dragged in The Kings of The Bible, I know very well why I interrupted you: you said the Pope's blessing is not the main purpose of our trip, and I asked you to tell us how we're expected to interpret that statement. I know you find a way out of everything and that if you wish to do so you'll muddle me up, but I would like to hear your explanation.'

The Senyor took her hand again. Unable to dodge the matter, he began with a good grace.

'First of all,' he said, setting his speech in order, as in the times prior to the Republic, 'you're forgiven for interrupting, which you did only once and not twice, I think.' He knew perfectly well that Dona Maria-Antònia had interrupted twice, but he was sorry that she had caught his reasons for letting go of her hand and ceasing to caress her index finger. 'Secondly,' he continued, 'I have not said that the Pope's blessing is not the main purpose or even the

170

only purpose of Joan's trip as well as yours. But in addition to being a Pope, Leo XIII is an illustrious personality and a skilful politician. I must write something about the man who has just opened the secret archives of the Vatican to the wise men of the world. I would like to meet him personally, and since he won't be able to grant us many hours, I must devote much thought to the questions I will ask. That is why I told you that the spiritual contemplation proposed by Joan can be interpreted in many different ways, Maria Antònia. You should pray, above all, because your creed is of a more magical nature, whereas mine, albeit within the boundaries of orthodoxy [at that point I looked at the Senyor, who met my stare] is more rational.'

'Until now, Tonet, everything was going very well, but I don't know why you have to drag magic into your argument. Neither Joan nor I have ever done any sorcery,' said Dona Maria Antònia.

And we tactfully changed the subject.

During the days preceding the audience, the Senyor wrote notes and seemed absorbed in his thoughts. I said mass at Santa Maria dei Miracoli and, as at Saint Roch in Paris, Dona Maria Antònia was usually the only member of my congregation. After mass, we walked around the sunny square a few times while we said our rosaries and then returned to the *albergo*, from which we would not move until it was dark and we returned to the church. We saw the Senyor only at mealtimes. Dona Maria Antònia made no comment. The day before the audience, as we left the church, she revealed her decision to me.

'Tomorrow I shall not go to visit the Holy Father with you, Joan.'

I was shattered by her words.

'Are you absolutely sure?'

She smiled faintly to herself, because she had already been thinking it over for days, and I should have guessed so. Instead of answering my question, she replied: 'The day after tomorrow there's a public benediction, and since that's all I'm really interested in, I'll go to Saint Peter's. For you and the Senyor, it's different.'

I understood that I was not to press her. The plural, 'you and the Senyor,' was a mere concession so as not to make even more blatant what was already perfectly clear. It was not on account of me that the Senyora refused to see the Pope. The Senyor must have also understood, because he refrained from inquiring as to her motives.

I tossed and turned all night long. The Neapolitans went to bed

171

late. They were merry as could be when they arrived and I heard them laughing through the wall. They were not alone: I thought I heard women's voices, too. I was not as easily shocked as some years before, but this was more than I could bear, so I resolved that the following day I would let the Senyors know. I heard falsetto voices followed by their salacious laughter. The thought of those boys being lost in a city full of vices such as Rome made me uneasy. Suddenly I understood my mistake: they were alone, acting out some sort of play. The discovery would have been a relief had the idea that they were completely alone laughing like that not been perhaps more painful to me than the assumption that they had company. Certain that I would be unable to sleep, I decided to knock on their door. They fell silent and opened right away. Standing on the bed was one of the students, wrapped in a pink bedspread, his face and eyes outrageously painted. The one who had opened the door was dressed as a Roman soldier. I begged them not to make so much noise and they burst out laughing uncontrollably.

'I would like you to meet Madame Angot,' said the boy dressed as a soldier. 'I'm her husband, and she runs off with every other man she meets.'

Madame Angot kicked and screamed on the bed with his hair full of feathers like a horse drawing a funeral carriage.

'*Io non la inganno que trois fois par settimana, signore Bartolo. E tutto normale in France, tutto normale, tutto normale!*'

I tried to restore order in that madhouse, reminding them that they were old enough to know better. The soldier pulled over a chair for me. His friend kept on screaming. The soldier grabbed one of his legs and made him collapse on the bed; then they both rolled onto the floor. I realized that they were drunk and I retired. For a few minutes I heard the sounds of a fight and some giggles through the wall. Then there was silence. I turned out the light and filled the silence and darkness with absurd scenes fired by my imagination.

When the following day we stepped into the carriage to go to the Vatican, I felt deeply uneasy. Like Dona Maria Antònia, I too would have preferred not to attend the audience. The Senyor told me: 'Look, Joan, I don't know how this interview will go nor how much time we'll have. You know I would like to speak with the Pope alone . . .'

The carriage made its way through the cobbled streets of Rome and I saw the old palaces parade by as if I were floating on a cloud. The

172

Senyor's last words snapped me out of my reverie. I told him I would not attend the audience and that I would wait for him at Saint Peter's. He gave me a slap on the back of my head that shocked me rigid, because it was an open carriage.

'Don't be ridiculous. We took this trip for your sake, so you could meet Leo XIII in person. All I'm asking is that if you see a chance to leave us alone . . . I don't know whether it will be possible. You're a smart boy and you'll do as you see fit.'

He fell silent and we arrived at the Vatican. At the foot of the Scala Regia decorated by Bernini was the Swiss Guard in their colourful Raphaelesque uniforms. Upstairs all the servants were ecclesiastics and wore long purple robes. We crossed sumptuous rooms full of important-looking people. After having shown our invitation several times, we were asked to enter a large golden room where a servant called us after a short while and took us to yet another room covered in red damask. There we waited for a while longer, and when the clock struck eleven, a priest walked over with a piece of paper in his hand and said politely: 'Would you be so kind as to come in? His Holiness is expecting you.' And he opened a door.

I will not describe my emotion. The Senyor, who walked ahead of us, stuck his head in and said in Mallorcan, with the same aplomb as if he had been in the courtyard of Bearn: 'I don't see anything resembling a Pope in here.'

The priest smiled and with a wave of his hand invited us to enter, closing the door after us. Then, behind a table that had been hidden by the door, we discovered Leo XIII; he was giving us our blessing. Despite my excitement, I was deeply struck by the resemblance between the Pontiff and Don Toni. Because that resemblance, Miquel, reminded me of another one I never would have suspected, one that has been mentioned with varying intentions in certain newspapers: that of the most saintly and illustrious man of our century and a certain sculpture by Houdon that stands in the hall of the Théâtre Français.

TWELVE

After the three bows demanded by etiquette, the Senyor bent down to kiss the Sacred Sandal, but His Holiness forestalled the gesture and offered his hand. The same scene was repeated with me. Afterwards, as if he knew the Senyora, he asked why he did not have the pleasure of seeing the Lady of Bearn. The question caught us by surprise, and the Senyor saved the day, claiming she did not feel well. Thus, the first words he addressed to Leo XIII were a lie. More than once have I reminded him of that, fulfilling my duty as a man of the cloth.

'But how could I explain such a complicated process in a moment, especially when he wouldn't have been interested in hearing about it?'

'I realize it would have been difficult, but I don't think anything can justify the lie. We could have told him it was due to complex reasons.'

'But in that case,' the Senyor argued, 'Leo XIII would have assumed that the Senyora didn't wish to see him, or that she was not a good Catholic; that falsehood would have been even worse than my version.'

'He may have assumed she was a little soft in the head.'

'Well, I told him she was ill.'

The Senyor's argument was irreproachable. However, I did find him lacking in regrets about having lied to the representative of Jesus Christ on Earth. Why not tell him all the truth, and confess that Dona Maria Antònia disapproved of her husband's rationalism, that being the reason why she had not wanted to come with us?

174

'Perhaps the Holy Father would have found a way out of the misunderstanding between your Honour and the Senyora . . .'

'Or maybe he would have told us to go climb a tree, Joan. Don't you see there are millions of souls out there? How can you expect him to tend to each one of them personally? If the Pope asked about the Senyora, it was out of courtesy, because on the note he received from the Embassy — and held in front of him during our entire conversation — there were three names and he saw only two of us come in. In case you ever leave Bearn, [those words, said with no specific intention, were deeply disturbing to me], you must get used to the fact that some questions are purely rhetorical.'

It was true that along with the important donation the Senyors had given to the Vatican, the Embassy had sent a protocol to Leo XIII, and the entire time I was present at the interview, the Pope consulted it, smiling.

'Mallorca,' he said, '*bello paradiso*. I was there once many years ago. What a splendid bay! Are the *bianchi molini* still turning? You live in Bearn. Those lands, if I am not mistaken, have been in your family since the Conquest?'

Don Toni was about to object, but Leo XIII continued: 'Bearn is an illustrious name. His Honour the Marquis of . . . Collera . . .' he kept on reading, but interrupted himself to ask what Collera meant, given that he was interested in etymologies.

The Senyor and I looked at each other.

'It's an old name,' said the Senyor.

The Pope was satisfied with his reply.

'I know,' he said, 'that you are a great publicist,' ('What the devil did that stupid Jacob write,' the Senyor mumbled.) 'And I also know that Don Joan is a lover of the Latin classics. Right over there,' he said, pointing to a little door. 'I have a small library with some valuable editions of Virgil.'

'Oh, Your Holiness,' Don Toni exclaimed, taking up the occasion, 'Virgil is one of his weaknesses.'

'He is also one of mine,' Leo XIII replied. 'The library is at your disposal.'

'It is known,' said Don Toni, 'that Your Holiness has opened the secret archives of the Vatican to the learned men of the earth. If Your Holiness permits, Father Joan [it was the first time he gave me that title] would be delighted to have a look at those editions of Virgil.'

'By all means,' Leo XIII replied, perceiving the Senyor's intentions. 'Go, Son, and examine the books at your leisure. We'll let you
know when the Lord of Bearn must take his leave.

I stayed in the library almost three quarters of an hour, until I was
called back. It was an octagonal room with light green *boiseries* framed
in gilded strips. It had a balcony overlooking a garden. The high,
arched ceiling was decorated with a fresco. Set in the walls, on four of
the eight sides of the room, there were bookcases with glass doors that
were also painted and gilded. In the centre of the room stood a round
table resting on four swans. It was the most harmonious ensemble
imaginable. They had closed the door, and I suddenly realized that I
did not know where I had entered. There was no visible lock or
doorknob. It seemed like magic, because only a moment earlier I had
walked in through one of those sections so beautifully covered in
boiseries. Finally, when I had started to get restless after pacing up and
down, I happened to lean on a moulding and a door swung open onto
a storeroom full of folders and ink bottles. I closed it, comforted by
having discovered the secret, and cautiously opened another section. I
was blinded by a ray of sunlight. The Pope and the Senyor had
vanished and instead of the wallpapered office with the desk, I was
facing a small room, a veritable friar's cell with an iron bed, a crucifix
and a high window revealing the top of a cypress tree. Hanging from
a hook were a white habit and a scourge. I stepped back in terror, as if
I had violated a secret. Could it be true that Leo XIII, the enlightened
Pope, as the Senyor called him, who looked so much like Houdon's
statue, took mysticism to the same extreme as a medieval monk?
Silence is enjoined on us in all matters of such personal intimacy. Years
before, in Bearn, I had listened to an entire conversation between the
Senyor and Dona Xima. It had been an uncontrollable urge. This time
I was again tempted by the Senyor's conversation and my conscience
offered a thousand reasonable excuses. Was it not my duty to watch
over the well-being of a soul that I have never succeeded in
understanding? Spying could perhaps shed some light on the matter
and help me in my mission. But in no circumstances can straying from
the course of morality be justified. I forced myself to concentrate on
the editions of the classics and not go over to the sections I had not yet
investigated. Believe me, it was not easy, but I will always have the
satisfaction of having refrained from committing a criminal act in the
chambers of the Vatican.

176

Amidst the solace I received from such considerations, God would have it that a book should give me a painful surprise, because, upon leafing through Eclogue II, my imagination, perhaps excited after a night of insomnia and the memory of the Neapolitans, suddenly discovered Corydon uttering concepts so indecent, so different from the metaphysical interpretation I had been taught at the seminary, that I thought I was dreaming. Even now I dare not attribute certain tendencies to the great poet of Mantua, and prefer to think of them as the product of a misinterpretation. Over centuries, ancient works have been subjected to many changes. Heraclitus tells us we cannot look at a river twice, because its flowing water is never the same. Everything is true and ephemeral. Who could ever be sure of owning the definitive edition of things?

I sat down at the table, determined to pray as I waited to be called back. I finally felt oriented. I was sure I had walked in through one of the sections on the right. Straight ahead I saw the perspective of a majestic garden full of fountains and statues, but I was unable to forget the view from the friar's cell: a lonely cypress against a bright blue sky.

A clock struck twelve. A few moments later I heard a noise and a servant appeared on my left. Again my sense of direction had failed me. Leo XIII gave us a warm goodbye.

'You are young,' he said, 'and I know you have talent. The Church has high expectations for young priests like you.'

Again we crossed the rooms and halls. A lady was speaking with two cardinals. Her face was covered with a veil and I could not make out her features. My heart missed a beat. As we walked by the group, one of the cardinals introduced her: '*La marchesa d'Acqua Tinto.*'

I let out a sigh of relief. And with no further incidents, we returned to the *albergo*.

THIRTEEN

The Senyor preferred not to talk about Leo XIII. Both Dona Maria Antònia and I, sitting in the railway carriage that crossed more than half of Italy in less than twenty-four hours, expected him to tell us some details about the audience. Instead of doing so, the Senyor spoke about Michelangelo, Bramante and Julius II. Dona Maria Antònia was apprehensive. She also preferred not to bring up the matter that was on all our minds. Only once did her practical yet scrupulous sense prevail over her apprehension.

'Tonet, you should have asked him if lying to the government is considered theft.'

She had never liked paying taxes. The Senyor, who basically felt the same way, tried to justify them just to play devil's advocate.

'The government needs money. Otherwise, how could it support its soldiers and its ships?'

'We all need money. They should ask for it politely, not demand it. If the government's poor, it should accept whatever it's given.'

'When Charles V came to Mallorca,' he said, going off at a tangent, 'he demanded nothing, but everyone gave him one thing or another. In Bearn it cost us more than seventy sheep.'

'See? I think that's the way it should be,' Dona Maria Antònia replied; 'everybody should give what they can, but there shouldn't be all these demands we have nowadays, which are really nothing but bad manners.'

He tilted his head and made his typical vague hand gesture, which in that case meant: 'I give up.' Deep down he was pleased to see his feeble defence of socialist states refuted. He believed that modern politicians represented the worst of every family, manipulators with no education or aesthetic sense worth speaking of; however, that aversion had more to do with his views as a writer than with his sense of justice. Politicians and philosophers perceive the world in different ways. The former are men of action; the latter search for truth. Even the most pagan intellectual is closer to God than most politicians, who invariably have to lie in order to fulfill their objectives. Therefore, he was a nonconformist in regard to power. However, in that instance, at the very thought that he should have asked Leo XIII about such problems, he could not hide his vexation.

'What would you have expected the Pope to reply, my dear? A lie is a lie, any way you slice it.'

He closed his eyes. She and I looked at each other.

'He's tired,' she said, and turned to look out at the landscape. But I could not be sure that she saw it go by nor was it true that the Senyor was tired. He did not want to be distracted; he wanted to be alone, and for that purpose he had uttered in only a few minutes two insubstantial sentences, more typical of a Marquis of Collera than of an educated man like himself.

What may have been on his mind as the train ran at forty kilometres an hour crossing picturesque Tuscany and fertile Liguria did not seem easy to discern, but he eventually revealed it to me. I was sure he would do so, and preferred not to press him to confide in me. It will remain a mystery why he chose not to make any reference to his private interview with the Pontiff for several months. Evidently he must have asked many questions in the course of that interview, and the conversation must have been very weighty. The Senyor may have seemed superficial, yet he was only so regarding style and form. His temperament was not frivolous and he was concerned about so many spiritual matters that on their account he had neglected the administration of the estate to the point of losing his entire fortune. However, he could not tolerate the solemn or the portentous and never exposed a serious idea without previously elaborating on it and disguising it in such a way that it would appear more insubstantial and airy.

'Do you believe,' he sometimes said, 'that Madame Pompadour was an empty-headed woman, because she dressed in pink? The one who favoured such a belief was Frederick of Prussia, and he had his reasons for doing so. He called her *Cotillon* II (for him, Maria-Theresa

179

of Austria was *Cotillon* I). The revolutionaries distorted her meeting with Kaunitz at the villa of Babiole to fit their purposes. I understand that the name, Babiole, which means toy, threw them off, as they were unworldly people, but what was actually discussed were serious matters, such as the *renversement des alliances*, that is to say, the reconciliation of the House of Bourbon with the House of Austria. If the Republic and the two Napoleonic Empires had abided by that policy, Prussia would not have invaded France thirteen years ago and France would still own the regions of Alsace and Lorraine.'

I believe it is entirely possible that the Senyor did not make up his mind to speak of Leo XIII, who had definitely impressed him, until he recovered his serenity and his natural tone, his pleasant villa of Babiole. That was only my assumption. If this were indeed the case, one must think of how dangerous such a sentimental transmutation (I almost dare say such a 'translation') can be for truth. To what extent can one separate form and content? During the months that had elapsed in preparation for that interview, the Senyor, with his artistic passion for composing, must have endlessly retouched the concepts he exposed, or at least their atmosphere, their tone, changing them gradually, with the best of intentions, into something fundamentally different. The example concerning the policy of Madame de Pompadour is not entirely convincing, because although it is true that the facts have proved that the *renversement des alliances* might have been beneficial, we must assume that neither the Marchioness nor the abbot Bernis had planned that far ahead, and that *Cotillon* II, as the King of Prussia claimed, was acting only on the inspiration of her vanity, striving to be treated as a 'friend' by Maria-Theresa of Hapsburg. The clothes end up making the man. The ideas attributed to Leo XIII in the Senyor's *Memoirs* should be considered with great reservations. I, for whom God had reserved the grace of contemplating the Pontiff's private cell, with his scourge hanging from a hook on the wall, am a witness that the paganism attributed to him by the Senyor is inaccurate. The fact that he may keep certain ancient sculptures in the Vatican Museum does not imply his approval of their reprehensible symbolism; in fact, most of such works are in the Secret Museum, hidden from curious or lascivious eyes. That is something the Senyor does not seem to understand when he attributes to the Pontiff the sentence that 'art ennobles everything', and others in the same vein. Neither is it possible that upon hearing the Senyor's proposal ('Faith

180

leads to Truth or Error, whereas Reason leads only to Truth') Leo XIII smiled graciously, as if he were being told that the weather was sunny outside, and started talking about Bernini's fountains.

The voyage was uneventful. Most of the time we travelled alone. After daybreak, near the French border, Italy saw us off in the form of an exuberant lady covered in veils and jewels who was leading a girl of eight or ten by the hand. Her arrival was preceded by musical phrases directed to the conductor, who saw them in. Then all the colours of the Renaissance unfolded before our eyes: '*Intra, bambina, saluta questi signori. Bon giorno, signori. Capiscono l'italiano? Ah, benissimo! Romanesi? Spagnoli? Ah, la Spagna, quel paese così bello, così meraviglioso . . . E da quale comarca? Forse andalusi? Adoro l'Andalusia . . .*'

And she hummed a few bars from *Il Barbiere di Siviglia*.

'What a bird-like disposition!' the Senyor said softly.

She was a large bird with the feathers of a peacock. Her face was a rainbow. In only a few minutes she told us intimate details about her life that were rather vulgar and did not quite hang together. The train ran in and out of tunnels. The Ligurian landscape is dramatic and full of surprises. Light white clouds floated by, followed by black, menacing ones, and the brightness they created gave way to a miraculous light, like the rays that fall upon a saint rising out of the mist on an old altarpiece; a minute later it would become a spring haze spreading its sweetness to the nearby hills. There were moments when the storm seemed about to break; we heard distant claps of thunder and the wind carried the freshness of wet earth; the sun came out, laughing merrily until the haze so beautifully captured by Botticelli sifted its rays and lavished us for a few seconds with a rain so fine that it only succeeded in lining the compartment windows with droplets as tiny as grains of sand. Then the sun shone again.

'I know I've been criticized,' the lady said, 'but do I have to lock myself up in a convent just because my husband left me? No, no. *La vita è bella.* I'm still young. I want to enjoy myself. I live for my daughter. However, no one has been able to say anything about me. I'm an honest woman . . .'

She dried a tear and laughed and cried alternately. When we reached the border we said our farewells. The Italian lady embraced and kissed Dona Maria Antònia. When we had already parted, she stepped back: '*Ho ancora una parolina a dire, signora. Lei ha la bellezza degli trent'anni.*'

And she gave her one last kiss.

FOURTEEN

We arrived in the City on the twelfth of January of 1884, with much on our minds and little in our pockets. In ten weeks we had spent the considerable sum of one thousand six hundred *duros*, in other words, everything we had been given for the sale of the pine forest. The olive harvest looked meagre and all that could be done to pay the interest on the mortgages was to draw up a new one. All these misfortunes did not seem to bother Dona Maria Antònia, who seemed more optimistic every day.

'You'll see, Joan; with one good year it will all be solved, and you'll be able to cancel this last debt. How much did you say we had to borrow? More than one thousand *pessetes*?'

'One thousand *duros*, Senyora. Five thousand *pessetes*.'

'Well, then, ask for a good crop and that's the end of that.'

The Senyor looked up: 'Ask for a good crop? From whom?'

'Oh, Tonet, sometimes you ask the strangest questions!'

And that was the end of that.

Their niece and nephews had come to wait for us at the pier, and despite the distance between them and the Senyors, they treated us most cordially. However, their smiles were insincere. Dona Magdalena had lost her husband. She lived with her two unmarried brothers in the old quarter near the Cathedral. Since I had always heard they were penniless, I was surprised to see that they lived quite well, and the dining room where they served us a cup of hot chocolate was full of silver. Dona Magdalena was elegantly dressed, perhaps a little excessively so; despite her mourning (it was still not three years since her husband's death) all she talked about was the opera and the aristocracy. As soon as we had finished our breakfast, the two brothers excused themselves, claiming they had some matters to take care of. We then discovered that they were working for the Agricultural Bank.

'They were tired of doing nothing, and they were asked to join, so . . .'

'Work is not dishonourable,' said Dona Maria Antònia, implying that she felt it was so to some extent.

'For years I've been saying,' added Don Toni, 'that the nobility is on its way out.'

To show off her importance, Dona Magdalena started talking about the Marquis of Collera.

'Last week he arrived from Madrid. Sometimes he has coffee with the boys. He's asked me several times how your audience with the Holy Father went.'

'The Holy Father treated us very well,' said the Senyor, 'but Jacob has a big mouth. Well, it makes sense that he should be considered Spain's foremost orator. What on earth is the point of claiming I'm a great publicist when I haven't published a thing in my entire life?'

'Tonet,' replied Dona Maria Antònia, 'that's hardly appropriate just now. As a matter of fact, it would be nice if you went to thank him.'

At that moment the door opened and the Marquis himself appeared. He was the very image of a gentleman.

'My dear relatives,' he said with assurance, thinking he was flattering the Senyors (in fact, they were not related). 'My dear relatives, I just heard about your arrival. Tell me, tell me.'

'I was just thinking,' said the Senyor, 'of going over to thank you and scold you a little, too. Why did you tell Leo XIII that I was a publicist?'

The Marquis laughed.

'Don Toni, do you really think that just because you're locked away in Bearn we don't find out about your endeavours? Your Honour will go down in history as the foremost writer on the Island and perhaps in the Kingdom. You can be sure of that.'

I was taken aback by his benevolence, for I realized it represented some sort of protection. The Senyor also noticed it and smiled.

'That may be, but you'll have to wait for me to die first.'

'What morbid thoughts!' the Marquis exclaimed, embracing him with the joviality of a worldly man. 'Your Honour will live to a hundred. You'll see us all dead.'

'Don't be so sure. Politicians and parrots never die.'

'Excuse him, Jacob,' his wife intervened. 'You know how he is. He's in one of his wild moods.'

'The day before we left,' the Senyor continued, 'I wrote a commentary about you. I quoted that speech of yours that begins, *Poetry, poetry, If only I could dive into the magic world of poetry*...

The Marquis had taken the comment about politicians and parrots very well, but when he heard Don Toni quoting his speech he lost his sense of humour. I think he was more intelligent than people believed him to be. He suddenly changed the subject.

'I didn't want to tell him,' said the Senyor when the visitor had left, 'that the Pope asked about the etymology of the word Collera ...'

'The etymology of Collera?' asked Dona Magdalena.

'Yes. As you know, a Collera is what you put on hors ...'

'Rome is lovely,' the Senyora rapidly interjected. 'The Galliera Museum ...'

'The Galliera Museum is in Paris, Maria Antònia.'

'There's the Capitoline Museum ...'

'That's more like it.'

Dona Magdalena asked us to stay for lunch, but the Senyors decided to leave. Tomeu had come to fetch us with the carriage. We arrived in Bearn after four, when the sun was beginning to set. On the way there, Tomeu told us the latest news: an Englishwoman had just rented a house in the village. They asked her for eight *duros* a year, but she thought it was a weekly contract and gave the owner eight *duros* every Saturday. It was the talk of the town. All she ate was lean meat and she did not like anything cooked in oil. She was a painter ...

'And she's painting me,' Tomeu added, not without some vanity.

Tomeu was about seventeen at the time, and we had always considered him an ugly boy. He had been born in the house, a dark child with big ears. Accustomed to his shabby state and rude manners — he was only used to talking to animals — we did not realize that this savage was becoming a rather handsome young man, proud and determined, even though his scant intelligence kept him from defining the object of his determination. The painter, who had been recommended to the Senyors, saw him in a different light. Instead of judging him from a past she did not know, she did so based on his present self, which no one, with the exception of Catalina, had known how to appreciate. I have already mentioned the scandal caused by her painting in which the boy appears surrounded by nymphs. The strange thing is that she had sketched only a portrait of his head and part of his chest, and covered in an undershirt at that; but since these artists know so much, in the painting she depicted him completely naked. Tomeu, who is a good lad, was so embarrassed when he found out that he hid in the hayloft and did not eat for a day and a night. The priest came to see us and complained about our having given our consent — we who were so innocent — and even though we did manage to convince him as to the truth, others were not as easily convinced. I happen to know that Dona Magdalena was among those who objected the most.

'Since he was just in Italy and thinks she's such an artist . . .'

The painting had already been finished when we arrived from Rome, and the author exhibited it a few days later, but there is no stopping a nasty rumour. Six or seven years later, the baneful attraction Tomeu was to elicit, this time with no artistic excuse, in an unlucky woman, would unleash a mental seizure that contributed to her death and, in a haphazard manner, to that of the Senyors, as well as to the ultimate fall of the House of Bearn.

Miss Moore, as the Englishwoman was called, was a slightly deranged lady with a head full of strange ideas who appeared at the estate carrying a letter for the Senyors the very same day we arrived. Dona Maria Antònia had a pot of tea brewed and Miss Moore talked all afternoon long. To make a long story short, which she certainly did not do, she had come to explain that she had been very modest and shy until the age of forty-five and then visited Florence and felt transformed.

'*The Piazza della Signoria!*' she exclaimed with a cynical candour that I found astonishing, 'Oh, sir, those phenomenal statues, those naked nymphs and athletes in the sun, with all their attributes in full view! It was the month of May. May in Florence, sir . . . Flowers and butterflies . . .' (She always addressed the Senyor; fortunately, Dona Maria Antònia had nodded off in her armchair.) 'I had gone there from London, where it was always raining . . . I fell ill when I returned to the hotel. A few days later, in Naples, I experienced a most extraordinary adventure. I hope you'll understand. Next to my *albergo*, located in a small square with a flower market, there was a tobacconist where I used to buy postage stamps from a young lady. That morning — the air was warm and the roses in the flower stalls looked like a red waterfall — the lady wasn't there. At the back of the store sat a man of about thirty. His hair was black and curly' — as she said that, she looked at me — 'he was wearing a green shirt unbuttoned at the collar; he was strong and tanned. I looked down, asking after the lady. "*Signorina ... è un maschio*," the man replied, and laughed, showing his white teeth. Indeed, an old man appeared to wait on me. Oh, sir, you're an educated, sensitive man; I'm sure you'll understand. At forty-five I was still a modest young lady from a good family. I had never heard an incongruity the likes of that one. The bold smile and the word *maschio* established a sort of complicity between that young man in his prime' — and upon saying this she looked at me again — 'and me, a faded, wilted Englishwoman. My eyes only grasped bright colours: green, red, white ... Red roses, white teeth on dark skin, the metallic green of his open shirt ... I felt intoxicated. The doctor they sent for at the *albergo* asked me if I had spent much time in the sun. It had not been the sun, but one sentence ... A few brash, banal words that opened up an entire new world to me ... and I was forty-five years old! Forty-five years, lost forever. I resolved not to return to England, and ever since, sir ...'

Don Toni nodded. I felt embarrassed and sorry for her. In the course of the conversation I had tried to leave the room discreetly, but she asked me to stay.

'Please don't leave, if you don't mind. I find your presence so soothing ... Now, do you understand why I paint?' she asked, addressing us both. 'I'm a late-comer to the world. I can only be a spectator ...'

'*Carpe diem*,' exclaimed the Senyor when we were left alone. 'Puritanism has done a lot of harm, Joan. I have known people to go straight from chastity to utter folly with no transition. Protestants ought to read Horace.'

FIFTEEN

Miss Moore came back twice, but after the scandal regarding her painting, she was no longer welcome as far as Dona Maria Antònia was concerned, and the Senyor simply had no interest in her.

'She's batty,' he said. 'Dostoevski or Ibsen would make one of those fashionable heroines out of her. If she comes back, tell her I'm out.'

His request was not easy to fulfil because in a place like this the Senyors could be nowhere else but at home. There was no need to do so, however, because Miss Moore did not return. She led a truly eccentric life, writing letters all the time and only going out for walks at night. I learned from the village priest that she tried to go into the church with her head uncovered and the sacristan had to send her out.

'I don't understand your language,' she said in English.

'Well, you ought to learn it,' the sacristan replied in Mallorcan, with sense enough to take her by the arm and lead her to the door.

On the other hand, she also showed humanitarian feelings. When she heard that Madò Coloma had fallen ill, she went to see her and took care of her like a Sister of Charity. During a few days she edified the village with her conduct. Then rumours started about her motives not being charitable but rather aimed at a grand-nephew of Madò Coloma's whom the foreigner wished to paint. It finally transpired that she had hit the ailing old woman. When they heard the news, the Senyors sent Madò Francina to see the old lady, and the servant came back in a state of shock.

'It was a scene straight out of the classical theatre,' the Senyor told me. 'We were in the piano room and the Senyora was trying to play *Il re pastore*, which she can no longer remember, when the housekeeper came in screaming like the trumpets in *Aida*, asking where we were. All that was missing was for her to say in verse:

> *Pine and sigh, dear women,*
> *the whirlwind is here.*

The Senyora stopped playing and looked up at me. "What's that, Tonet?", "The whirlwind is here." She closed the piano and crossed her hands on her skirt, as if she were posing for a picture. Madò Francina entered in a state of distress and shouted at us from the doorway demanding justice like Inès de Vargas in Zorrilla's legend: "Senyor, you must have that foreigner leave at once! It's your Honour's fault for letting her stay in the village! I only demand justice!" I didn't respond so as not to ruin her speech. Dona Maria Antònia, who has no interest in psychology, turned to the woman. "Well, well!" she said in the soft tone she uses when she's angry. "What on earth is this screaming about? You are being impertinent, talking like that in front of the Senyor. Go to the kitchen and make yourself a cup of orange-blossom tea." "Let's hear what it's all about," I added, fearing that Madò Francina would obey and we would never hear her story.'

The Senyor found such things amusing. The fact was that the foreign lady had hit Madò Coloma. Her grand-nephew, who tried to interfere, also got a beating.

'She broke the kettle,' Madò Francina continued, 'and on her way out she kicked the goat, which will never give milk again. That woman will be the end of Bearn, and it will all be your Honour's fault.'

They managed to send her down to drink her orange-blossom tea, and the Senyor, who knew about these things, sprinkled something into it. From what I learned later, it was bromide.

The cause of the scandal had indeed been a portrait the foreigner intended to paint of Madò Coloma's grand-nephew. The old woman, having heard the story about Tomeu's portrait, tried to stop her. The village priest went to the City hoping to see the Governor in order to have the foreign woman thrown out of the country; but the Governor, who was a liberal and who had apparently sold himself to the Masonic lodges and to English gold, viewed the matter in a very different light. He believed art was above all and that in her country, if not in ours, Miss Moore was a woman of importance.

It is lamentable that with a king as good as Alfonso XII on the Spanish throne, public morals depended on the whim of a few politicians with no scruples whatsoever. I hope Mr Sagasta will forgive me, but if he is indeed loyal to the crown and a true monarchist he never should have played the sovereign the dirty trick of presenting him with a Masonic governor. At the time I write these lines, after King Alfonso's death and during the reign of a lady who is exemplary in every sense, his efforts to keep up with the times seem very dangerous to me. Cuban separatism is already rearing its ugly head and no one can foresee how the sensitive problem of our sovereignty overseas will end.

If the Senyor had lived to read these lines, he would say that the final outcome will be the loss of the colonies, and, in addition, that it will be within the natural order and the logical evolution of time. He was a rationalist to such a degree that everything that could be included in a general system seemed to him, in principle, acceptable and fair. Based on this philosophy, he did not perceive the ruin of his household or his lack of progeny as a tragedy. He was convinced that the nobility would have no place in the next century; that although there would be rich men and scientists, people would cease to think of them as archetypes and that Marxism, perhaps under a different name, would be the system of the century to come, at least in Europe. But needless to say, for him Europe was the World. That was an unquestionable dogma.

'Don't you understand,' he once said when I told him about my curiosity concerning Oriental cultures, 'that only here will you find all possible ways of life? If you're interested in primitivism, in Castile and certain villages in Italy you'll see fakirs and religious charlatans. Even in Paris, the author of *Hernani* and novels as absurd as *Les Misérables* is a real charlatan. He even dares to prophesy in prose and verse. Whereas you will never find an Abbé Prévost or an Anatole France in Africa or India.'

Even though his disdain for what he called 'Orientalism' seemed unfair to me (the Old and New Testament came from the East, after all) I cannot deny that his words, as on so many other occasions, had a strong impact on me. In all countries, even in the most civilized cultures, one finds individuals as primitive as the Negroes from the heart of Africa. Despite all the education my benefactor tried to give me, I was one of those people. Jaume's tragedy, or murder, one could say, would prove my point. I now realize that I acted on some unclear impulse, worthy not even of a primitive man, but of a beast. The case of Miss Moore, educated and upright until the age of forty-five, would also show us to what a degree nature can impose itself upon culture and that a single human being can present the same evolutionary variations one would find in two lands as different as Great Britain and the island of Madagascar. Man reproduces in himself the entire history of the universe.

Miss Moore did not leave the village, although no one was very pleased by her presence, and she stayed as long as she wished, with the approval of the Governor imposed by Sagasta and perhaps by other less obvious powers. Defying the hostility she inspired in the villagers, Miss Moore impassively continued to take her solitary walks in the company of a most peculiar dog, eating her meals and sleeping at the strangest hours, making sketches, writing down observations in a notebook, peering into people's doorways and generally behaving as if she lived in a conquered land.

SIXTEEN

Some time after we returned from our travels, it became increasingly obvious to me that Dona Maria Antònia's mind was beginning to decline. God instils harmony in all His creations. It would seem at first sight that a person of the Senyora's stature ought never to grow old. It also seems that the sun ought never to set. But if noon is splendid, so is dusk sweet, and the nights are full of tenderness.

I remember that in Marseilles I had a chance to observe a strange device: a music box that worked on electricity and that also doubled as a magic lantern of sorts. It lit up on the inside revealing on a large sheet of glass a beautiful landscape at dawn. The morning light appeared behind Mount Vesuvius and then the sun rose in the sky to the notes of an enchanting Neapolitan song. The trees were emerald green, the sky was transparent, the sea looked like damask. When the sun set, the colours were muted, but as they lost liveliness, their beauty was only renewed, changing and complementing the charm they had before: everything lost its edge as if it were seen through a fine mist and the musical notes slowed down. The happiness of noon was followed by the loveliness of the quiet hours before rest, and when the sun, already set on the left, shone its last rays and the music drew to a stop, the souls of those who had been following the spectacle felt ennobled and comforted like one who has followed the natural process of things completed and fulfilled.

The Senyors' life could have been as harmonious as day and night and my existence almost as tranquil as theirs had it not been for the notion of Hell that always makes me tremble when I think of Don

191

Toni. I have already said that I have no worries regarding his wife. They had embarked on entirely different quests. She always followed familiar roads and it was as inconceivable for her to go astray as it was for her to reach any glorious fate, for that matter. Whereas the Senyor strove to discover new territories and unknown doctrines, as did some saints and quite a few heretics. I do not know what posterity will decree respecting the character of the last member of this branch of the Bearns, and I say the last because the one in Mexico has no descendants and it does not seem likely that Dona Magdalena's brothers will ever marry. There is no question in my mind but that the history of Mallorca, not very rich in writers (with the exception of a few truly fine poets) will have something to say. And yet, what will that be? Fate may have it that the parliamentary brilliance of a Marquis of Collera, representative in the Assembly and master at the simple art of social pyrotechnics, will eclipse the Senyor's work for a long time. He certainly believed so and did not seem to be deeply affected when the first street in the new part of Palma was called Collera instead of Bearn. Since he was truly dedicated to his writing and absorbed in his work, he had few hours left for resentment. Nonetheless, I do believe that criteria as objective as his cannot accept such a distortion of values with no resistance. And what about the Holy Church? What position will the Church adopt upon judging the Senyor? He claimed that Leo XIII had approved the general plan of the *Memoirs* and did not object to the notion of Good and Evil complementing each other. One would have to know how his question had been worded and exactly how the Holy Father had stated his reply. The Senyor's work, however full of shocking passages, does not openly attack any particular dogma; however, his style is captious. I have at times found it confusing and it would undoubtedly mislead others as well. Only God sees things as they are and can judge with full knowledge of the facts.

These last few winters, the Senyors got up late; Mass was never said before ten in the morning, usually in the small oratory on the upper floor rather than in the chapel. Naturally, the workers could not attend, but the Senyors had no scruples about depriving them of the celebration of mass. My benefactor, who had nothing to do, did not attend either, except on days of obligation. While I waited for the Senyors, I prayed by the fireplace in the drawing room, which is, as I have already said, a spacious room with two balconies overlooking the most unkempt, pitiful greenery one could ever imagine. The large garden stolen from the woods one hundred years ago has been slowly returning to its origins over the past thirty years of neglect. Lentisks, oaks and wild olives stifled the roses and the dahlias. The wild oleanders survived and boldly raised their poisonous flowers like bad children raised under the whip. That garden was particularly beautiful (and I must say *was*, my God!) in the autumn, when the mist heightened the tender greens and covered the fields in sweetness. It was at its loveliest on rainy days, seen through the window by the fireplace.

'If it weren't improper, I wouldn't move from here,' said Dona Maria Antònia, 'even to go to lunch. What a pity that Margalida went and died on you, Tonet,' — she placed no malice in that *on you* — 'just when she'd started learning to play the piano. Wouldn't it be nice to listen to a little *Barbiere di Siviglia* at this moment?'

'*Il Barbiere di Siviglia*,' replied the Senyor, lost in his lucubrations, 'is stolen from Mozart's *Le nozze di Figaro*, which is based on a work by Beaumarchais.'

She was scandalized at what she considered a hasty judgement.

'What on earth are you talking about? Do you think Rossini was likely to plagiarize two unknown composers? You say the nastiest things, Tonet.'

'Why do you say Mozart and Beaumarchais are unknown?'

'Because I don't know them,' Dona Maria Antònia placidly replied.

She held long conversations with me when the two of us were alone. She was very old, and yet at times her features seemed to light up with youthful mischief. At those moments it seemed as if she were half a century younger. I cannot help but describe one of her metamorphoses, as mysterious and poetic as those found in Ovid. The miracle took place one afternoon when Don Toni stated that the good seats were numbered in modern theatres. We were in the garden. She walked over to him smiling.

'How would you know that they're numbered, Tonet?'

The Senyor was about to reply. She repeated her question even closer up, with a smile of purity and mischief.

'What do *you* know? How would you know that they're numbered?'

She looked like a seven-year-old girl. The Senyor stared at her and waved at me so I wouldn't interrupt her. I understood he was reliving the days when they used to play together in that very garden. Her eyes were blue and glassy, and she spoke without listening, gleefully repeating the same words: 'What do *you* know? What do *you* know, Tonet?'

They had gone back in time and stopped, freezing a past moment as if it were a daguerrotype.

The apprehension she had once felt towards me and that had led me to say something improper ('I am an offence to you, Madam') which she had chosen to ignore seemed to have faded altogether. Now that her mind was failing, her heart revealed itself as it really was, simple and honest.

'Do you know what we went through when I was a little girl, Joanet? A disease had ruined the vineyards and my father fell into debt. It was serious. Besides, I don't know how many acres of pine forest burned . . . I can't remember. There were two years when we didn't even have turkey for Christmas, and once I couldn't have a new dress made for Corpus Christi. I certainly haven't forgotten that. Can you imagine? I had just turned fifteen. Now I realize that we didn't have turkey to save money. Now I know; my parents didn't tell me then. We did eat roosters, because we raised them ourselves. And living in the town house of Bearn four years in a row when we had a house in the City must have been for the same reason. And I was supposedly a rich heiress. Those were my riches . . . imagine that! We've all had our ups and downs, Joanet. What do you think? Maybe you . . .' She was about to talk about my childhood, but her instinct made her stop herself. 'There you have it. I was told living in the village would be good for my health, when I'd never been ill in my life. In those days the Senyors didn't like to admit that they had no *cèntims*' — following the old custom, she always said *cèntims* when referring to money, even if the amounts were thousands of *duros* — 'as if it weren't common knowledge . . . The town house of Bearn is gloomy, don't you think? All you can see are the walls of the church. But I liked it. I used to think — I did a lot of thinking — that I ought to marry the Senyor so as to join the two estates again. Besides, we'd been brought up together. The problem is that when there are so many marriages in the same family, the children can come out stupid or mad. But we had no children. That's why I can never thank God enough for everything turning out so well, Joan. When I think that we have more than we need and that we don't owe a single *cèntim* . . .'

194

We were swamped in debts. I was the only one who knew how hard it was to pay the interest on the mortgages.

'I've been happy with the Senyor,' she continued. 'There was more than one nasty rumour about his liking young girls, but they were all lies. We went to Paris on our honeymoon. I have also been to Rome and Geneva, and to Portugal, too, I think. I'm not sure about that ... I should ask him. Doesn't the Tagus go through Lisbon? See? Then I have been there. The Tagus' waters are green. In Lisbon there's the *Casa del Labrador*, or *del Príncipe*, with the best carriage museum in the world. Did you go to Rome with us? I thought so. The Senyor fought with all the coachmen, who weren't the least bit respectful. One of them tried to kill his horse once. The gondoliers in Venice are also awfully nasty. I've always been afraid in Italy, even though I didn't show it. Outside Rome there's a sanctuary with a Virgin Mary who grants you children if you worship her ... We went there, but we had no children, because it probably wouldn't have been right. If they might have been idiots or simple-minded it's better not to have had them. Isn't that so? Look at Don Felip ...'

Dona Maria Antònia, once so determined and self-assured, now spoke in a questioning tone. She paused for a moment and I took the occasion to see if I could discover anything about that man.

'Is it true that he went mad when he started dressing dolls?'

'Yes. He was very fond of girls. May God forgive him.'

She stopped abruptly and I did not get one more word out of her.

SEVENTEEN

For no particular reason, some superstitious villagers believed that Madò Coloma, the old woman who lived alone up on the hill, would be murdered. Indeed, one day she was found dead at the foot of her bed, and it looked as though she had been strangled. Her nephews, warned by Trinxet, arrived when she was still warm and saw that theft could not have been the motive of the crime. Nothing was missing from her house: neither the goat, nor her clothes, nor even her gold chain, although it had been broken and the pendant was not found. Everyone was terrified, and the people who had thoughtlessly predicted the murder were as surprised as everyone else. Who could have any interest in killing a woman who was no longer in this world? However, people need to point fingers and it was soon known that *sotto voce* two names were being discussed. The first was the English painter. The second (and God knows I was hardly surprised, because I had come to expect it) was the Senyor.

I will never cease to wonder what has done most harm in this world, whether malice or stupidity. In this case, ignorance was the main culprit of the nonsense that was being said about Don Toni.

'He stays awake all night long,' some said.

'He invokes the Devil.'

'He never goes to Church.'

I can assure you that on the days of obligation he never missed the celebration of mass. As far as his practice of sorcery is concerned, I can think of nothing more ridiculous than applying such an accusation to a man so deeply affected by the *illuminati* and who had borrowed the

196

remark from Diderot, 'Reason is a very weak light; along comes a necromancer and puts it out.' As his lack of popularity increased, the facts were distorted, and they even went so far as to accuse him of lending money when in fact it was the villagers who lent money to him, as I already mentioned, and always at high interest.

Nobody was able to discover the source of another rumour, according to which the pendant stolen from Madò Coloma was Masonic, and far-fetched though the connection may have been, the Senyor's name was brought up once again. I took that mysterious death as a warning, almost as a premonition. Evil creeps in when we least expect it, and we are all exposed to its fury. Let us pray to God and trust only in His mercy. That rule, which as a priest I have always preached, was applied better by Dona Maria Antònia than by myself.

'I don't know,' she used to say when she heard us discussing politics, 'why you worry so much about those things. Don't you see that whatever shall be shall be? If we only thought about what happens from day to day and didn't try to have the future at our disposal I think everything would be better. Why are they fighting a war over Cuba? Wars are sinful, apart from the fact that one risks losing them.'

Like the Senyor, she no longer chose to perceive the differences between great things, which all seemed the same to her, whereas she attributed great importance to the ones we usually qualify as little. She did not understand how Don Toni could spend so many hours writing 'for no particular reason'.

'I'm writing about you, Maria Antònia,' he answered on one occasion. 'And about my writing, I'll say, to quote Corneille, that it will preserve the memory of your eyes and that I shall

> *dans mille ans faire croire*
> *ce qu'il me plaira de vous.'*

'Oh, Tonet! Did Corneille think his poems would be read a thousand years later? Besides, what do we care about what they think of us one thousand years from now? I'd like to see what you're writing. Are you only writing about me?'

'I also mention other ladies, but they all lead me back to you. I've never been unfaithful to you.'

'Oh, Tonet . . .'

'I mean I've never been unfaithful to you with anyone who didn't resemble you.'

Dona Maria Antònia seemed to meditate.

'Well, then, why were you unfaithful to me, if they were the same ...? Or didn't you know beforehand?'

The Senyor shook his head.

'No?' Dona Maria Antònia inquired. 'You don't know until afterwards? Now that we brought up the subject, in what way do I resemble Dona Xima?'

'You're both kind-hearted. You both would have offered me a place at your table.'

'And Miss Bernal?'

'Her feet were just like yours.'

'And that Italian lady?'

'She fluttered her eyelashes the same way you do.'

I was about to retire, given the intimate turn the conversation had taken, when Dona Maria Antònia noticed and looked at me mischievously, with the best smile of her youth.

'Joan, don't you think the Senyor is always joking?' she said, pulling my sleeve so I would not leave. 'Pull up a chair and help me roll a ball of yarn.'

It is true that the *Memoirs* are an homage to Dona Maria Antònia. 'I can assure you,' the author writes, 'that I have always found her in each one of the women with whom I have betrayed her, so to speak.' Her husband sees that as a symbol of conjugal fidelity. However, was such a statement of crime really necessary? He himself answers the question: 'Once I had realized that Maria Antònia was morally and psychologically my true wife, proving the fact became unnecessary, just as one doesn't need a thermometer if one knows one's body temperature.' I believe, having seen with my own eyes, that each adventure drew him closer to his wife. Nonetheless, it is not easy to accept his paradoxical statement that one cannot be sure that Philemon was faithful to Baucis precisely because he had never betrayed her.

'That,' I dared to say, 'is like proclaiming that light is dark.'

'The Greeks,' he replied, 'succeeded in proving that snow is black.'

The Greek sophists, naturally. Zeno also proved that movement did not exist. Was the Senyor a humorist, making fun of absolutely everything? Despite appearances, it would be wrong to judge him so. His love for womankind, embodied in Dona Maria Antònia, and for

198

letters, to which he devoted half of his life, present him as the opposite of a sceptic. On occasion I was surprised to see him defend some of the villagers' lowest superstitions. For instance, he believed in the effects of the moon and changes in the weather on people's health and mood. It is true that he may have believed so out of mistrust towards the official scientific truth.

'All medicine,' he said, 'is sorcery. If it were a science, doctors would be able to treat their patients at a distance, just as engineers build bridges without leaving their offices, merely by applying precise rules. There would be certain pills for headaches, other ones for coughs, and so forth. And yet we find that there isn't one kind of headache, but many, and that there are as many illnesses as there are people. Doctors have to "guess" in each case. Haven't you heard people say that a doctor has "guessed" what was wrong with them?'

I took the occasion to tell him some of the rumours that were being spread around the village concerning Madò Coloma's death, the pendant she had worn on a gold chain and the Senyor's supposed sorcery.

'They think I killed her?' he asked.

I was astonished, because that was not what I had said.

'It's all rubbish, Senyor; it's best not to listen to it.'

'You're wrong,' he replied. 'It's quite curious. I would like to know the process by which an old advocate of the Enlightenment like myself can be turned into a sorcerer in the eyes of the people.'

God knows that I also would have liked to know. I mentioned the light in his room after midnight and the candles that were burned in the house, which amounted to a fine sum of money by the end of the year. He listened to me patiently.

'Yes,' he said. 'It doesn't take much. Three hundred years ago, an abbess who died in the odour of sanctity appeared before her daughters and told them she was condemned. "One day," she explained, "while I was praying with my hands crossed, I thought that my hands were beautiful" . . .'

I reminded him that the Church did not recognize that apparition.

'I know,' he replied, 'but many people do without finding it the least bit extraordinary that a poor nun should receive such a cruel punishment for having admired her own hands. The pendant Madò Coloma was wearing,' he added, 'was indeed Masonic.'

I was astonished.

'How does your Honour know?'

It took him a moment to reply. Then he said: 'Because I gave it to her many years ago.'

'To Madò Coloma?'

He smiled sadly.

'Madò Coloma was young once, too. And one of the times I went to France, I became a Freemason. Come, now, Joan, don't fret. I was only with them for a while. I don't know what Freemasonry was like at other times. In my time it was utterly ridiculous. Coloma — Madò Coloma,' he quickly rectified — 'fell in love with the pendant and I gave it to her along with the chain. I also let her have that plot of land. It all happened a long time ago.'

There was a deep silence and I could not break it. Madò Coloma, considered almost a saint, had in fact been a sinner? The Senyor, with his usual cunning, read my mind and tried to comfort me.

'It isn't that bad, Joan,' he said, caressing me kindly. 'Apart from the pendant, there was nothing ... More than fifty years ago, my God!' Then he repeated twice. 'Nothing, nothing ...' and very softly, as if to himself, he added: 'Almost nothing ...'

I looked up.

'Why did your Honour compare her to Dona Maria Antònia the day we went up to visit her?'

'You have a sense of veneration,' he answered, 'and that says very much for your generosity. It's strange that a man as strong, as handsome and as marvellously endowed as you can be so humble and respectful. After all, you're young.' He spoke slowly, and for an instant I thought that instead of saying I was young he was going to say I was nothing but a servant. 'The years will teach you,' he continued, 'that all things have their similarities, and that in the end everything is necessary.'

I asked him for permission to retire and the Senyor pointed to a chair.

'Sit down and listen,' he said. 'That'll teach you to ask questions. When the Senyora and I were reconciled, more than twenty years ago, she went through a difficult period. Nobody noticed because we knew how to hide it. There have been other deranged people at Bearn.' The eighteenth-century shadow of Don Felip, with his light blue uniform and a rose in his hand, seemed to float up, graceful and elegant, like a painting by Van Loo. 'Whenever she signed her name, she wrote

"Xima". Since it happened several times, she began to feel haunted with fears and became neurasthenic. The doctors in the City were at a loss, so I decided to write to Charcot, explaining all the background, part of which he already knew, as he had met Xima and me in Paris. I even sent him photographs of the Senyora, one full face and one profile. Charcot told me what I already knew: that my wife's distress was due to an inner shock. But he added something that had not occurred to me; in her illness, for fear of losing me, she identified with my niece, whom, according to Charcot, she resembles physically and corresponds to in the moral aspect as the positive would to the negative of a photograph.'

'And did your Honour take those statements into account?'

'Now that her mind is going,' the Senyor continued, 'and she is far more relaxed, you've seen how she even asks me directly in what way she resembles Dona Xima.'

'That doctor in Paris who passes judgement without seeing his patients must be quite frivolous indeed.'

The Senyor looked at me. Then he said with the composure so typical of the Bearns: 'If tomorrow it doesn't rain, we can go hunting for thrush.'

I arose and this time he did not detain me. I needed to collect my thoughts and pray. As the years went by, I thought I glimpsed in all those analogies and harmonies of opposites advocated by Don Toni a dangerous return to oriental fatalism.

That crime, those mysteries and that confusion against the background of the apparent peace of Bearn felt like a premonition. Could it have been the prelude to what in military terms we would call a mobilization of the troops? The Senyor had just let me know he did not wish to discuss anything but thrush. Even if he had not changed the subject, that afternoon I would not have asked him whether he believed in the identity of God and the Devil. I would have feared some outrageous reply.

EIGHTEEN

I believe that at times I may be unfair, but my inability to define the Senyor has always tormented me. I cannot even comfort myself by attributing some of his eccentricities to old age. His intelligence only increased as the years went by and while his passions dwindled he perfected his knowledge of people and things. His mistakes were thus even more difficult to forgive. I imagine that the peace he exuded in the last years of his life was more apparent than real; for Dona Maria Antònia, who died in the grace of God, it was quite the contrary. Her decline (more human than the Senyor's intellectual vigour) was observed with irony and tenderness by her husband; for a priest it was also a source of satisfaction.

'The newspaper's very interesting today,' she sometimes used to tell me over breakfast. 'Do you know what it says? "Is it possible to go to the moon?" – "Mountain climber saved by a dog" – "Harem women are very expensive". I'll have to read all this carefully.'

Then she never did, because she forgot to do so. The thought of the comfort of her room, right next to the large drawing room with the fireplace, was deeply satisfying to her.

'Here,' she said, 'I have everything I need. I'm not lacking a thing.' After thinking a while, and not finding anything else worth mentioning (although everything was important to her) she decided to open a curtain: 'See? A clothes hanger, a truly useful item . . .'

Her optimism was such that she once claimed to have discovered how to square the circle.

'Do you think it's that difficult? I don't think one has to be a Greek sage to know how to do it. You make a circle of yarn on a board and then you stretch it out with four pins until it makes a square.'

Her common sense triumphed over theoretical difficulties. Towards the end of her life, with her mind in a state of complete disarray, she made some sad, scandalous statements. I don't know whether the Senyor's scepticism had a part in her raving.

'I can't be sure that I'm a Bearn, Joan. My God, so many things may have happened ... I know I am my parents' real daughter, because my mother was a saint, but what do I know about my grandparents? There have been so many stories ... The Senyor may have found things in the archives, but he never says a thing. He's so secretive ...'

We were in the garden that was slowly becoming a forest. It was a misty morning. Dona Maria Antònia was holding on to my arm and looking at me affectionately. Had she lost her mind or was she humbling herself like a good Christian so I would not feel belittled? At times the thought of her fast-approaching death made her wish to erase from her soul the lack of affection (which after all was natural) she had shown towards me for some time. Furthermore, she had grown stubborn, and since she deplored any form of injustice, at times she could not stand her husband's scientific objectivity. I remember her the last time she lost her temper. It was concerning the Emperors of Turkey.

'They had a special kind of etiquette,' the Senyor explained to me. 'When an ambassador requested an audience, the Emperor called his vizier and said: "Feed and dress this ambassador." Once that had been done, he ordered: "Let that animal in."'

Dona Maria Antònia, who sat by the fire and appeared to be sleeping, looked up.

'You call that etiquette, Tonet? Where on earth do you get these things from, may I ask? I simply can't believe that a king, even if he's a heretic, could say such indecencies. And if he did, that's no reason for you to repeat them. I don't believe it. I simply don't.'

She was indignant and we had to distract her by talking about Rome.

'Tell me, Tonet,' she asked, 'why didn't I go to see the Pope with you?'

'Because you had a cold,' the Senyor calmly replied.

'That's right. What a pity!'

Aside from a few outbursts such as the one I just mentioned, her life became more and more placid as we drew closer to the final events. Did I mention that Madò Coloma's death was a sort of prelude to the end soon to come? It is easy to prophesy a *posteriori*. The truth is that those months elapsed in the most delightful serenity. The last winter (Your ways, my Lord, are inscrutable) was the mildest we ever had. I mentioned at the beginning of this second part that as Dona Maria Antònia's discipline relaxed, it did so with such skill that its disorder seemed like a new order. The Senyors woke up later and later each day, and their schedule was thrown out to such a degree that breakfast was almost at lunchtime, and lunch was moved up to mid-afternoon, the time when the Senyora had in past years taken her cup of lemon verbena and her biscuits; she now either missed that refreshment or decided not to have supper. The hours slipped through our fingers. We never left the upper floor nor received any visitors, and yet we never had time for anything.

I write to you from the same rectangular drawing room that connects on the right with the Senyor's room and on the left with Dona Maria Antònia's. I have already said that on one of the longer walls of the rectangle, the one opposite the entrance to the house, there is a fireplace with a balcony overlooking the garden on either side. I must remind you of the setting where my story finally unfolds, Miquel. At nine, either Tomeu or myself, if he was out working in the fields, lit the fire. Then I devoted myself to my prayers until the Senyor got out of bed. Above the fireplace there is a large mirror surrounded with the sort of classical décor reminiscent of the Trianon or even more of the small palace of La Moncloa. That mirror reflects the door in such a way that as you're sitting by the fire you can see someone arrive without turning around. Simultaneously, the balcony windows offer a view of the garden that is becoming a forest, and one can sit there, warm and dry, and watch the rain falling outside. Gold damask curtains hang from the magnificent doorways and French windows. The furniture is upholstered in light blue, with sprigs, in the French fashion. It will seem strange to you that the Senyors spent every day in a room like that. I had tried to convince them to move into the smaller room by the landing which is used as an anteroom to the archives, because my benefactor had the bad habit of carrying his inkwell with him all around the house and the upholstery in the drawing room is delicate. I was not successful and I now think that

204

having no children they did well to enjoy what was entirely theirs, like a legacy from their ancestors; it provided them with comfort while maintaining the illusion of their past grandeur. I must tell you, Miquel, that in this very drawing room they were on the verge of not having enough to eat. For months nothing but broad beans were served at Bearn, and we all ate the same food as the farmers, except for an occasional cake or glass of sherry, which I tried to make available to the Senyors.

As I prayed, poking the fire, I witnessed the preparation of their morning routine and heard them emerge into the light of conscience from the depths of sleep.

'Has the clock already struck nine, Tonet?' came the hesitant voice of Dona Maria Antònia from the left.

'I think it did a while ago,' came his answer from the right.

There was a moment of silence followed by the Senyora's comment of surprise, half concerned and half delighted, speaking softly, as if to herself: 'My goodness! Time simply flies in the morning ... And it feels so nice to be in bed ... I suppose I must start thinking about getting up.'

Then there was the sound of a bottle tinkling against the marble of her dressing table, followed by a waft of perfume. The Senyora wiped her forehead with rose water to wake herself up. In the mirror above the fireplace, Tomeu advanced, tall and dark, walking over to the doorway on the right.

'Senyor, would you like to drink some coffee?'

That expression, to 'drink some coffee' was a habit we couldn't break. 'Animals drink coffee, assuming they like it,' the Senyor told him. 'People *have a cup*. They have a cup of coffee or a glass of milk. Try to remember the next time.' It was a lost cause, however.

'Come in, Tomeu. What's the weather like?'

And he disappeared to the right holding a cup of coffee with both hands, as if it weighed several pounds. With his African hair and his dark skin, it looked as if the sun of a beautiful Mallorcan day had burst into the bedroom, locked in his physical structure. Catalineta went over to the door on the left and asked Dona Maria Antònia if she wanted to have breakfast.

'Haven't I already had it?' the Senyora replied. 'I thought you'd brought me hot chocolate and an *ensaïmada*.'

'No, Senyora. That was yesterday.'

'Oh . . . it was yesterday . . .'

'There are still some *ensaïmades*. Would you like one?'

'Come in and open the window. I certainly would like one. Who wouldn't? They're so good!'

Tomeu listed the events of the day to the Senyor.

'The young mule won't eat. She doesn't want hay or alfalfa.'

'What does she want?'

'She'll only eat grain.'

'What a fussy animal she's turned out to be! Come in and open the window.'

Catalineta arrived, pale and ethereal, with Dona Maria Antònia's breakfast, and as she set down the tray, she asked with her most candid smile, despite the fact that it was still a couple of weeks before Carnival: 'Senyora, will you give me permission to dress up?'

'She certainly is fussy,' said Tomeu's firm, masculine voice from the right. 'And it's your Honour's fault for spoiling her with sugar lumps.'

'Maybe it's your fault for not walking her enough.'

'That's because your Honour won't let me whip her.'

'Would you like me to whip you?'

'If I deserved it, I would, Senyor.'

'That's a good answer. Watch out, then.'

There was a pause and I returned to my prayer book.

'And what kind of costume will you wear?' the Senyora asked. 'I'll lend you my wedding dress. No, I don't want an *ensaïmada*,' she added, forgetting that she had asked for it. 'Ask Tomeu to tell the Senyor on my behalf that he can eat it.'

Catalineta's voice took on a mysterious tone: 'The Senyor won't eat a thing; he only *drinks* coffee.'

She was in love with Tomeu and it was impossible to make her speak properly. The *ensaïmada* passed from the girl to the boy and to the Senyor's room. In the ensuing silence I made out his clear, low voice: '*Ensaïmada*? I wouldn't dream of it. Eat it and don't say a thing. Quick, the Senyora's about to call you. Now she'll want you to tell her if it's nice out.'

'What's the weather like, Tomeu?' Dona Maria Antònia's clear voice inquired.

Catalineta came to the rescue of her beloved.

'It's raining, Senyora.'

'I didn't ask you. I'm speaking to Tomeu. Has he lost his tongue? Goodness, what a disaster! We'll have to send for a doctor from the City.' In a theatrical aside, she added to herself: 'They think I'm stupid, and I'm neither that stupid nor that soft in the head.'

She had moments of great lucidity. At times she seemed to be observing herself from the outside, like the Senyor.

'We don't really have many problems,' she told me. 'As a matter of fact, we don't have a single one.'

And a few moments later, lifting her head and adopting the inquisitive tone so frequent in her ever since we returned from our travels, she added: 'I wonder if something will happen . . .'

She did not say it out of fear as much as to have others assure her that she was wrong. I was the one who was panic-stricken. It was obvious that such a good life had to come to some kind of terrible end. If it did not happen spontaneously, we would take it upon ourselves to stage the tragedy. How would the misfortune present itself? Illness, disagreements, war, total ruin? The sword of Damocles does not threaten only tyrants: all of Humanity lives in the fear of the Evil that seems to be necessary to attain Goodness, or, in other words, Eternal Salvation.

NINETEEN

Those long hours by the fireside . . . how sweetly their two lives went by, seemingly so close to peace — and I do not mean that of the approaching grave, but the blessed peace of the chosen few. Memories seem as nebulous as the sky or the mountain of Es Teix that rose up on the north side of the house outside the balconies of the blue and gold room. Dona Maria Antònia confused dates, travels and facts, so her stories were tinted with the poetry of dreams. The Senyor came to the rescue undoing her mistakes and restoring the truth, making me feel in a different way the poetry that according to Pythagoras is found in numbers and in the harmony of the stars. The fog alternately drew and opened its curtains over Es Teix and on the two lives that tried to stop time and freeze the Absolute once and for all. The Senyor had told me that nothing is as absolute as that which is conventional, and that the platinum meter in Meudon is a meter for the simple reason that we call it so. Once again the name creates the Universe. He knew that those remembrances, those travels and anecdotes were the products of his fantasy and of the words he used to forge them.

'Nobody,' he said, 'has really seen the Place de l'Etoile and the eleven avenues that branch out from it. One can only see it if one imagines it drawn out on a ground plan, as did the architect who designed it. If one tries to see it by standing in the square, one can't grasp the whole thing and only catches unconnected pieces. The Place de l'Etoile is only beautiful with one's eyes closed.'

I lowered mine to remember that one night, almost twenty years back, near the downstairs fireplace, the Senyor contemplated Dona

Xima, dressed in white, entering the box at the Paris Opera. 'You could see me clearly from far away with your eyes closed?'

I can assure you, Miquel, that this drawing room where I now write, where I have lived with the Senyors and where I continue to seek shelter, is no longer the same. When I look at it I can barely recognize it and only in the night does it appear in the solitude of my room just as it was in the last few years; in my dreams, I can still hear those conversations in scattered pieces, chasing after days long gone.

'. . . What did they charge us for that pheasant at the Palais Royal, Tonet?'

'The Restaurant Véfour. The one with red carpeting.'

'Tomeu says the young mule refuses to eat.'

'I don't trust those Venetian gondoliers.'

'Rossini copied Mozart.'

'What do you know, Tonet? How would you know if the seats are numbered?'

Es Teix was covered in shadows and that premonition of a storm heightened the indoor peace of the drawing room.

'It looks as though it might snow,' the Senyor said. 'We're lucky we have this fireplace.'

Opening my eyes to tell Tomeu to fill the woodshed I snap back into reality: never again will we have to light the fire. I fall asleep again and the kind ghosts that triumph over time keep on speaking softly.

'Wouldn't you like to hear *Manon*?'

'The Hohenzollern were never kings.'

'I didn't recognize them. That's why I was so polite.'

'Marry them, Joan.'

'It's nice to know that we don't owe anyone a *cèntim*.'

'It's twelve. Should we say our three Ave Marias?'

'Light a candle . . .'

After lunch, which was served in the same room, Dona Maria Antònia used to fall asleep again. I used to take those moments to try to draw the Senyor towards religious practices.

'How long has it been since your Honour last made a confession?'

'That depends on what you call a confession. I think I make confessions all the time. Besides, I'll try to make my *Memoirs* as accurate as possible.'

I pointed out that a confession is not a mere listing of the acts committed, but rather an acknowledgement that requires pain and the

209

intention of not repeating the sins. He skilfully eluded the subject.

'At my age? How do you expect me to run off to Paris with a young girl now?'

'Yes, but what if you were thirty or forty years younger?'

'Forty years younger ... There are certain things you simply cannot understand.'

'I was sent off to a seminary when I was a child, Senyor.'

He looked at me, sitting up straight in his armchair.

'I realize that I'm selfish,' he said, 'but I have trouble putting myself in other people's shoes. That's why I'll never be a good novelist, which is what I would have liked to be. I can't imagine how a young, strong, healthy man like you ...'

It was not the first time he alluded to my supposed physical superiority and I thought it my duty to interrupt him.

'Your Honour is forgetting that I'm a priest.'

He took me by the arm and caressed it firmly, as if he were giving me a massage.

'I'm sure you're sincere,' he replied. 'One is always learning new things, even at eighty, Son.'

He seemed so engrossed that I dared not add a word. We were both thinking about that tremendous scandal, that mortal and dazzling beauty that had once shaken the capital of the world.

'You know that the Emperor gave her a town house near the Etoile. She had ruined Campo Formio. Her success didn't last very long: before the end of that year the Empire collapsed.'

'Didn't you think of her the last time you were in Paris?'

'I tried not to. We'd stopped writing quite a while before.'

I was surprised, because I did not suspect that they kept on writing after the Senyor was reconciled with his wife. He read my mind.

'She wrote me a few times giving me news and asking me for money. The revolutionaries burned the Tuileries and the town house at Etoile went with it. In my *Memoirs* I describe her flight from Paris. Can you guess how she got out? She fled with Eugenia de Montijo. It's not publicly known, nor would it be right to divulge it out of respect towards Eugenia, who is an aunt of the House of Alba. Naturally, over time, what is now gossip will become history.'

I could not overcome my astonishment. The Senyor added: 'Between you and me, I'll tell you that the Empress was terrified. They say she didn't want to leave the Tuileries, but that was because

210

she didn't know where to go and because the *communards* had besieged the palace. Then Xima appeared and they left in disguise through the Place Saint-Germain l'Auxerrois and took a hackney to the house of the Empress's dentist, an American by the name of Evans. By now it's a known historical fact. However, what they left out is that Evans didn't help them escape from Paris out of loyalty towards Eugenia de Montijo, but because he was Dona Xima's lover. Don't say a word about this for the time being, Joan.'

'But the Empress . . .'

'She knew everything,' he interrupted. 'Such are the wonders of the Earth.'

Then he started telling me for the hundredth time about the première of *Faust* and the brilliance of Gounod.

'In a century like ours, which has produced so many musicians, one could say that Gounod is not an innovator. However, he's an inspired and skilled composer who works with the materials supplied by others. Wagner has undoubtedly revolutionized many things, but he lacks Gounod's sense of proportion, he doesn't know when to stop. Some call that genius. I call it obstinacy. What does it matter, in a delicate palace such as the Petit Trianon, if Gabriel didn't put in a single column or window that hadn't been invented long before? None of those elements were the least bit innovative; everyone had seen them before. That's precisely why Gabriel was able to use them so expertly.'

Dona Maria Antònia opened her eyes.

'Don't you dream of starting work on the house. I don't like having masons around; they get dust all over the place.'

'We were talking about operas.'

She threatened him with a mixture of amusement and vexation: 'Tonet, Tonet, I don't like to hear about operas.'

'Now don't start bringing up things of the past.'

'Of the past? I'm not sure they are.'

'Don't you thing *we're* something of the past?'

She fell back into her reverie, mumbling: 'I know he has repented. Since he has no choice . . .'

TWENTY

On Shrove Sunday, after what for me had been a very agitated week, misfortune started to rear its ugly head: somebody had spread the news that Dona Xima had just arrived in the City. With the excuse that I was going to see the priest, I ran down to the village. It was raining and the paths were like rivers. I spoke to almost everyone in the village only to end up more confused than I had started. Some travelling merchants had brought the news and vanished. Nobody knew exactly what village they had left for. Their stories had been distorted: two old women claimed that a lady who was related to the Senyors had come begging for money; others asserted she was the Queen of France.

I returned in distress. Despite the confusion, it was obvious that it all referred to Dona Xima. I could not sleep all night long. What would she be like now? In Paris I had dreamt of her in different forms, before she was embodied in a ravaged woman in front of the church of Saint Roch. 'I owe twenty-four francs for the room,' she told me. She was wearing an old pair of shoes with crooked heels. I had seen lettuce leaves peeping out of her cloth bag. The Queen of France . . . a beggar . . . It could only be her. And assuming she had decided to come back to Mallorca, it was obvious that she would try to see the Senyors. Now past fifty, it was time for her to play the part of the penitent. Yet did I have a right to assume that her repentance would necessarily be fake? One of the greatest poets of our times* wrote in a painfully sceptical poem:

*The paragraph that appears in the original is the following: 'One of the greatest poets of our times, Don Ramon de Campoamor, whose glory can only be compared

212

que después que se extinguen las pasiones
yo he visto sorprendentes conversiones
a la moral y a la virtud cristianas. _*

All of Campoamor's wit cannot prove that there are no truly repentant sinners, touched by the grace of God. That this divine grace tends to appear when the mortal graces have dwindled offers a subject that is easy prey to the irony of unbelievers, whereas those of us who have faith know that the flesh is ephemeral and only the soul is everlasting.

On Monday the weather was fine. The sun was as bright as in summer. I was calm when I awoke; my anguish had lodged itself so deeply within me that nothing could make me lose my composure. I entrusted myself to God's will and opened the window to look out. Catalina and Tomeu were talking in the courtyard.

'The Senyora says we should dress up as bride and groom,' she said.

'You and your big mouth,' Tomeu replied. 'Now the Senyor knows that I was planning to pull a prank on him. I was embarrassed.'

'Do you really think he wouldn't have recognized you?'

'You can be sure!'

'Watch out! He might have thought you were a pretty girl!'

'Pretty or not, I would have got some money for sweets out of him.'

'With those hands and those shoulders of yours . . . I don't know. At least you've got a nice waistline.'

'Get off. Go away.'

I remembered that Catalineta had mysteriously confided in the Senyora about Tomeu's plans.

'No, I don't want him to play pranks on the Senyor,' Dona Maria Antònia had replied. 'That's the last thing we need, now that he's calmed down. Why doesn't he dress up as a groom? You put on my wedding dress and the two of you take a walk around the courtyard. I'll look at you from the window.'

After the fire of passion has died down/I have seen surprising conversions to Christian morals and virtue. (Translator's note).

---

to that of the painter Horace Vernet . . .' I have chosen to moderate such a strange and hyperbolic judgement that could adversely affect the reader's view of Don Joan's personality, a man of culture and talent, and yet also a man of his time. (Editor's note).

Those words, uttered with the best of intentions, were slightly irresponsible. The Senyor, who knew better, had taken the farmboy aside and scolded him in his own way. 'Be careful with Catalineta. Sooner or later, I find out about everything around here, and I don't want to hear about it.'

'I swear . . .'

'Don't swear. You're such a scatterbrain . . . You can't even remember to shut the door.'

That was a tacit authorization for all kinds of transgressions, even though it was true that Tomeu lacked the wits to see it as such. However, he did have an instinct for doing things without permission, and more than once I had found myself in the position of having to tell the Senyor, who, as he had just said, preferred not to hear about such matters.

Hours later, unwittingly, he was forced to hear everything, because it is not enough to close your eyes before evil to avoid its influence. We were sitting by the fireplace when the Senyora walked in with Catalineta.

'Let's see if you recognize this bride who's come to visit. Take a good look at her.'

She looked beautiful. In the white dress, with her eyes lowered, she was a living image of purity. The orange blossoms in her hair were no finer than her skin. The Senyor stared at her for a moment and then said harshly: 'I think that train's too long.'

'It's my dress, Tonet,' Dona Maria Antònia retorted. 'Why, don't you remember?'

'How could I forget, my dear? Where's Tomeu?'

The girl lowered her eyes even more. The Senyor was suddenly amused.

'What if you lost your groom?'

'I don't need one.'

'Don't say that. I happen to know . . .'

Shame and anger brought her to the verge of tears. Dona Maria Antònia interjected: 'Don't embarrass her, Tonet.'

'Don't embarrass her? Why doesn't she do things right, then?' he said under his breath.

She burst out crying.

'See, Tonet? You always have to say the unkindest things! I don't know why you had to go and pick on this poor girl.'

214

'Let it be, then. If I must give a warning, it will be in English: *Be good, and if it is not possible, be careful.*' He left the room. Catalineta, on the verge of a nervous fit, was sobbing out loud.

'I didn't understand what he said, Joan,' Dona Maria Antònia said. 'Did you?'

'Yes, Senyora,' I told her sadly, 'but I can't translate it just now.'

She started to lose her patience.

'Stop crying, now. Why are you crying if you didn't even understand what he said?'

'But I did!'

'Well, what did he say?'

'He said he knew about it, and it's all a lie.'

'Catalineta, what are you talking about? What's a lie?'

The girl was stamping her feet like a little child. The crown of orange blossoms had fallen to the ground.

'What the Senyor said ... it can't be true!'

'How would you know what is and what isn't true, you silly girl?'

At that moment Tomeu came in. I do not know whether he had heard something, but he looked rather shocked.

'Come over here, Tomeu,' the Senyora said.

The bride screamed in the midst of a nervous fit: 'Don't mention him! I don't want to see him!'

Dona Maria Antònia turned to her, twisting her neck. Fragile and small, she looked like a porcelain doll.

'Well, well, what sort of manners are these?' she said, calmly. 'Is this what you've dressed up as a bride for? Joan,' she added, 'take this little mule down to the stable and send up the cook. She won't see me for three days. And she'll never serve me breakfast again.'

It was true, God knows, that she would never serve the Senyora breakfast again. I sent the girl to the kitchen and then took Tomeu aside to question him. I was slightly nervous.

'Speak up. I think you owe us an explanation. What are these lies about?'

The Senyor was staring at us from his room with a smile on his face. Dona Maria Antònia had vanished.

'I haven't done anything wrong,' Tomeu mumbled.

'Who says you have?'

'I swear ...'

'Very well,' the Senyor interjected. 'Tell us what it is you swear.'

'I . . .'

The Senyor seemed amused.

'Question him, Joan. I'd like to know . . .'

I asked the question directly.

'What happened between you and Catalineta?'

'Nothing.'

'Well, then, why was she crying?'

'I don't know.'

'You haven't the faintest idea.'

'No.'

The Senyor sat down by the fire.

'The fact is, Joan,' he said as he stoked the fire, 'that this idiot may not even know. Just in case, I think we ought to marry them. Marry them, Joan.'

'But . . .'

'Can't you see they've had Easter before Palm Sunday?'

There was a strange, disturbing glint of mischief in his eye. He started writing things down in a notebook and waved to us to leave. I came across his notes later on, but they had been crossed out in such a way that I could decipher nothing but a few syllables that seemed to spell the name Catalineta.

I took Tomeu to the room by the landing in the hope of finding out the facts, but this attempt was no more successful than the first.

'Very well,' I finally said. 'Do you want to marry her?'

'She says we haven't got any clothes,' was his reply.

I was horrified to be faced with such stupidity, such innocence or such evil.

'And what if you have a child?'

'Maybe we won't.'

'Aha! Then you mean . . .'

But he meant nothing, absolutely nothing. I looked at him. He was handsome, strong, dark, and bold. One curl fell across his forehead. As his beauty increased, his intelligence only seemed to diminish. (A fortnight later the doctor from Inca cleared up any possible doubts and I married them as soon as I could.) In the midst of our exchange, the Senyora walked in.

'Why didn't you get dressed up?' she said. 'Oh, goodness, I don't know how you dare look so shabby in my presence. Now I understand

216

why Catalineta didn't even want to hear your name. Go away and don't come back until you look presentable.'

After these words, proof of the arbitrariness of human criteria, she proposed that we play a game of cards.

'I think,' she said, 'that the Senyor has been cheating lately. I can't trust him, and the worst part is that he always has an explanation and tells you that what's black is white. I know him all too well, better than you could possibly imagine. Once, when we were children, he kissed me. He was very naughty. I have never told a soul. We were in a dark corridor.'

The Senyor, dozing off near the fire, appeared not to be listening, but mumbled in his sleep. 'Corridors are made for kissing . . .'

She continued: 'He often came to the town house at Bearn to play with me. He was short, dark and naughty. I don't know what I fell in love with, Joan. Naturally, ever since we were born, our families had decided that we'd be married. Their interests were so much a part of it . . . They said that if we didn't marry we might have an awful lawsuit and end up penniless. Isn't that ridiculous, going to court to end up penniless? But you know that many noblemen do so. Besides, it was only natural that the house at Bearn and the estate should be reunited. I don't know why, now that I think of it: once we're dead, with no children . . . But then again, who else could I have married? We've had a good life. In all these years, we've had no real misfortunes. He's very good, particularly now. God always knows how to work things out, doesn't He? He makes us good when we're old so we can go to Heaven. I think Tonet will go to Heaven, don't you agree? What do you think?'

It was the first time that in speaking to me she called him by his name instead of referring to him as the Senyor. She gave me an anxious glance; she needed to be comforted. It would have been a crime not to do so.

'The Senyor is good.'

She was only senile every now and then.

'I know,' she replied, 'but we all sin. Do you think he has repented of his mistakes.'

That question tortured me.

'Yes, Senyora,' I replied.

Her face lit up with happiness.

'See? Now everything's erased and we can die in peace. All I hope is that God will let us stay together.'

A moment earlier the Senyor had been nodding off in his armchair, but for some reason I suddenly wondered whether he was only pretending to sleep. I pointed to him inquisitively and Dona Maria Antònia smiled.

'Can you hear us, Tonet?'

He snored faintly. It was obvious that he was awake.

'He can't hear us,' said Dona Maria Antònia. 'Today I finished a novena to Jesus Christ for a peaceful death, because we probably won't live much longer.'

I replied that they were in good health and that they could still live for many years.

'May God's will be done,' she said. Then, in a transition that seemed brusque and yet was not so because it merely reflected an inner rhythm, she added: 'I certainly don't work much. I don't do a thing. All I do is play cards, which is a vice, and walk around the garden and stare out of the balcony ... Lord knows how long ago I started to crochet a bedspread! I think it was when Tonet and I made our peace again.' — She said Tonet for a second time. — 'I wonder if I'll get it finished before I die.'

She did not. Never again did she take it in her hands, but God granted her what she desired: the death of the righteous and never to see her husband's grave.

TWENTY ONE

Around noon it started raining again and after lunch we sought the comfort of the fireplace, where the Senyors soon fell asleep. I opened my breviary and began to pray. I lifted my head now and again to listen to the silence, that marvellous silence that could be shattered by misfortune at any moment. 'If you have riches,' says Thomas à Kempis, 'do not be proud of them, as they do not last; only God is everlasting.' I was waiting for the storm to break; I was sure it had to happen and was not the least bit surprised when a voice called up from downstairs: 'Don Joan, you have a visitor.'

I left the drawing room. Downstairs stood Dona Xima in a pitiful state. She was soaked to the skin; her shoes were covered in mud. She was much thinner than when I had seen her in Paris outside Saint Roch. At first sight, her thinness made her look young and graceful, but in fact she was a wreck. Her face was covered in herpetic red blotches. When she saw me she tried to smile.

'You didn't expect this visit, did you, Joan? How are my aunt and uncle?'

I was dumbfounded. I finally managed to say: 'You've arrived on foot . . .'

She gave me an inappropriately mischievous glance, as if she still considered herself a desirable woman.

'I thought I'd get some exercise,' she said. 'I left the horses in the village so the coachmen wouldn't get wet. I love the rain!' She hummed:

Il pleut, il pleut, bergère,
presse tes blancs moutons . . . '

Her face was all made up. She spoke incoherently and gesticulated, twisting her mouth as if she suffered from a nervous disorder. Her fickleness and her lack of common sense were precisely what had made her fashionable in the French society of the Second Empire twenty years earlier, when she was beautiful and fascinating. To that extent do our senses lead us astray. When she laughed, her mouth twitched even more and her expression became downright painful.

'Please be so kind as to wait a moment. I'll tell the Senyors you're here.'

I found Don Toni awake and he looked at me with curiosity. I made a gesture asking him to speak softly, pointing to the Senyora.

'No, no. She might as well know. What could Xima want now? Maria Antònia, Xima's downstairs.'

The Senyora sat bolt upright in her chair. I witnessed the transformation: her skin turned the colour of earth and the muscles in her face relaxed.

'Oh, Tonet,' she said in a shrill voice, 'what will we do now?'

'Whatever you say.'

'This is horrible! It's the worst thing that could happen to us. I'd already heard that she was trying to pull something on you . . . '

'But, dear . . . '

'Everything was so nice and peaceful . . . In this house, now that we never leave these mountains . . . '

Her eyes had filled with tears. The Senyor looked at her and then at me without understanding what had happened. He had spent his entire life trying to eliminate every marvellous element from his existence and now the marvellous had taken revenge by presenting a conclusion he could no longer understand. Why had Dona Maria Antònia had that premonition? It was obvious that fate had finally caught up with them. Only God is Eternal; the rest comes to an end, and the end had arrived. The small, fragile woman went over to her husband's side.

'Does she want to take you back to Paris?' she asked softly.

He kissed her tenderly.

'Joan, tell her to leave. Did she come on foot?'

'Yes, Senyor. In this rain . . . '

220

Dona Maria Antònia stopped crying. She had recovered her countenance and her concern for the practical aspects of life.

'On foot? Then what does she need all those carriages and liveries for?'

'Carriages?' said the Senyor. 'She's a pauper now. Didn't you know?'

'Xima, a pauper? No, I didn't know. Weren't we the ones who were penniless? What happened to her?'

'We've talked about it a thousand times: the *Communards* burned down her house, the Emperor died . . .'

'Poor Xima, I had no idea! Did you know, Joan? Is she wet?'

'Soaked to the skin.'

'Well, that's just terrible,' she said sharply. 'Send her in so she can get warm.'

'Do you want her to come up?' the Senyor inquired.

'What else? Send up a bottle of sherry and a piece of *ensaïmada*. A pauper? Such a beautiful, elegant lady . . . Oh, my God!'

Suddenly her sadness disappeared and she put her hand on her husband's shoulder.

'You've always had good taste, dear,' she said.

I sent Dona Xima in and retired to say my prayers. I could not concentrate, and when about half an hour later I returned to see if they needed anything, they were chatting contentedly by the fire. In front of them was a little table with some pieces of *ensaïmada* and glasses. They were talking about Paris.

'Is that famous restaurant still there? I can't remember . . . What was it called, Tonet? It was near the Louvre. Don't you know which I mean? We ordered pheasant and they brought it in with all its feathers. . . .'

'The Restaurant Véfour, in the Palais Royal,' the Senyor replied.

'They had very handsome twin waiters.'

'Twins? Goodness, no! They were just dressed the same.'

'Dressed and combed the same way, in tails. Do they still serve there?'

Dona Xima laughed with a glass of sherry in her hand.

'If they were really that handsome, they probably serve some purpose.'

Dona Maria Antònia did not seem to understand her niece's cynical reply. Suddenly she asked: 'Tell me, is the Emperor dead?'

Dona Xima was taken aback. The Senyor smiled and came to her rescue.

'You must be out of work now. You were his secretary, weren't you?'

'Thank you, Tonet,' Dona Xima said softly, and added in a louder tone: 'I handled his Spanish correspondence.'

'What I still don't understand,' the Senyora said, 'is why you went to Paris when you were so young.'

Dona Xima twisted her mouth in a gesture that tried to be a smile. Suddenly she stood up and came over to me as if she were going to tell me something, but she quickly sat down again. The Senyor asked how the Emperor had died.

'He wasn't able to bear the defeat.'

'What defeat are you referring to?'

She fluttered her eyelashes the way she had in her youth.

'I don't understand, Uncle Tonet.'

'What happened to that twenty-year old dragoon?'

Dona Xima hummed:

'Il repose au Père Lachaise
par un prix exorbitant.'

'He died?'

'Who died?' the Senyor asked.

'One of Louis Napoleon's assistants.'

Dona Xima wiped away a tear.

'And Campo Formio?'

'He rebuilt his fortune. Now he's the leader of the Socialist Party. He won't have anything to do with me.'

'And what about Offenbach? You had a good voice. Didn't you sing in operettas?'

'I've lost my voice. I've also lost my figure, my youth . . .'

Dona Maria Antònia looked at her affectionately: 'But you're just a child, Xima.'

'You see me in a good light.'

'But you're just a little girl. So beautiful and so elegant . . .'

Her niece burst out crying in hysterical sobs.

'Stop, Aunt Maria. I'm finished; everyone's abandoned me. I should have died long ago.'

'There, there, child . . .'

222

When she calmed down she told them about her situation with some coherence. In the City she had been thrown out of the inn because she could not pay her bills. Her acquaintances no longer greeted her in the street. The night before, she had slept in a confessional in the Cathedral.

'Goodness gracious,' said Dona Maria Antònia, 'I didn't know it was possible! You didn't even have enough *cèntims* for an inn? Have you forgotten who you are? Don't you have anything at all? You had some jewels ...'

'Yes, Aunt Maria Antònia. I used to spend all my money on diamonds. I'd been told they were a good investment.'

'Well, then, sell your diamonds.'

'I sold them a long time ago.'

The last few years had been horrible for her; her only comfort had been the thought of suicide. For that reason she never travelled without a little box with three poisoned chocolates that had been given to her by some criminal. With those chocolates, she explained, one could never die of hunger, because upon eating them one fell asleep and never woke again.

'Smell them, Aunt Maria Antònia. The chocolate must be delicious.'

She laughed as she showed them to the Senyors. It almost looked as though she were offering them. Dona Maria Antònia took one, and I, without thinking, grabbed her hand.

'I don't intend to kill myself, Joan,' she said. 'I feel fine in the world of the living.'

Dona Xima was pleased again, for no apparent reason, and hummed a song. Suddenly she started discussing business. A doctor had proposed that they form a partnership to sell a cure for tuberculosis that consisted of injecting horse's blood into the patients, but first one had to give the horses the disease. One needed capital for that.

'Who is this doctor?' the Senyor asked.

'Well, I don't really think he's a doctor, but he's very knowledgeable.'

'Giving horses a disease ...' said Dona Maria Antònia. 'Such noble, necessary animals.'

'But it's in order to heal people, Aunt Maria Antònia. If I only had ten thousand *duros* ...'

'I don't like the idea,' the Senyor decreed. 'Can't you think of anything else?'

223

'Yes. I could open an inn.'

'That's better. A good inn, with a bathtub and everything. We could help you out, couldn't we, Maria Antònia?'

'Certainly. But I do think you should only take in ladies who are travelling alone.'

Don Toni pointed out that inns usually take in both ladies and gentlemen.

'In that case, it's out of the question,' his wife retorted. 'Xima has always been a good girl and I wouldn't like her to be criticized now.'

Uncle and niece glanced at each other. Dona Maria Antònia continued: 'Ladies travelling alone, only if one knows who they are and where they come from . . . Provided they go to church . . .'

'If we start making so many demands, there's no knowing how things will go. Travellers don't like . . .'

'In that case they can go elsewhere; we don't need them. There's no reason why Xima should put up with any sort of riffraff. She can stay with us and keep us company.'

Dona Xima kissed her hand.

'Oh, thank you! But it can't be. You would always remember . . .'

'Hush,' said the Senyor softly, 'I think she's forgotten.'

'But didn't you say you were penniless?' her aunt insisted. 'Besides, I think a young girl oughtn't to run an inn. Isn't that so? We'll ask Joan. Don Joan, I mean,' she corrected herself; 'We call him Joan because we've known him since he was a boy, you know.'

Despite her madness, Dona Xima stared at me with what was left of her worldly impertinence.

'Don't worry, Aunt Maria Antònia, to me he will always be Don Joan.'

I felt my blood rushing to my face and stared her back in the eye.

'I was once the swineherd of Bearn, Senyora.'

The Senyor looked up from his outdated newspaper to reprimand me: 'Don't be arrogant, Joan. There are certain kinds of humility that I don't like at all.'

'We are all the product of our actions,' said Dona Maria Antònia.

'Well, well. That isn't entirely true either,' the Senyor replied, and hid behind his newspaper again. A moment later I heard him murmur:

'What in the devil's name is this? It says the King went hunting, and he's been dead for years!'

TWENTY TWO

When we finished supper I locked myself in my room. I had barely been able to pray all day long. I was finishing my duties when Dona Xima appeared. I looked at the clock; it was close to midnight. I opened the door and she threw herself at my feet. I cannot put what she said in writing. Even if it were not under the seal of confession I would not do so. She kissed my hands and wet them with her tears. During that scene, which left me shattered, she was lost in despair; her repentance seemed sincere. She did nothing but praise the Senyors' kindness and the mercy of the Lord who had taken pity on her soul.

'This is the beginning of a new life for me,' she said when I had absolved her.

I allowed myself to be deceived, maybe because her deception was sweet. I felt as though that sinner's repentance preceded a great danger, not only for her, but for all of us.

'Now that your life is resolved and you are determined never to give in to sin,' I told her, 'you absolutely must destroy the chocolates that would have provided you with damnation rather than the rest that you seek.'

She told me that she had already thought of that and that she would throw them out of the window, but it seemed to me that such a momentous and symbolic act required a little more solemnity, apart from the fact that they could have harmed any child or animal that happened to walk by.

'You'll give them to me tomorrow after Communion,' I told her. 'I'll expect you at the chapel at half past seven. Devote the hours that are left to meditation, with the box in front of you, and when you've received Communion you'll give it to me and I myself will throw it in the fire.'

Morning was breaking when we parted. She did not appear in the chapel at the appointed time, and after waiting for her quite a while, I was greatly surprised to see her talking to the Senyor by the fireplace. I stopped on the threshold and stood there. Her silhouette was thin and graceful; she still looked young. For a moment she threw her head back and laughed, closing her eyes, in an improper abandon that reminded me of the sentence she had uttered a long time back by the other fireplace downstairs: 'You know I'm nothing but a stray.' I was about to retire when the Senyor called me: 'Come in and sit down; you'll frighten Dona Xima, so tall and dressed in black like that.'

She greeted me with a wave of her hand.

'Don Joan is going to lend me a cassock as a costume.'

I thought I heard a note of irony in her *Don*.

I pretended not to have heard her and sat at the opposite end of the room to open my breviary. They continued their conversation.

'What I would like to know,' my benefactor said, 'is how the Empress decided to run away with you, after everything that had happened. You've always been a liar, Xima.'

'Who, me?'

'Yes. You never take anything seriously. I wouldn't like to have been deceived by you in my *Memoirs*.'

She started singing:

> '*La paix est faite,*
> *ma foi, tant pis . . .*'

The Senyor continued: 'You left by the Place Saint-Germain l'Auxerrois.'

'And from there,' she replied, 'we took a boat.'

The Senyor interrupted her angrily: 'You took a hackney.'

She was still singing when Tomeu brought in a bundle of wood.

'That devil over there,' said the Senyor as he got up to leave, 'has charmed a young girl.'

Dona Xima looked at the farmboy with an expression of wonder I will never forget.

'You women are always the same. He really is ugly, you must admit!'

226

'But, Tonet, he's exquisite!'

Don Toni had gone off to his room, and he no longer heard her. Dona Xima boldly approached the lad.

'You're from Bearn?' she asked with a smile.

'Yes, Senyora.'

'How old are you?'

'I'll be twenty-four at Easter.'

'Then you're twenty-three. Why do you want to be older? Because you charmed a young girl?' she inquired with a provocative gaze.

Tomeu looked down and did not reply. She continued her shameless questions, even though she was well aware of my presence.

'Do you like living here?'

'Yes, Senyora.'

'What sort of work do you do?'

'Whatever I'm told.'

'You must get up very early.'

'At daybreak.'

'Haven't you ever been a soldier?'

'I got out of it because my mother's a widow.'

'Have you ever been to the City?'

'I'll go for the Easter fair.'

'Are you engaged?'

'No, Senyora.'

'And why is that?'

'We haven't got any clothes.'

'Would you like to live in a city? You could be a valet, with a beautiful uniform.'

'A what?'

'A servant, but you wouldn't work.'

'How's that?'

'An elegant coat covered in golden braid.'

'But what would I do?'

'Greet people. Or if anyone smoked, you'd light their cigarette.'

'And that's all?'

'And answer if you're asked a question.'

'What if I didn't know how to?'

'It doesn't matter! All you have to do is answer graciously with a smile.'

The conversation was taking a dangerous turn that disconcerted

227

me. Less than five hours earlier, that very same woman, prostrated at my feet, in tears of despair, had stated her firm resolution to change her ways. I coughed to state my presence but she looked at me indifferently; to that degree had she forgotten her resolution.

'Answer with a smile? What if they got angry?'

Dona Xima had a poetic expression on her face. She was relaxed and almost looked beautiful. Suddenly she went up to Tomeu.

'How is it that you're missing a tooth? I'll have to get you a false one.'

She had taken his head between her hands and stared into his eyes. He broke away in terror.

'No! I've heard they get them from dead bodies.'

TWENTY THREE

The succession of events began to quicken. On Tuesday after lunch people in costume began to arrive. I have already explained how the Senyor allowed them in due to an unspoken agreement with the late village priest who did not approve of the celebration. The new priest, Don Francesc, was less strict, but the villagers had become used to celebrating the ball at the estate and nobody saw any reason for changing the custom.

It was a beautiful afternoon. From my window, the garden that was turning into a forest announced that spring was soon to come. The sky was blue damask. Such a sky, my Lord, and such a splendid sun. And the stunning nature surrounding us was so indifferent, concerned with nothing but itself ... It looked as if summer were already beginning. Bees were flying about and buds were swelling on the tender branches of the trees; the ground would soon be covered in flowers. A bird sang voluptuous notes from an oak and was answered from another faraway tree. Everything — flowers, bees and birds — was rhythmic and harmonious. Yet beneath the apparent harmony lurked deep misfortunes: birds destroyed the insects, sheep devoured the flowers. High above, in the sky, I saw a falcon descend upon a dove. Nature followed its happy course amidst inevitable destruction. Both killer and victim laughed, until the latter's life was shattered in a shriek of terror. On one such afternoon, on Golgotha, Jesus Christ had a moment of weakness: 'My God, why hast Thou forsaken me?'

The end was drawing near. Convinced that I could do nothing against fate, I began praying with such deep longing that exhaustion closed my eyes and I fell sound asleep. By the time I awoke, night had fallen. The fields were silent, whereas the house seemed to vibrate with the shrieks of masked figures, shrill as those of swifts in the sky. The courtyard was full of people. Only the old folks and the cripples had stayed in the village. Everybody was wearing a mask, and many were wrapped in sheets and bedspreads in such a way that it was difficult to guess their sex or age, which resulted in many doubtful situations. Those of us who watch carnival from behind the scenes, in other words, from the confessional, are well aware of its dangers. The Senyor never wished to take them into account, unreceptive as he was to everything he did not like. One year, after the party, one silver spoon and two ashtrays were missing, but he made light of the matter, even though it was serious not only because of the value of the objects but also because of the evil implied in any act of theft.

As I walked around the house I observed the disarray that prevailed in the family seat of the Bearns as in a final apotheosis. The fire had gone out in the kitchen and the cook had disappeared. However, I did see two hams on the table and a flask of our best wine, which that morning had been full and was now empty. I went to speak to the Senyor, who was half asleep by the fireplace.

'Come here, Son,' he said when he heard me.

I told him about the wine and he shrugged his shoulders.

'Let them be, let them have a little fun,' and he fell asleep again.

'Aren't you feeling well?'

'I feel wonderful,' he replied.

Dona Maria Antònia advanced, fragile and pleased.

'It sounds as though they're having quite a time downstairs. Are you asleep, Tonet?'

'Yes.'

'Oh, goodness ... I'd never seen anyone answer in their sleep before. Listen to the people at the ball: "Tweet, tweet, tweet ..."' they sound like birds.'

A group appeared in the doorway shrieking and asking for sweets.

'Go away,' said the Senyor with his eyes closed. 'Go to the kitchen and they'll give you some sherry.'

Upon hearing that, they rushed downstairs. Some of the people in disguise were already venturing into the private quarters. I noticed that a couple had slipped into the Senyor's study. They had probably used the spiral staircase that came up from the garden, and I had to intervene to chase them out.

In the courtyard the ball had begun. A tall man, certainly no one from the house, gave out ham and wine to the guests. They had lit a bonfire and the shouts and laughter increased. I was not so much distressed by that scandal and squander as I was by the couples seeking intimacy in dark corners. I returned to the drawing room. Since it was useless to talk to the Senyor, I sat at one end where I could not be seen. Three figures peered through the doorway. They were dressed alike, but one of them, the smallest, could have been a woman. She kept on speaking in a falsetto and took the initiative in a most indecent sort of seduction. From my corner I could only catch half the words they said.

'What is all that chatter about?' the Senyor mumbled.

Not even they knew the answer. They were much like the birds I had heard after lunch announcing that spring was soon to come.

'Come, you must ask me to dance,' said the one I suspected to be a girl.

'First we have to be sure that you're a female,' said the other two, laughing.

There was silence. Then I heard muffled laughter.

'Let's see . . . Show me your hands. A fine male!'

They laughed again. The Senyor replied in his sleep: 'A fine male and you're fondling him . . .' he said between clenched teeth. 'They ought to be ashamed, but they aren't,' and he fell back to sleep.

I stood up and they ran off as soon as they saw me. I followed them from a distance. At the bottom of the staircase, someone was trying to hide a silver candle holder in his robes. I grabbed it back from the masked figure. Dona Xima rushed over to me nervously.

'Joan, where's Tomeu?'

'Why do you need him?'

'Because he's sworn that he'll marry me.'

She was extremely agitated. From the very first moment I had thought Dona Xima was disturbed. Now I was convinced that she was mad.

'Don't say such things, Senyora.'

'Let's go to see my aunt and uncle at once,' she replied, as she ran off. I did not dare follow her. A few moments later, the Senyor called me, just as I had expected.

'What is this nonsense Dona Xima tells me, Joan?'

She started screaming and speaking incoherently.

'You don't have to shout at me. I'm not deaf,' the Senyor reminded her. 'You won't marry Tomeu because he doesn't want you and because I would never allow it.'

She went wild. Standing by the fireplace, she spewed forth one insult after another. It seemed as if she were about to have a seizure. 'He loves me! He told me so!' she repeated, and she may even have believed it. She had forgotten that she was a poor wretch with half a century behind her. Fate determined that she was to hear the truth with her own ears. In one of her pauses Tomeu's voice reached us loud and clear, coming up from downstairs: 'That old woman who came the other day is mad as a hatter. She looks like a witch. Can't you hear her screaming?'

Dona Xima turned pale; those cruel words had snapped her back into reality. She seemed to hesitate and then she took the box of poisoned chocolates from her breast. I arrived just in time to stop her from putting one in her mouth and forced her to drop them next to the fireplace. During the brief struggle the top had fallen off the box, but I cannot be sure whether it still contained the three chocolates she had shown us the previous afternoon or whether one was already missing. She tried to fight me off with genuine fury, crying out Tomeu's name between sobs. I held her by the wrists and when she saw that she could not move she started writhing like a soul possessed. When I finally let go, she ran away. We never saw her again. We heard later that she had been picked up by the Civil Guard on the road and taken to the hospital in the City; she was dead by the time they arrived. This is my last memory of Dona Xima, Miquel. Even more ill-fated than the Duke of Gandia, what I lost that ghastly night was not her, but the image of pure beauty, which in my mind will forever be associated with horror.

Dona Maria Antònia walked in slowly.

'Oh, Tonet, if you look out ... All of Bearn is here. Don't you want to see the ball? Catalineta is crying by the fireplace. Let her cry, let her cry,' she added with satisfaction. 'She'll never serve me breakfast again.'

A moment later she added: 'Tomorrow I'll give her this bracelet. Don't you think I ought to, Tonet? Oh, goodness ... I lost my rosary.'

She looked for it on the mantelpiece, and that must have been the moment when she absent-mindedly took one of Dona Xima's chocolates. A while later she fell into a drowsy state which did not strike me at first. When we saw it was bedtime and she had not moved, we tried to wake her up; she did not respond, and only then did we realize that it was serious. There was no doctor in the village, and the barber, who often made house calls, had broken his leg the day before. It was very late. The last guests had gone and the house was so silent that you could have heard a pin drop. I chose not to wake anyone. I went down to the kitchen to brew some strong coffee and when I returned to the drawing room I found her in her husband's arms.

'This is the end, Joan,' he told me sadly.

We managed to give her a bit of hot coffee and she came to. The Senyor also seemed drowsy, and I attributed it to the shock; however, it was difficult for him to lose his consciousness. In a moment of lucidity, Dona Maria Antònia asked us whether she was dying. She was not the least bit uncomfortable, and felt fine, 'as if I were in Heaven,' as she herself put it. We assured her that she had simply fainted (I was trying to convince myself that this was true) and I gave her absolution. She seemed serene and brave. I thought that my words had deceived her, but it was not so. She took the Senyor's hand in hers and suddenly said: 'What will become of you, Tonet?'

Her light eyes looked like glass, dry and anxious. We were dumbfounded. She immediately recovered: 'Well, you'll amuse yourself with your papers.'

She tried to embrace him and smiled. Death was claiming her. And yet, does death truly exist? It does not according to Ovid, and for the Church it is a 'transition'. That last embrace reminded me of the poem in the *Metamorphoses*. For a few seconds her fragile, trembling limbs seemed to become branches, as in the fable of Baucis. Was it the breath of transformation that rushed through them before they lost their human form? Her eyes closed and she was taken to her heavenly rest. Only then did I think to count the chocolates. The box was empty. I looked at my benefactor. He was asleep.

'Senyor!' I cried, 'what has your Honour done?'

'Nothing,' he murmured with his eyes closed.

'Dona Xima had left three chocolates in this box.'

He did not reply. What had happened while I was in the kitchen? Undoubtedly the Senyor, seeing the state his wife was in and knowing she had lost her memory of recent events, had come to the same conclusion I had and went to count the chocolates. He must have been deeply distressed to see that some were missing, and being the pagan that he was, he had chosen suicide over the loneliness of an existence he lacked the strength to face at his age. I recalled a conversation we had a few days before, as we walked through the woods: 'I think that with the pages I'll give you today, the *Memoirs* will virtually be finished. Everything has been said in the best possible way: I don't know how to write any better. When you publish them' — never, Miquel, did it occur to him that I might not do so — 'you will naturally find some oversights in my style and perhaps a few grammatical liberties and transgressions. Be careful when you correct them, Son. Remember that I'm not a scholar nor a writer in the proper sense of the word, but rather a man who had no children,' — and upon saying this he squeezed my arm tenderly — 'and who would like to survive for some time by perpetuating all that he loved. I have made a particular effort to portray Dona Maria Antònia, describing her charming childhood, her maturity full of talent and the serenity and mental disorder of her last stages, which at times brought back to life the eight-year old girl I had played with as a child. That's what I intended, and to do so I have at times had to sacrifice grammar and morals in exchange for accuracy. You don't have my permission,' he added, laughing, 'to change more solecisms than those concerning spelling. I'm not interested in the problems of z's and s's. As far as syntax is concerned, it is mine, the one that best meets my needs. All in all, I consider the work finished. I know the money I gave you will be enough for its publication, which shouldn't be luxurious, but simply correct. Publish it in Paris.'

He was sad, and I guessed the reason why. He confirmed my suspicion without my having to ask.

'Now my life no longer has a purpose.'

'You have the Senyora,' I told him.

The Senyora no longer existed, and the *Memoirs* had been completed. The idea of his suicide came back to me.

'Senyor,' I said, 'the box is empty. If your Honour has eaten one of these chocolates, you must confess this very instant. Your eternal salvation depends upon it. Did your Honour try to commit suicide?'

He did not open his eyes, but it seemed as if he smiled faintly.

'Did your Honour eat one of the chocolates that were above the fireplace? If you can't answer me, make a sign with your hand.'

He gave a hesitant wave that could have been interpreted as a denial and I felt there was hope after all.

'So you confess that you didn't try to kill yourself?'

This time his hand denied it more clearly.

'Do you ask God's forgiveness for all your sins, do you repent and authorize me to omit from your *Memoirs* all that the Council of Moralists considers pertinent for the better service of God and the benefit of your soul!'

I said no more because he had lost consciousness. He slept until dawn, when he opened his eyes and momentarily recovered his speech. I wanted him to confess, and as he had done before, he referred me to his work.

'My writings, Joan, are my confession. I'm not afraid. God is good.'

I remember the tone of his words as if it were now.

'Your Honour's life has been so beautiful, despite your mistakes. Repent and ask for forgiveness.'

'I suppose,' he interrupted, sitting up, 'I am guilty of having envied Jacob Collera.'

He wavered and I held him. He was dead.

EPILOGUE

Yesterday afternoon I was told that some gentlemen wished to talk to me. They were two members of the 'Prussian Imperial Centre for Masonic and Theosophical Research.' On their cards was the old emblem of the Rosicrucians, a cross surrounded by a crown of roses. One of them, a stout, plethoric fellow, went by the name of Dr Wassman. The other one, whose name I did not understand, was introduced to me as his secretary. They told me that having heard of the death of the Lord of Bearn they had come as delegates of the Prince Bismark in order to inquire into certain matters that were of interest to the old chancellor.

Disconcerted by the unusual situation, I asked them in to the drawing room, and once I had served them some sherry and closed all the doors they exposed the purpose of their visit. They expressed themselves in correct, scientific Spanish, and only their accent revealed their German origin. They were provided with folders and as they spoke they consulted various documents. The object of their interest was Don Felip, and they began by showing me his birth certificate, issued in the City of Mallorca on April 16th, 1780.

'At the end of the eighteenth century,' they said, 'the Rosicrucians represented the eighth degree of Freemasonry, and you undoubtedly know that Don Felip de Bearn was a Freemason.'

I took the blow without batting an eyelash.

'In the Bearn family,' Dr. Wassman continued, 'there have been several Freemasons. The Prince . . .'

I cut him short.

'I was born in this house. I have spent half my life in the archives, and I know them inside out. The Prince, the founder of the Empire, has more important matters to attend to than an obscure Mallorcan family.'

I undoubtedly pronounced these words too vehemently, because the two men felt obliged to apologize.

'We beg you to forgive us,' they said, 'and hope you believe that we speak in earnest. The archives of this estate, which you know inside out, were expurgated by Don Toni de Bearn, according to our knowledge,' — they checked a document — 'in 1866, a few years after you entered the seminary. But we are digressing from our initial point. Our studies only concern Don Felip.'

'Assuming the archives were indeed expurgated,' I interrupted, 'I doubt that this is the best place for your research. Besides, I'm afraid I must tell you that my ministry does not allow me to collaborate with Freemasonry.'

'Many Freemasons,' they replied, 'are Christians, and as far as our sect is concerned, following Rosenkreuz, we have adopted the sign of the cross.'

'They may call themselves Christians, but they do not abide by the dogmas of orthodoxy, and are therefore heretics.'

'That is true,' they replied in unison, as if I had uttered words of praise.

I could not understand how a right-wing figure such as Bismarck could be in contact with the Freemasons, or how the Prince, who had just resigned from his office as Chancellor and was not on good terms with the young Kaiser, could speak on behalf of the Prussian Imperial Centre for Masonic and Theosophical Research.

The doctors smiled.

'The matter may not be that simple. The Prince proclaimed the Empire on January 18th of 1871, crowning William I at the Galerie des Glaces in Versailles. It was a blow for the Hapsburgs. Sedan had more of an impact on Vienna than on Paris. The Hohenzollerns owe a lot to the old Chancellor. Prussia owes him even more.'

We continued talking and I must admit that they proved extraordinarily learned and cultured. However, not always could I make much sense out of their statements. For a moment I even wondered whether Kaiser William I's enmity with Bismarck was only apparent, and whether he was secretly continuing to act as chancellor.

'Far from it,' they replied, 'the Kaiser is a liberal and the Prince is a conservative. Bismarck is not only a military figure; he is also a great politician who managed to fool Napoleon III and, in a sense, William I, too. You probably heard the story of the Ems Telegram, which started the war of '70, a story worthy of becoming as famous as Cesar Borgia's *bellisimo inganno* of Sinigaglia. Although he is a conservative, the Prince is also opposed to the old, traditionalist Hapsburgs. Every creed is a force that can be applied in many different ways, depending upon the circumstances. The Prince is a conservative in Germany because he does not wish to lose the empire founded at Versailles, and at the same time he favours Freemasonry so as to contribute to the disintegration of Austria.'

The pragmatism so cynically exposed by my guests did not please me, although I abstained from making any comments. William II and Bismarck were enemies and yet tacitly shared the desire to exterminate the House of Austria; but I was not entirely right this time either.

'According to the Kaiser,' Doctor Wassman said, 'the disintegration of Austria must be brought about in some entirely different way than the one the Prince proposes, which consists of an outdated conservatism in the style of Francis Joseph that will ultimately exhaust the country's vital resources; and the Hapsburgs really do seem incapable of facing the problems of this century.'

The more I listened to them, the more confused my ideas became.

'In that case, how can the Emperor favour . . .'

'The Emperor does not favour Freemasonry; he presides over it. As supreme arbiter, he recognizes its existence without fostering it.'

'And without condemning it, either.'

'Just as he does not condemn,' the Doctor replied, 'railways or stagecoaches, even though they compete with each other. Besides, the problem has two aspects, if not more, and although there may be some truth in William II's point of view according to which the personal power of the Hapsburgs must be increased in Austria in order to neutralize the country, that excess of power, degenerating them even more and accelerating the fall of the dynasty, could coincide with an uprising of the Austrian people, which must be avoided at all costs.'

I filled his glass again, because I noticed the wine made him talkative, and he continued.

'Whereas the problem is different in France: that country reemerged too fast after the defeat of Sedan. It would not be absurd to assume that freethinking Masonry, which would perhaps insure the unity of the Austrian Empire, could contribute to breaking up the decadent and undisciplined French. The same could happen in Italy, another young nation which must be taken into account.'

The man made a pause and in terror I thought that what both the conservatives and liberals of Prussia were striving for was the destruction of Europe. I found the conversation increasingly astonishing.

'The Prince, if you'll excuse me,' Wassman continued, 'has always opposed the Church — this is another aspect of the problem — in the religious war known as the ''Kulturkampf,'' and that is yet another reason for him to join us. The ''Kulturkampf'' also has two sides to it: on the one hand it is nationalistic, Prussian, and leans towards the supremacy of the German Empire forged ''of iron and fire'': as you can see, at first impression nothing could be further from the liberalism proposed by the Rosicrucians, even though, on the other hand, the Prussian hegemony is based on an intuitive, vital, purely magical element which is not foreign to us. You already know that during almost two centuries we have called ourselves ''The Invisible.'' Christian Rosenkreuz himself practised necromancy and at the beginning of the fifteenth century he was a precursor of modern physics.'

The doctor noticed my surprise and gave me an unsolicited explanation.

'Modern science comes from magic,' he said, 'and it could even be said that it is, in essence, pure magic. We know nothing about the causes of electricity, for instance, a source of energy we use all the time. The Universe is full of mysterious forces which the Supreme Being makes available to man when he deserves them, or,' — he smiled — 'when man is audacious enough to capture them. I must remind you that a German friar stole lightning from the gods with the invention of gunpowder. As freethinkers, we proclaim democracy and human liberty and will impose them with violence if necessary, because we will not let anything stand in our way. We're anti-Catholic and support the advocates of the ''Kulturkampf.'' Catholicism — and once again I hope you will excuse me — is the main enemy of Bismarck's Empire. Therefore the Kaiser and the prince have a common enemy, and in that sense are allies, yet merely in that sense. When the common enemy succumbs, what will become of their friendship?'

He was excited from the alcohol and perhaps also from his own speech. He made another pause and I realized that as soon as their enemies were eliminated, the Prussian fire would destroy itself.

It was getting late and starting to rain, so I felt obliged to suggest that they stay for supper. I resolved not to ask any questions, because I had observed they were not immune to the Binassalem wine and assumed that in the course of the evening they would pour out their hearts, which indeed proved to be true.

'These old Mallorcan estates,' they said, 'have great charm. Is it true that Bearn is for sale?'

I briefly explained the situation, which was hardly a secret anymore.

'Will it be difficult for you to leave this place?'

'I was born here,' I replied, 'and I would have liked to die here, too, but God has willed it otherwise.'

The man sat there studying me for a moment and then said: 'Maybe not. There's something we would like to discuss in that respect, too,' and he emptied his glass of wine. 'How much do the debts amount to, if I may ask?'

'Close to seventy thousand *duros*, all in all.'

The secretary took out his pencil and wrote down some numbers on a piece of paper. Then he handed it to the Doctor and whispered something in his ear. I thought I heard the word *marks*.

'*Das ist nicht zu viel*,' the Doctor mumbled. And then, turning to me, he added: 'The figure of Don Felip is considered extremely interesting in Germany. We are compiling a complete history of Freemasonry.'

I let them know that there was no reference to the subject in the house archives.

'As I mentioned before, we know that the archives were expurgated due to certain circumstances . . . We are only interested in the dolls' room. That is where the real archives are.'

Unable to control myself, I stood up.

'I'm surprised that you know about that, too. The Senyor has forbidden that the matter be mentioned. I've never been in the dolls' room myself. In more than a quarter of a century, no one, not even Don Toni, has set foot in there.'

The Doctor ignored my vehemence and I sat down again.

240

'Don Toni de Bearn,' the Doctor slowly continued, 'corresponded with the Rosicrucians of Prussia between 1862 and 1866. Then he broke away from us and from Freemasonry, which was our ally until the war of 1870. Naturally, he was considered suspect and we watched him. On his part it was not a violent separation, and I say "on his part" because defections are not forgotten in Freemasonry. I will read you part of his last letter, written on January 8, 1866. It says: "I have decided to leave your organization. Consider me disillusioned rather than antagonistic. I admire your faith and yet do not share it. You need not worry about the secrets you have entrusted to me. Today I am putting them under lock and key in the dolls' room, along with the collections and correspondence of the perverse and diabolical Don Felip, whose soul is probably in limbo. 'Silence in matters which we cannot understand,' as they say in Catalunya. As long as I live, nobody will ever enter that room, but I cannot bring myself to destroy these documents that may determine the history of tomorrow, assuming tomorrow does not present more pressing problems. I have no right to decide over the future. After my death I am sure that Don Joan Mayol, now a seminarist and in due time, God willing, chaplain of the house, will know how to act as he sees fit." As you can see,' the Doctor continued, 'his attitude is that of a sceptic who declines all responsibility and resolutions: that is what our credo prosecutes the most. It was discovered that Don Toni had given a Masonic pendant to a peasant woman instead of returning it to the organization, as was his duty. Well, that old woman already . . .'

The Doctor, who was rather excited, let out a cackle and seemed to be about to add something, but reconsidered it and continued: 'As I was saying, the Prince is interested in Don Felip, an exceedingly complex character related to some courts at the beginning of the century. Professor Freud of Vienna, one of Charcot's young disciples, has also gone to Bismarck to find out about this extraordinary Bearn who at the same time had an affair with Queen Maria Luisa of Spain and a — very close friendship with the young and vigorous Don Manuel de Godoy.'

I blushed and made no comment.

'We have some of Godoy's intimate correspondence,' the man continued, 'that make reference to the reasons why Don Felip was forced to leave the Army, and we also have Don Toni's letters, including the last one which I just read to you. Therefore we know that the real archives are not the ones you know ''inside out'',' — he emphasized that expression — 'but the ones in the dolls' room. Therefore, sir . . .'

His secretary whispered a few words in German and the Doctor changed the course of his speech.

'You are absolutely sure that your late master did not set foot in the dolls' room for a quarter of a century?'

'Almost positive.'

'*Sehr gut*. Based on that statement, I would like to make a proposal on behalf of the Prince: we could purchase this estate, which in fact belongs to its creditors, and name you administrator for life, since you'd regret having to leave it . . .'

'In exchange for opening the dolls' room.'

I could feel my heartbeat. 'Dear sir, aside from other considerations, although mortgaged, Bearn does legally belong to the Senyor's nephews and niece, who could get back the estate.'

'You know they have no money. We have all the information. In any case, if you would prefer that we speak to them directly, we have no objection. We can obviously approach them with the same proposal we just made to you, and that would greatly simplify matters. They'd be sure to accept.'

He was right. Thoughtlessness, frivolity and greed would lead Dona Magdalena to reveal happily the intimacies of Bearn to the Masonic lodges. The danger was great and I realized that I had to buy time and avoid severing the negotiations no matter what it took.

'Your proposal,' I told them, 'is so generous,' — I was pale with shame — 'that it takes me by surprise. You needn't bother visiting the Senyors' relatives, since I will be as pleased as they to oblige you.' I pretended not to see the smiles on the faces of my guests. 'But I'm so overwhelmed that I beg you to give me a few hours to consider the matter.'

I immediately proceeded to insinuate that if we were to reach an agreement it would be convenient to draw up a written contract and they offered to deposit a sum right away with a notary as a down payment. I managed to act dumbfounded and take advantage of the uneasiness I truly felt to fake the confusion of a fish staring at its bait. They took me for a greedy peasant, and thus, without saying so outright, I gave them the impression that, overwhelmed with joy, I was accepting their proposal. They were convinced to such an extent

242

that, contrary to what I had expected, they did not think of asking that the doors of the dolls' room be sealed shut until they had examined the documents.

'You have until tomorrow morning to make your decision,' the Doctor replied, believing it was already made. 'We will expect your reply at ten o'clock.'

'I am most grateful. It would be impossible to examine the papers at night. Tomorrow, in broad daylight, we will take care of everything. And now, assuming it is not too late, I think we could open another bottle, if you'd like.'

They poured out extravagant courtesies believing that my suggestion was some sort of toast or unspoken ratification of our pact. Besides, there were not immune to the generous Binissalem wine, to which they paid lavish compliments. I took my hypocrisy to the extreme of praising the dark beer of their homeland. The conversation continued amidst an embarrassingly fake cordiality. Whoever said that Northerners were laconic and reserved? My guests drank a drop too much wine, and hoping to encourage them, I followed suit, although in moderation. At no point did I lose my self-control, and God willed, for His greater glory and for the good of the Church, that an inexperienced peasant should triumph that evening over two outstanding historians, the secret agents of Bismarck.

It is true that I have a rather vague recollection of the things that the wine or the satisfaction of thinking that they had me under their control inspired in my guests. According to them (and God knows how comforted I was by their statements) Don Toni had severed his relations with the lodges at the beginning of 1866. Assuming he entered the order around 1862, which according to my visitors was when his correspondence with the Rosicrucians began, it would follow that he was affiliated with them for less than four years. This conclusion coincided with what the Senyor had once told me: "I was a Freemason, but only for a short time." I tried to discover whether Dr Wassman knew the story of Dona Xima, and whether she had also had dealings with the Rosicrucians. The Doctor, by now quite drunk, laughed out loud.

'Of course she did! She was the lover of Napoleon III, and he was a great defender of Prussia. She came to Mallorca recently on a special mission.'

He gave his companion an ironic glance. I was taken aback.

'A special mission?'

'So special that you must allow us to keep it a secret.'

'Was Dona Xima a Freemason?'

'Perhaps.'

'And there are people who would assign a mission to a madwoman?' I insisted, trying to press him for more information. Yet the Doctor was not completely drunk.

'Sometimes madmen . . . ,' he smiled.

'Consider the example of the Illuminati,' his secretary exclaimed.

'Or that of the Stylites, who now are called the Catatonics.'

'Or of tranvestites, who are also important . . .'

They ignored me as they bounced sentences back and forth between them. All their seriousness and pomposity had disappeared.

'Transvestites?' I asked.

'Or captains who like to dress dolls.'

'Or seduce queens.'

'Or . . .'

Without letting him finish his sentence, I grabbed the secretary by his jacket: the Doctor laughed and embraced me, partly to hold me back and partly to make light of the incident.

'You are strong,' he said as he felt my arms.

'Excuse me,' I muttered in confusion.

The scene had upset me. I attempted to perform an act of contrition without successfully setting my spirit at ease. For a moment I saw my existence as being sterile and confined, and feeling that I had powers that seldom converge in a single individual (youth, strength, intelligence — that is how the Devil has tempted me) I told myself that it was unjust to sacrifice my entire life, and in my desperation I doubted both God and my benefactor. I think a fight with my visitors would have given me tremendous physical pleasure, but even this pleasure, which is common for other men, was forbidden to me. 'Why should I not behave like a farm boy,' I asked myself, 'if I have not a gentleman's name?' A farm boy of Bearn. I have sometimes noticed that women looked at me with desire. The unlucky woman that you know about would have committed the wildest follies for me. And yet the earthly beauty she attributed to me is not more than that of a farmer or a cart-driver. On any path in Mallorca you can find peasants with black eyes, curly hair and the same wild look as me. If the face is the mirror of the soul, I too should have been a peasant: a

244

man like Tomeu, who lived and will die in these mountains. Such were the thoughts that crossed my mind. From that moment on, my memories are confused. The sentences uttered by Dr Wassman and his secretary were incoherent, but their incoherence was tainted with horrifying insinuations.

The moment they left, I ran to wake up Tomeu, and after lighting a fire we went up to the dolls' room through the oratory and the hidden staircase. He was pale as we walked upstairs. I can assure you that I have never known exactly what was in that room, so hastily did we throw everything in the fire — dolls, folders and papers. In less than a half an hour the flames devoured an entire universe in exchange for which the Prince Bismarck would have granted me the usufruct of Bearn, the one thing I love most on this earth. Once the sacrifice had been consummated, I felt calm in my utter nakedness and the conviction of having interpreted my benefactor's wish.

This morning at ten o'clock sharp the emissaries again appeared at the door. I immediately led them to the dolls' room. As I crossed the oratory, I collected my thoughts for a moment, thanking the Lord for my determination the night before. The visitors were deeply surprised when they did not find a single paper. They opened the empty drawers and closets as if they could not believe their eyes.

'But how can you explain this, Father? Only ten hours ago you assured us that no one had ever set foot in this room. What could we call a mystery like this?'

I allowed myself a note of irony.

'In Egypt they would call it "the Veil of Isis".'

The anger in their faces quickly poured out in insults. They accused me of having deceived them. I let them abuse me, and when their injuries finally subsided I replied: 'Last night, when I assured you that I had never set foot in that room before, it was true. That is all I have to say.'

Standing in the doorway of the courtyard Dr Wassman said to his secretary loud enough for me to hear: 'The usurpers have destroyed all the proof of their bastardy.'

The circus magician had just lifted the cape covering the fairy: she had disappeared.

They vanished in laughter.

'The Veil of Isis . . .' Now that the dolls' room has been destroyed,

I will vainly attempt to discern whether it had been hiding dark mysteries or whether that veil covered nothing but a wall. The Senyor said that Don Felip was probably in limbo, but did he really believe so? I have already written that one ought not to be misled by his light treatment of grave matters. That enlightened man who would allow nothing to shock him was not, in fact, able to stand the idea of a Bearn expelled from the Army for the strange madness of dressing dolls. That Don Felip was by no means a mediocre man is proved by his renown in the courts of Europe. The enigma of his life which is still a source of concern to the Rosicrucians and the disciples of Charcot has been consigned to eternal oblivion. The darkness surrounding the death of my benefactor is even more tragic. It is difficult to judge the man. Even I, who have known him so well, have been frivolous in accusing him of frivolity and presenting him as an epicure without problems. That blessed existence, which at my more bitter moments I have compared to my own, was reduced to burning his library and seeking refuge in irony. He had to create his own world in his *Memoirs*. In that sense, circumstances were no kinder to him than to me. To what degree he succeeded in feeling free amidst the contingencies that forced him to amputate what appeared to be the most genuine part of his personality is too great a question for my pen.

I do not even know whether he killed himself. To my question, 'Do you confess that you did not try to kill yourself?' he replied with a gesture of denial which I interpreted as an answer to the second part of the question, but it may have referred to the first. Thus, the Senyor (I will never know) may have denied the denial, implying that he had indeed committed suicide. On the other hand, when yesterday evening Dr Wassman implied that the Freemasons had not forgiven him, and alluded to Dona Xima's special mission, he seemed to open the door to an entire new series of speculations, assuming he did not do it to confuse me. Who will ever know the truth? The Senyor died without making a confession. His fate, or rather that of his soul and his bodily form which are to appear in front of the Supreme Judge, is already decided. Yet the problem of his spirit remains, that noble, autonomous breath destined to last through the centuries, as did the ideas of Plato. That spirit has been captured in his *Memoirs*. For many years he lived only to write them. I am not forgetting his great love for Dona Maria Antònia, because his wife and the *Memoirs* are virtually one and the same thing. Other women may appear in them, but he claimed that his adventures had been nothing but rehearsals for the definitive possession. ('The fidelity of Philemon, like the chastity of Hippolytus, is only lacking the proof of comparison,' he wrote in chapter XXI). In this sense, the book, so scandalous in certain instances, constitutes as a whole a homage to his wife. If it is destroyed, we would destroy the most faithful testimony of conjugal love, thus giving a confirmation in a certain sense to the heretical beliefs according to which Good and Evil go hand in hand. Nothing appears certain in the personality of Don Toni de Bearn. There is reason to believe that he preferred Saint Augustine during the first stage of his life rather than the second. However, did he ever openly profess that preference? I defy anyone, Miquel, to point out a single antidogmatic statement in his work. There is no denying that he sinned: notwithstanding, it is doubtful whether he died outside the bosom of the Church.

And with this doubt, more honest in my opinion than many deep convictions, I draw my story to a close. Through Father Armengol, who has been assigned to Toledo, you will receive a copy of the *Memoirs* for you to examine and submit to His Eminence the Cardinal, with the understanding that if his judgement should be contrary to the last wish of the deceased, I reserve the right to take the matter to Rome. If it happened that there my voice were not heard either, I could appeal to no one else on Earth and would have to retire to await my death in some secluded monastery. '*Adhuc sub judice lis est,*' writes Horace in his *Ars Poetica*. After losing these lands of Bearn, with their charming and terrible secrets, and after burying the spirit that my benefactor has chosen to leave us in his work, I would still be left with the comfort of trusting in the supreme justice of God.

LLORENÇ VILLALONGA was born in Palma de Majorca in Spain in 1897 and died in 1980. Fluent in Spanish and Catalan, he wrote fifteen novels, five books of short stories, and five volumes of drama, in addition to over five hundred articles for newspapers and magazines. *The Dolls' Room* is widely considered to be his greatest work, and a masterpiece of post-war Catalan fiction. His narrative preoccupation with his personal and ancestral past has been compared to that of Marcel Proust and Giuseppe di Lampedusa.

DEBORAH BONNER received her BA degree from Cornell University and since then has worked as a translator in Catalan, Spanish, and English in Barcelona and New York.

SELECTED DALKEY ARCHIVE PAPERBACKS

PETROS ABATZOGLOU, *What Does Mrs. Freeman Want?*
MICHAL AJVAZ, *The Golden Age.*
The Other City.
PIERRE ALBERT-BIROT, *Grabinoulor.*
YUZ ALESHKOVSKY, *Kangaroo.*
FELIPE ALFAU, *Chromos.*
Locos.
IVAN ÂNGELO, *The Celebration.*
The Tower of Glass.
DAVID ANTIN, *Talking.*
ANTÓNIO LOBO ANTUNES, *Knowledge of Hell.*
ALAIN ARIAS-MISSON, *Theatre of Incest.*
IFTIKHAR ARIF AND WAQAS KHWAJA, EDS., *Modern Poetry of Pakistan.*
JOHN ASHBERY AND JAMES SCHUYLER, *A Nest of Ninnies.*
HEIMRAD BÄCKER, *transcript.*
DJUNA BARNES, *Ladies Almanack.*
Ryder.
JOHN BARTH, *LETTERS.*
Sabbatical.
DONALD BARTHELME, *The King.*
Paradise.
SVETISLAV BASARA, *Chinese Letter.*
RENÉ BELLETTO, *Dying.*
MARK BINELLI, *Sacco and Vanzetti Must Die!*
ANDREI BITOV, *Pushkin House.*
ANDREJ BLATNIK, *You Do Understand.*
LOUIS PAUL BOON, *Chapel Road.*
My Little War.
Summer in Termuren.
ROGER BOYLAN, *Killoyle.*
IGNÁCIO DE LOYOLA BRANDÃO, *Anonymous Celebrity.*
The Good-Bye Angel.
Teeth under the Sun.
Zero.
BONNIE BREMSER, *Troia: Mexican Memoirs.*
CHRISTINE BROOKE-ROSE, *Amalgamemnon.*
BRIGID BROPHY, *In Transit.*
MEREDITH BROSNAN, *Mr. Dynamite.*
GERALD L. BRUNS, *Modern Poetry and the Idea of Language.*
EVGENY BUNIMOVICH AND J. KATES, EDS., *Contemporary Russian Poetry: An Anthology.*
GABRIELLE BURTON, *Heartbreak Hotel.*
MICHEL BUTOR, *Degrees.*
Mobile.
Portrait of the Artist as a Young Ape.
G. CABRERA INFANTE, *Infante's Inferno.*
Three Trapped Tigers.
JULIETA CAMPOS, *The Fear of Losing Eurydice.*
ANNE CARSON, *Eros the Bittersweet.*
ORLY CASTEL-BLOOM, *Dolly City.*
CAMILO JOSÉ CELA, *Christ versus Arizona.*
The Family of Pascual Duarte.
The Hive.
LOUIS-FERDINAND CÉLINE, *Castle to Castle.*
Conversations with Professor Y.
London Bridge.
Normance.
North.
Rigadoon.
HUGO CHARTERIS, *The Tide Is Right.*
JEROME CHARYN, *The Tar Baby.*
MARC CHOLODENKO, *Mordechai Schamz.*
JOSHUA COHEN, *Witz.*
EMILY HOLMES COLEMAN, *The Shutter of Snow.*
ROBERT COOVER, *A Night at the Movies.*
STANLEY CRAWFORD, *Log of the S.S. The Mrs Unguentine.*
Some Instructions to My Wife.
ROBERT CREELEY, *Collected Prose.*
RENÉ CREVEL, *Putting My Foot in It.*
RALPH CUSACK, *Cadenza.*
SUSAN DAITCH, *L.C.*
Storytown.
NICHOLAS DELBANCO, *The Count of Concord.*
NIGEL DENNIS, *Cards of Identity.*
PETER DIMOCK, *A Short Rhetoric for Leaving the Family.*
ARIEL DORFMAN, *Konfidenz.*
COLEMAN DOWELL, *The Houses of Children.*
Island People.
Too Much Flesh and Jabez.
ARKADII DRAGOMOSHCHENKO, *Dust.*
RIKKI DUCORNET, *The Complete Butcher's Tales.*
The Fountains of Neptune.
The Jade Cabinet.
The One Marvelous Thing.
Phosphor in Dreamland.
The Stain.
The Word "Desire."
WILLIAM EASTLAKE, *The Bamboo Bed.*
Castle Keep.
Lyric of the Circle Heart.
JEAN ECHENOZ, *Chopin's Move.*
STANLEY ELKIN, *A Bad Man.*
Boswell: A Modern Comedy.
Criers and Kibitzers, Kibitzers and Criers.
The Dick Gibson Show.
The Franchiser.
George Mills.
The Living End.
The MacGuffin.
The Magic Kingdom.
Mrs. Ted Bliss.
The Rabbi of Lud.
Van Gogh's Room at Arles.
ANNIE ERNAUX, *Cleaned Out.*
LAUREN FAIRBANKS, *Muzzle Thyself.*
Sister Carrie.
LESLIE A. FIEDLER, *Love and Death in the American Novel.*
JUAN FILLOY, *Op Oloop.*
GUSTAVE FLAUBERT, *Bouvard and Pécuchet.*
KASS FLEISHER, *Talking out of School.*
FORD MADOX FORD, *The March of Literature.*
JON FOSSE, *Aliss at the Fire.*
Melancholy.

FOR A FULL LIST OF PUBLICATIONS, VISIT:
www.dalkeyarchive.com

MAX FRISCH, *I'm Not Stiller.*
Man in the Holocene.
CARLOS FUENTES, *Christopher Unborn.*
Distant Relations.
Terra Nostra.
Where the Air Is Clear.
JANICE GALLOWAY, *Foreign Parts.*
The Trick Is to Keep Breathing.
WILLIAM H. GASS, *Cartesian Sonata and Other Novellas.*
Finding a Form.
A Temple of Texts.
The Tunnel.
Willie Masters' Lonesome Wife.
GÉRARD GAVARRY, *Hoppla! 1 2 3.*
ETIENNE GILSON,
The Arts of the Beautiful.
Forms and Substances in the Arts.
C. S. GISCOMBE, *Giscome Road.*
Here.
Prairie Style.
DOUGLAS GLOVER, *Bad News of the Heart.*
The Enamoured Knight.
WITOLD GOMBROWICZ,
A Kind of Testament.
KAREN ELIZABETH GORDON,
The Red Shoes.
GEORGI GOSPODINOV, *Natural Novel.*
JUAN GOYTISOLO, *Count Julian.*
Juan the Landless.
Makbara.
Marks of Identity.
PATRICK GRAINVILLE, *The Cave of Heaven.*
HENRY GREEN, *Back.*
Blindness.
Concluding.
Doting.
Nothing.
JIŘÍ GRUŠA, *The Questionnaire.*
GABRIEL GUDDING,
Rhode Island Notebook.
MELA HARTWIG, *Am I a Redundant Human Being?*
JOHN HAWKES, *The Passion Artist.*
Whistlejacket.
ALEKSANDAR HEMON, ED.,
Best European Fiction.
AIDAN HIGGINS, *A Bestiary.*
Balcony of Europe.
Bornholm Night-Ferry.
Darkling Plain: Texts for the Air.
Flotsam and Jetsam.
Langrishe, Go Down.
Scenes from a Receding Past.
Windy Arbours.
KEIZO HINO, *Isle of Dreams.*
ALDOUS HUXLEY, *Antic Hay.*
Crome Yellow.
Point Counter Point.
Those Barren Leaves.
Time Must Have a Stop.
MIKHAIL IOSSEL AND JEFF PARKER, EDS.,
Amerika: Russian Writers View the United States.
GERT JONKE, *The Distant Sound.*
Geometric Regional Novel.

Homage to Czerny.
The System of Vienna.
JACQUES JOUET, *Mountain R.*
Savage.
CHARLES JULIET, *Conversations with Samuel Beckett and Bram van Velde.*
MIEKO KANAI, *The Word Book.*
YORAM KANIUK, *Life on Sandpaper.*
HUGH KENNER, *The Counterfeiters.*
Flaubert, Joyce and Beckett: The Stoic Comedians.
Joyce's Voices.
DANILO KIŠ, *Garden, Ashes.*
A Tomb for Boris Davidovich.
ANITA KONKKA, *A Fool's Paradise.*
GEORGE KONRÁD, *The City Builder.*
TADEUSZ KONWICKI, *A Minor Apocalypse.*
The Polish Complex.
MENIS KOUMANDAREAS, *Koula.*
ELAINE KRAF, *The Princess of 72nd Street.*
JIM KRUSOE, *Iceland.*
EWA KURYLUK, *Century 21.*
EMILIO LASCANO TEGUI, *On Elegance While Sleeping.*
ERIC LAURRENT, *Do Not Touch.*
VIOLETTE LEDUC, *La Bâtarde.*
SUZANNE JILL LEVINE, *The Subversive Scribe: Translating Latin American Fiction.*
DEBORAH LEVY, *Billy and Girl.*
Pillow Talk in Europe and Other Places.
JOSÉ LEZAMA LIMA, *Paradiso.*
ROSA LIKSOM, *Dark Paradise.*
OSMAN LINS, *Avalovara.*
The Queen of the Prisons of Greece.
ALF MAC LOCHLAINN,
The Corpus in the Library.
Out of Focus.
RON LOEWINSOHN, *Magnetic Field(s).*
BRIAN LYNCH, *The Winner of Sorrow.*
D. KEITH MANO, *Take Five.*
MICHELINE AHARONIAN MARCOM,
The Mirror in the Well.
BEN MARCUS,
The Age of Wire and String.
WALLACE MARKFIELD,
Teitlebaum's Window.
To an Early Grave.
DAVID MARKSON, *Reader's Block.*
Springer's Progress.
Wittgenstein's Mistress.
CAROLE MASO, *AVA.*
LADISLAV MATEJKA AND KRYSTYNA POMORSKA, EDS.,
Readings in Russian Poetics: Formalist and Structuralist Views.
HARRY MATHEWS,
The Case of the Persevering Maltese: Collected Essays.
Cigarettes.
The Conversions.
The Human Country: New and Collected Stories.
The Journalist.

My Life in CIA.
Singular Pleasures.
The Sinking of the Odradek Stadium.
Tlooth.
20 Lines a Day.
JOSEPH McELROY,
Night Soul and Other Stories.
ROBERT L. McLAUGHLIN, ED.,
Innovations: An Anthology of Modern & Contemporary Fiction.
HERMAN MELVILLE, *The Confidence-Man.*
AMANDA MICHALOPOULOU, *I'd Like.*
STEVEN MILLHAUSER,
The Barnum Museum.
In the Penny Arcade.
RALPH J. MILLS, JR.,
Essays on Poetry.
MOMUS, *The Book of Jokes.*
CHRISTINE MONTALBETTI, *Western.*
OLIVE MOORE, *Spleen.*
NICHOLAS MOSLEY, *Accident.*
Assassins.
Catastrophe Practice.
Children of Darkness and Light.
Experience and Religion.
God's Hazard.
The Hesperides Tree.
Hopeful Monsters.
Imago Bird.
Impossible Object.
Inventing God.
Judith.
Look at the Dark.
Natalie Natalia.
Paradoxes of Peace.
Serpent.
Time at War.
The Uses of Slime Mould: Essays of Four Decades.
WARREN MOTTE,
Fables of the Novel: French Fiction since 1990.
Fiction Now: The French Novel in the 21st Century.
Oulipo: A Primer of Potential Literature.
YVES NAVARRE, *Our Share of Time.*
Sweet Tooth.
DOROTHY NELSON, *In Night's City.*
Tar and Feathers.
ESHKOL NEVO, *Homesick.*
WILFRIDO D. NOLLEDO,
But for the Lovers.
FLANN O'BRIEN,
At Swim-Two-Birds.
At War.
The Best of Myles.
The Dalkey Archive.
Further Cuttings.
The Hard Life.
The Poor Mouth.
The Third Policeman.
CLAUDE OLLIER, *The Mise-en-Scène.*
PATRIK OUŘEDNÍK, *Europeana.*
BORIS PAHOR, *Necropolis.*

FERNANDO DEL PASO,
News from the Empire.
Palinuro of Mexico.
ROBERT PINGET, *The Inquisitory.*
Mahu or The Material.
Trio.
MANUEL PUIG,
Betrayed by Rita Hayworth.
The Buenos Aires Affair.
Heartbreak Tango.
RAYMOND QUENEAU, *The Last Days.*
Odile.
Pierrot Mon Ami.
Saint Glinglin.
ANN QUIN, *Berg.*
Passages.
Three.
Tripticks.
ISHMAEL REED,
The Free-Lance Pallbearers.
The Last Days of Louisiana Red.
Ishmael Reed: The Plays.
Reckless Eyeballing.
The Terrible Threes.
The Terrible Twos.
Yellow Back Radio Broke-Down.
JEAN RICARDOU, *Place Names.*
RAINER MARIA RILKE, *The Notebooks of Malte Laurids Brigge.*
JULIÁN RÍOS, *The House of Ulysses.*
Larva: A Midsummer Night's Babel.
Poundemonium.
AUGUSTO ROA BASTOS, *I the Supreme.*
DANIËL ROBBERECHTS,
Arriving in Avignon.
OLIVIER ROLIN, *Hotel Crystal.*
ALIX CLEO ROUBAUD, *Alix's Journal.*
JACQUES ROUBAUD, *The Form of a City Changes Faster, Alas, Than the Human Heart.*
The Great Fire of London.
Hortense in Exile.
Hortense Is Abducted.
The Loop.
The Plurality of Worlds of Lewis.
The Princess Hoppy.
Some Thing Black.
LEON S. ROUDIEZ,
French Fiction Revisited.
VEDRANA RUDAN, *Night.*
STIG SÆTERBAKKEN, *Siamese.*
LYDIE SALVAYRE, *The Company of Ghosts.*
Everyday Life.
The Lecture.
Portrait of the Writer as a Domesticated Animal.
The Power of Flies.
LUIS RAFAEL SÁNCHEZ,
Macho Camacho's Beat.
SEVERO SARDUY, *Cobra & Maitreya.*
NATHALIE SARRAUTE,
Do You Hear Them?
Martereau.
The Planetarium.
ARNO SCHMIDT, *Collected Stories.*
Nobodaddy's Children.

SELECTED DALKEY ARCHIVE PAPERBACKS

CHRISTINE SCHUTT, *Nightwork.*
GAIL SCOTT, *My Paris.*
DAMION SEARLS, *What We Were Doing and Where We Were Going.*
JUNE AKERS SEESE,
  Is This What Other Women Feel Too?
  What Waiting Really Means.
BERNARD SHARE, *Inish.*
  Transit.
AURELIE SHEEHAN,
  Jack Kerouac Is Pregnant.
VIKTOR SHKLOVSKY, *Knight's Move.*
  A Sentimental Journey: Memoirs 1917–1922.
  Energy of Delusion: A Book on Plot.
  Literature and Cinematography.
  Theory of Prose.
  Third Factory.
  Zoo, or Letters Not about Love.
CLAUDE SIMON, *The Invitation.*
PIERRE SINIAC, *The Collaborators.*
JOSEF ŠKVORECKÝ, *The Engineer of Human Souls.*
GILBERT SORRENTINO,
  Aberration of Starlight.
  Blue Pastoral.
  Crystal Vision.
  Imaginative Qualities of Actual Things.
  Mulligan Stew.
  Pack of Lies.
  Red the Fiend.
  The Sky Changes.
  Something Said.
  Splendide-Hôtel.
  Steelwork.
  Under the Shadow.
W. M. SPACKMAN,
  The Complete Fiction.
ANDRZEJ STASIUK, *Fado.*
GERTRUDE STEIN,
  Lucy Church Amiably.
  The Making of Americans.
  A Novel of Thank You.
LARS SVENDSEN, *A Philosophy of Evil.*
PIOTR SZEWC, *Annihilation.*
GONÇALO M. TAVARES, *Jerusalem.*
LUCIAN DAN TEODOROVICI,
  Our Circus Presents . . .
STEFAN THEMERSON, *Hobson's Island.*
  The Mystery of the Sardine.
  Tom Harris.
JOHN TOOMEY, *Sleepwalker.*
JEAN-PHILIPPE TOUSSAINT,
  The Bathroom.
  Camera.
  Monsieur.
  Running Away.
  Self-Portrait Abroad.
  Television.
DUMITRU TSEPENEAG,
  Hotel Europa.
  The Necessary Marriage.
  Pigeon Post.
  Vain Art of the Fugue.
ESTHER TUSQUETS, *Stranded.*

DUBRAVKA UGRESIC,
  Lend Me Your Character.
  Thank You for Not Reading.
MATI UNT, *Brecht at Night.*
  Diary of a Blood Donor.
  Things in the Night.
ÁLVARO URIBE AND OLIVIA SEARS, EDS.,
  Best of Contemporary Mexican Fiction.
ELOY URROZ, *Friction.*
  The Obstacles.
LUISA VALENZUELA, *He Who Searches.*
MARJA-LIISA VARTIO,
  The Parson's Widow.
PAUL VERHAEGHEN, *Omega Minor.*
BORIS VIAN, *Heartsnatcher.*
LLORENÇ VILLALONGA, *The Dolls' Room.*
ORNELA VORPSI, *The Country Where No One Ever Dies.*
AUSTRYN WAINHOUSE, *Hedyphagetica.*
PAUL WEST,
  Words for a Deaf Daughter & Gala.
CURTIS WHITE,
  America's Magic Mountain.
  The Idea of Home.
  Memories of My Father Watching TV.
  Monstrous Possibility: An Invitation to Literary Politics.
  Requiem.
DIANE WILLIAMS, *Excitability: Selected Stories.*
  Romancer Erector.
DOUGLAS WOOLF, *Wall to Wall.*
  Ya! & John-Juan.
JAY WRIGHT, *Polynomials and Pollen.*
  The Presentable Art of Reading Absence.
PHILIP WYLIE, *Generation of Vipers.*
MARGUERITE YOUNG,
  Angel in the Forest.
  Miss MacIntosh, My Darling.
REYOUNG, *Unbabbling.*
VLADO ŽABOT, *The Succubus.*
ZORAN ŽIVKOVIĆ, *Hidden Camera.*
LOUIS ZUKOFSKY, *Collected Fiction.*
SCOTT ZWIREN, *God Head.*

FOR A FULL LIST OF PUBLICATIONS, VISIT:
www.dalkeyarchive.com